Readjustment

Tom Peavler

iUniverse, Inc.
New York   Bloomington

Readjustment

iUniverse books may be ordered through booksellers or by contacting:

iUniverse
1663 Liberty Drive
Bloomington, IN 47403
www.iuniverse.com
1-800-Authors (1-800-288-4677)

ISBN: 978-1-4401-5256-6 (pbk)
ISBN: 978-1-4401-5257-3 (ebk)

Printed in the United States of America

iUniverse rev. date: 10/13/2009

Readjustment

It was the largest funeral in the storied history of Mexico. Presidents and dictators have been put to rest with far less show than that which was provided for the alcalde. Politicians, generals, and celebrities of all kinds were in attendance. The alcalde's three sons from the States had arrived the day after the old man's death. The youngest had not arrived from his home in Panama. The three sons from the States went immediately to the home where they had spent their youth before leaving to seek their fortunes in the underworld of the States.

The eldest of the three was Diego. He bore little resemblance to his father. He was by far the shortest of his brothers, and he had inherited none of the physical grace of his father. There was a sure sign of strength in his broad shoulders and thick torso.

Carlos was the next in line and showed more of the de los Santo's characteristics than his older brother. He was taller by six inches, and in both his eyes and hair bore more of a resemblance to the alcalde.

Jorge was the given name of the third, but for some reason early on in his life he had been given the name of Pancho. He had a look about him that would have kept anyone from buying a used car from him, something about the eyes and a tiny twitch on the left side of his face. Even with these imperfections, he resembled his father more than Diego.

Diego knocked on the door, and when Charley answered the knock, Diego introduced himself and his brothers and was invited into the house. The four went into the den where Charley introduced them to Alice. He told them of the funeral arrangements and informed them that the service would take place tomorrow if their younger brother could make it there from Panama.

Diego asked, "So how's the business with the carburetors goin'? The old man was sure that you guys were gonna make a fortune off that thing. Was he right?"

Charley noticed that Diego's command of the English language was good but in no way resembled the preciseness of his father's. The effect of living in the States, no doubt. He was not yet ready to tell them all he knew about the state of affairs with the business, or that he was the sole heir of the business. He knew instinctively that they would not be thrilled to find that their father had left everything to a Yankee and had not left them anything.

Charley replied, "I guess everything is going okay, but I haven't paid much attention since the alcalde's death. The last I knew we were doing all right, but then I never was a bean counter. The old man had total control of the finances. I was just the idea man."

"Yeah, the old man always kept tight control of the money. That's one of the reasons we all decided to try to make it somewhere else. When can we get a look at the books and the old man's will?"

"Well, I guess you can look at the books when the funeral's over. The old man's lawyer can let you see a copy of the will tomorrow or the next day, but I really don't want to talk about it now. There'll be plenty of time to discuss that after the service. Any idea when your younger brother will arrive?"

"No, I'm surprised he wasn't the first one here. He always was the old man's favorite. You mind if we clean up now and get a little shuteye? It's been a long hard trip."

"No, that'll be all right. You guys know your way around the house. Just find yourself an empty room and make yourselves at home."

They grabbed their bags and headed up the stairs. After a short silence, Alice almost whispered, "Well, what do you think?"

"I don't know, but one thing for sure. They sure aren't goin' to like the looks of the old man's will. What do you think?"

"I don't like the looks of the oldest one. He's obviously the leader, and he doesn't look at all like his father."

"Yeah, and you gotta remember that these are the guys who blew up a board room and a super tanker. We know what they are capable of. Scary, isn't it?"

"Yeah, but things have always been pretty scary. Ever since we headed down here we've been in danger."

"You're right. I think I need to have a chat with Terry and Hans to see if there's anything we can do to ease the situation. If not, I guess we'll just have to hunker down and be prepared for anything they decide to throw at us. I'm not gonna let that bunch push me around, and I don't think I could ever be a partner with those guys."

Later that day a knock on the door announced the arrival of the fourth of the alcalde's sons. He needed no introduction. He was the spitting image of the pictures of the alcalde himself when he was that age. They had seen his pictures in the yearbooks that the alcalde had shown them of his time spent at the University of Texas at El Paso. His name was Juan like his father's, and his command of the English language quickly reminded them of the alcalde. He was dressed in a dark and very expensive suit. He asked if his brothers had arrived, but he did not seem overly anxious to see them. He did say, however, that he would like to view the body of his father, something his brothers had never mentioned. Charley told him which funeral home was in charge of the body and the service, and after asking for a drink of water he left in a limousine that had been waiting outside.

Flowers by the hundred continued to arrive throughout the day. The sudden surge in the Mexican economy had made the alcalde a national hero. Rich and poor alike credited the boom to him, although it had been an American who had created the carburetor that had been the thrust that had both locally and nationally given rise to sudden prosperity.

When the three older brothers came down from their afternoon naps, Charley told them where their father's body could be viewed and told them they were headed there. Once outside the house, Charley and Alice met Hans and Terry and headed out to the site of the factory which only the alcalde had been able to envision. Stopped at the gate by armed guards, they were allowed on the site when they were recognized. Charley took the other three to his huge private office. Very little conversation had taken place on the way to the factory. Once inside the office, Charley began, "Well, I guess it's time for a council."

"Of war?" Hans asked.

"I don't know. You tell me. You saw the three who arrived here earlier today. How do you think they'll act when they find out the old man didn't leave them anything? They don't seem like the type to just walk away from what we got going here. I think we better be ready for the worst."

"What would that be?

"Hard to say. We know at least one of them is awfully good with explosives. I'm sure the other two are no strangers to violence."

"We don't meet with the lawyer until tomorrow, so I guess we have until then to get ready."

"We can double the security around the plant, but I don't imagine they came down here ready to blow the place up. Besides, like you said, they don't know yet that the old man cut them out of the will. I don't think we really have anything to worry about until they get back to the States. I'm sure they want to be a long way off when the trouble really starts, if it does. What do you make of the younger brother? He certainly doesn't resemble the other three."

"Naw, but he does look more like the old man. I know for a fact he was the old man's favorite. The alcalde seemed more disappointed when he couldn't talk him into coming back home to take over the family fortune than he was with the other three. I'd like to have a little one-on-one conversation with him before we meet the lawyer tomorrow."

Alice said softly, "I'll go up and see if I can set up a little private conversation."

When they returned home, Alice went quietly up the stairs, and the men split up and headed for what once had been the old barn. Charley picked up his driver and personal bodyguard and told them he wanted to return to the plant. Hans and Terry went into the barn to discuss possible measures to take if things did not go smoothly with the brothers.

At the head of the stairs, Alice met Juan as he was about to go downstairs. She called him by name, and he looked up and smiled in a manner that definitely reminded her of the many smiles she had gotten from his father. She motioned him with fingers to her lips to be quiet and pointed down the stairs. He followed her wordlessly until they were in the dining room. She finally said, "Charley said he'd like to have some chat with you without your brothers. He's headed out to the plant. Would you like to go out there? I can get you a ride if you'd like to go now."

"That would be fine. How far is it out there? I've done more traveling recently than I care to."

"Oh, it's not much of a trip. Fifteen minutes tops. I'll call Hans or Terry to give you a lift."

She walked halfway to the barn and called out to Terry. He heard his name called and headed back up to the house. He caught up to her before she returned to the house and asked her what she wanted. She told him, and he went back to the barn to get Hans. Both men went back to the house to escort Juan out to a waiting car. An awkward silence prevailed on the whole trip to the plant. The security guard let them in and told them that Charley had gone to his office. He pointed to a light burning in the main office. When they got there, Terry knocked gently on the door and Charley said, "Come on in. Alice called and told me you guys were headed this way."

They entered sheepishly and stood almost in the doorway until Charley motioned them to sit in the three plush chairs facing his own. Charley made direct eye contact with Juan before he spoke.

"Juan, I'm gonna get right to the point. Your father left everything to me and Alice. I don't know if that disappoints you, but I have a hunch that your brothers are not going to be pleased when they find this out. What do you think?"

"I think you're right. I haven't spoken to any of them for more than three years, but I know them well enough to know they think they're going to get the lion's share of the business. I'm sure they won't take this lying down. I don't know what kind of connections they have down here, but I know they are well connected with powerful people in the States."

"Yeah, we know that, too. We know that they blew up a major oil company's boardroom and sank a super tanker. What they can do to us down here is what I really want to know. How disappointed are you that the old man didn't leave you a share?"

"Not very. I could have had a huge piece of the action if I had come home years ago when the old man wanted to retire. I knew what his main crop was, and I didn't want to get involved in the drug trade. It got my mother killed and almost cost the old man his life on more than one occasion. He had lots of powerful friends, but he made some powerful enemies along the way. For all the old man's charm, there were many who hated his arrogance and his insistance on sticking to the traditional way of doing things."

"Yeah, we butted heads on that once or twice, especially when my son wanted to marry his niece. It's funny how adaptable he was in some circumstances and how he refused to budge an inch when he thought honor was at stake. A modern Don Quijote in some respects."

"I think my brothers thought if they waited long enough, he would let them have it all when he died. I'm glad they were wrong."

"And why is that. You don't like your brothers?"

"Well, let's just say we were never very close."

"What exactly is the job you have now? Your father told us you worked out of Panama, but he never really told us what you did."

"I work for a major corporation that specializes in building roads all over South America. We are a multi-national corporation, and I am fortunate enough to have climbed far enough up the corporate ladder to be a vice-president. Thanks to my father's influence, there's a chance that some day I might even be president and CEO of the company."

"Tell me what you can about your brothers. I'm afraid there's going to be big trouble when they find out what's in the old man's will."

"No doubt. I'm certain you've heard of the old Italian group called cosa nostra. Well, a lesser known group calls itself cosa nuestra. It means the same thing, this thing of ours. It has the same type of organization the old mob had, but they have branched out now and are no longer confined to a certain city like Chicago or New York City."

"Were you aware that they were the ones who blew up the board room of Universal Oil and sank one of their super tankers?"

"I wasn't certain when it happened, but I certainly suspected that they were involved when I got a telephone message from the old man."

"Are you aware of what the oil companies tried to do to us?"

"Yes, he told me about the attempts on your life and all the other things they've tried to put your enterprise out of commission."

"Is there any chance you might give up the opportunity to become the president and CEO of your present company to hold the same titles with us? I know this is sudden and that we barely know each other, but we don't have a lot of time to get ready if there's going to be trouble. Your father handled all the paper work and the dealing with the Japanese that really got us where we are today. You obviously have some of the same skills the alcalde had or you couldn't have risen up the corporate ladder as fast as you have."

"I'd have to think about that. I'd have to look at the books and see what your prospects are. I stand to become a very wealthy man in my present position, something I would not give up lightly just to keep my brothers from taking over."

"Good, I can see you are a very practical man, just like your father. He always said of his four sons, you were the only one with any business sense."

"He nagged me harder than the other three to come home, as he put it, to preserve the honor of the de los Santos name."

"Yeah, we heard a lot about the honor of the de los Santos' name. He was almost fanatical about it at times. Well, early tomorrow morning I can have our lawyer bring the books here to my office and you can take a look and see where we stand. Later, tomorrow afternoon, I'll let your brothers in on the bad news that they made a long trip for nothing if they thought they were going to inherit anything. By then you should know if you want to join us or not."

"Okay, I'll take a look, but I promise nothing."

All four men left together in the same limo that Charley had taken before the other three arrived. There was very little conversation on the way home and none after they arrived back at the house.

Early the next morning, Charley ordered a breakfast catered for eight of his guests, his wife, and two top security men. He told the brothers that the lawyer would be there at ten for the reading of the will. The three older brothers smiled at this announcement while the youngest merely nodded. After breakfast, the three elder brothers excused themselves for a walk around the homestead. Charley wondered what they might have been discussing last night while he was at the plant.

Shortly before ten the lawyer arrived, carrying nothing but a small briefcase. Charley introduced him to the brothers. The lawyer seemed hesitant to read the will and tried to make small talk until Diego finally told him to cut to the chase and get on with it. He shrugged and pulled a piece of paper from his briefcase. Then in a voice that quavered a little he said, "This is the last will and testament of Juan Carlos de los Santos. All of my holdings in the de los Santos and Johnson Corporation I leave to my friend and partner, Charles Johnson. All of my farm ground and real estate I leave to the families who are now residing on those properties. For my house and the land which goes with it, I leave to my niece and her husband Billy Johnson. To my four sons who refused to return and accept the responsibility of ownership, I leave the sum of ten pesos each and the good de los Santos name." It is signed by myself and three other witnesses."

Up until the reading of the will, the three eldest brothers had been standing sheepishly like teenagers waiting to receive their allowance. A look of shock was soon replaced by a look of hatred directed straight at Charley. It was the eldest who spoke out.

"So you screwed the old man out of all of it. How did you do it? I can't believe he left everything to a goddamned Yankee the way he hated all you people. Well, if you think we're gonna take this laying down, you got another think coming."

"I never screwed your old man out of anything. It was his idea to have this man draw up both our wills at the same time. He was my sole heir to all the business if I was the first one to die. He did leave some cash to my wife and son since they held jobs within the business."

"Yeah, how much cash would they have got?"

"Well, it was a substantial sum, but less than one per cent of the business. He thought they were entitled because of the risk they took to be with us at a time when the oil companies and the whole American government were after us."

"And how about us? Was there no risk in blowin' up boardrooms and super tankers?"

"I don't know about that. I'm sure he took that into consideration, but he was really pissed when none of you would come home when he asked you to. You guys could have been major partners if you had returned."

"True, but how about you? Couldn't you still cut us in if you wanted to?"

"Yeah, I suppose so, if I wanted to, but I don't. Sorry. It's nothing personal, just business. I have all the security I need, and I can't see what else you could add to the corporation."

"So, that's the way it's gonna be, huh?"

"Yes, you guys can stay until the funeral is over and a little longer if you choose, but there's nothing here for you from the corporation."

The eldest led the way as the three stormed out the door. Once outside, Jorge motioned for the limo which pulled up beside them and waited as they climbed into the back seat. Inside, Charley turned to the others and shrugged as if to say good riddance. Nothing in his demeanor gave away the cold chill that he felt when the look of hatred had been directed toward him. He had learned from the old man that it is best never to show one's adversaries any sign of fear or weakness. The color was gone from Alice's cheeks, and both Terry and Hans looked worried. Juan smiled as he noted the reaction to the commotion his brothers' sudden departure had left on the others. He waited for a short time before saying, "They'd be even madder if they knew how much money they're not going to get to share. I've had time to look at the books, and while I'm sure there's more to look at than what I've seen, I've seen enough to realize that there's more potential here than there is in my present position. If the offer is still open to join the company, I accept."

"Well, that's the best news I've heard in a while. Yes, the offer is still open, and I'll have all the books open for you to examine. We've got to finalize with the Japanese. They are the key to being just rich or filthy rich. You'll have to look through the alcalde's papers to find out what's under negotiation. He thought if he could swing the deal he was workin' on with them that Perdido could easily replace Detroit as the car manufacturing capital of the world. Any car which came off the assembly line without our carburetor would be a dinosaur."

"Does your carburetor or as you call it, your adjustment, really do what the old man said it would do?"

"If it didn't, we wouldn't be talking about it. The possibilities are almost unlimited. I'm sure the oil companies will jack the price of a gallon of gas to make up for the loss of revenue caused by the increase in mileage, so everyone who drives a car without our adjustment is going to be in a real bind. No one in their right mind would consider buying a car without our adjustment unless they were independently wealthy. All the older cars will be forced to come down here to be adjusted. I couldn't see all this, but your father certainly could. He had vision. No one but he could ever have envisioned what the adjustment could mean. I guess it's about time I introduced you to these gentlemen. This is Terry, a long time friend of mine. We worked together back in the States, and he helped my son Billy to escape from the pursuit of the oil company thugs after they murdered my older son and his family. He is my head of security. This other gentleman is named Hans. He was sent here by the oil companies to kill me, but then he decided to throw in with us. He helps Terry to protect us all. He was the man who took care of the notorious hit man, Toyota Man."

"Yes, I heard through the grapevine that Universal's number one assassin had been taken out. I didn't know he got it here."

"I'll have Hans and Terry tell you all about that sometime in the future. Right now we have more important things to do."

"When can I get a look at the old man's private papers which include his dealings with the Japanese?"

"They're locked up inside his study, and I don't have the combination for it. I guess we'll have to figure out some way to get it unlocked."

"No problem. I know the combination."

"Great. That'll save us some time. As soon as you can, set up a meeting with them. They've already sent their condolences about your father, and I felt from the note attached that they were worried that whatever agreement they had with your father might fall through. You've got to assure them that nothing has changed with his death, and that we still intend to carry out whatever they had agreed on."

"I don't have any knowledge of the Japanese language. Will that cause any problem?"

"I don't see how it could. Your father didn't speak any Japanese either, but he spoke the language of money. Do you speak that language?"

"I think so. I told you my present employer deals in billions. If that isn't thinking in the language of money, I'll try to think bigger."

"I'm sure you will. That's why I offered you the job. Let's go to the old man's study and see if you still have access to his safe."

The two went into the study alone. Juan went over to the safe and knelt down. He spun the combination lock around four times and waited for the click which unlocked the lock. He looked up at Charley and said, "No, he never gave me the combination, but once I peaked over his shoulder and watched as he opened it. I have very good eyesight and an even better memory."

"Have you ever unlocked this safe before?"

"No, I've never had any occasion to, but I always thought knowing the combination might come in handy."

Juan fumbled around inside the large safe until he found what he was looking for. It was in Spanish, so Charley had no idea what was written on the outside of the folder which Juan removed from the safe. He said, "This looks like what I've been searching for. I hope so. I'll take this out and look it over carefully. If this isn't it, I'll come back later and look over some other stuff."

They left together and Juan stopped in the living room while Charley continued on outside.

Juan smiled as he looked over several pages which the folder he had extracted from the safe contained. These pages were clearly what he was looking for. They contained all of the past and present negotiations that his father had conducted with the Japanese car makers. Charley was right. The potential here was far greater than his present job. Now he had to decide if the risks involved were worth the undertaking. He knew his brothers would try to take over, and failing that, they would try to destroy the whole operation just for spite. The danger was considerable because he knew that his brothers would show him no mercy if he sided with this Yankee. Still, his present job, though lucrative, had very little in the way of excitement. He knew that his father had lived on the edge for many years and in both looks and temperament he was his father's son.

****

The phone awakened Charley early the next morning. The excited voice he heard on the other end of the line was Terry.

"Well, it's started already. I just heard from the guards at the gate of the plant. Hans suggested we get some dogs to do a little sniffing of the cars as they entered the plant, just in case somebody had any idea of slippin' in some plastic explosives. He was right. We nabbed a local with enough explosives in the trunk of his car to take out the plant and most of Perdido along with it. We managed to keep it quiet. I don't think it frightened any of our customers away. Hans is in the process of interrogating the guy right now. He said he's got ways of makin' the guy tell who paid him, as if we didn't already know."

"Yeah, I'd be surprised if it turned out to be anyone other than Juan's brothers. Where are they holding the guy?"

"Down at the jail. Do you want to be there for the questioning?"

"Yeah, unless it gets ugly. I know some of the methods Hans has described would make my stomach turn."

"Yeah, I think I'll just stay here at the plant in case they try something else today. Do you want an escort out to the jail?"

"No, I can manage. Let me know if anything else is happening. I don't think they would try twice in the same day, but you never know about these guys."

"Okay. I'll see you this evening if nothing else happens."

Charley walked outside and yelled loud enough to awaken the driver of the limo who had taken the quiet of an early morning as an opportunity for a nap. He leaped from the front seat and opened the back door. Charley stepped inside and told him to head for the jail. He offered no explanation, and the driver asked no questions. On arrival, he told the driver he need not wait, that he would catch a ride home with Hans. Inside the jail he saw Hans standing in front of a small Mexican youth who appeared to be in his early twenties. Also seated next to the suspect was

Enrique's brother Tomás who was acting as translator. Charley asked, "Well, what have you learned so far? Has he admitted anything at all?"

"Oh yes, we've had quite a little chat. At first he was quite reluctant to have any conversation at all with us. Said he had no idea what was in the trunk of his car. Said his brother-in-law had borrowed the car yesterday and only returned late last night. I told him I was skeptical. It was amazing what a little pressure on his testicles did to revive his memory. He suddenly recollected that three rather distinguished looking Mexican men had offered him $50,000 to deliver the package in his trunk. They never told him what was in the package, and he didn't ask. Do we need any more information than that?"

"No, I think that's really all we needed to know. Did they pay him, or was it just a promise to pay that they never intended to keep if he stayed close enough to the car to go up with the rest of the plant?"

"They gave him $5,000 and promised the rest by tomorrow

"Did he have the money on him?"

"Yeah, what do you want me to do with it?"

"Give it to the guard and the dog who found the explosives. They deserve it more than anyone else. How are you, Tomás? Do you see your brother often?"

"Yes, he comes by often in the new pickup truck that he bought. He is so proud of it. He has shown all the neighbors what can be accomplished if they work as hard as he has."

"If you see him today, tell him to stop by the house."

Back at the house, Alice was finishing up the breakfast she had fixed for Billy and Luisa. They sat at the table while she finished up the dishes that had been left in the sink. Both at the table were still in their nightclothes, neither having seen any prospect of leaving the house today. Neither had been informed of the alcalde's will which had made them the owners of the house where they now resided. Alice decided it was time they knew.

"You guys want to hear some great news? You weren't at the reading of the will yesterday."

"Yeah, I know. We weren't invited."

"Well, there's a good reason you weren't. I'll tell you about that later, but would you like to know what was in the will?"

Both nodded at each other. Neither spoke while they waited for Alice to continue. She hesitated and then said, "Well, you two are now the proud owners of this house and the land that goes with it. Billy, you also have considerable cash. What do you think about that?"

They stood and hugged each other before either could speak. It was Luisa who finally broke the silence. "That's wonderful. We also have some news. I think I am with child. Can you arrange for a visit to the doctor so we can be sure?"

Now it was Alice's turn to be at a loss for words. "Of course, but I'll have to check with Charley first to see if it's safe for you to go out of the house for a check-up. If he's against it, I'll arrange for the doctor to come here and check you."

"Now can you tell us why we weren't at the reading of the will?"

"Sure, Charley just felt that the brothers might be angry enough to go into a rage when they found out they were getting nothing, You've already been shot once, and he didn't want to risk it."

"And were they that angry?"

"Not at the reading, but there's been an ugly incident at the plant this morning. I don't have all the details, but I'm sure you father will be glad to tell you all about it when he gets back."

"Was anybody hurt?"

"I don't think so, but Charley left here in a hell of a hurry, and I haven't heard from him since he left early this morning. I'm sure he'll be tickled pink to think about being a grandfather again."

"I hope so. I was hoping for a little peace and quiet after the death of the alcalde, but I guess that was too much to hope for."

"Yeah, I'm about to the point where I'm not sure there'll ever be any peace and quiet. I guess we just go on and hope for the best."

She walked over to the table and hugged them both before returning to the sink to finish the dishes. She would ask Charley if they could visit the doctor. If so, she wanted to go with them. The thought of shopping for baby clothes made her smile. She hoped someday to shop for such things for a child of Charley's, but a grandchild would be the next best thing.

When Charley returned shortly that afternoon, Alice could not wait to tell him the good news. She was surprised at his lack of enthusiasm. The worry lines in his face to which she had become accustomed were now more prevalent than ever. She waited for an instant before she asked him what had caused his hasty departure that morning. He told her about the near-miss at the plant, and the grim look on her face now matched the one on his own. He saw the change in her expression and forced a smile to try to ease the tension. She returned the smile and went to him for a hug. They sat down at the table, and she poured him a cup of coffee.

"Aren't you glad about the baby? I thought you'd be thrilled."

"I am. It's just that it's hard to imagine raisin' a kid under these circumstances. It's gonna be a full scale war with the brothers. I was afraid of that. Maybe I made a mistake when I didn't offer them a piece of the action. I know their father didn't trust them, so I figured why should I. Maybe I should have put off the final decision until later."

****

Back in the U.S., the brothers were holding what was to be the first of many strategy sessions. They had received the news that their first attempt to bomb the plant had failed. Diego was more upset than the others. He scowled as he paced back and forth

between his younger brothers. The loud profanity which punctu-
ated his rant was a far cry from the smooth English that always
characterized his father's speech, even when he was angry and
frustrated.

He almost screamed, "I tried to tell you both, but you wouldn't
listen to me. You guys think you know more than me about
how to handle such things. I tried to tell you we should have
had a back-up plan, that their security might catch the kid with
the explosives, but no, you guys were so sure it would work, or
maybe you were just too scared and wanted to get the hell back
here before he tried to…"

Carlos interrupted, "We left hurriedly for a better reason than
that. You know Pancho and me better than to think we ran away
for fear of that pipsqueak gringo."

"Oh yeah? Then why did we leave in such a panic?"

"Because we were afraid that you would let your temper do something really foolish like shoot him and the lawyer."

"That might have been better than running away."

"See? That's what I'm talkin' about. You don't seem to realize that
there's a lot more people involved than just Johnson."

"Oh really? Who?"

"His security, his family, all of his employees, but more impor-
tantly, the whole Mexican government. Don't you realize that
they are not goin' to just let us walk in and take over a billion

dollar project and move it to the States. You just don't see how big this thing is. The Mexican government thinks this may be its answer to the whole country's economy. It goes far beyond just a way to get better gas mileage."

"And what makes them think it's such a big deal?"

For the first time Pancho got into the heated discussion. Before Carlos could reply he said quietly, "It's the Japs."

"What? What the hell do they have to do with this?"

"Don't you realize that with the deal they worked out with the old man that soon every car being produced in Japan will be built right here in Perdido? Perdido will soon replace Detroit as the car manufacturing capital of the world."

"Is that a fact?"

"I know you don't think so, but from all the information I've been getting, that's the way things are shaping up. One company comes to Perdido now because it's cheaper than they can put 'em together in Japan and ship 'em over here. The old man wouldn't let 'em have access to the carburetor unless they manufacture the cars in Mexico. With the competitive advantage that first company would have, all the other companies would be forced to move here quickly. Can't you see that it would be virtually impossible to compete with a company whose cars are very similar to your own, but theirs get more than three or four times the gas mileage yours do?"

"Well, what can we do about that?"

"I think the thing we gotta do is make the Japs a little uneasy about investing such a huge sum of money into such an unstable location."

"Then it's up to us to see that the location becomes unstable."

"I think maybe you're finally beginning to see the light. The fact that we were unsuccessful with our effort to bomb the place wasn't the worst of it. The worst part was that there was no publicity about the attempt. They did a really good job of covering up the whole thing. If the Japs knew about it, I'm sure they might have some second thoughts."

"So what do you recommend we do now?"

"We've got to come up with something that will attract a lot of world wide attention, even if the attempt is a flop."

"Got any brilliant ideas?"

"Not yet, but I'm thinking about it."

"Well you better come up with something pretty quick, or I'm gonna go back to the old-fashioned way of influencing people."

****

Back in Perdido, Juan sat pondering what his brothers might try next. He knew well they would never give up. He knew of their ruthlessness because the alcalde's blood which flowed through their veins, also flowed through his own.

Charley came in and interrupted his thoughts. He asked, "What have you heard from our Japanese friends?"

"They tell me they have heard rumors that an attempt was made to blow up the plant."

"And what did you tell them?"

"I told them it only proved that our security system was so fool-proof, that there could never be any real threat to the plant."

"And did they buy it?"

"I don't know. I have a hard time reading these guys. There's no emotion in their voices, and I can't read anything in their facial expressions either. What do you think my brothers will try next?"

"That would be hard to say, but I'm guessing it will be something that would attract a lot more attention than just one person with explosives. Right now I'm going to check with our security people. I've got a hunch that the next thing they try might involve some of the locals. If not right here in Perdido, then maybe in one of the larger towns around here, maybe even Mexico City itself. I'll put Hans on that right away. I'm going out this afternoon with my wife and daughter-in-law to a doctor's office."

"Why? Is either sick?'

"No, we think my daughter-in-law may be pregnant. Is there a doctor here in Perdido that you could recommend?"

"Yes, if Dr. Schmidt is still in business, he would be my first choice."

"Schmidt? Doesn't sound very local. What's his story?"

"His father didn't repatriate when WW2 ended. He left the States and moved here and married and raised a family. The doctor now is his eldest son. He's not a specialist, just a GP, but he's had lots of experience, especially with delivering babies. I'll give him a call and set up an appointment. He delivered my brothers and me."

"Sounds good. I'll tell Alice and Luisa. Think they can get in today?"

"No doubt. He'll squeeze them in if I ask him to. Will this be your first grandchild?"

"No, my eldest had a son, but he and his wife along with my grandson, were all murdered by the agents of the oil companies."

"Sorry to hear that. You must be very anxious about this grandchild."

"Yes, I may not have many more chances at immortality. I hope it's a boy, but as long as it's healthy, it won't matter."

"How does your son respond to the thoughts of parenthood?"

"He's more excited than scared. He knows how hard I took the loss of my son and grandson, but he's also a little scared because of the threat from your brothers, and maybe a little worried about a child from a mixed marriage being accepted here in Mexico."

"Has he accepted the fact that he may never be able to return to the States?"

"I think so. He used to talk about returning someday, but recently he hasn't said anything about it."

"And how about your wife? What's her attitude?"

"She can hardly wait. She has always wanted children of her own, in fact she still thinks that someday she and I might….but her biological clock is ticking pretty fast, I think."

"Until we get things settled with my brothers, I think being a parent is going to be quite a chore, don't you?"

"Of course, we'll just have to do the best we can. I guess the first thing to do is get ahold of my security team. What is your immediate plan?"

"Right now I'm going to try to get in touch with the Japanese and try again to reassure them that the rumors they have heard have been greatly exaggerated, and that there is no real danger to the plant. If we can get them to go forward just a little bit, it may make my brothers try something risky and stupid. I'll let you know as soon as I can when I have the prenatal appointment set up. Don't forget maximum security for any of the family who leave the premises for any reason, and that includes yourself."

"Thanks for the warning. I'll take all the precautions that I can. We've been doin' that for a long time now. Call Alice and tell her that she and Luisa will be goin' to see the doctor today. She'll want to get herself and Luisa all dolled up before they go. I'm headed out to the plant for a check on a couple of things. I may not see you again today, so follow your own advice and take care."

"I shall."

At the entrance to the plant, Charley ran into both Hans and Terry. He pulled both men aside and told them he thought the brothers might try something that would attract a lot more publicity than a single man with explosives had created. He told them to tell their operatives to keep their eyes and ears open for any gang activity in any of the town around Perdido, even as far away as Mexico City.

Terry asked, "Why? What have gangs got to do with our problems?"

Hans stepped in and said, "It's only logical to think that with their connections with the locals they might try to use that in a way that might be damaging or embarrassing to us. We'll check with all of our connections and let you know if anything unusual is going on."

"Do you have any connections as far away as Mexico City?"

"It just so happens that I do. When I was employed by the oil companies, I did a job or two for them in the City, and I'm pretty sure some of my old friends are still around. I'll find out before the sun goes down if they've heard of anything unusual goin' on."

"Do that, and let me know what you find out. Terry, do you have any moles here in Perdido?"

"Yeah, I've got about a dozen on the payroll, and they report to me twice a week to collect what I pay 'em. I'll call a special meeting for this afternoon and let you know tonight if they've heard anything."

"Okay, I'll probably be at the house after I take Luisa and Alice to the doctor."

"Why, is anything wrong?"

"No, just a prenatal check for Luisa."

"Congrats, boss man. I hope it's a boy."

"I'll talk to you guys before bedtime tonight."

Charley walked back to his bulletproof limo escorted by two of his most trusted bodyguards. He got into the back seat and told the driver to take him home. The driver nodded and wasted no time in gunning the big black Caddy back toward the safety of home base.

When Charley walked in the door, he could tell by the smile on her face that Juan had already told her about the appointment with the doctor. She had already changed into an outfit he had not seen before. Her hair was combed neatly, and he thought he detected the aroma of a new perfume. She gave him a big hug before he could say a word.

"You've obviously heard from Juan."

"Yes, I can hardly wait. Are you going with us? Are you going to change clothes?"

"Yes, to the first question, no, to the second. Why should I change? I'm not going there to be seen. I'm just there to escort you two."

"I know, I just thought...

"Yeah, I know, you haven't seen me in anything but work clothes for a long time, and this just might be a special occasion that might call for a little celebration. Okay, I'll change. What do you want me to put on?"

"I really don't care. Just put on something nice."

"Do I have time to take a shower?"

"Yes, we're not due at the office for about an hour and a half. I've got to go check on Luisa and see how she's getting along. She's more worried about how Billy will look than I am about you, even though he won't be going with us to the doctor today."

"She has more reason to worry. The poor boy never had a mother to teach him how to dress, and he hasn't had a wife long enough to get proper training."

She left Charley standing in the middle of the room as she left to check on Luisa. He heard giggling from the closest bedroom and wondered what was so funny. No matter, he thought as he headed for the shower. *My wedding clothes would look a little* too formal, but I've surely got something that would satisfy the ladies.

He came back to the living room wearing a pair of dress pants, a new pull over shirt, and a matching vest. Alice looked at him closely and then nodded her approval. She and Luisa both smiled as he stepped between them. He offered each an arm which they accepted as he headed for the door. They got into the back of the black limo that was flanked both front and back by a carload of bodyguards.

Charley asked, "Where are we going? Do we have an address?"

"Yes, Juan gave me the address, and I wrote it down. Here, you hand it to the driver." She handed the slip of paper to the driver who glanced at it and nodded. After all three vehicles had come to a stop in front of a small medical clinic, the occupants of the lead car got out and went to the front door. Then one of the men signaled the middle car to proceed. Luisa got out first, followed by Alice with Charley bringing up the rear. The men in the third car got out but did not follow the others. They had been told to keep a close watch on all three vehicles to be certain no explosives could ever be planted.

Inside, a nurse dressed in white, led them into a small waiting room. She spoke in Spanish to Luisa who listened and nodded. She turned to Alice and said, "She says the doctor will see us next."

"Us? I thought we were here for him to examine Luisa. What's this us? Does this mean I've got to sit out here by myself while you two are in with the doctor?"

"Yes, that's exactly what it means. I think you can survive that. You've survived worse."

Charley groaned and sat down with the other two. Only one elderly gentleman was already seated and waiting to be seen. Charley thought he's going to be disappointed if he thinks he's next. He remembered other trips to the doctor's office when his sons were young and the frustration of waiting long after the time of the appointments. He thought about maybe looking at a magazine but quickly realized they were not only out of date but also in Spanish. He crossed his legs, sighed deeply, and shook his head. Alice said calmly, "Be patient. She said we'd be next. Relax."

"Okay, I'll try."

Ten minutes later the nurse returned and motioned to the ladies to join her. They left Charley sitting in the same attitude he had assumed as quickly as he had sat down. It seemed like an eternity, but in reality it had only been about twenty minutes. When they returned to the waiting room, both were beaming. Charley jumped to his feet and almost ran the short distance between them.

"Well," he said, "What's the verdict? Is she pregnant?"

"Yes, we are."

"We? What's that supposed to mean?"

"We, Charley. That means Luisa and I are pregnant."

"What the hell are you talkin' about?" How? When?"

"I think you know how, Charley. As to when, do you remember the picnic we went on?"

"Of course I do, but why haven't you said anything?"

"Because I wasn't sure. I haven't been regular for a long time. I didn't want to worry you with a false alarm."

"So when are you due?"

"In about five months. He didn't set an actual date."

"And how about Luisa?"

"In about six months."

"Do you know the sex of either child?"

"He doesn't have the equipment to perform a sonogram. He said we'd probably have to go the City to have that done. Are you happy, Charley?"

He hesitated for just a second and then said emphatically, "Of course I am. I just wish we could concentrate on the baby alone instead of all the other things that are going to be happening in the near future."

"I know the timing stinks, but I'm still so happy it just doesn't matter. I've wanted a baby all my life and now, after I'd almost given up hope, I have a chance to have a child with the only man I've ever really loved."

"How about you, Luisa? Are you as happy as Alice?"

"Yes, I know Billy will worry, but there is nothing I can do about that. We will just have to be as careful as we can."

"You guys know it would be dangerous for you to travel to the City for a sonogram. I think for the present you're just going to have to wait it out like the locals do."

"That's okay. It doesn't really matter. Just as long as it is healthy, a boy or girl will be great."

"How about you, Luisa? Does the sex of the baby matter to you?"

" No, I feel exactly as Alice does, but I know Billy would like for it to be a boy."

"Well, then we are all agreed. It's going to take me a while to get used to the idea, but I'm sure when it sinks in, I'm going to be one of the happiest men in all Mexico. What could be better than a child and a grandchild within a month of each other, huh?"

"Nothing that I can think of, love. The only thing that could make it better would be a little peace and quiet. Is there any prospect of that happening?"

"Probably not before the children are born. We're working on a long term solution, but for the present, we just have to take it one day at a time, I'm afraid. Why didn't Billy come with you today, Luisa?"

"I wasn't sure either, and I didn't want to worry him."

"Yeah, I think I've heard that one before. Well, let's head back to the house so we can share the good news."

When they arrived back at the house, Luisa ran on ahead to tell Billy what she hoped was good news. She had already disappeared upstairs before Charley and Alice had dismissed their escort and made their way into the living room. Just outside the house, Charley grabbed his wife and gave her a big hug and a lingering kiss. When the kiss ended, Alice asked, "Are you really happy, Charley? I could end the pregnancy if you're really unhappy."

"Don't even think about it. The timing is strange, but I truly am happy for you and me and the baby. I hope you have an easy time of it. I know it's never really easy, but I hope you aren't plagued with morning sickness the way my first wife was. She had it pretty rough."

"It won't matter as long as the baby is healthy. I've gone through some pretty rough times during drug rehab. If morning sickness is nothing more than a lot of throwing up, I know I can get through that."

"You know there will be times when I can't be with you, may not even be there when the baby is born."

"Yeah, I know that, but it doesn't change my mind a bit. You'll be with me in spirit, and I know you'll be with me as soon as you can. Luisa will be with me, and we can share this experience together. I think it will bring us closer together. Maybe I'll even get a little closer to Billy, too. I think that would be great."

"I hope you're right. Let's go upstairs and see what Billy's reaction is to the whole thing."

When they got upstairs, Charley knocked on the door before he and Alice entered. Billy came quickly to Alice and gave her a hug and a peck on the cheek. Then he went to his dad and gave him a big hug. Simultaneously, each said a single word, "Congratulations."

****

Two days passed before anything of import happened. Back in the States, the brothers de los Santos were in serious disagreement about what course to follow in trying to persuade their father's one time partner to give them a piece of the action. Diego was in favor of anything violent, including the assassination of Charley, his family, or anyone else he felt stood in the way. The two tried to explain to him that murder or blowing up the plant would probably queer the deal with Japanese and thus make a takeover much less profitable for whoever wound up in control of the company. Carlos tried to reason with Diego, but it had always been difficult to do so. As a boy he had always tried to settle all disagreements with his fists. As he grew older, he gave up his fists for knives and guns or explosives. He had none of the tact or the ability to compromise like his father. He was tough, but he had none of the qualities of leadership. He was loud, crude, and often an embarrassment to his brothers. His father could hardly believe that he had sired such a son. If not for the undying love he had for his wife, he might have accused her of infidelity. As a boy he had learned that there was little love for him from his mother and none at all from his father. He had learned early on to hate almost everything his father stood for. All of the old traditions and folderol about family, he thought were wastes of time. About the only way he resembled his father was his love of power and the belief that power could not be maintained without large amounts of money. He got along all right with the other two brothers as long as they pretended that his roll as oldest brother gave him the final say in any major disagreement. He had always hated and been jealous of his youngest brother, for he had seen early-on that he was his parents' favorite. Named after the father and resembling him more in physical appearance, he had always been a source of anger. Their father had tried from time to time to get any of the older brothers to leave the U.S. and return to Mexico to take over the family business and maintain the family tradition of running the land surrounding Perdido. None had been willing to return, though they knew the marijuana business, which was the largest part of the de los Santo's enterprises, was lucrative. They also knew that it was dangerous, because the old man had made some important enemies along the way, some even responsible for the death of their mother. All three had been happy when the youngest had also refused to return to Perdido because they knew how much this must have vexed the old man. They knew that Juan was doing well in legitimate business in Panama, while they preferred to use their connection with the American mafia to try to make it to the top. The one thing they had agreed on was that it would not be profitable to return to the dryland farms which produced little more than a decent marijuana crop and barely enough of subsistence farming to support the poor locals who paid homage to the de los Santos name.

After a short silence, Diego erupted, "Alright, I've had enough of this bullshit. You two are supposed to be the brains of this outfit. It was you two who masterminded the blowup of Universal's boardroom and one of the super tankers. Now you're tellin' me we can't touch this prick who's livin' in the old man's house. How can that be?"

Carlos replied, "Because we had the element of surprise. None of the oil company people had any idea we were about to hit them. These guys know in advance that we are probably going to try to hit them. That's why their security is so much tougher than the oil company's was."

Jorge chimed in, "That's right, brother, and don't forget they're gettin' a lot of help from the government. Those bastards in the City know that if the Japs move in, there will be lots more graft and corruption to spread around. They're tryin' to make it look like they want this company to succeed for the good of Mexico. That's a laugh. We all know they don't give a shit about the good of Mexico as long as they can line their pockets with Japanese gold."

"Well, this is the way I see it. We don't want the Japs to back out completely. We just want to slow things down until we get a chance to get a controlling interest in the company. Maybe just a major scare."

"And just how do we go about that?"

"I've got an idea. Do you still have any connection with any of the street gangs we used to run with before we moved north? If you do, I have a plan."

"Yeah, I still know some of the people. One of the gangs owes me a big favor for supplying them with grass a couple of years ago when weed was hard to find."

"Well, I thought maybe a demonstration there at the plant. You know, just a well-meaning bunch of Mexican kids who are afraid that with the coming of the Japs that there won't be any really good jobs for the people around Perdido. It could start out as a peaceful demonstration, and then turn into a full-scale riot. They know how to provoke law enforcement people. With any luck at all, we could have several major injuries, maybe even a fatality or two. Nothing really major, but enough to insure that the whole thing would show up on the 6 o'clock news. What do you think, brothers?"

Diego smiled and then nodded and said, "It might work, but I would still rather try something a little rougher. This is not gonna cause them to come running to us."

"I know that, but it might make the Japs wait a while before they commit the kind of money it would take to move their operation to Mexico. We don't want to scare them away, just hold off a while so we can get some leverage."

"Well, personally, I'd like to leverage that candy-ass little brother of ours to the cemetery. You know if it wasn't for him, the Yankee would be willing to make a deal. But you know him, just like the old man. Always with the big idea. Before this is over, I'm gonna deal with him, once and for all."

"Don't underestimate him, brother. He may not have the *cajones* that the old man had, but he is sharp. He has political connections in both Panama and Mexico, and he has access to a lot of money. That can be a lot of trouble for us because we've always thrived on big money and the help of powerful politicians."

"I'd like to see some of that aristocratic de los Santos blood out on the ground. I will see how blue his blood is before this is over, I can promise you that."

"When the time is right, I agree. Right now, it would probably frighten the Japs away, and that we don't want. Your time will come."

"I can wait for now, but not too long. It seems like I been waiting most of my life for a chance to do the little *vendejo*."

****

Three days later, an agent of the de los Santos' brothers walked in to the headquarters of the Fuegos, the worst of the street gangs in Mexico City. He asked the man at the bar where he could find *Feo Grande*, the Big Ugly, leader of the gang. The man motioned toward a room in the back. He knocked loudly before entering, not wanting anyone inside to shoot through the door in panic if someone came through unannounced. When someone spoke from inside, he entered cautiously. Sitting behind a rundown desk was a huge man of no more than 20 years of age. It was obvious how he had gotten the name Big Ugly, for in addition to his huge size, his face was pockmarked and scarred.

"What can I do for you?" he said in slurred Spanish."

"I'm not sure, really. A better question might be what I can do for you, amigo."

"And what might that be?"

"Depends. How would your gang like to make $100,000?"

"Great," he said without enthusiasm. "Who do we have to kill?"

"Probably no one. How many members do you have at present?"

"Depends. Who wants to know?"

"Diego de los Santos. Do you know the man?"

A short puase while he scratched his head and nodded. "Yeah, I remember him. He's the dude who got us weed a while back when times were really tough. What's he got to do with all this?"

"Well, he'd like you guys to do him a favor, a favor for which you will be well paid."

"You still talkin' $100,000? If you are, keep on talkin'."

"Are you familiar with the town of Perdido?"

"Yeah, that's the place where the dude fixes everybody's carburetors for big mileage, we heard. Is that true or just talk?"

"True. Could you get as many as 50 members to Perdido for a demonstration?"

"Probably, but what do we do when we get there? We hear security there is pretty rough. I don't think we could get in and trash the place."

"That's not what we want you to do."

"So what's the point?"

"We want you to carry signs that say the company in unfair in hiring too many foreigners and not enough Mexicans for the jobs at the plant."

"And that's it?"

"Not exactly. The local law enforcement will no doubt come to try to break up the demonstration. At first we want you to do nothing but argue with them. Then as the argument begins to heat up, we'll need some action. We want you guys to do battle with the locals. No guns. We don't want anybody killed on either side. Just a lot of noise and maybe a little blood. There will be television cameras there, filming the whole thing. If they want to talk with you after it's over, you just blame it on the locals and explain it was supposed to be a non-violent demonstration."

"And when would we get paid?"

"The day after the demonstration. Can you get the 50 guys?"

"Might take a couple of days. Is that a problem?"

"No problem. I'll leave a check with you for the amount we discussed, dated for a week from today. If you do what we ask of you, you can cash the check. If you can't do the job, or we don't see you on TV, then we stop payment on the check."

"Suppose we do the job, and you stop payment on the check anyway, huh?"

"Always a possibility. Tell the guys the job pays $1,000 a piece. Keep the rest for yourself."

"Yeah, but if you stop payment after they've done the job, they'll skin me alive."

"True, but you've done business with Diego before. Has he ever stiffed you before? Every once in a while you just have to say 'What the fuck' and take a chance. Has there been anyone around lately offering you a chance to make $100,000?"

"No, give me the check and I'll set it up."

****

Two days passed with no problems. None of Terry or Hans' snitches had reported any suspicious gang activity. Then on the third day, Hans called for a meeting of security. Terry asked Hans if he had heard anything out of the ordinary.

"Yeah, one of my snitches in the City tells me that a gang called the Fuegos has started bragging about a big score they're gonna make in the very near future. The figure being tossed around is $100,000. We know none of the locals have enough money to create that kind of talk, so I think we better get somebody down there to find out what's really going on. It might just be talk, but I don't think we can take any chances."

Charley said, "I agree. Do you have any way of checking this out before they have time to organize anything?"

"Yeah, I got a couple of well paid informants who'll let me know by this time tomorrow. I'll need a little more cash, because spyin' on these guys could be kinda risky."

"Money is no problem. We gotta find out what these guys are planning to do. Is there anything else we need to discuss?"

"Yeah, I think so. If they move against us, what measures are you willing to take to stop them?"

"What exactly do you mean by that?" Charley asked.

"I mean if the group proves really hostile, can we simply eliminate the whole gang?"

"Eliminate? Do you mean…?

"I think you know what I mean. If this whole gang is never heard from again, I think the government in the capital will be sending us a 'Thank you' card."

"Then are you asking me permission to 'eliminate the whole gang?'"

"I guess you could call it that. Not only would it solve a problem we're having in the present, I think it would make an excellent example to all the other gangs who might be inclined to try something like this at a later date."

Terry spoke up, "I gotta agree with Hans. I know it sounds harsh, but Billy and I already got hit by these bastards, and I don't plan on ever lettin' them have another shot at me."

"I never thought I'd live long enough to be one to condone the death of a bunch of teenagers."

"Well, don't forget, Charley, that when you're killed by a teenager, you're just as dead as if an adult killed you."

"I can't argue with you, there. I guess you guys will have to use your best judgement on the level of violence. One thing, though. Let's try to keep as much of this out of the media if we can. This kind of publicity can't possibility do us any good."

Hans was quick to say, "We'll do the best we can. If at all possible, we'll try to head them off before they even get to Perdido."

"Where will you try to head them off?"

"We'll have roadblocks set up for about the only two ways they could come into town. There are good places on both roads about six miles out. If we can stop them there, there won't be any publicity"

"Sounds good to me. Keep me informed."

Back in the City, Feo Grande was having little trouble rounding up 50 who were anxious to earn a thousand dollars American in a single day. He smiled as he thought of the $50,000 he would earn if things went as planned. Even if everything went wrong, he was in no personal danger, for he had not even considered getting on one of the two old busses he had commandeered for the transportation to Perdido. He'd even had the busses checked mechanically to see if they could make the trip without breaking down. He had supervised the construction of the signs the boys would carry as they demonstrated outside the plant. He knew that several would be carrying pistols, even though he had warned them not to. Some never went anywhere without the small caliber pistols they had owned since grammar school.

The trip would take hours. A stop or two for gas and something to drink. These old busses had never been air-conditioned, and the weather had turned off unseasonably warm. Tempers would be short by the time they arrived in Perdido. The stage was set for more violence than they could have anticipated.

Six miles outside Perdido, Hans was waiting with 30 men. All were armed with fully automatic weapons, a nice mixture of M-16's and AK-47's. He has set up a roadblock and had been waiting impatiently for three hours when the busses finally came into view. He had half of his men covering the door of each bus. One of Hans' men had a bullhorn and told all of the passengers to dismount and form a single line. For more than a minute, no one moved. Then the door of the first bus opened and men began to slowly file out. Only the driver remained on the bus. Now the door to the second opened, and even more slowly the men began descending and forming a line. The officer with the bullhorn told them if any of them had weapons to throw them to the ground. There was a slight hesitation before three from the second bus pulled out pistols and fired them at the man with the bullhorn. He fell to the ground and never was aware of the hail of bullets from the automatic weapons which systematically mowed down every single man in both lines. Then, after the firing stopped, Hans ordered two of the men to open fire on the drivers inside the busses. That completed, he walked down the line and used his pistol to finish off anybody who showed the slightest sign of life. He then walked back to the fallen body of his deputy and saw that the man was dead. He instructed his men to start loading the bodies back on the busses. He had two of his men take the places of the dead drivers and told all of his patrol to follow his car.

More than a mile off the highway, this strange convoy came to a stop in front of a very large cave, large enough to house both of the busses with room to spare. Two of Han's men placed the explosives at the mouth of the cave and retreated back to their own vehicles where they used the ignition to set off the blast that closed the cave forever. Then Hans gathered them all together to address them.

"Men, what you have seen here today never happened. The death of one of our own will be explained as an accident. You know nothing about busses or gang members or caves or explosives. If you are questioned by anyone about the events of this day, you know absolutely nothing. If your tongues begin to wag, there are other caves nearby where your body will be laid to rest. Do you understand what I am telling you?"

A resounding chorus of "*Sí, Capitán*" was the final word as they mounted their cars and headed back to Perdido.

****

In the City, Feo Grande was becoming extremely nervous. He had been watching the news on TV for many hours, enduring the mind numbing repetition of the same stories which the network presented on a day in which nothing of importance was happening. He scowled and spit a huge stream of tobacco juice into a half full can of beer. He would have liked some conversation with one of his lieutenants, but all of them had been anxious to make the trip to Perdido to earn the $1000. He wondered what the worst case scenario might be. What if all the gang had been arrested and bail had been set at such a high price that he could not obtain their bail. Was that the worst? No, he thought. What if they failed to keep their part of the bargain and put a stop on the check they had left with him? Not only would he be unable to get the $50,000 thousand which had been promised to him, he would be left trying to explain to fifty very unhappy gang members why he could not deliver on his promise to them. Yes, that would be the worst. He never dreamed he was now the leader of a gang that had virtually no members.

Even after two days had passed, he still could not imagine what had gone wrong. He called every one of the few remaining gang members to ask if they had any word from their comrades. He could not go to the police and report them missing. They certainly would not go all the way to Perdido to try to find a gang they hoped would never be found. Their only concern might be job security since the crime rate was bound to go down with the Fuegos no longer a part of the system. Maybe he could steal a car and make the trip to Perdido, to see what had happened. Yes, that would be the best course of action to take to be certain what had happened.

After his confrontation with the Fuegos, Hans was not anxious to tell Charley what had happened. He knew Charley would be happy that the brothers' latest ploy had failed, but he was also aware that his boss had a weak stomach when it came to disposing of adversaries. When the threat had been personal, as it had at his wedding, he had been able to pull the trigger on a man who he thought had shot his son, but he had been a little squeamish about the death of Toyota Man. So, he could not tell what his reaction might be when he learned the fate of the Fuegos. His own experience in working for the oil companies had left him callous to the death of people he did not know. He would lose no sleep over the vermin he had buried in the cave outside Perdido. His former employers would have applauded his action, but he wasn't sure how Charley would react. He had been told that the level of violence would be left to his own discretion. He was almost certain that the three shots fired by the gang members would be justification for his order to kill them all. He had no way of knowing how many of the others were armed, and it made no sense to wait until others of his guards had been killed to find out. It was strictly a precautionary measure. Men like Charley, who he liked to refer to as civilians, found killing very difficult to understand. It was something they read about in the papers, but a thing that never touched their lives directly. He knew Charley would not criticize him for his action, but he also knew that he would never understand completely what had compelled him to take such drastic action. As he entered the study where Charley was mulling over some papers, he came to attention, almost a military pose.

"You need something, Hans?"

"Yes, if you got a minute."

"What's on your mind?"

"We've just thwarted the brothers' second attempt to raise hell at the plant."

Charley dropped the papers he had been holding and looked into Hans' eyes. "Tell me about it."

"Two bus loads of thugs from the City were on their way here. We stopped them several miles outside Perdido. We ordered them to throw down any guns they might have. Several of them pulled pistols and opened fire on my deputies and me. We had no choice but to return the fire. One of my men was hit and died almost instantly. When the shooring stopped, none of the thugs were left alive."

"You killed them all?"

"I'm afraid so. I anticipated that the next bunch we face would have automatic weapons, so I armed my men with the same. When thirty men open up with automatic weapons, I'm afraid there's not much chance of survival."

"How many were there?"

"We didn't count them, but my best guess is about fifty."

"And you just left them beside the road?"

"Of course not. All of the bodies and the busses have been disposed of in such a manner that I doubt they will ever be discovered."

"But won't some of them be missed?"

"I don't think so. All of them were members of a notorious gang in the City. The authorities won't waste any time or money trying to find a group that they'll be glad to see disappear."

"But how can you be sure the bodies and the busses will never be found?"

"One can never be sure, but I've done my best to see that they'll never be discovered."

"And how did you manage that?"

"Are you aware of the large caves located some six or seven miles south of town?"

"Yeah, so?"

"We put all the bodies and the busses inside on of the caves and used explosives to close up the entrance."

"Won't there be tracks leading from the highway to the cave?"

"There might have been if I hadn't foreseen such a thing. I had one of my men drag the area to remove any sign that vehicles had ever been there."

Charley nodded. For a moment he was speechless. He thought he had become immune to the thoughts of the deaths of others. He remembered the shock of the blow-up of the oil company boardroom and his surprise at the sinking of the supertanker. But those were the work of the alcalde. He had not even been aware that those two events would tale place. He had no direct connection to either event, but it was he who had given Hans the authority to use whatever level of violence that he thought necessary. In an instant, he began to realize that this would not be the last of the killings

"It's okay, Hans. I wish we didn't have to be so bloody, but we have to if we want to survive. What do you think will happen next?"

"I have no idea. We'll just have to be prepared for anything they try to throw at us."

"How did you find out they were headed our way? It couldn't have been just a lucky guess."

"I have a mole in the City who keeps me informed of all gang activity. He told me the gang was going around bragging about a chance to make a $100,000. I knew that kind of money could only have come from the brothers. I was right."

"Does Terry know about this?"

"Not yet. He was guarding the other road in case they tried to slip in the back way. He had a group identical to mine, armed the same way. I'm sure they would have met the same fate if they had tried the other route."

"Anything in the news yet about this?"

"There hasn't been a thing, either national or local. The men who did the shooting know that to speak to anyone is tantamount to suicide. I'm sure it will drive the brothers crazy trying to find out what happened. I'm pretty sure this wasn't a suicide mission on the part of the Fuegos. I think it was meant to be a publicity stunt to frighten off or slow down the Japanese."

"Don't mention this to Billy or the women. In their condition they don't need this kind of news."

"I really don't think it would matter much to either one. Luisa has known for a long time how ruthless her uncle was, and Alice has been shot at enough to know the score, but I'll keep it mum if that's what you want."

"You're probably right, but for right now, Terry and I are the only ones who need to know."

Hans left Charley's office feeling pretty good. It had gone better than he expected. Maybe Charley what beginning to see what it would take to stay in control He bumped into Billy who was about to enter the room just as Hans was leaving. He nodded and continued on his way. Billy went directly to Charley and said, "What's this that me and the wives aren't supposed to know?"

"How much did you hear outside the door?"

"Not much. Just enough to know there's something you don't want me and the women to know."

"Well. We had a run-in with some thugs that had been sent to make trouble at the plant."

"What's such a big deal about that? We've had worse than that. Must be more than that."

"Well, maybe a run-in wasn't a very good choice of words. Hans headed off two bus loads of these thugs about six miles out. There was a lot of shooting on both sides. Casualties on both sides."

"Why haven't I heard anything on the news about this? I'd think with casualties it would certainly be newsworthy."

"Hans is pretty good at covering things up. He thought the publicity would be bad for us, you know, with the Japanese and all."

"Dad, there's something I gotta say. You know that Alice and I are the owners of the corporation if anything should happen to you. Because of that, I don't think you should be keeping any secrets from us."

"You're right. I never really thought about it in those terms. It's just that…….."

"I know. The pregnancies and all that, but they'll just have to suck it up and be tough. Luisa and I have talked about it, and I think she's tough enough to handle the truth on just about anything. I know Alice is. So tell me what really happened today. I got a feeling you left out some pretty important details."

"You're right. You're entitled to know the whole truth. Here's what really happened." From that point on, Charley told his son as many of the details as Hans had given him

Back in the States, the brothers were holding a conference. Diego, as usual, was angry and loud. He had been on edge ever since he'd heard about the plan to use the Fuegos in a way to at least embarrass the owners of the plant. He had only given lukewarm support to the whole concept. He shouted, "I told you they couldn't pull it off. Too young, too stupid. Why can't we at least find out what happened to the crazy motherfuckers?"

Carlos tried to calm him, "Relax, brother. What have we lost? Only a little time. I put a stop on the check we left with the leader. He'll surely get in touch with us soon and tell us what happened."

Jorge chimed in, "Maybe they just chickened out. That would be a logical explanation for why they aren't in the news."

"I don't fucking believe that for a minute. Something has happened that we need to know about. Don't we have any operatives left in that part of the world?"

"Of course we do. They just don't know anything. According to them, nothing has happened. We just need to be patient for a day or two more before we do anything really radical."

"I'm tired of waiting. I think we ought to go down there and find out for ourselves."

"I think we can wait a day or two. If we haven't heard anything by then, I agree we need to make a trip."

"One more day. I'll wait that long and no more. If you don't want to go along, I'll do it myself."

"Relax, brother. When you go, we'll go with you."

****

Terry could tell something had happened today even before Hans a chance to tell him any of the details. When Hans told him in more graphic detail than he done with Charley, Terry did not feel the sense of revulsion that had encompassed Charley. He had seen the cold-blooded nature of Hans before, so he was neither surprised nor made queasy by the details of the slaughter. He asked, "How did Charley take it when you told him?"

"Better than I expected. I was afraid he might come unglued when I told him there were no survivors. But he seemed to take it in stride. I could see he was upset, but he didn't say much. I think he's beginning to realize what he's up against. I can see you've had a change of attitude since you first met me. You hated me a lot more than you seem to now. What happened?"

"I've seen what these people are capable of. They're the scum of the earth. I still can't have your attitude about killing people just for the money, but I've made it a personal thing. The bastards took a shot at me before, and that really helps me hate them on a personal basis. Them or anybody they've hired to do their dirty work are fair game to me."

"Yeah, I know it's hard for you civilians to think about killing for a vocation. I forget that sometimes. I tried to tell you right off that there was nothing personal in the job I was hired to do when I came down here to take care of Charley and anyone else who stood in the way of the oil companies. Universal Oil paid me very well for the service that I provided. A man gets used to a certain standard of living. After a while you just can't go back to a regular job that wouldn't let you maintain the style of living you've become accustomed to. For some reason, I think I adapted to my line of work rather easily. I liked the money, I liked the loads of free time between assignments, and sometimes I even liked the adventure of it, you know, living on the edge, so to speak."

"So why did you come over to us? Just to save your hide?"

"Yeah, originally that was it. But I never really liked the assholes I worked for. They never showed you any respect, no matter what you did for them. They thought as long as they paid you well, that was enough. I also realized that no matter what they paid you, it was only a drop in the bucket to what they were making. I got thousands sometimes, but I know they got millions. Call it professional jealousy or whatever. I never could make myself like the bastards. Until I made a deal with the alcalde, I never thought I could continue in my line of work for someone I liked. Believe it or not, I really like the people we're both workin' for now."

"You know, I think I told you once before that I didn't think we'd ever be close friends. I'm still not sure we ever will be. I do have a lot of respect for the knowledge and expertise you have in dealing with the scum we're up against. I'm not sure I could have dealt with that gang the way you did today. Maybe, I just don't know. I think maybe I could have ordered the deputies to open fire on the gang, but I'm not sure I could have taken a pistol and finished off the wounded."

"Look at it this way. I couldn't just leave a bunch of wounded bodies out there. The bodies had to be disposed of. Now, if I hadn't finished them off, just loaded them back on the bus with the others, they would have died a much slower death inside the cave where they would have either bled or starved to death. To me, it was more an act of mercy than anything else."

"One way of looking at it, I guess. Do you always rationalize things like that?"

"Not always, but it does help if you can persuade yourself that the people you kill don't deserve to live. These guys were headed here with guns. We know that. Exactly what their mission was, we can't be sure, but when they agreed to take the money from the brothers for whatever reason, that was enough for me to put them on the expendable list."

"How old would you say they were?"

"I don't know. Teenagers mostly. It doesn't make any difference. They could have been just as dangerous to us regardless of their ages."

"I suppose. What do you think their next move will be?"

"Impossible to say. They'll wait a little while longer. Trying to figure out what happened to the gang. Then, it's my guess, if they can't know for certain what happened, they'll make a trip to the City to try to find out. Diego, the oldest of the three, has less patience than the other two. He's the leader and he won't wait for long. I don't think they'll try anything big until they have some idea what happened. That may take a while, but we just can't be sure."

"What do we do while we're waiting?'

"Try to get as much information as we can from the moles and spies that you have. They were the key to knowing ahead of time what the gang was up to. Don't be afraid to pay for information.

It's money well spent. Not all the information you get will be valuable, but just one little piece of information can make up for all the worthless stuff you're bound to get."

"No problem. Charley picks up the tab for all of that anyway. It never comes out of our pockets."

"He probably has no idea what we spend for information, but right now, I don't think money ever crosses his mind."

"It used to, but with the success of the plant and what the old man left him, he has no reason to think about it."

"Yeah, I think with the two pregnancies and trying to protect what he already has is enough to occupy his mind."

"I'm headed now to check with some of my informants. I suggest you do the same."

Charley had decided to take Billy's advice and tell Alice what he knew about the slaughter of the Fuegos. He was surprised that she took the account so calmly. He guessed she was beginning to share his callousness about the deaths of people they didn't know. She said, "So not a single one of the survived, huh?"

"I guess not. Hans said all the gang and the bus drivers were taken to the cave. There were no survivors. Does stuff like that upset you? Would you rather I kept things like this to myself?"

"No, love. I'd really rather know what's going on, even if the news is bad. I can take it. I really don't know about Luisa. I think she's having a tougher time than I am with morning sickness. But she is tough. She stood up to her uncle when there were very few people who had that kind of courage."

"It's really a shame that both of you picked such a miserable time have babies. This should have been one if the happiest times of your lives, but I don't see how that's possible now."

"It gives both of us an even bigger reason to carry on, more than just the love we have for our husbands. Maybe you guys picked a really bad time to become fathers."

"You're right, as usual. We have to accept our share of the blame for our present situation."

****

A day had passed, and Diego could no longer be put off. He had already arranged airline tickets for himself and his brothers. He had packed one small bag with two changes of clothes. He did not plan on staying long. His curiosity about the fate of the Fuegos had been gnawing at him for days. His impatience was not shared by his brothers, but they could contain him no longer. They feared if they did not accompany him, he might do something rash or ill-advised that might ruin any chance they might have had at sharing in their father's good fortune.

"Come on, you two. The fucking plane takes off in a little more than an hour. You two gotta know the airline security is so tight we can't take any weapons with us. That scares me. But I've arranged to have a piece waiting for us as soon as we get off the plane."

"Bro, do you really think we're gonna need the heat? I thought you were just gonna go down and find out what happened."

"If they managed to get rid of the whole gang, don't you think they could do the same to us just as easily? No matter, I won't feel right until I have a gun under my belt."

"Just promise me that you won't do anything crazy until we get back. Down there, they have all the advantage. We got a lot to do to even up the odds before we try to hit them again."

When they arrived, they went straight to the address which the agent who had arranged the deal with the leader of the Fuegos had given them. Only one person inside the building fit the description of Feo Grande. Dressed as they were, in contrast to the other occupants, Feo Grande knew who they were even as they approached. The conversation was all in Spanish with Diego doing most of the talking.

"Is there somewhere we can talk a little more privately?"

"Yeah, here in that room."

They left the main room for a small office where he did what little business he had. Once inside, Diego made no pretense of civility.

"Okay, motherfucker, what happened? Why haven't we heard a goddamn thing from you or someone who can tell us what happened? You better have some damn good answers."

He could see from the bulge in Diego's trousers that he was carrying a gun. He was certain the other two were also packing. His voice quavered. He had not known such fear since he was a small child.

"I don't know for sure. I really don't know. No one does. They just disappeared. They left here on two busses. There were fifty of them. They never made it to Perdido. I've checked, and no one I've talked to says they ever saw any of them or the busses in the town. They must have been stopped before they arrived in the town."

"Have you looked along the route they took to see if you could find any trace of them? Fifty men and two busses just can't disappear into thin air."

"I sent several of my men, and they can't find a trace of them anywhere. No tire tracks, not an article of clothing, nothing. I don't know what else I can do."

"What do you think, brothers. Is this huge tub of shit tellin' us the truth? Or did his whole chickenshit outfit lose their nerve and just steal the busses?"

"For some reason, brother, I think he's tellin' the truth. Perhaps we should contact some of our own men and let them conduct a more thorough search before we decide."

"Probably a good idea. In the meantime, you better be available when we get through lookin'. Don't think about takin' any long trips before we get back to you."

They left hurriedly and took a taxi back to the downtown hotel. As soon as they checked in and made their way to their suite, Carlos got on the phone. He talked for no more than five minutes in explaining that he wanted the route between the City and Perdido combed for any clue that might reveal the fate of the fifty and the busses. He gave the man a promise of a nice reward if he could report back his finding within two days.

They relaxed for a short time. Diego stretched out on one of the beds while the other two began a game of gin rummy. None of the three had spent a night in the City for many years, and no one was considering going out for the evening. Too dangerous.

****

Juan disembarked from the huge airliner that had just landed in Tokyo, he wondered if he would not be better served if he had an interpreter. He knew that the leaders of Japan's largest car manufacturer could provide him with one if it proved necessary, but he thought that arriving here without one of his own might make him appear to be a rank amateur in the field of negotiation. He did not want to lose face.

He took a taxi to the huge skyscraper which was the corporate office of what he hoped would soon be a partner in his enterprise. In his haste to assure them that all was well at the plant, he had not even bothered to make an appointment. He was certain when he told them who he was, he would have no problem getting an audience with the upper echelon of the company. He hit a snag with a secretary whose English and Spanish were limited. It took ten minutes before he could connect with someone who recognized the name and led him into the office of the head of the corporation. They exchanged bows and handshakes, and he was relieved to find out that this man's English and Spanish were as good as his own. He had decided beforehand to use English if he had a choice.

"I'm so very glad to see you, Mr. de los Santos. I was truly sorry to hear of the death of your father. He was a man of great vision. I was looking forward to a long and prosperous relationship for us both. What news do you bring from Mexico?"

"Well, the news I bring should please you. There is no reason now to think that any business dealing you had with my father cannot be completed with me and my partners. Nothing has really changed. I have become the leader of his enterprise. Mr. Johnson has made me CEO of all his operations. He is still the owner of the plant, left to him in my father's will. I am hoping that any agreements you made with him can be extended to include me."

"And that is our hope as well. You are surely aware that the Japanese economy at this time is not exactly, how shall I say, robust. The stock market had been in serious decline now for some time. We are now suffering from previous excesses, and also from some serious errors in judgement by our present government. A move on our part would be a risky proposition. Tell me, am I correct in assuming that you are not your father's only son?"

"No, you are correct. I have three brothers, all of whom reside in the United States.

"And how did they react when they found out they had not been included in their father's will?"

"I'm sure they were most unhappy, but not necessarily surprised. For years my father had been trying to get one of the three to return to Mexico and help him with some of his other enterprises. Their refusal was no doubt the reason for their exclusion from the will."

"But how did you escape his wrath? Were you not a resident of Panama at the time of his death?"

"Yes, but I had made him a promise to return within the next two years. And you must realize that my father left very little to me directly. Mr. Johnson and his family are the heirs to most of my father's fortune. They have chosen me to represent them as CEO of the enterprise."

"We have heard that your brothers have already tried to make trouble for you at the plant. Is this true?"

"Your information is correct. We apprehended a man with a small supply of explosives. He never even got close. Our security is so tight that no one could possibly get past our guards with explosives. The man never did confess who had hired him, but we are relatively certain that it was my brothers. It grieves me to say, but my brothers are connected to organized crime in the U.S. But you must also realize that my father had close connections with the Mexican government, and they also have a vested interest in seeing the success of our enterprise. My country, like yours, is in economic decline. Your move to Mexico could well be the tonic for both our countries. I'm sure we can count on the government to supply us whatever we need to ensure our security."

"I see. That is refreshing to hear. We also have heard of possible interference of a gang from Mexico City. Is there any truth to this report?"

"I have heard these same rumors, and they are groundless. They were probably started by my brothers in an attempt to slow any move you might be considering. I'm sure you will be deluged with such rumors in their attempt to slow down any real progress. Do not worry."

"I'm glad to hear these things. I think within a week we can sign the final papers which will allow us to begin our move. I shall relay the information you have given me to the rest of the board of directors. I shall recommend the move."

"I'm glad to hear that. I shall relay this information to Mr. Johnson so he can ready the ground for you."

A final bow and a handshake, and Juan was back on his way to the airport.

****

Upon his arrival back in Perdido, Juan could hardly wait to tell Charley the outcome of his trip. He found that Charley failed to share his optimism. He shrugged and turned away from Juan.

"What's the matter? I thought you'd be more pleased."

"I am pleased, it's just that I've never been able to accurately judge these people. Even your dad said he had that problem, too, and he was great at being able to judge people."

"That is true, he was, but I think maybe I inherited a little of that. I didn't get to the position I held in the business world by not being a good judge of people and their motives. I know about the Japanese and their supposed treachery, but it's been a long time since Pearl Harbor. I think some time this month we'll see the beginning of their move to Perdido. Can you be ready for them if that's the case?"

"I couldn't say. You'd have to check with Hans and Terry to see if the security is ready. The land where they plan to build is ready. I don't think we have a big enough labor force here in Perdido, but I think with a little advertising, we could get a big enough group of unskilled laborers. There's plenty of unemployment close by. Will they provide the architects and skilled people? I can have all the heavy equipment they'll need to clear the ground in less than a week."

"Yes. I checked over the old man's papers, and that was part of the original agreement. They also promised to hire at least 60% Mexican workers and to provide the training necessary so our people will have a chance at the better jobs later on."

"Do we have that in writing?"

"Yes, we do. I found a copy of the agreement in the old man's papers. Some of the stuff between them was faxed, but I'm almost certain it's all legal."

"I hope you're right. What will the brothers try if they see we're beginning to start on the plant?"

"Hard to say. If they listen to Diego, it will certainly be something violent. That's all he knows. The others will try to dissuade him, but that's a very tough job."

"I'll get in touch with Hans and Terry and let them know they may soon be in charge of the plant construction. Anything else?"

"I guess not. How are the two ladies doing with their pregnancies?"

"Alright, I guess. It's been a long time since I had a pregnant wife. Alice hasn't complained, and I don't see Luisa very much. Billy hasn't said anything, so I guess everything is okay."

Billy had not seen much of his wife lately. He had been too busy trying to tie up some loose ends at the plant. He was still the unofficial complaint department, and although there were few complaints, he had learned in a very short time how to diffuse the most irate of those who were unhappy with their adjustment. He had learned quickly that the offer to refund the money to anyone who complained was almost certain to quell the complaint. An offer to re-do the adjustment was much more often accepted than the offer of a refund. Gasoline prices had been steadily rising with no end in sight for the increases. For those, who for whatever reason, did lots of driving, the adjustment was a terrific bargain. The initial outlay of cash to have the adjustment performed was well within the reach of the average American consumer, and also affordable for many of the Mexican middle class.

Billy walked into the bedroom and found his wife sitting on the bed. Her eyes were red, but she was not crying when he entered the room. He asked in almost a whisper, "Is anything wrong?"

"No, I'm alright. I just worry that my cousins will make more trouble than we can deal with. Juan is the only good one in the bunch. The others are in many ways like their father."

"I thought you liked your uncle."

"I did, but I was never blind to his faults. He was always power hungry, and ruthless when his authority was challenged. He could be very cruel. I know these cousins to be made of the same stuff. They have none of his charisma or grace, only the bad qualities."

"You knew these men?"

"Yes, I was very young, but I remember Diego's cruelty to animals and also to his brothers when they crossed him. I fear they will never leave us alone until they get what they want or we kill them."

"Well, that's a possibilty. We have some guys on our side who are not afraid to kill if necessary."

"I know. Are you one of these?"

"I don't know. I've never killed anyone, but I think if anyone was threatening you, me, or Dad, I could do it. How about you?"

"Yes, especially with the baby. I know you'll think this is funny, but there were many times when I thought I could kill my uncle. I even went so far one time as to plan his murder."

"You're right. That is funny. How were you gonna do it? Were you gonna shoot him?'

"No, I never had access to a gun, and I was watched, day and night, so I never had a chance to get one. But I did have access to poison, and I was often asked over to his house to prepare one of his favorite meals. Does it frighten you to know your wife is capable of such a thing?"

"No, do you think you could use a gun or a knife if you had to? I don't think we'll ever get close enough to our enemies now to poison them."

"Yes, I think the de los Santos blood which flows through my veins is the same which has made killers of my family for centuries. My ancestors slaughtered the Aztecs when they first arrived in Mexico, and they have a long, if not glorious, record of killing ever since."

"You know, I wondered about Dad, whether he could do it. But Terry told me how on the night of the wedding, he shot a man in the head at very close range. The man was already dead, but he didn't know that. He's never talked to me about it, but Terry and your uncle did. I know Hans has killed lots of people. I told you how he killed Toyota Man, and Terry told me how he finished off all the wounded of the Fuegos and the bus drivers before disposing of the bodies. I'm sure he's a match for your cousins when it comes to cold-blooded killing. I never in my wildest dreams ever imagined that some day I would be discussing with my wife whether or not we had the nerve to kill someone. Did you?"

"Only my uncle. Even though I hated my cousins, I never really thought about killing them until now. Let's talk about something else. Have you decided what name you will give your son?"

"I kinda narrowed it down to two. Either Charles after Dad or Jack after my brother."

"But not William after you?"

"Definitely not. Let's lay down and take a nap.

The brothers were still quarreling. Diego was still in favor of some Mission Impossible scheme to hit on the leaders of the newly formed corporation which had not included them. His brothers were just as determined to try something else. They did not know how long they could postpone Diego's blood lust. He screamed at his brothers, "How much longer am I gonna have to put up with this shit? You guys keep tellin' me that my way won't work, but you don't seem to have any ideas of your own."

"Relax, brother. I've been thinking all day, and I've finally come up with something that might slow them down."

"And what might that be?"

"Hear me out. I've got a friend who works for one of the big car magazines. What if we could persuade him to write an article that claims that a lot of people who went down to Mexico to get the magic adjustment are now finding that it overheats their

engines and causes major damage. Wouldn't that slow down the
Japs?"

"Maybe, but as far as we know that's a crock of shit. All the people
we've talked to says it does just exactly what he says it will do."

"That's not the point, brother. We're not trying to put them out
of business. That wouldn't be good for us. We just want to slow
them down until they relax their security and we can get a foot
inside the door. If the Japs decide not to come at all, it might not
be worth the effort to try to muscle in on their thing."

"Do you think the guy will write the article?'

"He will if we make him an offer he can't refuse. I can arrange
that. The magazine comes out this week. That should give him
enough time to get what we want in there published."

"Okay, set it up. I can wait that long."

****

The magazine did indeed come out the next week, and the cover
story was the failure of the adjustment. A survey, the article
claimed, had shown that a majority of the Americans who had
the adjustment performed on their cars now discovered that they
had been struck with engine failure due to over heating, all in
less than 10,000 miles. Though the process was guaranteed, most
had decided not to return to Mexico because of what had been
described as instability in that area.

The Japanese were aware of the article before Charley. They wasted no time in contacting him. They were visibly upset. Charley did his best to smooth things over. "I knew something like this was bound to make you guys nervous, but you must realize that we've driven a lot more miles than these guys claim they have and we've never had a single incidence of what they're claiming."

"Perhaps we should wait a while before start the move. What do you think?'

"I've got a better idea. Why don't I fly to your place and perform an adjustment on several different models of your cars. Then you can put all of them through the most rigorous test you can imagine. If you find even one case of overheating on any engine you manufacture, I'll let you guys out of any contract you've signed with us. I'm pretty sure this is just another ploy by those in the States who are just now realizing what you'll do to their sales when your cars go to market with my adjustment. What do you say? Is there any better way to decide who's telling the truth about my adjustment?"

"No, I guess not. How soon will you be here?"

"No more than two days. I'll bring an assistant with me. Will you get a good hotel for us, close to where we'll be working? Two or three days at the most should be all that we'll need to adjust as many cars as you think necessary."

"We shall await your arrival with great anticipation. We are still in hopes that we can work this out together."

Charley knew exactly the man he would take with him to perform the adjustment on the new Japanese cars. It must be his first student, Enrique. He had not kept in touch in recent days, but he was confident that he would both understand the importance of their assignment and quickly be able to handle any difficulties these new models might present. He knew the promise of 100% perfection on all models had been an act of rashness, but he knew of no other way to prove to the doubters that everything he had ever said about his adjustment was true. Speed was also a factor. He did not want the Japanese to hesitate. They were on the brink of the big move, and once started could not be halted. He decided to visit Enrique personally. He called a driver and a bodyguard and told the driver to take him to the farmhouse where he lived. Enrique was surprised to see his old friend and benefactor. He invited Charley to sit at table with them, but Charley declined.

"What brings you to my humble abode, amigo?"

"Business, I'm afraid. I'll get right to the point. I've just had a long conversation with our friends from Japan. They've read some nonsense in an American car magazine which claims our adjustment does great harm to an engine. I told them I can prove it's a lie by coming over there and performing an adjustment on as many of their cars as they like. We need to get it done in a hurry because they are almost ready to make the big move to here. I'm afraid this is a part of Juan's brothers' efforts to slow us down. The sooner we can convince them that the article is crappola, the sooner we'll have them building their cars right here in Perdido. I see outside your house a new pickup. How's the adjustment working on it?"

"Great. It does better than a hundred miles to a gallon, and the engine purrs like a kitten. What can I do to help you?"

"I need someone to go with me to Tokyo. Will you go with me?"

"Of course. I can get my brother to look after things here until we get back. How long will we be gone?"

"Three or four days."

"Why did you choose me? There's other guys who do the adjustment as well or better than me."

"Because I've never done an adjustment on these brand new models they've come up with. I'm sure I'll be able to figure out if I need to make any changes from what I've done on the other models, but once I figure it out, I want you there so I can teach you if there's any differences. You picked up the original faster than anyone else we've ever tried to teach. I'm confident together we can get it done faster than I could alone. Have you ever flown?"

"Not commercially. I've been up in small planes a time or two. I didn't get airsick, if that's what you're worried about."

"Normally, we'd both need passports, but I'll tell our friends when we'll be there, and I think they can arrange for us to skip the formalities. We'll be flying in a private jet to avoid all the security at the airport. Pack enough clothes for four or five days."

"When do we leave?"

"Tomorrow at six. Will you be ready?'

"Of course. Are you sure you haven't got the time to sit down and eat a bite with us?"

"I'd like to, but I've got a few details to take care of before we leave."

As he got up to go to the door, he noticed the frightened look on the face of Enrique's wife. He imagined he would see that same look on Alice's face when he told her about his early departure tomorrow morning.

He decided to take Hans along with them for security. He had been to Tokyo before and perhaps that might be useful if they had to get around the town, but the biggest reason was his ability to spot trouble before it actually happened. The charter jet had no more passengers than the three men headed for Tokyo. Their luggage included a large supply of the several elements needed to perform an adjustment. One suitcase apiece made up the rest of the cargo. The pilot, co-pilot, and one attendant were the only others on board. After a bumpy take-off, the flight smoothed out. Hans was the only one with any real experience at flying in high-speed aircraft. He had long since made it a point to try to sleep through long and boring flights. He had no interest in the conversation between Charley and Enrique. The talk centered on the possible difficulties of performing the adjustment on models of cars they had never seen. Enrique was by far the more nervous of the two. He would have preferred to have stayed in Mexico, but he felt obligated to the man who had gotten him out of the rut of dry land farming. He paid close attention to the schematics of several models he was certain they would be asked to adjust. He asked a few questions and tried not to show his lack of confidence in his own ability. Han's snoring during one of the lulls in the conversation caused both to laugh. Three hours into the flight they joined Hans in slumber.

An intense thunderstorm caused the pilot to alter the direct route he had plotted for the trip. The bumpy ride awakened all three. For the first time Hans became a part of the conversation. He related two other trips he had made while in the employ of the oil companies. He did not relate the gory details of the deaths of the men he had been sent to deal with. He talked about the landscape and some of the fun things to do in the city. When the change in course had smoothed out the flight, he resumed his nap.

On landing at a small but private airstrip, they were met by a large limosine which took them to the corporate headquarters of the company. They were ushered into the CEO's office without fanfare. The formal bows were exchanged, and all three men asked to be seated.

"So glad to see you and your friends, Mr. Johnson. How was your flight?"

"No problem. We hit a little turbulence, but our pilot detoured around most of it."

"I'm sure you must be tired after your long flight. We have you logged into a beautiful suite in one of our finest hotels. We will take you there immediately after we finish here. You can begin your adjustments tomorrow, if that is satisfactory?"

"Sounds good to me."

"Is there anything you would like before we escort you to your hotel rooms?

"The only thing I can think of is a list of all the models you want us to adjust and the schematics of the fuel systems. We haven't had a chance to look at the latest models."

"I'm sure that will be no problem. We will have them delivered to your room as soon as we get them. Is there anything else?'

"Well, I don't know about the other two, but I'm getting a bit hungry. Is the food at the hotel good?"

"Some of the finest that Japan has to offer, either in Japanese or American cuisine."

"Then I guess we'll be getting to the hotel. Will you pick us up tomorrow and take us to where we can begin the adjustments?"

"But of course. What time would you like for us to pick you up?"

"Around 8 o'clock our time. I know that's an awkward time for you because of the time difference, but I don't want to get caught up in jet lag. Will that cause any problems?"

"Not at all. We'll pick you up at 7:30 your time. That will allow you to begin work by 8 o'clock."

They got up and made their bows and were led out of the office by a man who escorted them all the way to the hotel. Charley and Enrique were impressed by the luxury of the rooms to which they were taken, but Hans had seen it all before.

"You two ever eaten Japanese food?"

"I haven't. I don't know about Enrique. Anything you'd like to recommend?"

"I like the sushi, but I know these people serve some of the best steaks in the world. I'm told they fatten them on beer. The cost of steaks is prohibitive to most of the populace, but I'm sure our tab will be taken care of by our hosts."

"Then steak it is for me. How about you, Enrique?"

"Steak will be fine. I like mine well done, I think. I've had steak so seldom I don't really remember how I like it cooked."

"Want a baked potato to go with your steak?"

"I guess so. I'm not really all that hungry. Probably just a bad case of the nerves."

"Let me do the ordering, then. Charley, how do you like your steak?"

"Medium rare. I want lots of sour cream on the baked potato. Italian dressing on the salad. How about you, Enrique?"

"The same for me will be fine."

Hans went to the phone and called room service. The man who took their order spoke perfect English. He told them their order would be ready in 30 minutes.

The food arrived even sooner than the man had promised. Charley had to admit that Hans was right. It was the best steak he had ever eaten. Enrique's lack of appetite was evident. He ate most of the steak but left the salad and potato almost untouched. Hans made no comment about the food. He left nothing on his plate.

They turned in early, and Hans was the only one who slept soundly. Morning came, and there was no need for the wake-up call that Charley had requested. Room service served a large American style breakfast. Once again Hans had more appetite than the other two. Charley and Enrique put on comfortable work clothes, and Hans wore a business suit which camoflaged the pistol he always carried. They were met in the lobby by a delegation who escorted them to a limo. An immaculate work area had been cleared inside the plant. Two workmen carried the parts they would need to make the adjustments

"We will leave you alone now to do your work. If you need anything, ring this bell, and we will attend to you. Do you have any requests for lunch?"

"I think hamburgers will be okay. We won't be taking much time off for food."

Charley saw what they would be up against for the next two days. He saw six different models of cars, two pick-ups and two SUV's. He had decided to perform all the adjustments himself with Enrique's job to assist and double-check every move he made.

He saw the look of relief on Enrique's face when he was told he would not have to perform any adjustment on his own.

Only one of the cars was any different from those of previous models. They finished with five by early afternoon. The sixth, however, was a high performance engine which had been radically altered. Three different attempts proved fruitless. Charley's frustration was growing. He slammed one of the tools to the floor and cursed. Enrique had an idea, but he was afraid to offer any unsolicited advice. Finally Charley asked, "You got any bright ideas?"

"Maybe if you reversed the order of the 4th and 5th procedures it might work."

"Okay, I'll give it a try. Couldn't be any worse than the mess I've made of it so far. I'll have to undo what I've done.'

He worked more slowly than usual in reversing the process of what he had already done. Then, after taking Enrique's idea, he opened the door of the car and started the engine. This time the sputter and the miss of the previous attempts were gone. The engine ran smoothly.

"That's why I brought you along. I know you could do these adjustments as well as me, but I can see you're more comfortable doing it this way. I might never have thought of reversing the process. Thanks. Let's call it a day."

He rang the bell for the second time. Lunch had been the only other occasion. When the attendant came in, Charley told him they were through for the day. They left their tools in anticipation of continuing the job tomorrow. They were met outside by the CEO.

"How did your day go? Did you run into any unexpected problems?"

"Only one, and we solved that. How do you propose to test the adjustments we've done?"

"We can put them on our computers and simulate 100,000 miles of driving. It will tell us what the mileage would be, and if there was any undue stress on the engines. We can tell in two days if there is any merit in the claims in the American magazine."

"I don't know what we'll run into with the SUV's. I know we've got to get them right because the American government is raising hell about the low mileage the SUV's are getting. If we can double their mileage, I'm sure we could just about monopolize the whole thing. Ford, GM, and Chrysler have all increased the horse power of their engines, but they haven't done a damn thing to improve their mileage. They won't until Congress forces them to do it, but I think that day may be coming soon."

They rested for a while before ordering dinner. Hans went for the sushi again, and the other two men for fried chicken, American style. Hans turned in earlier than usual. He said he was bored and wished he were back in Perdido. Charley and Enrique discussed what they had accomplished during the day and the problems they overcame on the 6th adjustment. Charley left another wake-up call before retiring, but he was certain they wouldn't need it.

The next morning was a repeat of the first—greetings from the headman and a quick trip back to the work area. The only difference was the attendant who waited on them in the work area. He seemed four inches taller than the one who had attended them the day before. Neither Charley nor Enrique seemed to take any note, but Hans seemed puzzled by the switch. He said nothing, but he moved closer to the workmen than he had the day before. The attendant left the area and they began to work on the SUV's.

The work was tedious. Charley was in unfamiliar territory, but he pushed on. He experimented a little and by noon had solved the problems. He rang the bell for the attendant to come and take their order for lunch. He came and told them it would be at least 15 minutes before he could bring what they had ordered. About 10 minutes later, he opened the door, and he was carrying a large tray covered by a large white cloth. Just as he was approaching the mechanics, Hans pulled his weapon and shot the attendant between the eyes. As he fell to the floor, all could see that underneath the white cloth there was no food, only a large caliber pistol.

No one spoke for an instant. Charley was as speechless as he had been when Hans had killed Toyota Man. Enrique was shaking, but Hans did not seem to be visibly upset.

"How did you know?"

"I knew he wasn't the same man we had yesterday. Why would they change? This is a very sensitive job you guys are doing, and I was almost certain they wouldn't let just anyone get this close to you guys. But I think that more than anything else it was his eyes. It's really hard to describe to you civilians the feeling you get when you know something is about to go down. He said at least 15 minutes, and he was back here in 10. He couldn't have got what you guys ordered in that short of time, so for what other reason could he come back, except to kill you?"

"Did you see the gun before you shot him?"

"No, I only saw the shape of the gun."

Now the area was overrun by workers, managers, and later by the police. They pulled the three American aside and began their questioning. They asked Hans to give them his gun which he reluctantly did. The CEO arrived and pushed his way through the officers. His apologies were extreme. He told the officers that he would take the statement of the Americans and deliver it to them as soon as it was completed. They had a small conference and agreed to let the CEO get their statement.

"You must know that this man was not one of ours. We have just now recovered the body of the man who attended you yesterday. It was hidden in the tool room. He must have taken the man's uniform and assumed his duties. I'm so grateful that you are unharmed."

"It isn't the first time we've been targets. We should be getting used to it by now. Have you got any idea who he was working for?"

"I'm sure our police will be able to find out. We will inform you as soon as we know. Will this hinder you in finishing the job you came here to do?"

"No, but I think we'll call it a day and try to finish up tomorrow. We could have finished today, but my nerves are a little raw, so I think we'll head back to the hotel."

"Very well. We will have the limo pick you up at a different door just in case."

Back at the hotel, Enrique could not shake off the effects of the shooting. He threw up twice before lying down on his bed. Charley and Hans talked a while before there was a knock on the door. Hans took another pistol he had brought along from his bag. He whispered to Charley, "Don't stand in front of the door." Then he approached the door from the side and asked, "Who is it?" The voice from the other side was that of the CEO. Hans recognized the voice and unlocked the door. He came into the room and once more apologized for what had happened.

"The police have identified the man. He is a hired assassin for whom they have been searching for years."

"And have they been able to find out who he was working for?"

"No, but they are almost certain that it was no one here in Japan. At first we thought it might have been one of our rival companies who would suffer greatly if we have the adjustment and they do not. We cannot be certain, but it is believed that the man was hired by Americans. They have tracked down a huge sum of money which was deposited into a Swiss account."

"Yeah, we know who has that kind of money. At first I thought he might have been hired by the alcalde's other three sons, but from the amount of money, I'd say it has the smell of Universal Oil."

"I agree. What do you think we should tell the women when we get back home?"

"Might as well tell them what happened. It's bound to make the papers anyway, don't you think?"

"I suppose so. Maybe they'll get used to it eventually."

The CEO excused himself and the trio began to dress for bed. Only Hans slept soundly. He knew that events like today were just job security so long as he was at the top of his game.

****

The limo picked them up at the same time, and by noon they had completed all of the adjustments. They had taken their belongings to the job site so they could leave from there and go directly to the airport. They shook hands and were glad to get back inside the jet which was ready to roll as soon as they had boarded. Once seated, Charley and Enrique began to feel as relaxed as Hans. Charley said, "I wish I'd asked how long for them to simulate the mileage on their computers."

Hans replied, "Don't worry. They're as anxious as you are to put to rest the lies of the magazine. He'll call you as soon as he has anything to tell you."

Enrique said, "I'll be just as glad to get back home again. Plain tacos will taste better to me than any of that fancy stuff we had in the hotel. I guess I'd forgotten that I'm still a target. Since all the mechanics at the plant know how to do the adjustment, I thought maybe I was no longer in danger, but I see now that that's not the case."

"As long as you're close to me, there'll always be some danger. Would you rather I didn't call on you any more for help?"

"That's a hard question to answer. I wish my help might never be needed again, but if it is, I'll always be ready to do whatever you want. If you hadn't had faith in me, I'd still be strugglin' with dry land farmin'. It all happened so fast that I can hardly remember what it was like before. I just remember that it wasn't nearly as nice as drivin' a new truck and eatin' regular."

"Yeah, and I can't remember what it was like when I was just a mechanic with a dream, workin' in Chicago. I ask myself all the time if I had it to do over, would I."

"And how do you answer the question?"

"It depends. On days like yesterday, when I was close to being shot, it's an emphatic 'no way.' But there are times when things are going well that I wouldn't change a thing. How about you, Hans? Do you ever wish you'd gone into another line of work?"

"I never even think about it. It doesn't do any good to think about what might have been, so you just do the best you can and live with it."

"I suppose so, but still I wonder. Most people never have a shot at what I do. I think that's why I decided to go ahead with it. The safe thing to do would have been to sell my patent to the oil company people and live comfortably on the proceeds. But that sounded kinda boring. Beside, I had this idea that maybe I could help all the 9 to 5 guys of the world to have a better life if they weren't getting ripped off by the oil companies. I think if I'd known how powerful they are, I wouldn't have had the courage to challenge them. My lawyer tried to tell me, but I wouldn't listen. He was willing to risk it, and I got into a thing where I couldn't back down without looking cowardly and foolish. I wish I knew how many men have died just to keep from looking cowardly or foolish."

Hans chimed in, "Believe me, there's been lots of them. I've taken out a few. There's just something about testosterone that will not allow a man to look cowardly or foolish."

"I suppose so. I'm anxious to get back and talk to Terry and see if he's had any trouble."

****

Charley was thankful that Perdido had been peaceful during his absence. Terry relived his own close call with Toyota Man when Charley told him how Hans had taken care of the Japanese assassin. He said, "You know Hans is a hard son-of-a-bitch to like, but you gotta give him credit. He does his job. I bet the oil company people were sad to lose his service."

"Yeah, but you gotta remember they sent Toyota Man down here to get rid of him because he failed to kill me. I guess you never go into a slump when you work for them."

"I suppose not. How did every thing go with the adjustments?"

"About like I figured. No real problems. We hit a snag on the SUV's, but we managed to work our way through it. Enrique helped me when I was hung up. He's a good man. He's scared to death, but I can't hold that against him. We'll be hearin' from the Japanese in a day or two, or I miss my guess. You know they brought something to my attention that I never thought about. I knew we had the brothers and the oil companies for enemies, but I never thought about the other Japanese car companies as a threat. They were the first suspects of the Japanese police after Hans took care of the assassin. I never realized what a hurtin' it's gonna put on the other car makers."

"No kidding? I guess you gotta stand in line if you want to take a shot at us, huh? I hadn't thought about that, either. It just adds another bunch to the list of people who want to see us dead."

"Has anybody been snooping?"

"No, I don't think so. How did Enrique hold up with the shooting and all?"

"I guess okay. I think considering the sad state of the Japanese economy, they wouldn't mind if they could capture more of the automobile market globally, no matter which Japanese car maker had the lion's share of the market."

"That makes sense. I'll start looking through Dad's stuff and see how to get in touch with the tabloids. What should I tell them?"

"Tell them we'll pay their expense down here and give them an even bigger story than the one they broke before. That ought to be enough to get'em down here. I'll decide how much to tell 'em when they get here."

When Charley got back to the house, he took Alice into the study and told her what had happened. He was surprised at how calm she remained when he told her of the attempt on his life. "You don't seem upset."

"And why should I be? This isn't the first time. You've had closer calls than that. When you were shot in the arm, when they missed you and hit Billy at our wedding, when Hans killed Toyota Man. I guess I'm just getting used to it. I've almost resigned myself to the fact that I'll have to raise your son alone."

He laughed. "Well, as one of the richest widows in the world, you won't have any trouble finding him a new father."

She smiled and said, "Probably not, but I much prefer the one he has now. Shall we tell Luisa? She's not as used to this as I am, and I wouldn't want her to miscarry your grandson."

"I'll tell Billy and leave it up to him. He knows better than we do what might upset her. How are you feeling? Have you felt the baby move yet?"

"Yes, he's kicked me in the stomach several times since you've been gone. I wish you could have been here for his first kick."

"Yeah, I'm sorry I had to be gone. I hope I won't have to make any more long trips in the near future."

"Me too. I've missed you. I know you'd like to be here all the time, but I know you may have to do lots of traveling before this is over."

"Right on both counts. I hate any kind of traveling, but I think I hate flying the most. Wouldn't it be ironic that after all the close calls I've had to die in some stupid airplane crash?"

"Let's not talk any more about dying or close calls. Let's go to bed and make love."

****

The very next day the people from the tabloids arrived. Charley escorted them to the plant and showed them around. They were greatly impressed with the size and the scope of what they were shown. Charley gave them some slightly inflated figures on how many adjustments had been performed to date and how many they were expecting in near future. Then he hit them with a bombshell. A Japanese company was moving its center of production to Perdido. He refused to tell them which of the Japanese companies would be moving, but he assured them it was one of the biggies. Then he related the scam of the auto magazine that had claimed that his adjustment would ruin the motors of those that were adjusted. He told of his trip to Japan and the success of all his adjustments on the new models. Then he told of his close call with the gunman and left little doubt that the oil companies were at the bottom of the failed attempt. He was extremely complimentary to his hosts in Japan. He made it perfectly clear that in no way did he blame them for his close call with the gunman. When they asked how soon the Japanese would be arriving, the only answer he could give them was "soon." They left in a rush to get their scoops to press.

****

It was less than a month before the land that would contain the new Japanese car plant had been purchased and cleared so that construction could begin. Terry and Hans remained as head of security, and Billy was put in charge of hiring the local labor force that would be needed in the early part of the construction. There was no shortage of men applying for the jobs when they heard what the wages would be. The Japanese had promised to train a large percentage of the workmen who would be a big part of the skilled labor force when production actually began. Billy was glad that he had been given a job that he knew was extremely important. There could be no sabotage or the jittery Japanese might pull out before the thing ever began to take shape. He took the advice of Hans who told him to hire a detective agency to run a background check on all those who met the initial requirements before they were given clearance to go to work. He worked long hours interviewing the applicants before turning over the list of those he approved to the detective agency. Several he had earmarked for hire were turned down by the agency as too risky. The ones eliminated had either lied about their past or there were holes in their past which could not be accounted for. By the time the heavy equipment began to arrive, Billy had enough men hired for the construction to begin. Three large construction companies had been chosen from several that had bid on the job. Each company had been given a section of the plant to work on. No one company in Mexico was big enough to have completed the project within the time frame needed. The plant had to be completed in months, not years. The next year's models were scheduled to come from Perdido, not Tokyo

****

As the project got under way, the population of Perdido began once more to explode. Once again the construction of motels, hotels, restaurants, fast foods, and tourist trap things was rampant. And with this, also came with what always comes with rapid expansion—hookers, dope dealers, and grifters of every description. Once again with the help of Hans, Terry had been forced to expand the local police force to deal with the every day problems of law enforcement. It wasn't exciting work, but Terry didn't mind as much as Hans. The latter found such mundane things beneath him. He preferred keeping a close eye on the security of the plant and the construction of the new auto works. He was content to let Terry take care of the little things as long as they did not smack of something sinister.

The only thing that bothered Terry about his new responsibility was that it gave him very little time to spend with Teresa, the young hooker he had persuaded to give up whoring to become his mistress. He had put her into a nice house of her own, one large enough to include the girl's mother without sacrificing their privacy. He had bought the house before the values of real estate in Perdido had skyrocketed. When he had purchased the house, it was somewhat isolated, but more recently, other structures had sprung up. Nevertheless, the new places were not shabby, and most were of new homes of the Japanese workers who had recently been imported.

Terry had learned to deal with the riff-raff of Perdido, and he had almost forgotten what life had been like before he had impulsively agreed to follow his friend to Mexico. He smiled when he thought of the days back in the States when he was a nobody, simply a mechanic who was trying to make a living. Now he was a somebody, the closest personal friend of the richest and most powerful man in Perdido, or maybe in the whole of Mexico. He was powerful, and all the locals knew that his word was law. He was not feared in the same manner as Hans, but he knew he would never be able to take the lives of other people as casually as a man who made a living out of killing. He reflected briefly on how Hans had taken care of the wounded members of the Fuego gang, how easy it had been for him to walk up to the wounded and finish them with a single shot to the head.

The strain of the extra time spent in watching over the heavy equipment which had begun arriving each day had started to take a hold of him. He promised himself that tonight he would enjoy some tequila and a night with Teresa. He had made the same promise twice this week, but something had come up each time, and he had been forced to forego his evening of R and R. If something came up tonight, he made a vow that it had better be something big, or Hans and the deputies could handle it.

****

Back in the U.S. the boardroom of Universal Oil was filled with executives, even those newly promoted due to the deaths of so many caused by the huge explosion. Each had before him on the long table a set of papers that had been passed out by a secretary before the meeting began. Only a few scattered whispers broke the silence. The chairman was reluctant to begin the meeting in earnest until the group had a chance to digest the information on the papers. He finally cleared his throat as an indication that the meeting was about to begin.

He stood up and began, "Gentlemen, I think you've had enough time to digest what is most important in the papers before you. You can see at a glance that the volume in sales of unleaded gas has dropped off substantially in some areas. There can only be one reason for this decline. Motorists are driving more now than they ever have, yet we see a big decline in retail sales. We know that hundreds of thousands of our customers have run off to Mexico to be given what they call an adjustment. Now we have even worse news than that which is before you. We know that one of the major Japanese carmakers is moving its entire operation to Mexico. When they become established there, it stands to reason that all the other Japanese manufacturers will have to follow suit. They simply cannot stay in competition with a company that can provide three times the gas mileage they can produce. Do any of you have any ideas about what we can do to halt this trend?"

The man sitting closest to the chairman rose to his feet and asked. "Is there any way we can create an artificial shortage of oil to justify the high prices at the pump?"

"Yes, in the short term, that might work for a while, but there is another important consideration. If the price continues to escalate, the people will become restless and uneasy. Inflation will follow, and the people just might vote our friends out of office and replace them with people who are not so friendly with us."

A younger man at the end of the table rose to pose a question, "Isn't there a limit to the number of Japanese cars that can be imported into the United States?"

"That would be true if the cars were indeed manufactured in Japan, but as long as they are manufactured in Mexico, the NAFTA treaty lets them ship anything they want up here with no tariff."

An older exec remained seated and asked, "What will our Big Three car manufacturers do if this happens?"

"That is uncertain, but if they do nothing, it is most certain they will be out of business completely in two years. I'm sure that as we speak they are in meetings just like the one we are having now to try to come up with a solution."

Another older exec stood and asked, "Have we tried to get a suitable replacement for Toyota Man? It would seem to me that a man of, how should I say, his "abilities" would be useful in these troubled times."

"A good question, and the answer is 'Yes'. We have hired those who specialize in much the same type of work he was famous for. Unfortunately, the security since we first sent him to Mexico has increased so much that no one now thinks it is feasible to hit them. They are protected not only by locals, but also by the state, and soon the nationals will be in place"

"And who is responsible for such tight security?"

"Unfortunately, he is one who was once in our employ. He was sent there to get rid of the man responsible for the adjustment. He failed, and we sent Toyota Man down to relieve him, but he was lucky and recognized him in time to kill him. Since his failure, we now find no one willing to take a similar risk. They consider it a suicide mission, and to date we have found no one in the mood for that kind of thing."

"Are there any others we might consider allies in this besides Detroit?'

"Another good question. We have reason to believe that the three oldest brothers de los Santos are quite angry at being left out of the old man's will. We know they have strong ties to organized crime. Perhaps those connections might be of value to us if we cannot come up with a peaceful solution."

"Is there absolutely no chance that we can buy these people off? I'm sure we could make it worth their while."

"A good thought, but after the deaths we caused in the family, I'm certain they cannot be bought."

"How about the patent?"

"It's rock solid. No way around that, but even if there was, we don't want to go there. If everyone had the use of the patent, imagine what that would do to our volume at the pump."

"Do we have any influence with the Japanese government that might halt or even slow down the move to Mexico?"

"Now that's an area we haven't completely explored so far. I know we have some friends there, but their economy is struggling so badly now that a monopoly of the American car market must seem like a godsend to them. Still, there are some that we might be able to buy. We'll be looking into that more closely in the near future. You can bet on that. Any other questions or comments?"

"One more thing. How about our own government? Surely they aren't willing to sit idly by and watch our Big Three go under, are they?"

"I'm sure they will help us if they can. The problem is their help must be covert. They can't be put in a position of trying to bully their neightbors. They have the potential to be a prime oil exporting country. We need to keep that in mind, knowing that our Arab sources cannot always be counted on. The problems we face at this time are extremely complex. The geopolitical situation is very unstable, as well as the local problem that we face. If there are no more questions, I shall adjourn this meeting until a week from today. Gentlemen, good afternoon."

****

Three months passed swiftly. The construction of the plant on the site of where the first Japanese cars were to be built in Mexico progressed rapidly. Urban sprawl was evident wherever one looked. The Perdido that the alcalde had loved had vanished, and in its place stood the makings of a metropolis. Construction of new housing could not possibly keep pace with the demand that increased daily. Homeless people roamed the streets during the day, and at night they could be found sleeping in storefronts and alleys. An old abandoned building now served as a makeshift jail for those convicted of petty crimes. For those who came looking for work in Perdido and could find none, the situation was desperate. Purse snatching and petty theft were the most common offenses with which the local law enforcement was forced to deal. Burglary was on the rise, but most of the new affluent homeowners had purchased guns. Three persons had been shot after breaking and entering.

Construction had also begun on the new house for Charley and Alice. The alcalde had made them a present of the land, and they had planned the new home down to the last detail. Charley made visits to the site at least twice a week and tried to tell Alice about any new progress. Her pregnancy and Charley's fear for her safety kept her confined in the house which was now the property of Billy and Luisa. Both ladies made regular trips to the doctor for prenatal care. Both had had sonograms and were informed that each would be the mother of a baby girl. Neither husband seemed disappointed that a son was not in the near future. The building of the Japanese plant occupied most of their time and left them not nearly as much time as they would have liked to spend with their wives. Alice seemed to understand, but Luisa could not help complaining that she needed more time with her husband. At the end of a long and grueling day, Billy came home almost exhausted. Luisa met him at the door and was in tears. She said, "I'm so glad you're home. My morning sickness has stayed with me all day. I can't seem to keep any food down. I hate to complain to Alice because she never seems to have the problems that I do."

"You can't help the way you feel. I wish I could be here with you more, but...."

"I know. You have your job to do. Your father needs you more than I do. He depends on you as much as anyone, and he has far too much to do."

"Still, a man should be with his wife at a time like this. Do you think you should see the doctor more often?"

"No, I'm told that what I'm going through is normal. Most women have the same problems that I'm having. I guess Alice is the exception that proves the rule. I know Charley spends even less time with her than you do with me. Have you thought about a name for your daughter?"

"Well, here's a thought. How about Carlotta after Charley and Alicia after Alice? What do you think?"

"It sounds great. Can you stay here for the rest of the evening?"

"I had a few things to look into, but I guess there's nothing that can't wait until tomorrow. Let's just relax for a while."

****

In Japan the legislature was in a heated debate. Many thought that moving a major car company to Mexico was a huge mistake. They argued that the loss of jobs would be bad, and that if rival companies followed suit, it might be catastrophic. The small majority countered with the argument that a monopoly of the car market in the long run would outweigh any short-term losses. The CEO of the movers was holding his breath for fear they might force his company to return to Japan. He had already gone too far and spent too much money to turn back now. If he succeeded, he might well go down in Japanese history as the man who saved his country from financial ruin. If he failed, he would be forever known as the man who bankrupted the largest corporation in the country.

In Mexico City, the government was all smiles. There was no organized opposition to the move from Japan to Perdido. There was an alarm, however, that there might be those who, for whatever reason, might not want the move to succeed. For that reason, there was a motion that the governing body should allocate troops to the Perdido area to insure the safety of both the plant and the workers there. The taxes to be paid by both the company and its employees would generate far more revenue than the expense of the troops sent to watch over the place. The measure passed with only two dissenting votes.

In the States, the possible impact of the move was seen only by a few. Most could not see how having the competition from Japan move to Mexico would have any impact on the American economy. A few had traveled to Mexico and had their cars adjusted. They knew that American made cars without the adjustment could not possibly compete with those who were getting the kind of mileage they now enjoyed. Only those elected from states where the manfacture of automobiles was important seemed to realize the importance of the move to Mexico. The others were far more concerned with the relationship of the U.S. to the oil exporting countries of the world. Trouble on the horizon with OPEC nations seemed a far greater concern than one car company moving to Mexico.

Meanwhile, the brothers were biding their time, Carlos and Jorge patiently, and Diego, fuming as usual. Diego had seen the failure of the negative advertising campaign and continued to insist that violence was the only way to halt what was beginning to seem like the inevitable. It took all the years of experience the other two had in dealing with their brother's rashness to dissuade him from senseless acts that could only have harmed their cause. His latest fiasco was to try to enlist as many soldiers of fortune as he could for a psuedo military strike against the plant. Their arguments against such an action and a shortage of hard cash were the only things that stood in his way. After all, it was not in the best interest of those employed by organized crime to see that the brothers became instant millionaires. The risks of exciting the wrath of both the American and Mexican governments made such a military move far too risky. The mob's sentiments may have favored them, but their money was not so inclined

Business at the plant was brisk. Not only were more and more ordinary citizens bringing their cars for the adjustment, but first the trucking industry had seen the light and arrived in droves, followed closely by the military. All branches of the military were quick to see the advantage they might have with vehicles that required only 20% of the gas they now used. Because of the volume these two provided, the mechanics at the plant were working overtime to try to keep up. A reduced rate for those who brought in more than 30 vehicles made the traffic even heavier. Enrique was the general foreman and the man most responsible for the overall operation. He had gradually acquired the air of authority that was necessary for his position but unnatural to his disposition. He found it difficult but necessary to be harsh with those who worked beside him. There were a few who had gotten used to the good life too soon. Some had already forgotten what it was like before they had passed the test to become the adjusters and had begun to receive the good pay that went with the job. Some had to be let go, and it was Billy who took care to keep a file of all those past employees who might harbor a grudge against the company. These were people an enemy might try to employ with acts of sabotage, for they knew where security was most lax and where the most damage could be done in a short period of time. When Charley came to make his daily visit, Enrique met him before he got into his office. He said, "I had to let three men go today. Two were chronically late for work, and the other had a lot of complaints from people whose carburetors he adjusted."

"No need to apologize for that. We need people we can depend on. It's too bad when some don't measure up, but we gotta do what we gotta do. Do you think it's possible that any of them might cause trouble?"

"I don't know. They were all pretty upset. I think I might rehire the two who were late if they promise to do better, but the other guy I never did like and couldn't see how he passed the test to become an adjuster."

"Well, you do whatever you think best on the rehires, but don't put a guy back on line who does a poor job on the adjustment. We can't afford the negative publicity."

"Yeah, I know. How's everything on the home front? How are the wives?"

"Okay, I guess. I'm taking them in for a check-up later today."

That afternoon Charley and a single deputy accompanied both women to the doctor's office. Both the women were excited and chatted nonstop all the way while the men remained silent. When they arrived, Charley got out first to assist the ladies in exiting the car. He made a single step when the shot rang out. The bullet broke the window on the passenger side and was embedded in the back seat. The deputy and the driver both jumped into action. Both pulled guns from the holsters they wore and looked anxiously for a target. From the top of a small building the driver spied a man with a high-powered rifle pointed in their general direction. He motioned to the deputy, and both men aimed and fired. The man dropped the rifle which came tumbling to the ground. They raced toward the building, but the man slid down from the roof of the building and ran toward another small building adjacent.

Charley pulled both women inside the doctor's office and hesitated briefly. He fought to control his desire to see what was happening on the other side of the wooden door. The relative safety inside proved hard to overcome, but after a short time when he had heard no more shots, he crawled out the door to see what was happening. He could not see from his prone position either of his two men or the assailant. He dared not elevate himself for a better look for fear of making himself a better target. After a minute or two, he crawled back to the station wagon and got in. He grabbed the radio and sent a mayday to Hans or Terry.

Terry answered, "Is that you, Charley? What the hell is goin' on?"

"It's me alright. How fast can you get your ass down here to the doctor's office? I'm here at the clinic. At least one guy with a rifle took a shot at me. Both of my guys are in pursuit, I think. I can't see any of them from where I am in the car. Bring all the help you can get."

"Roger, I'm on the way."

He was there in less than five minutes and with him were four others. They pulled up in back of the station wagon and dismounted from all four doors. Terry jumped into the front seat with Charley to get a better idea of what they might be up against. Charley pointed to the building from which the lone shot had been fired. He told him he wasn't certain in which direction the man had fled. As far as he knew, there been only one man in the attempt. Terry leaned out of the car and told the men to spread out and head in the direction of the building from which the shot had been fired. He warned them to be careful not to fire at one of their own men. He told the leader of the group to use his walkie-talkie to keep them informed of what was happening.

Terry said, "God damn it, where is Hans? He's always better at shit like this than me."

"My guess is he's on the way. Sometimes he looks so bored with the routine that I think he actually enjoys crap like this."

"I know he does. He told me that the best thing that happened recently was his chance to blow away the Jap that was after you. He smiled all the way through the execution of the Fuegos. Makes me really glad that he's one of us."

Several shots could then be heard. Charley asked, "Why the hell doesn't that idiot with the walkie-talkie tell us what the hell is goin' on?"

"He might be so busy dodging bullets that he hasn't had a chance to fill us in. Hey, you on the other end of this thing! What the hell are you guys shootin' at! Come back."

The voice on the other end replied, "We got him holed up inside the next building over. One of our guys got nicked, so you might want to call for an ambulance. It's not serious, but he has lost a lot of blood."

"How many are there?"

"Only one as far as we can tell. He seems to be armed with only a pistol, but he's in a place that's hard to get at. Should we rush him or just try to wait him out?"

"Just keep him there till Hans gets here. He'll let you know what to do then. Just be sure you got the place surrounded and keep him there until Hans is on the scene."

"Roger, out"

"Where was Hans when this went down, do you know?"

"The last I knew he was headed toward the construction site. I'm certain he's on the way."

No sooner said than Hans pulled in behind the station wagon. He had only one other deputy. He crawled toward the wagon and then opened the rear door and slipped inside.

"What the hell is goin' on?"

"One guy took a shot at Charley as he was takin' the ladies to the doctor. As far as we can tell, it's only one guy, and we got him cornered in that building over there. Four of our guys have the place surrounded, so he can't get out. One of our guys has been hit, but we think the guy is armed only with a pistol."

"You okay, Charley?"

"Yeah, I still lead a charmed life. It was a clean miss. You can see from that hole in the window that that shot didn't come from a pistol. He dropped a weapon when my guys first took a shot at him. My guess is he started with a scoped rifle."

"Is there any chance he might have other weapons stashed in that building?"

"Well, I guess there's a chance. We can't be for sure, but the only thing he's fired recently is a pistol."

"Well, I gotta get up there to find out what's happening. Tell the guys I'm headed that way and not to take a shot at me."

"Okay"

He slipped out the back door and dodged his way along, making use of every bit of cover between himself and the nearest deputy. He joined that man and asked essentially the same questions he had asked before. There was no additional information to be gained from that source. He asked where the next deputy was stationed and the man pointed to a spot behind a thick hedge. Once again he began a zig-zag course which took him to the second deputy. The man told him the assailant had not fired a shot in the last several minutes and thought he might be out of ammunition.

"That's possible. Do you want to lead the charge to see if he's really out of ammo? I didn't think so. Stay put until I tell you different. Do you understand me?"

"I do."

"Where's the next man stationed?'

He pointed to a small building close to the one where the man had holed up. Once again he made his way cautiously toward the third deputy. The second deputy's opinion about the scarcity of ammo was proven incorrect as three shots were taken at Hans as he made his way toward the small out building. He arrived unharmed and found the third deputy keeping himself well out of harms way.

"Why didn't you return fire when that son-of-a bitch took three shots at me?"

"We were told not to do anything rash until Hans gets here."

"God damn it, I am Hans. Who the hell did you think I was, the Lone Ranger?"

"Sorry, sir. I didn't know it was you."

"Well, you know it now, and if that asshole shoots in my direction, you better open up or it will be your ass. Do you read me?"

"Loud and clear."

"Where's the fourth guy?"

"He's around in back of the building. There's no door on that side. But there's a window. He's keeping that covered."

"I'm headed that way. You better give me some cover if he opens up again."

"I will, you can count on me."

"Bull shit!"

He was quickly out of the line of fire. He was not shot at again. He found the fourth man hiding behind a tree. He only nodded when Hans approached. It was a man that Hans knew well, and he was glad that their leader had joined them.

"Has the man fired anything at you?"

"No, I haven't even seen him. I don't know if he even knows this window is here. I'm just here to stop him if he tries to get out on this side."

Just then a bullet hit the tree. "I guess he must have found the window, wouldn't you say?"

"Yes sir, I would."

"Here, hold my cap up on the tip of your rifle. If he takes a shot at that, I'll get a shot at him."

The deputy did as he was told. He put Han's cap on the tip of his rifle and held it up in plain view of the window. A shot rang out from above, and Hans got off a quick shot of his own. The man tumbled to the ground, and his pistol went flying.

"Are you sure he had no partners?"

"We never saw anyone but his one man."

Hans crawled toward the fallen man. Thirty feet from the body he discerned some movement and correctly surmised that the man was only wounded. He started to finish him off but stopped just short. First, he would like to know who had hired this stupid son-of-a-bitch. The man was barely conscious and bleeding profusely from the shoulder. The man had landed on his side and crawled a step or two on his stomach. Hans put the cuffs on the man and shook him down for another weapon. Then he stood and told the fourth man to tell the others that the danger was over. He remained with the captive until Terry and the others arrived. Charley had decided it was best to remain with the wives.

Hans said, "I want to be the one to question this stupid piece of shit. I'll find out in a hurry who put him up to this. My first guess would be the oil companies, but they usually hire people who can shoot straighter than that."

Charley couldn't refrain from saying, "Don't forget. You took a shot at me on my wedding night, didn't you? And you missed."

"No, I killed the man who missed you. You're lucky it was him shootin' at you instead of me. I couldn't possibly have missed at that range."

"Do you ever wish he'd shot straighter and you were still employed by them?"

"Never. Protecting you is a lot safer than the jobs they wanted me to do. Besides, I've even grown to like you. That's a danger in my line of work. I took more chances today than I normally would to get a shot at him."

"That's why you get the big bucks, amigo."

Hans couldn't help laughing. It had been a long time since anyone had called him "amigo"

Terry asked, "Should we send for an ambulance for this turkey?"

"No, I'll just slap a tourniquet on the arm, and we'll escort this son-of-a-bitch to the hospital. That'll save the meat wagon a trip. How bad was the deputy hit?"

"Just nicked him. He'll be all right. No more widows to contact from this caper."

"You want to go with us to the hospital?"

"No, I think I better stay here with the ladies. You can tell me later if you find out who sponsored this escapade."

"Oh, I'll find out alright. If he hasn't died by the time we get him to the hospital, he'll be glad to tell me everything in a hurry. You can be sure of that."

At the hospital, the wounded assailant was taken immediately to the emergency room. Hans was definitely in charge. He told the attending doctor to stop whatever he was doing and look at the wounded and bleeding shoulder of the man on the stretcher. The doctor recognized Hans from other cases that he had brought in. He was aware that Hans stood very high in the pecking order in Perdido. He stopped bandaging a man with a superficial knife wound and turned his attention to the cuffed prisoner. He saw the bullet wound had made an exit, and there was no reason to look for the bullet. He placed an antiseptic salve over the wound and applied a bandage. He turned to Hans and said, "He's lost a lot of blood from the looks of his complexion. He'll need a transfusion soon."

"Can the transfusion wait? Is he in serious danger of dying in the immediate future?"

"I don't think so, but he will need some blood."

"Then let it wait. I need some answers from this man. If he gives me the right answers, he can get the blood. If not, don't waste the blood."

"Whatever you say.

Hans had the prisoner placed in a wheel chair. He rolled the man to an office and invited only one deputy to join him. The man was semi-conscious, but Hans had already decided not to wait for the man's condition to improve before he began the questioning.

"Hey," he screamed at the prisoner. "I know you can hear me. Now listen. Do you know who I am?"

The man merely nodded. He looked pale, but the look of fear upon his face was not lessened by the loss of blood.

"What is your name?"

"My name is Carlos Garcia y Ortega."

"Why did you try to kill those people today?"

"I was fired from my job at the plant. It wasn't fair. I know I made some mistakes, but others made mistakes and were given new chances, but not me. They said, 'Garcia, we can't use you any more' Now my life is ruined. My fiance will not marry me. She will find someone who makes the kind of money I was making. It wasn't fair."

"But why did you try to shoot that man? He wasn't the one who fired you, was he?"

"No, but he was the one who hired the guy who fired me. I knew Enrique when he was nothing more than a dry land farmer, like me. I went to the school he taught where I learned to make the adjustment. I made lots of good ones. Lately I made mistakes, but they knew I could do it if they gave me a chance."

"How did you know this was the man who hired Enrique? Had you ever met the man you tried to kill?"

"No"

"So how did you know who he was and where to find him on that day?"

"I was told."

"By who?"

"I do not know the man's name. I had never met him before yesterday. He told me who the man was and where I could find him today."

"What else did he tell you?"

"He told me he would pay me $10,000 if I killed him. He gave me a $1,000 to try. He promised me the rest when I had done the job. Please, don't kill me."

"What did the man look like who paid you the money? Was he a Mexican?"

"He spoke Spanish very well, but he spoke mostly in English. He was dressed like an American. The money he gave me was American. I'm begging you not to kill me. I promise I'll try to help you find the man if you give me a chance."

"Where did you meet this man?"

"In a cantina where I often go to relax after work. He seemed to know that I'd been fired. I don't know how he found out about that. It had been very recent. Maybe he knew someone who worked in the plant."

"What else did he tell you?"

"He told me there was a very good chance that he would be taking two women to the clinic, that the women were pregnant and that there would be an armed escort. He took me to the back room and gave me a rifle and a pistol. He asked me if I knew how to shoot. I told him I had served in the army and that I was familiar with both guns. He advised me to plan an escape route after the shooting. I hoped when I got to the outbuilding that I could slip away before your men got the place surrounded. I was afraid to give myself up. I knew you would probably kill me."

"You were right. We very well might have. Where is the money the man gave you?"

"I hid it under the mattress at my house. I'll give it to you if you won't kill me."

"I'll think about it. What's your address?"

"It's in the new section of town. It's one of the nice apartments on Via Magnifica. It's called the Plaza. Apartment no. 10."

"Who else knew you had been fired from your job?"

"The three others who worked with me on the day shift surely would have known. I don't know how many others. Can I get the blood I need now? I've told you everything I know."

He wheeled the man back into the emergency room and told the doctor that the man could have his blood. He signaled to the deputy, and the man preceded him through the door to the parking lot. There he instructed the driver to head for home base.

"Back so soon? I thought it might take you a little longer."

"There wasn't a whole lot he could tell me. He didn't know the name of the man who hired him. He got a thousand up front to try and was promised 9,000 more if he succeeded. He said the man who gave him the money spoke both English and Spanish and was dressed like an American."

"Was money the only motive?"

"No, he was pissed because he'd been fired from his job at the plant. Not too many could have known about the firing so soon. I think maybe we better have a chat with three of his co-workers. We need to know who they've been talking to recently."

"Anything else?"

"Yeah, he told me where he lived and where he hid the thousand. If I find it, can I keep it? I need some cash to pay some of my informants."

"Yeah, that'll be okay. It'll save Billy havin' to get the money for you, and he's got a lot to do."

"I'm headin' out to the address he gave. I'll let you know if I find the money. Oh, yeah, one other thing. He knew Enrique personally before either of them got into the business. You might want to know what he could tell you about the guy."

"I'll make a point of asking him about it tomorrow. Is that all?"

"Yeah, I'm on my way."

He gave the driver the address the prisoner had given him and rode without conversation to the spot. The door to the apartment was locked, but he jimmied the lock with little difficulty. Once inside, he went to the bed and flipped the mattress. He found the money in a small plastic bag and had already decided there was nothing more to be gained by a further search. He went back to the car and told the driver to take him home.

The next morning Charley left early with his usual escort toward the plant. He went to an office that was now occupied by Enrique. He saw the look of surprise when he entered.

"Is there something wrong?"

"Did you hear about the shooting yesterday?"

"Yes, I heard no one was hurt on our side and that they caught the guy. Hans again, I suppose."

"Yeah, Hans again. The guy they caught said he knew you, had known you for a long time. Said you were the one who fired him. His name was Carlos Garcia. Do you know the man?"

"Yes, I hired him. He was marginal at best, but I knew he was a lot like me. I hoped he would get better, but it didn't work out. I had to let him go because of all the complaints we got on the adjustments he performed."

"Who else would have known about the firing?"

"Well, here in the plant, probably only the three guys he worked with. But they would also know in personnel. I let them know almost immediately so they could draw up his severance."

"Are the other three all on the job this morning?"

"Yes, them and the new replacement."

"Could you send them in here to see me, one at a time so I can ask them a few questions?"

"Sure, you want to do it right now?"

"Yes, I do. Go get the first one and I'll wait here. Don't tell them what it's about. I don't want any of this to go any further."

"Okay, I'll send the first one in as soon as I can walk down to their work station."

In about five minutes, the first of the three tapped on the door and then walked in. The look on his face was fear. He was almost afraid to look Charley in the eye.

"Don't look so frightened. I'm not here to chew you out or fire you. I just want you to answer a few questions for me, so relax."

The questions were short and to the point. Did he know the man before they worked together on the job, did the man have any friends working in the plant, had he said anything about the man's firing to anyone on the day he was fired. The answer was "no" to all three questions. Charley told the man to go back to work and send one of his fellow workers to the office.

The second workman appeared shortly thereafter with the same puzzled and frightened look. The questions were posed with the same responses. He was sent back with the same instructions as the first. The third man gave Charley no more useful information than the first two. He was pretty sure that neither of these three had been the one who let slip the information about the firing. That sent Charley to the personnel office.

When he got to that office, he ran into Billy. He was surprised but pleased.

"What are you doin' here, dad?"

"Well, I had a little question or two to ask, but since you're here, I'll let you ask them for me."

"Okay, who do you want me to ask and what do you want me to ask?"

"I want to know who knew about the firings yesterday."

"That would be only the guy in payroll. I can find out if there was any reason for anyone else to know."

"Do that, and then let me talk to whoever's in charge of personell."

"Okay. I'll be right back."

When Billy returned, he had the man in payroll with him. The man looked puzzled and frightened. Charley said, "Relax. Did anyone else in your department say anything about the three men who were fired yesterday?"

"No sir. That information was only between me and the director of personnel. Would you like to speak with him? I'll get him for you if you want."

"Okay, do that."

Shortly thereafter, the personnel director made his appearance. Charley asked him what he knew about the men recently fired. He shrugged his shoulders and said, "I didn't know any of them personally. But something strange did happen. A man called and did not identify himself and asked if any of our workmen had left recently. He said he needed mechanics and he knew that we hired only the best. He said the work would have nothing to with adjusting carburetors, just run of the mill mechanical work. I thought since these three were unemployed, it might be an act of kindness on my part if I could get them a job they were better suited for than here. I really hope I didn't do anything wrong."

"No, you didn't, but in the future you're not to release any information about the people who're employed here. If there are any more calls of that type, you're to inform me or Billy immediately. Do you understand? One more thing. Did the conversation you had with this man take place in English or Spanish?"

"English, with an American accent. Definitely not European."

"Thank you. That will be all."

When Charley got back to the house, he got Hans on the phone and told him what he had learned at the plant. Han said it sounded more like the work of the brothers than Universal or the Japanese. After his chat with Hans, Charley decided to have a talk with Juan. He went to the room that Juan now called home and knocked.

"Come in."

"Have you got a minute?"

"Sure, what's on your mind?"

"I was just wondering. Do you possibly have any recent pictures of your brothers?"

"Let me think. I don't have any, but the old man had some taken at a family reunion we had about two years ago. What's the point?"

"Do you think you might be able to find any of those pictures?"

"I might. I know where the old man kept all the photo albums. You still haven't told me why."

"Well, the guy who took a shot at me yesterday might be able to identify the man who hired him to do the job if it turned out to be one of your brothers."

"Yeah, that makes sense. I never thought of that. Well, if it was one of them, it would have been Carlos or Jorge. Diego would have tried to do the job himself. How did they find someone crazy enough to take a shot at you? How did he know where you'd be at the time?"

"The guy was a man that had just been fired at the plant. Someone called the plant and got the names of all the men we had recently let go. He said he wanted to hire them for some routine mechanic work. The man in personnel thought he was doing the men a favor, so he gave the man a list of three of our most recent dismissals."

"Now I'm certain that it couldn't have been Diego. He would never have been clever enough to think of something like that. Sounds a lot like the work of Jorge."

"You really don't like Diego much, do you?"

"No, I don't, and for good reasons. He tried to make my childhood and youth as miserable as possible. He was extremely jealous of my resemblance to the old man and also of the fact that my mother made it no secret that I was her favorite. He's not only ugly, he's also stupid. I'm surprised that he's done as well as he has in organized crime. I'm sure my brothers have had to keep him in check, or he would have been dead a long time ago."

"Well, I'm headed for the kitchen for a cup of coffee. I'll be there for a while, so if you find any of those pictures, bring'em to me and I'll pass'em along to Hans. He can take'em to the prisoner and see if he can recognize any of them.

"Will do."

He met Alice downstairs and asked if there was any coffee left over from breakfast. She said no, but offered to make some fresh, and he accepted.

They sat down at the table and waited for the coffee to brew. He told her of his conversation with Juan, and told her he would take any pictures of the brothers that Juan found to Hans so he could finish the interrogation of the prisoner.

"Will Hans kill the man?"

"I don't know. Maybe, if he thinks the man is lying. I know he's quite capable. He's killed men for less."

"He still gives me the creeps. I know he's saved your life more than once, but I can't make myself like him."

"I know. I feel the same way. Like him or not, we need him. He knows more than any of us how to anticipate what the others are likely to do. Forewarned is forearmed, so they say."

"Do you think there'll ever come a time when we won't need Hans or someone like him?"

"Not any time soon. Yesterday was a reminder that we can never let down our guard. Tell me, now. Exactly what did the doctor say about your and Luisa's condition?"

"He said I'm doing fine. He's surprised that I'm getting along better than Luisa. She's at a better age for having babies than I am. Did you know that?"

"I know lots of women are waiting until they are your age to start families. I also have heard that it's equally hard for teenagers like Luisa to give birth. The mortality rate for them is higher than it is for women your age."

"How do you know these things?"

"I can read something besides Car and Driver."

"Oh really? I had no idea. What's your source? Women's Day or Cosmopolitan?"

"Both actually. You leave them laying around the house. They make for pretty good readin' when you're sittin' on the toilet."

"And here I was thinking you were suffering from constipation when all the time you were improving your mind. I suppose that now you are an authority on sanitary napkins and disposable douches?"

"Hardly, but I have learned a few things about childbirth."

"What exactly have you learned?

"I've learned that it's usually better for the husband to be present for the birth of the child. I don't know about the breathing sessions and all that or the birth under the water, but I've tried to find out as much as I can. I didn't take much interest in the birth of my sons, but I'll try to do better with my daughter,"

"I'm glad. Did you really want another son?"

"Why should I? I've already had two sons. Don't you think it's about time I had a daughter?"

"I know. But you lost one and I thought…"

"Nothing could bring my son back. I loved Jack, and I still miss him but you having another boy wouldn't lessen the pain I feel when I think about him. I'll have to try to do better with Billy and my daughter."

"You still blaming yourself for what happened to Jack?"

"Sometimes, I guess. I never thought it would come to this when I first came up with the adjustment. I never set out to become the richest man in the world. I think the alcalde could see it happening, but I never in my wildesr dreams ever imagined something like this might be about to happen."

"I never did either, but there's no turning back now. I'd want to go on with what we started no matter what. Even if they tried to buy us out, I wouldn't consider it, would you?"

"Not after Jack and all the shots they've taken at me. I could never trust them. I trust Hans more than any of the oil people or the brothers. I have no problem in trusting the Japanese. They have a vested interest in this thing, the same as we do. If we fail, they go under with us."

"What kind of world will our daughter grow up in?"

"I can't answer that one. She could grow up as the pampered brat of one of the richest men in the world, or she might not grow up at all."

The next day Charley took the pictures that Juan had finally found the night before to Hans. He looked them over and decided it was a good likeness of the three he had met for the only time at the old man's funeral. He put the pictures in an envelope and went directly

to the hospital to see if the prisoner might be able to identify one of
them as the man who had hired him for the assassination attempt.
Hans had been worried that whoever hired the man might try to
silence him before he could identify the man who hired him. He
walked to the side of the bed where the prisoner lay sleeping. He
shook the man and then said in a loud voice, "Wake up!"

The man blinked once or twice and then grimaced as he recognized the speaker. He tried to turn away, but Hans took him by
the shoulder and pulled him back to where he faced him.

"I want to know something. Now I want you to look at the pictures
of three different men and tell me if any one of the three could be
the man who hired you. Do you understand what I'm saying?"

"Yes, I do," he almost whispered.

He looked at the first picture only briefly and then shook his head
from side to side. He said nothing. Then he stared a little longer
at the second photo, but once again shook his head. He looked
much longer at the third before finally saying, "That could be
him. I can't be sure, but I think it might be him."

"Alright, go back to sleep."

He left the hospital in a hurry and went straight to the plant
where he knew Charley would probably be. He telephoned ahead
to tell him to stay put until they could have a chat. He didn't like
to do business over the phone. One could never tell who might
be listening.

He sped past the guards after showing them a quick glance at his ID. He made a mental note to chew the guards who he thought had done an inadequate job of checking his ID. Fake ID's were easy to come by, and they should have spent more time checking his over. He had the driver park in the usual spot and told him to keep the motor running. He knocked on the office door and waited for a response.

"Come on in, Hans. What did you get from the prisoner?"

"Well, he couldn't make a positive ID, but he's pretty sure it was this one." He held up a picture of Jorge.

"Well, perhaps Juan was right. He said if it was one of them, it most likely would be this one. What now?"

"Well, I think we should have some blow-ups made of this picture and circulate them around town. It's doubtful he would still be in the area, but you never know. At any rate, if he shows up again, we'll have some idea what he looks like. We'll blow up pictures of the other two as well and let it be known on the streets that anybody who can help us nail these guys, will be in line for a large sum of money. How does that sound?"

"Sounds okay to me. You know a lot more about these things than I do. Did you get anything else?"

"No, that was it. I'll check on him later in the day and see if his memory has improved. He's not quite recovered from all that blood he lost, so he may be thinking a little strighter when he's had a little more time."

****

Back in the States, the two older brothers were waiting impatiently for the return flight of Jorge. He had not contacted them at all since he had departed to Mexico. They were in hopes that he could report the death of the one man who stood in the way of their hopes. When they saw him approach them, they knew from the look on his face that it had not gone as they hoped. Carlos helped him with his luggage and tried to hide his disappointment. Diego could not hide his impatience.

"Well, are you gonna tell us what the fuck happened, or are you just gonna stand there?"

"I'll tell you all about it as soon as we get back to your room. This is not a good place to be discussing such things."

They hailed a cab and headed back to the hotel room they had occupied for several days. When they had ridden the elevator up to the 14th floor, Diego led the way to their room. As soon as the door was unlocked, Diego screamed, "Alright, brother, what's the story?"

"Well, I found one of the workers who'd been fired from his job at the plant. I set him up with the guns and told him exactly where to set up shop. I found out from a nurse when he'd be takin' his pregnant wife to the doctor. He showed up at exactly the time I told him he would, but would you believe the stupid son-of-a-bitch missed?"

"I believe, so what happened next?"

"He got into a shoot-out with the locals and took a wound to the shoulder. He was captured alive and taken to a hospital."

"Is he still alive?"

"I can't answer that. He may be. I couldn't hang around much longer."

"Do you think he could identify you as the man who hired him?"

"I can't say about that, either. I wore a fake beard and mustache, but he got a pretty good look at my face."

"Do you realize that we'd be takin' a big risk for any of us to show our face in Perdido now?"

"Why so? They don't know what we look like. Why would we even be suspects?"

"Because that gutless fucking brother of ours by this time has no doubt found some of the old man's pictures of us and circulated 'em all over town. We'd be fools to go back there now. Anything else we try will have to be from a distance."

"You're probably right about that. I think we're going to have to attack this from another angle, Diego. We still need for the Japs to keep on coming, and if we keep tryin' to hit him, they may get cold feet and decide to stay at home."

"Do you have any more bright ideas, brothers? So far you haven't come up with shit."

"It may take a little time, brother, but we'll come up with something."

"You better. My patience is wearing thin."

****

In Japan the board of directors was growing more nervous by the minute. Rumors were flying about what the end result of the move would be. Not only the employees of this company, but also those of their rivals were beginning to protest. They could see that in order to compete, they too would be forced into a move that would allow them access to the adjustment. Until today, the protests had been scattered and disorganized, but today the streets were filled with people whose banners indicated that this was no spur of the moment thing, but a well planned and well orchestrated demonstration. Already police had been called in to quell the disturbance, but still the crowd grew larger and less manageable. The CEO rose to his feet to address the rest of the board for this impromptu meeting.

"Gentlemen, we must remain calm. We must not let the mood of the people outside cause us to make a grave error in judgement. We knew when we agreed to our present course of action that there would be a great many who would oppose our action. The loss of some jobs by our work force was bound to cause unrest within the industry as a whole. It may be that some of their fears are justified. There will be considerable unemployment, at least in the beginning, but the present state of the Japanese economy is such that if we do nothing, the end result will be far worse than the temporary disruption we may soon see in place. Therefore, it is my judgement that we must try to ignore the noise we hear from the outside and continue to make plans for the more distant future."

A vice-president rose and asked, "But what can we do in the meantime to ease the situation? We cannot count on the continued support of the national government. Their mandate is small, and these demonstrations may undermine what support we do have at this time. We must do something to stabilize their wavering support."

"You are right. Something must and will be done. Do any of you have any suggestions as to what we might do to lessen the tension of the people and the government?"

"Here is a thought. You, Mr. Chairman, should make an address to the nation on television. Tell the people that their fears are groundless, that any jobs lost through expansion will be regained when we control the car market. The huge amount of capital which will be generated by these sales will allow us to expand into other even more lucrative markets. There will be jobs for everyone in these new markets as Japan assumes the role of world leader in commerce."

"And what exactly are these new more lucrative markets that I am supposed to mention?"

"You need not go into detail. It will be enough, I think, to slow down the opposition long enough for us to make the transition."

"Thank you for the suggestion. Are there others who wish to speak at this time? If not, I shall close this meeting for another 48 hours."

****

Almost three months passed, and the time of the deliverance was almost at hand for both Luisa and Alice. The latter continued to enjoy her pregnancy while the former continued to suffer. As the time approached, Billy was able to spend more time with Luisa while Charley spent less and less with Alice. Charley had managed to shift some of the earlier responsibilities of Billy to others who had shown that they could be trusted and had even taken on some of the work himself to give his son more time with his wife.

It came suddenly. Luisa's water broke and she was rushed to the hospital. She was not in labor long before she gave birth to a slightly premature four and a half pound baby girl. She was healthy in every other respect, but she would not be allowed to leave the hospital until she weighed five pounds. Luisa would be allowed to nurse the baby if she chose to. She told the doctor she would like to nurse her daughter. Billy had been present for the birth, but Charley had not got the message in time to be there. He rushed there as quickly as he could and arrived shortly after the birth. He first congratulated his son and then went for his first look at his granddaughter. He was told that she resembled him somewhat, but it had always been his opinion that babies do not resemble anyone. It was enough that the child was healthy, and that Luisa was finally over the ordeal of pregnancy. He hoped his wife would have an easier time, and that the baby could leave with them soon. Staying here at the hospital spread the security he demanded for his family extremely thin. He would put Terry personally in charge of all the security here at the hospital. Terry now knew even better than Hans who could be counted on. He was in closer touch with most of the men than Hans. More and more the duties of the two men became well defined. Hans could take care of the national and international problems, leaving most of the local things to Terry. Before leaving the hospital, Charley wanted to have a few words with his son. "Billy, I just wanted to tell you to take it easy for a short time. You need to spend a lot of time with Luisa and the baby for the next few days. I want to warn you not get too lax with your own security. There's still a lot of people out there who would like to see you out of the picture. It might mean another assassination attempt or maybe even a kidnapping. Don't get so wrapped up in things that you forget and leave yourself open to attack. I need you now more than ever. When I have to be with Alice, you'll probably have to make some decisions. Others will look to you, and you've got to be ready to take over if something should happen to me."

"Okay, Dad, I'll try, but don't you think Juan could make better decisions than I could?"

"Maybe about some things concerning his brothers, but I still would rather have you make most of the decisions. You've been in on this from the ground floor and he hasn't. I trust him, but blood is thicker than water. You are my son, and that means a whole lot to me. I may not be able to spend as much time with you in the near future as I'd like to because of the babies, but don't ever think I've forgotten you."

"Okay, Dad, I won't. I hope Alice can have an easier time than Luisa did. I hope she won't be afraid to have another child because of how hard it was this time."

"Relax. She's Catholic. She'll want more. This is probably my last shot at parenthood. Alice might want more, but her biological clock sure must have just about run its course."

"Maybe not. Would you want another kid if she did?"

"I don't know. I haven't thought about it much. There's so many other things to think about that I haven't given that much brain room. I used to worry about how I could support a larger family, but now that's the least of my considerations. I just talked to my chief accountant yesterday, and I still can't believe what he told me."

"Tell me, Dad. What did he tell you?"

"Well, you might as well know. You are a millionaire several times over. Does that make you feel any better?"

"I guess. There's not a lot I can do with the money right now, but it's good to know that at some later date I can have about anything I've ever wanted. Do you think it's even remotely possible that we might be able to return to the States some day?"

"I can't really say. There was a time when I desperately wanted to go back, but now I've come to regard this place as home. Who can say what the future holds in store. I never once imagined any of what we have now would ever happen. It's hard to imagine that those who hate us will ever forgive or forget the misery we've caused them, but you never can tell."

****

Back in the States, the brothers had not been idle. Led by Diego, they had almost given up hope that anything but an armed insurrection could slow down the events in Perdido. It was Jorge who finally persuaded the other two that the answer might be found easier in Tokyo than Perdido.

He said, "Brothers, I think our best bet at this time might be the other car companies in Japan. They gotta know that if Perdido ever gets off the ground, it will be the end of them if they have to compete with the adjustment. Do we have any connection there?'

Carlos replied, "Not directly, but I'm relatively sure that some of our associates do. What do we want our connections to do for us if we get some?"

"Oh, I'm not sure, but I think provoking a little trouble in the streets might slow things down. The Japanese don't have a huge domestic police force and are hardly ever called on to put down domestic violence. We could start with a few peaceful demonstrations and then progress to some that got a little out of control."

"It might make them nervous and uncomfortable, but they've gone too far to turn back now. No matter what we do, they're moving to Perdido. You know it, and I know it."

"You're probably right, brother, but I think it might slow them down. Their government could help us out if things got a little too hot down in the streets."

Diego finally chimed in, "What the hell good does it do just to slow them down? What's the point? We need to take over the whole operation. I been tellin' you guys that for a long time. Delay does us no good that I can see. I told you then and I'll tell you now, we gotta show these people some muscle, or we ain't ever gonna see a dime out of all the millions the old man left our brother and the gringo."

"You might be right, Diego, but you'll have to be a little more specific. What exactly do you have in mind?"

"Well, check this out. You say the key may lay in Japan. I think you may be right, but instead of using what connections we have to start a street riot, why don't we try to get the help of one of the Japanese gangs? With all the Japs already in Perdido, a few more certainly won't arouse any suspicions. They wouldn't stick out. Maybe we could slip one or two inside the plant have them open a door or two to let some of the others in, and then see what mayhem they can create for my brother and his gringo friend."

"That may be the most sensible thing you've said since this whole thing began. I'll get ahold of Tony and Fats and see if they can give us a name or two that we could contact in Tokyo. I'm pretty sure they'll know somebody there who's lookin' for action."

"Yeah, you do that. If we need to contact them personally, I'll go along with you guys to help set something up."

"That probably won't be necessary. We can probably set the whole thing up without a trip over there. Anyway, you need to stay here if Carlos and I have to go. Somebody's got to stay here and mind the store, or the big boss is gonna get really sore at us, You've always been his favorite because you are a man of action. He's told us many times that we think too much and that he really likes the way you get right to the bottom of things. I'm sure you can do us more good here than in Tokyo."

"I think you're just blowin' smoke up my ass. You're afraid my temper might fuck things up if I went along, isn't that it?"

"Why brother, that's a terible thing to say. You? A temper? Isn't that the funniest thing you ever heard, Jorge?"

"It sure is, brother, it sure is."

"Oh, go fuck yourselves, both of you."

****

A week later a gang of six young Japanese were meeting with the Brothers in New York. They had been promised a large sum of money if they agreed to infiltrate the plant in Perdido. A much larger sum would be their reward if they were successful. They were warned about the danger, and especially to be aware of Hans.

The six were to go individually to Perdido and meet three days after the arrival of the first two. The place for their first meeting was to be a small bar on the outskirts of town, a bar which was unfinished and had been built to cater to the ever growing number of Japanese workmen. There, they would attract little attention. They had been provided with clothing that much resembled the clothing of the men who worked in the rapidly expanding plant. They were to spend a week scouting the location to find a point where the security was the weakest. The general plan was for two to slip in during a break in the night shift, overpower the guard at that location, and then let the other four inside. From there, three different sets of explosives were set to go off simultaneously, giving all six an opportunity to escape before the explosions. They were to leave Perdido the following day, each by a different route back to New York.

After the week of scouting, the leader decided that they should wait another two nights before implementing the plan. The weather for that night was forecast to be stormy and wet. A large front would be passing through, and the added darkness would help hide their entrance into the grounds of the plant.

The storm was approaching as the clock was striking the one o'clock hour. Dressed in black and armed only with knives and explosives, they made their way to the point where they had decided they had their best chance to gain entrance. There were two guards at that point, and both were outside the fence taking a smoke break. They were easily overpowered and silenced with knives. The bodies were dragged to a point where they would not be visible until the next morning. From that point they split up into three groups to plant their explosives. They made a quick check of the timers to make certain that all three blasts went off together.

The first group made their way down a hallway and quickly planted their charges in an office room and headed back to the rendevous point. They had gone undetected and waited impatiently for the other four to return.

The second group was not so fortunate. They ran into security and were challenged. They tried to explain their presence at that point, but the guards were not convinced. They asked for identification, and when these two could not provide any, the guards pulled their pistols and demanded that they follow them to a superior officer. The first made a move for the knife concealed in his belt, but the officer rendered him unconscious with a blow to the head with his gun. The second tried to run but was tackled by a guard who blew a whistle as the two struggled to the ground. The first officer rushed to the aid of his fellow officer and dispatched the second intruder with a second blow of his weapon.

The third group was even less fortunate. By coincidence, Hans had decided to make a late night inspection of the plant's security. He heard the whistle blow and was headed in the direction of the sound when he ran into the third group. They were trying to set their charge when they first saw him. He screamed at them to stop whatever they were doing and put their hands in the air. Both decided to make a run for it, a fatal mistake. Two shots from Han's pistol reduced the number of the gang to four. Hans moved on quickly toward the sound of the whistle. He did not even pause at the bodies of the fallen gang members. He rushed to the spot where the two guards were standing over the unconscious bodies of the second group.

"What happened here?"

"We challenged these two and asked for identification. They didn't have any with them, and he tried to pull a knife. I whacked him on the head. The other tried to run, and my buddy here tackled him and blew the whistle. I whacked him on the head, too.”

“A good job, men, I’ll see that you’re rewarded for your work here tonight. There may have been more than just the two groups. I’m pretty sure they were trying to set some explosives. We don’t have much time. Where are the dogs? If they were able to plant some, they’ll be goin’ off pretty soon. The dogs are our best chance to find any charges they may have set.”

The guard ran off to try to find the dogs, leaving Hans to guard the fallen men. They were back in less than two minutes. They found the hidden charges of the first group with less than a minute before the time would have blown them to Kingdom Come. The first group had heard the shots that Hans had fired and decided that they could wait no longer. They left hurriedly and retreated on foot until they were more than a mile away from their point of entry.

A Perdido deputy challenged them as they walked along in the dark. They pretended not to understand his questions, pleading a language barrier. They also walked with a stagger and used sign language to indicate they had been drinking heavily. The deputy laughed and motioned them to go on down the road. They kept up their staggering walk until they were well out of sight of the deputy.

Even considering the lateness of the hour, Hans decided that it would be best to inform Charley what had happened. He wanted to know if he should try to cover up the event so as not to worry the Japanese leadership. Billy answered the phone.

Hans said, "I hate to call you guys at this time of night, but we had something going at the plant tonight. Is your dad handy?"

"Yeah he's in the other room. I'll go get him."

He stumbled out of bed and almost hit the crib of the baby who remained asleep. He tapped on his father's bedroom door and said, "Hans is on the phone. He said something happened at the site He wants to talk to you."

Charley picked up the phone by his bed. "What's goin' on, Hans?"

"We had intruders break into the site tonight. There were at least four and I think possibly more. Two are dead, and two more were captured and knocked unconscious. I haven't had a chance to interrogate them yet. We found explosives they had set and narrowly avoided being blown to pieces. I guess my main question is, do you want me to cover the whole thing up so as not to unnerve our Japanese partners?"

"What do you think? Can you cover it up? Was enough noise made that you couldn't explain it if they called you on it?"

"I think I can cover the noise of the two shots I fired. The main thing is we'll have to make sure the guards don't say anything. I think if we make it worth their while, we can be sure of their silence."

"Okay, then. Let's try to keep it in the family, but Hans, and I mean this, under no circumstances are you to insure the silence of the guards by …… you know."

"What! Why boss, I'm horrified that you could think that I might.... you know. I'd never consider such a thing.

"Yeah, I know you wouldn't. You wouldn't even bother to consider it. You'd just do it! That's why I'm tellin you not to do it."

"Okay, anything else?"

"Get with me in the morning and tell me if you think you've been successful in covering it up. Good night."

The next morning, Hans knocked on the door as Charley was pouring his second cup of coffee. He came in and sat down at the table. Charley got up and poured him a cup and sat back down.

"Well, were you able to cover it up?"

"Yeah, I think so. The guards were tickled pink when I gave them a thousand each. I also told them they might wind up dead if they were ever tempted to tell what really happened."

"The cookie and the whip, huh?"

"Yeah, I guess you could call it that. It seems odd to me, but I have to admit that it works most of the time."

Later that morning, Hans stopped at the plant to converse again with Charley. He was busy with paper work when Hans knocked on the door.

"Have you had a talk with any of the Japanese at the site yet?"

"Yeah, I had a long chat with one of them this morning."

"How did you explain the noise of the two shots?"

"I told him we heard noises outside the entrance and that one of the guards got trigger happy and fired a couple of rounds into the air. The noise must have scared whoever was out there because the noise disappeared and that was the end of the whole thing."

"Are you sure he bought it?"

"I think so, but the Japanese are really hard to read. Their faces rarely let you know what they're thinking."

"Even the alcalde said the same thing, and he was a master at reading other men's thoughts. Well, let's assume they bought it until we know different."

"Suits me. Is there anything else we need to discuss at this time? If not, I'm gonna go down and have a little talk with the two we caught last night."

"No, that's really all I wanted to know. I thought you might want to grab a little shuteye before you talked to the prisoners."

"No, sleep can wait. I gotta know who sent these bastards. I know they're Japanese, but they could have been hired by Universal or Juan's brothers, as well as one of the other Japanese car companies. I guess it really doesn't matter who sent them, but I'd still like to know."

"Okay, let me know if you find out for sure. I'm a little curious myself."

Hans left in the company of one of the deputies who drove him to the jail where the two men had been held since last night. Both had swollen heads from the lick they had taken from the guard. Hans walked in quickly and with a wave of his hand dismissed the jailer. He strode toward the cage and motioned for them to stand up. He said, "I know you two bastards speak English, so don't try to play games with me. First, do you know who I am?"

Both shook their heads no. "Well, let me tell you then. My name is Hans, and I am the head of security here in Perdido. Perhaps you've heard of me." One shook his head in assent while the other just moaned slightly. "Now, I have a few questions that I want you to answer. I know you guys think you're really tough and all that macho bullshit, but it's only a matter of time until you tell me what I want to know. You can make it easy on yourselves, or you can force me to do things that I'd rather not. Chances are you will survive this thing if you cooperate. Play it tough, and I can guarantee that you will never draw breath as free men again."

He paused to see what effect, if any, his speech had had on them. One tried to maintain a stoic appearance, but the other was visibly shook. His body began to twitch, and his breathing became irregular. Hans could see that he would be the first to break under pressure. He grabbed the trembling man by the dark shirt he wore and lifted him off his feet. "Now, I want to know, who paid you guys to come over here and try that amateur bullshit you guys tried last night?"

The one who remained seated said nothing and showed very little emotion toward the threats which Hans had made, but the other was quick to say that the money and the job description had come from America.

"And how much were you paid?"

"Ten thousand each to come here plus expenses. Twenty-five more each if we were successful."

"How many people were with you last night?"

" Six. We heard two shots. Are there other prisoners?"

"No, two have escaped for the moment. The other two won't be returning to Japan or any place else. What were your plans for a return to Japan?"

"Each man was to go separately. I was to take a plane today. I do not know what plan the others had."

"And you, my brave friend, what was your escape route?"

He said nothing until Hans whacked him hard across the face. Then he felt Hans fingers close around his neck, and he tried to talk. Hans released just enough of his grip on the man throat to let him squeak out a word or two. "I was," and Hans gave him a little more air, "to take a bus to Mexico City and take a plane home in three days."

"And your two friends who got away, what were their plan for escape?"

"We were never told. Only that we were not to even be seen together after we had done the job. We were not to travel together, and they thought it best if we did not know what the plans were for the others."

He pushed the man away from him and motioned for the jailer to come and let him out of the cell. "That will be all for now, but I may come again, and if I find you have not been completely truthful with me, well, I'm sure you know what that means."

He motioned for the deputy to follow him out to the squad car they had arrived in. "Take me back to the plant. I gotta talk to Charley again. He'll want to know what I found out."

Charley was not at the office when Hans got back. He called the house and Billy told him that he had said something about his dad wanting to speak to Enrique, but he didn't know if he was going to his house or was going to meet him at the plant. He tried Charley's number at the plant but got no answer. He decided to try Enrique's house. He signaled once more for the deputy and gave him directions to Enrique's house. He was not at Enrique's house, so Hans headed back to the plant.

This time he found Charley on the way to his office. They walked together to that room. Once inside, Charley asked, "Well, did you find out anything?"

"Yeah, I got some information. There were only six of them. Two got away, two are dead, and we have the other two. They aren't really sure who put up the money, but it was in American currency. Ten thousand apiece for the attempt and twenty-five more each if they were successful. A little over $200 thousand total. I'm betting on the brothers. They could raise that kind of dough, and

I'm relatively certain that they have connections in Japan to set up something like this. I wouldn't rule out the rival car companies, but my money is on the brothers."

""How about Universal?"

"That's still a possibility, but I think they'd be more reluctant to get involved with the Japanese than the others. Still, I could be wrong."

"Do you think they'll try to hit us again from that direction? Or will they try something a little less dramatic?"

"Once again, it's hard to tell. I'm a little surprised they haven't tried some sort of government intervention. That would come from Universal. They've got some people in high places, but I'm not sure they would want to get involved in this. I know they tried to have you extradited once before on the phony murder raps. The old man quashed that, but I don't know if Juan has the *cajones* to stand up to big time State Department threats. What do you think?"

"Yeah, I think he has what it takes. There's a whole lot of his old man in him."

"Is there anything else we need to discuss before I start makin' my rounds?"

"No, that about covers it. Let me know if you get anything more out of the prisoners."

Diego was furious. The expenditure for the six gang menbers had really hurt. They could not afford many more fiascos. If that kind of money was to be spent, there had to be more results.

"Okay, got any more bright ideas, brothers?"

"Not yet. What's your idea? An atomic bomb?"

"Don't get smart with me, brother. If an atom bomb is what it takes, then I'm in favor of that."

"I'm not surprised, Diego, but what is the point of blowin' up the place? That's not going to put a single dollar in our pockets. What do you want? Money or revenge?"

"A whole lot of both, brother, a whole lot of both. It really burns my ass to think that our youngest brother might come out of this filthy rich while we don't get a cryin' dime. Can you live with that?"

"If I have to, yes, but I'm certainly not willing to concede anything yet. We have a long way to go before I'm willing to just give up. I know you haven't had a thought about anything that requires a little finesse. What kind of power play do you have in mind, if I might ask?"

"Okay, I'm glad you asked that question. I know my opinions don't carry much weight, but I think we should give some serious thought about hiring some mercenaries. You know, some real professionals, not these jerk-off gangs we've been dealin' with. The market for their kind of service has been real slow lately. I bet we could swing a better deal if I told them almost all of the payoff comes after the job is finished."

.

"Well, it's for certain we can't put as much up-front money into something like that as we did with the Japs. I don't even know how much credit we have with the big boss."

"Do you think the big boss is even aware of how much this thing could be worth? Maybe if we cut him in for a share, he might be willing to go with us big time."

"Yeah, he probably would, but I also know that anything he has a piece of eventually comes under his total control. I'd really like a shot at the big time before I let him start callin' the shots. How about you?"

"Sure, that would be best if we can swing it. But I also know that a small piece of millions is worth a whole lot more than 100% of nothing."

"I can't argue with you there, brother. Can we at least see what we might be able to do with mercenaries?"

"Sure, brother. Why don't you try to get in touch with those you know and see if we have any takers for what we have to spend?"

"Will do."

****

In Japan the situation was worsening. Every day more and more protesters were taking to the streets. More riot police were called in, and every day more arrests had been made until the jails were bulging. Still plans were proceeding for the complete evacuation of Tokyo in favor of the move to Perdido. Some of the anger of those who feared for their jobs had been quelled by the promise of even better jobs after the move was completed. After all, it would take just as many workers to produce cars in Mexico as it did in Japan. Those in middle management would be hit the hardest. It was for certain that many of the lower paying jobs would be filled by the Mexican work force, but if they could get a virtual monopoly on the American car market, they could create more job types of every description. The unruly mob that was gathered outside was the most vocal and potentially dangerous of any so far. Signs now suggested that those who were in charge of the move should be eliminated. Others said that this move might be worse than what had happened at Hiroshima and Nagasaki. The mobs were harder and harder to disperse each day. Some of the members of the board were weakening in their resolve to see this thing through to the end. It would take the iron will of the CEO to see that this did not turn into a financial disaster.

****

Finally Diego was to have his way. No more pussy-footing around. This time the move against the plant would be handled by professionals, not gang members. He had made contact with an organization in France which had the services of many former members of the Foreign Legion. Their home base was Paris, and Diego had been chosen as the one to meet with them to see if a deal could be worked out. He was thrilled to be the representative of the three. He had always resented the way the others dismissed any of his ideas. He thought to himself what a laugh it would be at their expense if he was successful after their schemes had failed. As he boarded the plane, he looked once more at the piece of paper which contained the address of the man he was to meet in Paris. He went to his seat, placed the small bag he carried in the overhead, and sat down and waited for the take-off. He hated flying, and he usually tried to sleep through as much of a flight as he could. He also hated any situation which did not allow him to carry a weapon. He felt naked without the .357 he had carried for years. He told himself that he would be back in no time and leaned against the window to try to begin his sleep.

When he arrived, he looked once more at the piece of paper with the address before he hailed a taxi. He gave the address to the driver and settled back for what he thought would be a 30 min-ute ride. When the cabby finally pulled up to a large frame house, he stopped and told Diego what the ride would cost. He paid in American and gave the driver a nice tip. He got no " Thank you" from the driver and hurried toward the front door of the house.

He knocked loudly until he heard a voice say "Come in". He was surprised to hear English spoken, for he fully expected most of the conversation to be between himself and a translator. He went in quickly and faced a man who appeared to be in his late 40's or early 50's. The man was slender and sported a thin mustache. When he spoke again it was without a trace of an accent. Diego relaxed, for he had been somewhat afraid that there might be a lack of real communication if things had to be translated.

"You must be Diego," he said.

"Then you must be Francois."

"Of course. Did you have a good flight?"

"I guess. I slept through most of it. I hate flying. Do you like to fly?"

"I never really liked it or disliked it. It's just something I have to do in my line of work. Do you have to fly often?'

"No, most of my work is in the States, mostly around New York"

"So tell me why you suddenly need the services of an organization like mine in Mexico."

"It's a long story, but I'll try to make it as short as I can. When my father died, he was co-owner of a plant which has come up with a way to increase the gas mileage of almost any car by 500%."

"Ah yes, I have heard about this "adjustment". Is it true that this thing really works?"

"Yeah, it is. They're makin' a goddamn fortune out of it. People from the States have flocked down there like you wouldn't believe. Now, most of Mexico has lined up as well. One of the major Japanese car companies is even moving its base of operations there. They'll have exclusive use of the "adjustment" for several years. That'll probably force the other companies to move there if they want to have it on their cars. It would seem that this could be one of the biggest financial things in the world."

"I see. So what exactly would you want us to do? Destroy the factory where the adjustment are made or the new plant that the Japanese will be building?"

"Neither, actually. We don't want to frighten off the Japs or destroy the plant. We only want to slow down the whole process of the move to Perdido."

"Why? For what purpose? What is to be gained by slowing down something that seems inevitable?"

"Well, you see, my father didn't leave my younger brothers and me a piece of the action when he died. He left it all to my youngest brother and the man who invented the adjustment. What we need is just enough to scare them into wanting to share a little of their good fortune with the rest of the family. Is that an unreasonable thing?"

"I guess not. I know your family has connections in New York. Your family consists of men of honor. It's said that you can be trusted to keep any contract that you make."

"Yes, we have that reputation, and I can assure you that any deal we make is a solemn contract. We never renege on anything that we've given our word to."

"Do you have any real plan of action?"

"No, that would be left entirely up to you and your organization."

"Can you describe the kind of security that we'd have to overcome to be successful?"

"Well, the man in charge of the security is named Hans. He was once the number 2 troubleshooter for Universal Oil. He took out Universal's number one nicknamed Toyota Man. He has a lot of deputies and can call on the state police if necessary. There's talk that soon he'll have the Federales at his disposal, so we need someone to take action in a hurry."

"Ah yes, Hans. We served in the Legion together before he found employment with Universal. We never thought he could handle anything as large as you now describe, but I see that we may have underestimated him. We knew him to be cold blooded. He could kill a man and never flinch. Have you tried others to do the job?"

Diego hesitated before replying, "We have tried two other groups, but both failed."

"Could you be a little more precise? What happened to those you tried?

After another hesitation, Diego continued, "Well, the first group we sent was a bunch of about 50 young Mexicans, a gang, you might say."

"And what happened to them?"

"Now, I know you're gonna find this hard to believe, but we really don't know. They just disappeared. They never made it to Perdido. We checked every which way we could, but no one could find a trace of them."

"Strange that so many could just vanish. Didn't the authorities make a search of the area?"

"Not a great search. They were relieved to not have to deal with that bunch any more. Still, we made a pretty thorough search on our own and came up empty."

"As I said, we may have underestimated Hans. Doing away with that many bodies is no small achievement. Who else have you tried?"

"We thought that since the Japanese were involved in this that they could maybe help us. They helped us employ a small gang of six to try to plant a few explosives at a few key points, just to put a scare in Mr. Johnson and my brother."

"And the results?"

"Two killed, two captured, two escaped. No damage to the plant."

"What went wrong? Were they able to breach the security and gain entrance to the plant?"

"Just bad luck, I think. The story we got was that a couple of guards stumbled onto one pair. They knocked these two unconscious and set off an alarm. Hans happened to be on night patrol and answered the alarm. He shot and killed two others and the last two escaped."

"Yes, Hans was always a good shot. So, now you come to us. Why did you wait so long?"

"I know it's embarrassing to me, but my brothers are supposed to be the brains in my family. They were the ones who set up these fiascos, not me. I wanted an organization like yours from the start, but they thought that you would be too expensive. That is why they sent me instead of coming themselves. They didn't want to admit what fools they'd been. We've spent a lot of money, our own money, and so far we haven't got squat."

"Well, maybe your brothers were right. Maybe we are too expensive. Do the top men in New York know all of this, and are they a part of the bargain?"

"No, they're not into this. This is a private affair that deals only with my family, not the crime family."

"Well then, how do you propose to pay us if you don't have the financial backing of the organization?"

"Well, you have to realize that the profits from this could run into the millions. If we can get our fair share, we'll have no trouble in payin' for your services."

"And if you are not successful?"

"It's a risk. You surely knew that all the time when you told us you would consider dealing with us."

"Yes, we deal in risks. That is our business, but we are handsomely rewarded for the risks we take. What can you offer us to take such risks?"

"I'd rather hear first how much you might need for such a thing, just to see if we could even begin to meet your price."

"Well I'd have to employ at least 20 men for a month. I'd say for transportation, weapons, and miscellaneous that I'd have to have $500,000. I'd need at least $250,000 up front, just to get things organized. I would expect the other $250,000 when the job is finished. Is that within what you thought it might be, or is this way beyond your means?"

"It might take us a little while to come up with that much cash up front. I know we have it, but a lot of our stuff is tied up, and we're not as fluid as we'd like to be."

"Well, then, when you put the up-front money in my hand, we'll call it a contract. You can wire the money here so you won't have to make a return trip. If you can't raise the money, we'll both just forget this conversation ever took place.

"Okay, I'll let you know within 48 hours."

Diego left and wished he didn't have to wait eight hours before he could begin his flight back to the States. He wasn't sure whether his brothers would be willing to go along for another $500,000 in an effort to try to get a piece of the pie.

When Diego's plane landed, he went directly to the hotel room where his brothers would be. He tapped on the door and waited for an answer. When Jorge said, "Come in" he opened the door and stepped briskly into the room."

"Well, brother, how was France?"

"Can the small talk. We got a lot to discuss. I met the guy. He's interested, but he wants a lot of jack up front before he'll even think about doing the job."

"And how much jack are we talkin' about?"

"$250,000 up front and $250,000 more when they finish the job. What to you guys think? Can we raise that much cash up front?"

"And an even better question is do we want to put up that kind of jack for something as uncertain as a hit on the plant? Their security is mighty tough. We know that. We've tried twice and spent a lot of dough, and what have we got for our money? Squat! Now we're supposed to put up another $500,000, bettin' on people we don't even know? Brother, I just don't know."

"Okay. I agree. We spent a lot of dough on schemes I didn't really like when we decided to go that way. The people we sent were amateurs. These guys are pros. I've gone along with the shit you guys came up with. I think it's about time we tried things my way. But we can put it to a vote. If both of you think it's a bad investment, then I guess I'll go along with you, especially if either of you geniuses has a better idea."

"What do you say, Jorge? I think it's too big a risk."

"Well, you're right. It's a big risk, but let's give our older brother a chance. He's gone to a lot of trouble to set this thing up. I think we can raise the first $250,000. Don't forget we made a ton of money off that last heroin shipment. We got another big deal comin' up. I think it would be enough to cover the rest of the deal if they're successful. I vote with Diego."

"Thank you, Jorge. I think Carlos will agree when this thing is over that you made a good choice."

"I hope so, brother. I really hope so."

****

Back in Perdido Hans had not been idle. He never failed to make several phone calls a day. Many of the calls were to places where he knew that men for hire doing espionage type work could be found. He had just finished a call to Paris and could hardly wait to tell Charley what he had just learned.

"Charley, I just got word from one of my contacts that a group of mercenaries has just been hired for a caper in Mexico. It probably will be headed by an old comrade of mine. We served in the Foreign Legion for a while. If it's really him, we could be in for lots of trouble. He hires only the best men, and he's usually well financed to buy the best of whatever he needs to do a job."

"Okay, then let's assume that he will be leading this thing. What should we do to be ready for them when they get here?"

"How much money are you ready to spend to be ready for all contingencies?"

"Have you got any idea how much money I have at my disposal as we speak?"

"No, I don't."

"Well, let me tell you, it's a lot more than you think. Just how much I don't even know, but it runs into the millions. How much do you think you'll need?"

"You really don't care how much I spend, do you?"

"Frankly, no I don't. Whatever it takes to beat these bastards is what I'm willing to spend."

"Wow, I've never had that kind of budget before. I think the first thing we should invest in would be at least three helicopters. That could get us a lot of advance warning. Also could be a big help if we got into a fire fight with that group."

"Where would you find pilots with helicopter experience?"

"I knew a few guys who flew in Viet Nam. I think I could lure a few out of retirement if the price is right."

"The price will be right. Whatever it takes."

"Okay, I'd like a lot more automatic weapons, AK47's and M16's, some grenades, a few mortars, a couple of 50 caliber machine guns and several SAM missiles."

"Sounds like World War III is about to begin."

"It could be, but it won't last long. If we can figure out ahead of time when and how they'll try to hit us, I think we can send them home with their tails between their legs. He's a shrewd campaigner, but if we have what we need, I think we can handle him."

"Then get what you need. If you need my authorization for any of the expenses, just tell me. You'll have it."

"Then from my point of view, this could be fun."

"Tell me something. If you were trying to hit us, what would be your plan of attack?"

"There's no doubt in my mind but that I'd try paratroopers. They could land at night in the vicinity, regroup, work their way on foot into range, hit the plant with whatever they had, then disperse to where the plane had dropped them for a quick getaway."

"And just how do you plan to defend against such an action if that is the way he chooses to attack?"

"First of all, I'll have all the men trained to use what automatic weapons we have. Then I'll have those pilots that I've hired flying those helicopters as soon as the sun goes down. I know he'll try it at night. He'd be a fool to try anything in broad open daylight, and believe me, he's no fool."

"Anything else?"

"'Yes, I'll have some men deployed with SAM missiles in the places I think he's most likely to make his drop. If I guess right, this will be the shortest campaign he's ever been in, and his last. One hit from the SAM , and the game is over."

"You do consider this a game, don't you?"

"Yes, in a way, I guess I do. I know this is serious business, but there is still the element of gamesmanship involved. His wits against mine. You can see that, can't you? We are both professionals, just doing what we get paid to do. It will be interesting to see which one of us does it best."

"Interesting is a strange word for it. But I guess from your point of view that it would be an accurate description. Is there anything else we need to discuss at this time?"

"I think not. I think I can get the helicopters in less than three days. It might take me a little longer to get the pilots I want, but no more than a week."

"And what if he hits us sooner than that?"

"Then I guess we're screwed, but he won't. Like any good military man, he'll want to scout the place before he strikes. I'd say we have at least two weeks to get ready, probably more than that."

"Well, then you better be gettin' it all together. Keep me advised if there's anything I can do to expedite things."

"Will do."

The money had been raised and wired to Paris. Men were arriving every day to become a part of the force that was to attack the plant in Perdido. Weapons and ammunition had been purchased. For three weeks, the men had been schooled in what would be expected of them at any given time during the assault. The plane to make the drop had been acquired. The plane would take off from Guatemala, and the escape route would be through the United States. There was a certainty the U.S. would not shoot down a civilian airliner if it properly identified itself. The landing would take place in Texas, Dallas if they could get clearance to land, Oklahoma City if Dallas did not work out. Bazookas would be the main weapon to hit the plant because they had good range and made very little noise. Any of the men could operate one. All of the men would carry automatic weapons in case they ran into resistance close to the plant. All were aware that if anything went wrong, during or after the attack, it was every man for himself. Most of the men chosen for this campaign could speak both English and Spanish. If they became bogged down in either Mexico or the United States, men who spoke the language had a much better chance to escape if they had no problem conversing with the natives.

As the plane took off from Guatemala, Francois was briefing his men one last time on what would be expected of them. He had tried to cover every contingency, but he knew well from experience that there was always the unexpected. Operation of any type, particularly those with big money attached, had been hard to come by in recent days. He knew the risks involved in a gig like this one were extreme, yet he felt he could not say no to that much money. The men also knew the risks, but the money and just the thrill of action had been plenty of incentive for them to take on an assignment like this one,

The men were getting fidgety as the plane approached the drop zone. They were double checking their gear, and having their last smoke before the attack was over. Conversation had ceased as the plane was headed for the two mile spot where they hoped to land and form up as a group. They never saw the SAM that hit the plane amidship and caused the giant explosion which sent the plane into a thousand pieces.

On the ground, Hans was ecstatic. He had heard about the plan from a source in Paris and had been waiting patiently for his old "friend" who had thought he never had enough brains to be a leader. He could hardly wait to tell Charley what had happened.

He did not wish to communicate news of this magnitude over the phone. He had the deputy drive as fast as he could to home base. He knew the family would be sleeping, but he thought this could not wait till morning. He rang the bell and waited for the light to come on. It seemed like an eternity until he finally heard Billy's voice say, "Who is it?" He identified himself and waited for the door to be unlocked. By this time Charley had joined Billy downstairs and stood there in his pajamas.

"What's the problem, Hans?"

"There's no problem. Our problem has been eliminated. Tonight our latest enemy made his move."

"And?"

"He and all of his friends have all their body parts strowed all over the land around Perdido."

"I thought I heard an explosion about twenty minutes ago. What was that?"

"That, my friend, was the sound of a SAM taking out the whole enemy force sent here from France. They were trying to come in the back door from Guatemala, but we were prepared. It only took one shot. That was it!"

"Were there any survivors?"

"Are you kiddin' me? Survivors? There couldn't have been any. If the explosion didn't get them, the fall to earth would have. I didn't see a single parachute open. No, there were no survivors."

"Did you even bother to look for any?"

"I have men out doing that just now. They will report to me if they find anything. They have instructions to collect anything which might be used to identify any of those on board the plane."

"Are you absolutely sure you got the right plane?"

"Of course it was the right one. We followed the flight from Guatemala by radar ever since it took off. They were going to hit us with bazookas, I was told. We're lookin' for the remains of any of those as well as the automatic weapons they no doubt carried. I'll get the full disclosure of what they found from the wreck in the morning. I just thought you might sleep a little better tonight if you knew this problem had been solved."

"Thanks, Hans. Is there anything else?"

"That's about it. Good night."

****

A crew of more than fifty deputies was indeed searching the area around Perdido. They had found several bazookas, though none could have been used in their present state as a weapon. Also found were the remains of several automatic weapons. A few large body parts had been collected, though they found no bodies entirely intact. Four different name tags were picked up, two French, one Italian, and one American. The impact of the SAM together with the explosion of the ammunition had created the jigsaw puzzle which was the remains of the aircraft and its passengers. An hour after sunup, the lead deputy decided that he should report to Hans what they had recovered while the others continued the search. He took with him two of the others and headed for the spot where he knew the boss would be waiting. He met them at the door and told them to take a seat. He sat and waited for the headman to make his report. He told Hans what they had found and told him the men were still searching. Hans could hardly stifle a laugh. He remembered Charley's questions about survivors and the possibility that they had hit the wrong plane. There could be no doubt now about either point. It had been the right plane, and there were no survivors. It was certainly a feather in his cap and maybe a lesson to those who might want to try something similar. This time he would wait until all the debris had been located before he went to Charley's house to gloat. He waited until late afternoon to visit the boss again. He had earned a nap, after the action of last night, and he had decided to take one.

Charley went to the plant, more to get away from the house than anything else. He was surprised to find that Juan was there waiting for him. He had the look of anxiety on his face. Charley sensed that he had already heard about the events of last night.

"Can we go into your office and talk?"

"I can see that something important is on your mind. What is it? You know about last night. I can tell that already. What's on your mind?"

"Well, you're right about that. I do know about last night, but I'm afraid I'm not the only one who knows. I've been inundated with telephone calls from people who are most unhappy about last night."

"And who would be these unhappy campers?"

"Where shall I start? First the people in Guatemala want to know what has happened to the airplane they leased to the French travel group. They claim it was leased to a bunch of vacationers who wanted to visit Mexico City. They can't believe it got so far off course as to be anywhere near Perdido. Next are the authorities in France. They understand that several of their citizens have been killed in a terrorist attack on a civilian airliner. What can I tell them about the whole affair? Next, it seems there were also a couple of Americans on board and the American consulate is very curious about the whole affair. We may have solved one problem only to find that we have created several others. I wish now that my father were here. He was much better at this sort of thing than I am. He was much more, how shall I say, diplomatic."

"He was all of that. He got me out of a lot trouble with the American government when they tried to extradite me on those trumped up murder charges. We made a flight to Mexico City to meet with a lot of American bigwigs, and he convinced the Mexican government that the whole thing against me was bullshit. If he hadn't done that, I'd be doin' time in an American prison right now."

"Well, I've already got meetings set up with all three governments today. Is there anything you can tell me that might help me explain what happened?"

"Yeah, I've been thinking of a good cover story ever since Hans told me what happened last night. If we have to tell the truth about it, we have recovered enough evidence to prove that these were not merely vacationers headed for a good time in Mexico City. However, we don't want to alarm out Japanese friends, so let's just tell them that we have proof that the people on this plane had been hired by an Arab terrorist group to make a huge hit on Mexico City. If Guatemala continues to make a big squawk, we'll threaten to disclose their part of the plot as co-conspirators. As for the French, who gives a shit what you tell them? They can go to hell. Most of the men on board the airplane were French, and we'll give them an international black eye if they don't just shut up. Tell the Americans that this was probably a ploy by the American oil companies to discredit the adjustment that's cost them so much money. If they'll buy it okay, and if not, you might have to tell them at least part of the truth."

"Well, at least that gives me something to work on. Are you sure the old man didn't give you a lesson or two in diplomacy? This sounds like something he might have come up with."

"I confess I watched him a great deal. I guess I must have picked up a thing or two. He had a lot more influence than I or anyone else ever imagined."

"Yes, he had a lot of powerful friends, but he also made lots of enemies along the way. Well, I hope I can sell this to them as easily as you've sold me"

"Is there anything else?"

"Probably, but I think this is about all I can handle for one day. I'll let you know how things are going before the day is through."

"Good luck."

.

****

Later that day at the Guatemalan Embassy, Juan was at the table with the ambassador of that country. The whole discussion took place in Spanish, although both spoke perfect English. The ambassador had a worried look on his face while Juan tried to hide the fear which had not diminished much after his conversation with Charley earlier that day.

"Señor de los Santos, what can you tell me about the incident which took place last night?"

"I can tell you that the Mexican government had no choice except to protect itself from the terrorist group which was about to attack our capital city."

"But how can you be sure this was a terrorist group? Our information was that they were merely a group of tourists headed on holiday to Mexico City."

"Perhaps your people should check more closely before they lease a plane to groups like this one. We have examined the wreckage closely, and we have no doubt this was a mission sponsored by Al Qaeda, the Arab terrorist group that hit the United States so hard on November 11."

"But how can you be so sure? We have information that the wreckage of the plane was so scattered that it would be impossible to identify those passengers on board."

"Your information is incorrect. It is true that the damage did not leave much for those who were trying to put a name on the passengers, but we found enough. We found dog tags on a few. Apparently the group was a multinational force. We have identified at least three different nationalities."

"And what would those three be?"

"French , Italian and American."

"May I assume that you found no evidence of any of my countrymen among the debris?"

"As of yet we have not, but the investigation is still underway. We cannot say with real certainty what we may find when the investigation is completed."

"I see. Then there is no reason at this time to believe that my country was complicit in any plot against Mexico, is there?"

"Only that on the flimsiest excuse you leased a plane to the terrorists. That in itself is enough to make my government uneasy."

"But we have excellent relations with your country. What motive would we have for such an act?"

"The Arabs who fund this type of operation have millions of dollars at their disposal. Placed in the right hands, only one or two people would have to look the other way at the leasing of an airplane to make such an operation possible."

"Then is your country accusing us of conspiring with these people to attack you?"

"Accusing, no. But we want you to know that we think you erred greatly in leasing the plane to that group. We admit no liability for the loss of the plane or to the deaths of those on board. We regret the incident, but our security is our primary concern."

"Of course, you are right. These are troubling times. Every country must be on guard against terrorism. I do have one more question before you leave. Would it be possible for someone from my country to examine all the remains which are recovered after your search is completed?"

"I cannot answer that question. It is not within my power to grant such a wish. You would have to take that up with our security people."

"I see. Well, I had a good relationship with your father. He was a good man. I hope this will continue with our talks in the future."

"That is my wish as well, ambassador. I'll see myself to the gate."

He left and went directly to the French embassy. He was not as nervous as he had been before. He remembered what Charley had said about the French before. If Charley didn't give a damn what the French thought, why should he worry? He knew that recent relations between France and the U.S. had not been cordial. The French failure to back the American effort to oust Sadam Husein had left a bad taste in the mouth of the American government. Charley had told him that he was surprised that the French could not see the stupidity of appeasement after how they had dealt with Hitler. He was angry that he was kept waiting for more than hour before he was let in to see the ambassador. This conversation was also in Spanish, although the ambassador's Spanish had a distinctive French accent.

"Good afternoom, Señor de los Santos. Sorry to have kept you waiting. Could I get you a drink of something before we begin our talk?"

"Yes, a glass of good dry wine would be appreciated. Would that be troublesome?"

"Not at all."

He rang a small bell that was on his desk and a servant appeared almost instantaneously. He told the man what Charley would like to drink. In a couple of minutes he returned with a glass of white wine. During the lull in the conversation, the ambassador fumbled with the papers on his desk. When the wine arrived, he looked up and smiled.

"I think now we should get down to the business at hand. We have learned that a most unfortunate accident took place here in Mexico last night."

"Accident? I know of no accident. You should explain."

"I was referring to the explosion which took place on board an airliner that carried several French citizens, I'm told."

For a brief moment Juan pretended he had not heard of the incident. Then he nodded and said, "Oh, yes, the explosion. I know of that, but you must believe me when I tell you it was no accident. The explosion came from a SAM missile fired at the plane by representatives of my government. We had advance notice that a band of terrorists hired by Arab radicals was headed for our capital city with intention of doing great damage that might cause loss of life. We thought it prudent to protect the lives and property of our people, so we instructed our security to down the plane. The reason for the big explosion was the amount of explosives which the plane was carrying, no doubt."

"Are you positive this was not just an aircraft carrying tourists on holiday as we have been led to believe?"

"I have no ideas who led you to believe this lie. Perhaps, the Arabs themselves have created this fiction. Your country seems more interested in maintaining good relations with these people than in containing their acts of terrorism."

"Oh my, that is quite an accusation. It is true that my country is not as eager to rush off to war as the Americans and the English, but we certainly want no part of anything that smacks of terrorism. We learned the true costs of war in our struggles with the Germans."

"It's a pity you didn't learn the true cost of appeasement. It's true that there were several Frenchmen on board the plane, but we offer no apology for the loss of lives or the aircraft that was taking them to our capital."

"And you have proof that what you have told me is correct?"

"I'm satisfied that it is nothing but the truth. If it were not, we should be offering you our sincerest apologies. We are not apologizing. We have no regrets about the outcome. Our only regret is that your country does little to check people like those on board before they can carry out their missions."

"Then I guess we have little to discuss. We shall contact you again when we have had a chance to examine all the facts."

"Until then, Ambassador."

He left the French embassy feeling much better than he had when he entered. He didn't like the French ambassador, and he could see why Charley didn't like the French. He had decided to wait until tomorrow to talk to the Americans. They had not made nearly as much noise as the other two countries involved, so he thought he would wait a while before contacting any government agency. He knew Charley would be anxious to learn of the attitudes of those with whom he had parlayed today. He decided that Charley would still be at the plant and told the driver to take him there. He was surprised to find the office locked. One of the secretaries told him that Charley had left minutes before he arrived. No one seemed to know where he had gone, only that he had left in great haste. He went to where he thought Billy might be but found that he too had left in a hurry. He asked if he could use a phone in one of the offices and called Charley's home number. No answer. He now became worried. Something must be wrong. Maybe Hans would know the answer. He was also unavailable. He decided to have the driver take him to Charley's to wait and see what was going on.

When he arrived, he knocked on the door. A nurse who had been recently hired to help Luisa with the baby came to the door. He asked her if Charley was there and she said no.

"Do you know where he is or when he might return?"

"I know where he is. He is at the hospital with his wife. I cannot say when he might return."

He turned around and signaled for the driver to pull closer to the house. He jumped inside the car and told the driver to head for the hospital. That would explain everything. Charley and Billy had to be there for the birth of the baby, and Hans would be there for security reasons. He felt relaxed once more as they sped down the road.

When he arrived, he went straight to the maternity waiting room. He saw Billy pacing the floor as if he were the father while Charley relaxed in old easy chair. I seemed as though it was role reversal. He seemed puzzled for a minute before he realized that this was Charley's third child. Billy was newer to the waiting room thing than his father. Charley motioned for him to have a seat beside him in a straight-backed chair. He sat down and didn't know what to say.

"How did it go today, Juan?"

"Okay, I guess. The Guatemalans are a little afraid we might link them to the terrorists. The French are bluffing. I can see why you don't like them. I hate their "better than you" attitude. I didn't make it over to see what the Americans are saying. Have you heard anything from the Japanese?"

"I've been pretty busy. Alice picked a good time to have a baby. But I guess the mother hardly ever picks the time."

"How long have you been waiting? Is she doing alright?"

"I think so. The doctors haven't mentioned any abnormalities, so I guess everything is okay. Billy, will you sit down? You're makin' me a nervous wreck."

"Okay, dad, I'm gonna walk down and get me a coke. Do you want anything, dad?"

"Yeah, get me a diet coke. Do you want anything, Juan?

"Thanks. I could use a cup of coffee, black, no sugar. Can you carry all that? I could go with you."

"No, I'll get a tray. You and Dad sit still and I'll be right back

As soon as he was out of sight, Juan asked, "Where's Hans? I thought he would be here."

"He is. He has this place surrounded with men. He's taking no chances on someone trying to get us here in this exposed place. He won't sleep at all until he sees Alice and the baby back at the house. He's still pretty pumped up about last night. You gotta give him credit. He knows how to do his job. When I see how he handles things, I often wonder that he wasn't successful when he tried to kill me. I think I must have been extremely lucky.

"I would say so."

A doctor came into room all in white and wearing a mask. He walked over to Charley and took off the mask. "Mr. Johnson, you are the father of a beautiful baby girl. She weighs seven and a half pounds."

"When can I see the baby and my wife?"

"Right now if you wish. Just follow me."

They left Juan sitting in the room and walked down a long hallway to the private room which Charley and Hans had both insisted that she be in. She was awake and holding the baby when they walked in.

"Hi, Charley. See what I got?"

"She looks beautiful just like her mother. Have you finally decided on a name?"

"Well, if it had been a boy, I thought Charles would have been good, but that's really weird for a girl. So how about Charlene? Neither of your sons was even close to being named after you, so I thought this might be a good time to give you a little recognition. What do you think?"

"Sounds okay to me. Will she have a middle name?"

"Of course, but here in Mexico it's usual to have several middle names. I thought Charlene Maria Luisa Johnson has a nice ring to it. What do you think?"

"If it suits you, it tickles me. With that many names she can surely find at least one that she likes."

"I hope so, but sometimes girls like to pick their own names, or they get stuck with nicknames in their childhood that they never can get rid of."

"Yeah, I know some guys who never outgrew some stipid nickname. I had one friend who was known as Stinky all his adult life. He said he just got used to it."

"How are Luisa and the baby? Who's home with them?"

"Hans has left a small army there to guard them, and on the inside is the nanny we hired to look after the baby until she gets stronger."

"Has there been any fallout from what happened last night? Has Juan been to the embassies?"

"Funny that you should use the word "fall out" after we scattered that plane all over Mexico. Juan had visited two of the embassies. The French are pissed and the Guatemalans are scared that they'll be accused of collusion with the terrorist. At least that was the impression that Juan had. I want you to get all this stuff off your mind and concentrate on Charlene. I like it. It had a nice ring to it. We'll take care of all the other stuff. You don't need to worry."

"How can I not worry when every day there's some new plot to kill my husband?"

"Oh, I'm afraid you exaggerate, my dear. They hardly ever try to kill me more than twice a week now."

"Don't make me laugh, Charley, It hurts, and besides, it's no laughing matter. Are the Japanese really coming?"

"Unless they've changed their minds in the last thirty minutes, they'll be puttin' their cars together here next year. It seems like half of Tokyo is already here."

He took her by the hand and kissed her gently on the cheek. She smiled and said, "Would you like to hold your daughter?"

"Yes," he said. He reached down and gently lifted the child into his arms. He held her up close to his chest until she made a slight whimpering sound. He held her in position for Alice to take her from his hands. "I've never really felt comfortable holding babies." He said. "Not with boys and certainly not with a baby girl."

"Baby girls are no more fragile than baby boys, and you don't seem to have done the boys any harm."

"I guess not. The doctor says for you to get some rest. He thinks you may be able to go home tomorrow. I hope so. Hans thinks they may try something again soon to retaliate for last night, and he can't wait to get you back home where he feels you'll be a lot safer."

"Okay, I'll try to get some rest. When will I know whether I can go home tomorrow or not?"

"No way to know that. It will all depend on how strong the doctor thinks you are."

He kissed her full on the lips and turned and said to Billy, "Let's go."

They walked by the waiting room and motioned for Juan to follow them. He hurried to catch up as they continued walking toward the exit. They got into separate cars as Hans had suggested and headed for home.

****

For five months things went smoothly for Charley and his family. His daughter and granddaughter were healthy, and his wife and daughter-in-law had recovered nicely. Since the night the plane had been shot out of the sky, there had been no more attempts to hit the Japanese plant where the new cars were scheduled to go on line in less than four months. At the plant, Charley's people churned out so many adjustments each day that his accountants could not even estimate the net worth of the company. It took three full shifts of eight hours a day to even come close to taking care of all the business. With the new Japanese cars all scheduled to have the adjustment as standard equipment before they were sent to the dealers, a new wing had been added to the plant to accommodate the new burst of business that was on the way.

Another giant boost to the already huge volume of business was the rush of military vehicles sent for adjustments. The older models as well as the ones fresh off the assembly lines crowded the highways in route to Perdido. There were no generals foolish enough not to realize the importance of gaining five times the previous mileage of trucks and personnel carriers. There would always be a demand for the armies of the world.

****

In Tokyo, confusion reigned. The loss of one of the biggest employers had shaken the whole economy. With rumors flying that the others were ready to jump ship, it was a strain on the local law enforcement to contain the almost daily riots. In a country which had not been known for violence since the end of World War II, it was a threat which this government had never seen. The more severe the punishment handed out to those who were arrested, the more the violence seemed to increase. But those in charge had waited too long to try to stop the movement. They had benefited earlier when the U.S. had exported many of its industries to Japan in an effort to find cheaper labor, and a more efficient way of producing a product. They knew they could never reverse the course of this trend by asking the population to reduce its standard of living. They had seen too much of the good life to ever return to the old way.

Twice the CEO had come close to assassination. Once a man had hidden in his car and tried to stab him as he was about to drive home from work. The second attempt came from a rifle shot fired from an adjacent building. The bullet had nicked his shoulder but had not kept him from going to his office each day. He was counting the days until he could leave for Perdido to cover the actual transition. The police had never made an arrest for the attempt on his life that had come from the adjacent building, and he was relatively certain that they had made no serious attempt to find the assassin. He watched the news on TV every day, but there was hardly a mention of any progress the police

had made in finding the man who had tried to kill him. He had
called another of the many meetings of his board of directors. He
was to tell them today of his decision to leave a month earlier for
Mexico than he had originally planned.

"Gentlemen, I'm glad to see you all here today. I shall not bore
you with a long or boring speech. My purpose for this meeting is
to tell you that I have decided to leave for Mexico tomorrow."

There was a buzz among those still seated at the table. They had
not anticipated this. They feared what might happen to both the
company and themselves with their long time leader in absencia.
A younger man at the end of the table rose and was recognized
as the next speaker

"Sir, may I ask the reason for your sudden departure. We were
told that you would not be leaving for at least a month."

"Of course you can ask, my young friend, but you probably will
not like or believe the answer. We are at a crucial juncture in
our move to Mexico. The next few days will see us actually go
into production in Mexico. I feel that my experience in such
things will be of more value than anything I might accomplish if
I stayed here another month."

"But if we have difficulties while you are there?"

"Then you will have to solve these problems for yourselves. I cannot stay here and have things go badly there, or it would mean
the end of the company."

Another older man stood and waited to be recognized. The CEO hesitated before nodding to the man as a signal to begin his opportunity to speak. He knew what this man had to say would not be pleasant, for he and this man had never been friends. At one time this man had been considered for the job that the CEO had held for so long, and he was now considered the heir apparent when he should decide to step down.

"Sir," he began in a sarcastic manner, "could your decision to leave early be based on other considerations? Something like your personal safety?"

"Are you challenging my personal courage in this matter? I don't think I have anything to prove to you or anyone else. Your remarks now and in the past concerning my personal integrity have been insulting. Do I have to remind you what this company was like when I took over the reins of leadership?"

"You often remind us whether you have to or not. We know of your past accomplishments. There is a statement which the American often use. 'What have you done for me lately?' I think now it might be good for our company to ask you the same thing."

"Then if you would be so kind as to be silent for a few minutes, I'll tell you what I have done. I have taken this company which has recently seen a tremendous drop in corporate profits and kept it afloat while others were sinking. At a time when our government could not bail us out any more with subsidies, I have once again taken the steps to put us in the forefront of the automobile manufacturing business. We have the opportunity, under my leadership, to open up the gap between ourselves and our competitors that should give us almost a monopoly."

"Or sink us completely."

"It is true that there are substantial risks involved in this move. I never told you otherwise. But since you like to quote Americans, remember this one, 'Nothing great was ever achieved without enthusiasm.' If we are content to play it safe and take no risks, we will live to regret that decision more than the upheaval that the move will create. When completed, the move will give us two and maybe three years of a head start over all the competition, foreign and domestic, which does not have the benefit of the adjustment."

There was a round of feint applause when he fininished this short speech. He watched the faces of all at the table to see how much support he really had. He was convinced that he still had a majority, however slim. The noise outside from the street reminded him that it was more than just the financial well being of the company that was at stake. The lives of thousands of his country-men would be altered forever, some not for the better. He had weighed this fact in his mind over and over before deciding that the greater good could be accomplished by the move.

Another younger man rose and waited for the signal to speak. He asked, "What exactly is the status of things in Mexico? We have heard rumors that there have been attacks on both our new plant and that of the plant where the adjustments are performed. Is there any truth to these rumors?"

"Yes, it is true, but the attacks have accomplished nothing. The security of the place is ironclad."

"Do we know who is responsible for these attacks?"

"We cannot be sure. There is more than one possibility. The first and most obvious is our rivals here in Japan. They know that if we succeed, they will have to give up the relative security here and make the same move that we have already made. The second would be the American oil companies. No doubt their revenues have shrunk dramatically since the advent of the adjustment. They are powerful and corrupt enough to try to quash the adjustment. You haven't forgotten how they hated us when we improved the average mileage in an American driven car by 30%. I'm certain that if they could have, they would have struck at us in similar fashion. You may not be familiar with the third possibility. There is a faction within the family with whom we first dealt, Juan de los Santos. He had four sons, three of whom we know are connected to organized crime in the United States. The youngest of these sons, also named Juan, has thrown in with Mr. Johnson and has become what we suspect is a part owner of the company. The other three sons have inherited nothing and for spite or greed have decided to muscle in to get at least a piece of the action, as they like to say. We cannot be sure which of these groups could have been responsible for the attacks. There may be other enemies that we are not aware of, but we know about these three."

The man who had posed the previous question remained standing and continued, "Has there been any progress by our own authorities in tracking down the people who have twice tried to kill you?"

"No, and I daresay there never will be. They are too much influenced by the noise you hear in the streets. I sometimes fear them more than I do the agents of our rivals. The police themselves have become so corrupt that unless one pays them a great deal of money, he is not likely to get much of an investigation of anything."

He watched closely again to see if there was general agreement with his last statement. Several nodded their heads, and he knew he had struck a responsive chord.

"At least in Mexico, we will be protected by a security force that is responsive to our needs. If we fail there, there will not be any need for their services. They will do their utmost to see that we are well protected and successful. Their economy is much the mirror image of our own. They need jobs, and they need a product to export that will insure at least their own short term prosperity."

He went to the window to look at the demonstration going on below. He watched as the police tried vainly to break up the mob that was headed for his building. He could hardly wait for his departure.

****

The brothers were unhappy. There was no doubt about that, but the unhappiest was Diego. He had not recovered from the fiasco with the French mercenaries, nor could he dismiss the scorn of his brothers over his failue to accomplish his goal. He paced nerviously back and forth while his brothers played gin rummy.

"Why don't you sit down and play some casino with us, brother? Pacing back and forth doesn't do any good."

"Right, and neither does sittin' on your ass and playin' cards all day. If I don't get some action soon, I'm gonna have a stroke."

"Right brother, you will have a stroke."

All three wanted part of the millions they knew were in the coffers of Mr. Johnson, his family, along with their younger brother. The money was the primary object, but wouldn't it be ironic if these three whom the old man had disinherited somehow raised the de los Santos name to an even higher level than the old man ever had?

"So, brother, have you come up with any more of your brilliant plans?"

"Caution, brother. One of these days I'm gonna have to beat the livin' shit out of you if you don't lay off on my stupidity."

"Is that a fact? Well, if your feelin' froggy, jump. Go ahead!"

"Cool it, you two. We don't need this kind of crap. It's not gonna get us anywhere. Listen up, both of you. I think I got some good news yesterday."

"Well, tell it slow so he can understand."

"I'm warnin' you for the last time, lay off. I'm not gonna tell you again."

"Yeah, yeah, yeah, go ahead brother. Tell us the news."

"Okay. I think we may get some help from the government."

"Really? Whose? Theirs or ours?"

"U.S. of course. The Mexican government is never gonna do anything that might help us, at least not intentioally. They say they're gonna look into the patent to make sure that what they have gives them the exclusive right to the adjustment."

"I don't see how that can help us. If they let the Americans use the adjustment, the Japs won't come to Perdido, and the company we want a piece of might not be worth squat."

"You're right about that, but I have it on good authority that the patent is rock solid, so there's no way the Americans can use the adjustment."

"So how does that help us?"

"They don't know what the outcome of the patent hearing will be, so if we can get in touch with them, we might offer to help swing the decision in their favor for a piece of the pie."

"How can we get in touch with them? I don't think any of us would be safe if we tried to go down there ourselves."

"I agree. That would be foolish. I think our best chance might be to charm our little brother into coming here to listen to our proposal."

"Yeah, I'd like to make him an offer he can't refuse."

"Don't start that macho bullshit. He could be a lot more help to us alive than dead. If we're ever gonna negotiate anything, we're gonna need a go-between. Juan is the only person both sides might trust."

"But how can we even get in touch with him to even make a proposal?"

"He surely has a personal E-mail. I think I can get a hold of that. I'll simply tell him we have a proposal that would be in the best interest of all concerned. I'll ask him to come here so we can discuss the details."

"Do you really think he's dumb enough to come here?"

"Yes, I do. Don't forget he's a lot like the old man. They have a certain amount of Don Quijote in them."

"Don who? What family does he run?"

"Oh, shut up, brother. Every time you open your mouth, you display your ignorance."

"I'm warnin' you, if you mention my ignorance one more time I'm gonna…..

"Will you two knock it off, for Christ' sake? I know a computer nerd who's good at getting' people's E-mail addresses. For a few bucks, I think he'll dig up Juan's address."

"Then why don't you give up that stupid card game, genius, and start tryin' to find this nerd so we can get something goin'."

"Because he sleeps during the daytime, and he doesn't like to be disturbed. As soon as the sun goes down, I'll be on my way to see if he can help us. In the meantime, don't do anything stupid."

"I swear I'm gonna….

The next day Juan received the E-mail from his brother. He was surprised because he couldn't imagine how his address had been obtained. He read the message twice before he decided to show it to Charley. He waited until breakfast that day before inviting Charley into his room He walked over to his computer and turned it on. He motioned for Charley to come over and take a look. He shook his head in bewilderment when he read the message.

"What do you suppose it means? What could they possibly have that would be beneficial to us both?"

"I have no idea. I haven't had any correspondance with any of them. I thought you ought to see this, though."

"You're not seriously thinking about going to New York are you? That sounds like suicide to me."

"I don't know. If there was some way we could get them off our back, it would make all our lives a lot easier. I know they want a piece of our action. I also know they would never be satisfied with just a piece. Once they get their foot in the door, either they or the people they work for, will try to take over the whole operation. That's the way they do business."

"I've heard that. Well, before you make up your mind, there's something I've got to tell you. If you go and they decide to hold you for ransom, there's very little we can do. We can't mortgage our whole future to rescue you. Keep that in mind before you decide to do anything rash."

"Okay, I will. What do you think I should do?"

"Christ, I don't know. I know it would be a lot safer to stay here where you're well protected than to go running off to New York."

"He left a return address. I'm gonna think about it for a while before I make my decision."

"A good idea. Let me know what you decide as soon as you make up you mind."

"I will."

Charley left the room and Juan stared at the message one more time before he decided to lie down on his bed and close his eyes. He mulled the thing over and over in his mind. Maybe it wasn't as dangerous as he had first thought. After all, if they had a proposal, there would certainly be some negotiating to do. He would certainly be safe until he could deliver whatever they had in mind back to Charley. If Charley turned them down, then it might be dangerous to go back and tell them the bad news, but a first trip didn't seem so much like a death wish. Then he remembered just how much his brothers hated him. Could this be just a ploy by them to get the chance they'd always wanted to kill him? No, Diego wasn't smart enough to come up with anything like this. Probably Jorge's idea. Even if Juan failed to get the handle on anything that might get his brothers to leave them alone, maybe he could find out what they were really up to.

At dinner that night, he winked at Charley and nodded his head in the affirmative. Charley shrugged his shoulders to indicate he wasn't sure what that meant. Juan got up from the table and said, "I've decided to go." Then he excused himself.

Alice asked, "What did he mean by that? Where is it that he's going?"

"To New York."

"But why?"

"To see his brothers."

"But why? That's crazy. They might kill him."

"He knows that."

"You can't let him go."

"Can't stop him would be better way to put it. He's made up his mind, and you know how the de los Santos are when their minds are made up."

"But you still didn't tell me why."

"He got an E-mail from one of his brothers telling him they have a proposal that might help all of us."

"What could they possibly have that would help us all? There couldn't be anything like that, could there?"

"I can't think of anything, but he wants to go up and see what they have on their minds."

"Can you talk him out of it?"

"I'm not even going to try."

Juan went directly to his room and went to his computer. He looked at the E-mail address and smiled. Somehow he just couldn't visualize his brothers in anything as high-tech as a computer and E-mail. He sent back an acceptance of their offer and asked where they should meet in the City. He got a reply almost instantaneously. They wanted his ETA so they could be there. He called the airport and booked the earliest flight to New York. Then he E-mailed back that he would be arriving at 3 p.m. the next day.

His flight to the City was uneventful. He saw Jorge waving to him as soon as he got off the plane. He waved back and headed in that direction.

"Welcome to the City, brother."

"I hope I haven't wasted my time and money on this wild goose chase. I'm a busy man these days, and I don't have time to play games."

"We're busy, too, Juan. Like you, I hope some good can come out of this trip. Let's head up to meet your brothers. They're anxious for your arrival."

They took a cab to the hotel and went directly to the brother's room. Carlos smiled and extended his hand, but Juan merely nodded. He could not hide the hatred he had harbored for his brothers for as long as he could remember.

"Let's get right down to business. I didn't travel this far just to exchange pleasantries. What do you have on your mind?"

It was Carlos who spoke up for the trio. "Okay, Brother, I don't know how well you guys keep up on things here in the States, but here's something we do know. Your friend's patent is being challenged by some powerful and and influential people. It will be heard very soon."

"So what's the point, Carlos? There have been other challenges before. This is really nothing new."

"I don't think you know just how powerful these people are who're making the challenge."

"I think I can guess. Either the oil companies or the American car companies. Am I right?"

"Yes, they are a part of it."

"Who else?"

"Some powerful politicians, at least three senators."

"So how do you guys fit into the equation? You guys aren't politicians, are you?"

"No, we aren't, but some people we know have a very powerful influence on some of those who have been elected."

"And these people wouldn't happen to have long Italian names, would they?"

"Right first time, brother. You catch on quick."

"I still don't see how this concerns you."

"Well, then let me explain. For a nominal sum we can arrange to see that the challenge has no chance of succeeding."

"And just how nominal would this sum be, if I may be so bold as to ask?"

"Well, you know our father's first lesson in business was that greed is a terrible thing. We thought 10% of the company would be fair."

"And just exactly what would we get for that 10%?"

"Well, in addition to quashing the challenge on the patent, we could exercise a lot of influence on the oil companies if they decide to go after you again. If you have labor problems with a new union, we could help settle that. We have experience in settling strikes. You see, once we have a vested interest in the company, it would be to our advantage to see you succeed, rather than fail."

"Well, here's another question. Is this deal between you and us entirely, or will there be others, namely the people you now work for, in on this deal?"

"No, brother, strictly between you and us. We'd like to get out of the businees we're in, but we'd need something pretty good to leave the kind of money we're makin' now. We're sure that 10% of your enterprise would be more than enough to compensate us for the loss of revenue here."

"I see. We'll, I have to tell you I don't have the authority to negotiate with you. Only Charley can do that. All I can do is take back your proposal and see what he has to say."

"That's all we're really askin' of you, brother. I think you might sway him a little, but whatever he decides, we won't hold you responsible."

"My return flight isn't until tomprrow, so I guess I'll go out and try to see a little of the town. After that, I have no reason to stay here any longer."

"That's too bad. You could have made your fortune here with us."

"I made my fortune in Panama, so I don't think I missed a thing by not coming to the States. I'll let you know as soon as I can what Charley has to say about your proposal. I don't think he'll even consider it, but you never know until you try. Adios."

He left and took a cab to to the other side of town where he had already booked a hotel room. He was not burdened with luggage, only one small bag that contained one change of clothes. He really had no desire to go sight seeing. He only wanted a chance to be away from his brothers as fast as he could. They had always left him with a queasy feeling when he had been forced into their company. Today had been no different. He felt the dislike from Carlos and Jorge and the burning hatred of Diego. He would have liked to phone Charley, but he knew that Charley did not like to discuss important business over the phone. He bought a copy of the Times and took it to his hotel room. He found an article on the second page that told of the upcoming challenge to the patent. There was a picture of three senators who were to lead the challenge. No doubt they had been bought and paid for by the automobile industry in Detroit. He also knew that Charley had on retainer the best and most expensive lawyers in the United States to protect his investment. He had never shown any anxiety over the challenges to his patent. From the beginning he had been assured that everything was in order.

He boarded the plane early and waited on board to plan what he wanted to say when he returned. He had no intention of trying to persuade Charley that it would be a good deal to try to do business with his brothers. He knew they could not be trusted. He also knew that the people they worked for would want a piece of the action. Under no circumstances could they become involved with these people.

Terry was there to pick him up when the plane landed in Perdido. He was somewhat surprised that Charley was not there personally to meet him. It meant he was not taking any proposal that came from that direction seriously.

He had Terry take him to his office at the plant. On the way he asked Terry if anything of importance had had occurred during his absence. He replied that nothing out of the ordinary had happened while he was gone. He asked where Charley might be and was told that he might very well be at the plant. On the way to his office he met a security guard and asked him if he had

198   *Tom Peavler*

seen Charley. The man told him that Charley was somewhere on the premises, but he wasn't sure exactly where. He went to the main office and asked if they would page him to the office. They complied, and he waited about five minutes until Charley made his appearance.

"Do want to talk here, or should we go to your office or mine?"

"Mine is closer. Let's go there."

They walked slowly toward Charley's office with no word between them until the door to the office was closed.

"So, what did your brothers have to say?"

"Well, they tell me the patent is up for a serious challenge, and they claim they could assure you that the challenge will fail, if you want to do business with them."

"And what would it cost to do business with them?"

"Ten percent of the company."

"Are they offering anything else for their service?"

"Yes, they claim they can keep the oil companies off your back and straighten out any labor problem you encounter in the future with unions."

"We pay our workers top dollar already, so they have no reason to form a union. The Japanese never seem to have any problems with their work force, so I don't see that as any incentive to do business with them."

"What do you know about the latest challenge to the patent?"

"I pay the best lawyers in the world to see that things like that can't derail us, so I'm confident there isn't a chance in the world that my patent can be overturned."

"I thought so, but I didn't let on that they couldn't be of any help. What do you think I should tell them when we meet again?"

"Well, I think it might be a good idea to string them along for a while. They won't try to hit us again for a while if they think they might get to own a piece of what we have."

"The challenge comes up in a very short while. Shall we accept any of the proposal they're offering?"

"Sure, why not? We can tell them we want six months to think over a written proposal. Only then can they become a part of our organization."

"What happens after six months?"

"Fuck them! They can wait till hell freezes over, but they will never be a part of anything I have control over. No matter what they offer, I'd never be a part of anything that included them."

"I'm glad we're in agreement about that. I know you hate them for what they tried to do to us, but you have no idea how much I hate them. They made my life a living hell for as long as we lived together. My mother tried her best to protect me from them, but she wasn't always around when they were at their worst."

"For whatever reason, I've never liked them since that first day I met them at your dad's funeral. I think your dad had even got to the point where he didn't care much for them either. The only time he spoke about them was to complain about the fact that none of them would come home to help relieve him of some of the duties he had. He thought they had little regard for the family name or tradition. He knew you were his only hope, but he'd almost given up hope that you would ever return to help him."

"He was right about that. I never would have come home until he was gone. I knew all about the marijuana sales, and I didn't want any part of that. He tried to keep things like that from me, but I knew it was the cause of my mother's death. I never really forgave him for that."

"Yeah, I heard a little about that. It was also the cause of his own death. He wanted out of the business, but the people he supplied weren't going to let him go. He fought with them because he knew he couldn't get things going on the scale he wanted with the possibilty of problems over drugs. He had the vision of what we have now. I couldn't see it, but he could. My mind could never comprehend what he saw as clear as a bell. Even today I'm amazed when I look at the way things have changed since I've been here. I can hardly recognize the town of Perdido that I first saw."

"I get that feeling, too. Well, what do you want to do? Shall I fly back to New York to tell them what you just said, or should I just E-mail them?"

"The E-mail would be safer, but your going in person might make our offer seem more sincere. I'll leave it up to you."

"Then I'll book another flight for the day after tomorrow. That will give them a chance to use whatever influence they have on the two senators. They love to throw their weight around, especially with politicains. I'm sure they'll be able to take all the credit for the failure when it happens."

"Okay, I've got to get ready for the arrival of the CEO of our Japanese friends. He'll probably get here tomorrow. He'll be a neighbor of mine when Alice and I get the new house finished."

"Well, there goes the neighborhood. Just kidding. How long do you think it will be before you can move in?"

"The architec has completed his work, and the builders are ready to begin any day now. We could have started sooner, but Alice wanted a special room for the baby. We started building on, before we even started building. Hans is the only one who'll be sorry to see us leave where we are now. He doesn't like all the trees nearby. He says they make too good a cover for a would-be sniper. He may be right, but you'll never get Alice to agree to cut down a single tree."

"I won't be long in the City. I don't know which gives me the creeps more, that town or my brothers."

Mr. Samura had never been to Mexico before. He knew when he agreed to move his company headquarters to Perdido that he would have to leave his beloved home in Tokyo. He had sent the man who designed his Tokyo home to Perdido to seek out a place where he could build another similar to the first. He had brought back photographs of the area, and Mr. Samura had chosen one and sent him back there to begin the construction of his future home. It would resemble his first home in as many ways as were possible, considering the huge differences in landscape. He would have a beautiful garden of flowers and a fountain filled with golden fish. There would be a heliport for helicopters to land so that he would have instant access to the plant should anything go wrong. He had arranged to have his wife and two teenage daughters moved there as soon as he felt settled. In the meantime, he would content himself with letters and long phone calls to those he loved.

He could not believe the speed with which his new plant was being erected. It did not seem possible that they would actually be producing this year's models of his automobile in a place that had recently been a grazing area for cattle. He shook his head in bewilderment as he observed for the first time the main area and all the smaller buildings that surrounded it. It didn't seem possible, yet there it was before his eyes. His new work force would enjoy the space that they never had in the crowded atmosphere of Tokyo.

He made his first real tour of the plant and was surprised that no one seemed to know who he was, or if they did, they did not seem to care. Everyone was so bustling that they did not have the time for anything except the task to which they had been assigned.

It seemed strange to see so many workers who were obviously not Japanese. The language he heard most around him was foreign. He made a mental note to begin lessons in Spanish and to refresh himself in the English he had taken in college.

He met with one of his most trusted foremen and asked him how he thought things were progressing. He asked if they would be able to meet the time line which called for this year's models to be produced here. With only a slight hesitation, the man reassured him that they would be in production on time if there were no unforeseen delays. In his mind he wondered if that meant any more attacks on the plant by those who would like to see him fail.

"Can you tell me what you mean by unforeseen delays? Terrorists attacks or what?"

"Maybe, but there may be other things."

"Such as?"

"Shipments of parts or other necessary items that are delayed. A breakdown in a place we have not anticipated. The distance that things must be shipped makes things uncertain."

"Do you fear more attacks on the plant? What have you heard recently?"

"There have been rumors of mercenaries sent to destroy the plant, but if the rumors are true, the enemy never reached us. Our security destroyed this force before they could fire a single shot at us. We have guards around the place around the clock. They are quite thorough. No one can even approach the site without being challenged. I feel as safe as one might when one knows there are people who would like to destroy you. How are things in Japan?"

"A mess. There are daily riots in the streets that the police cannot control. We have a very thin majority on the board that supports us. We must not have any early problems. We must be an unqualified success, or the whole thing will come crashing down upon our heads. I want to thank you for the support you have always shown me. If we are successful in this, you will be rewarded beyond your wildest dreams. You might even be the next CEO of this organization."

He smiled at that thought and wondered if the boss was just blowing smoke, or if he really was sincere with such flattery. He watched as the boss wandered on through the plant and stopped to talk to others as he made his first inspection of the plant.

****

Juan's second trip to New York was even shorter than his first. He did not even plan to stay over night. He carried no baggage on board the plane. He saw Carlos as soon as he deplaned and hurried toward him. He had a cab waiting for them and they went directly to the hotel.

"Glad to see you again so soon, brother. I hope your return signals something good for all of us."

"It might. I've had a chance to talk to Mr. Johnson about your proposal."

"And what did he have to say?"

"He thinks we may be able to work something out if you guys can be patient."

"Tell us more of what he said. We need something more definite than that."

"He thinks he can arrange to see that you guys get your 10% if you can wait six months. It would take that much time to get all the paper work done because of the Japanese. He also says the challenge against his patent must be dealt with, or obviously you won't be interested in owning 10% of a company that's going nowhere."

"What else did he say?"

"He fears retaliation by the oil companies for some of the measures he's had to take against them. I think you know what I mean. I've heard you guys were instrumental in the boardroom blowup and a super tanker that went down. They now attribute those things to him, and he's certain they would do anything to get even."

"Yeah, we know all about those things. The old man persuaded us to give him a hand when they were leaning pretty hard on Mr. Johnson. I don't think Mr. Johnson had either the brains or the balls to think up something like the boardroom or the tanker."

"He may not have had at the time, but let me tell you now that he has both the brains and the balls to compete with those bastards. He's got the Japs eating out of his hand, and the security he hired around him has taken care of some pretty bad hombres."

"Yeah, we heard about that French thing. That was quite a deal. How did he manage that?"

"He didn't. Hans did. Do you know about Hans?"

"Not a whole lot. We know he got Toyota Man. And we heard he got a hit man in Tokyo. He used to work for the oil companies, didn't he?"

"Yes, he did, and you can bet your ass they would like to have him back."

"Any chance of that?"

"I don't think so. They've made some big offers, but he doesn't trust them since they sent Toyota Man down to eliminate him. He knows there's lots of money to be made with this group if they are successful."

"How about you, brother? What are you gettin' out of all this?"

"I get a percentage, similar to the one you guys are asking for."

"Yeah, but we gotta split up ours three ways, so I'd say you stand to do better than us. What do you have to do to collect such a handsome sum?"

"A lot of legal work. You guys have no idea how hard it is to deal with the Japanese. They are really tough to deal with. They didn't really know they were holding the trump card when they agreed to come over here. They could have gotten a much better deal if they had held out a little longer. They realize that now, but it's too late. Now they are uneasy about anything we propose. They're afraid we're going to screw them like the old man did when he first drew up the papers. You have to give the old man credit. He knew how to do business. My main job is to see they don't fly the coop until we can get all the other Japnese companies to get in line and move closer to the adjustment."

Diego had said nothing until this time, but the mention of his father made him decide to join in the conversation. He said, "Yeah, I hated the old son-of-a-bitch, but I'll give him credit. He did know how to do business. I know some people who say you couldn't trade dollar bills with him without losin 95 cents."

"Yes, I've heard that too. Still there were always those who thought they could outsmart him. Very few ever managed. I think he must have taught Mr. Johnson a few things, because he's got things going pretty well."

"Then maybe we should be afraid to take his word that in 6 months he's gonna cut us in for a piece of the pie. Maybe he's just stringin' us along to see what benefit we can be to him. He knows that we can't do much about it if he reneges on the deal later on."

"I guess that's true. You have nothing but his word. That's all he can give you at this time, but let me tell you, if you have any chance at all of ever getting what you call a piece of the pie, this is probably your last chance. You might be able to destroy us, but there is no way you can ever be a part of us if you continue to harrass us."

"Can you take our word on it? That's all we can give you, so I guess it's just a matter of mutual trust."

"We'll see how the challenge goes on the patent. Do you still think you can influence the senators to give up the challenge?"

"At least two are in our pocket. That should be enough to quash the whole thing."

"Well, I got lots of things to do in Perdido. I'm on a turn around flight schedule, so I'm on my way back. Shall I tell Mr. Johnson that we have a deal if the challenge fails?"

"Yes, you can read about it in the papers in less than a week. We'll give the oil companies the word to lay off any more hits against you guys."

"Okay, then I'm on my way."

He smiled as he turned and walked away. He felt that Charley had read his brothers correctly. They were desperate for a piece of the pie, and he had just bought six months of freedom from assaults from two directions with his phony promise to include them at a later date. He was surprised that they could be taken in so easily.

With no real problems on the immediate horizon, things were happening at a remarkable rate in Perido. The grand opening of the show room had drawn such a crowd that they had been forced to stay open till midnight for the first two weeks. Americans came there in droves. They came to stay on vacations and planned to drive home in new cars that made the cost of the trip almost nothing. The economy of Perdido was at an all time high. The new motels were all boasting no vacancy signs, and the restaurants all had customers waiting to be seated.

Most of the people who were destined to be moved from Tokyo to Perdido had made the move. Things had settled down somewhat as more of the work force left the struggling Japanese economy for the boom that was in Perdido.

Car dealerships in the United States could not get the new models fast enough to satisfy the demand. The advertising that promised Japanese reliability, coupled with mileage that none of their competitors could even come close to matching, had put sales and profits at an all time high. This could not go unnoticed in Tokyo where every single one of their competitors had seen sales sink to less than half of what they had been last year.

****

Juan was worried. The six months grace they been promised by the brothers was fast coming to an end. He knew that even bigger things were on the way if they could maintain the stability here. He had already gotten feelers from two other Japanese carmakers concerning a move to Perdido. He felt it was only a matter of time before they would be moving to Perdido. He was afraid of what his brothers might try when they found they had been duped. He knew what Diego would want to do, and he wondered if the other two could control him. He felt he had to relay his fears to Charley. He rarely saw him these days as both were busy taking care of their own ends of the business. He called and asked if he could see him some time this day. The meeting was set for 10 o'clock the next morning.

"Come on in. I've been wanting to see you for several days now, just to ask you how things are going on your end. What's on your mind?"

"My brothers are on my mind. You haven't forgotten what we promised them almost six months ago, have you?"

"Of course not. Have you heard from them lately?

"No, but I expect to hear from them any day now, and I don't know what to tell them. Can you think of a way to stall them a little longer?"

"Maybe. What if I tell them that we are about to get two more car companies ready to move to Perdido? If they wait another three months, their piece of the pie will be a lot bigger."

"I've been meaning to ask you about that. What is the status of the other companies? Do we have a real chance to get them over here?"

"More than just a chance. I'd say it's a certainty if we can maintain stability here for a while longer. They can see they're in the toilet if they stay put. Their sales are down to almost nothing, and their stock is fast becoming worthless if they don't do something fast. I'd say they'll be ready to negotiate with us very quickly if nothing weird happens here in the next two months. I've had feelers already from two of the smaller companies, and I think the big boys will jump on board if these decide to make the move. I see the price of Arab oil went up again last week. Not enough to really matter, but enough for the oil companies to gouge the consumers with another major price hike. They're going to have to keep jacking the price to compensate for the mileage the cars are going to be getting now. It's not that much now because we don't control all of the market on the new cars, but when we do, they're in real trouble, and they know it."

"How long before they try to hit us again? Do you have any idea? Can your brothers keep them in check until we get something going with these companies?"

"I'm not certain they can. I don't know how much real influence they have or how much of what they told me was pure bullshit. We lie to them, and they lie to us. The first liar doesn't have a chance, they tell me. Maybe if they knew it was my brothers who blew up the board room and sank the super tanker, they might be ready to hold off for a while."

"I hope you're right. By the way, I've just approved a $500,000 bonus for you that has already been deposited in your account. Keep up the good work. There's no end of the money if things keep goin' our way."

"I'll do my best."

"I'm counting on that. Is there anything else on your mind?"

"Not really. I'll try to stall my brothers and let you know what they have to say."

When he left, Charley shook his head. Two more companies headed their way. Another bunch of headaches. He would have to negotiate the peace between the competing car companies. He would have to make promises to each that he knew he could not keep. Where was the simple life he once imagined that he would have if only his adjustment was successful?

The second of the Japanese companies was having a heated discussion concerning the longterm prospects for the company. It

was clear they could not maintain the status quo. Around the
table heated arguments raged. The CEO waited for some sem-
blance of attention before trying to bring the meeting to order.
He banged the gavel three times before he felt it was quiet enough
to begin."

"Gentlemen, you all know why we are here. Let's not beat around
the bush and pretend that we don't know what the situation really
is. Our company is ready to collapse. Bankruptcy is just arround
the corner if we don't take immediate action. You are all aware
of this, so don't try to act surprised. If you are not aware of this,
then where have you been for the last year? Our sales are off more
than 50% and our stock has lost 75% of its value. If we continue
on our present course, we will have nothing in less than a year.
Just to finish out this year will require some great sacrifices, but
before the next year's models go on line, we must do something
drastic."

The second in command stood and waited to be recognized.
When the muttering had stopped, he began, "Can you be more
specific about what sacrifices we must make to get by this year?"

"First, we must reduce our inventory. That means that we will
have to sell this years models for less than it costs to produce
them."

"And what else?"

"Each of us must take a huge hit on our own wages and bonuses."

"Does that include your wages and bonus?" asked a man who
remained seated.

"Of course it does. That question was an insult. I will require an apology. If none is forthcoming, I will ask you to leave this table and hand in your resignation before the end of the day."

The seated man rose, hesitated, bowed stiffly and said, "I meant no disrespect. I apologize for the question."

"You all must be aware that the cause of of our downfall has been the move to Mexico by one of our competitors. They not only have the advantage of cheaper labor, but the adjustment which gives them such gas mileage that we cannot even compete. The very best mileage that we can coax out of any model we produce will not give the consumer 50% of the mileage our competition can offer. It's only a matter of time until we go under if we don't take drastic action."

"And what might that action be?"

"I think you know the answer to that. We must do as our competitor has done. We must strike a deal with those in Mexico and move our base of operations there. If we go now, we might be able to rescue the company from doom. If we hesitate any longer, it will be too late."

"Is there any certainty that we can move to Mexico? Has the man who invented the adjustment been contacted? Will he make a deal with us that will let us compete?"

"We have begun preliminary negociations. They are willing to talk. We found that they do not have an exclusive agreement with our competition. That is much in our favor. Since they took the initial risk, they probably got a better deal than we can get, but any kind of deal will certainly be better than our present prospects."

"How about our employees? What will become of them?"

"Many of them we can take with us, if they are willing to make the move. Most will have jobs. If we stay here until we are bankrupt, none of them will have jobs."

"Will the government allow us to make such a move? They cannot be happy about their manufacturing base leaving the home island."

"Do you think they will be any happier if we stay until we are bankrupt? I think not. They have no solution to our problem, so we cannot expect any help from them."

"How about the mob that gathered around our competitor when they made their move?"

"They were contained. They didn't do anything but make a lot of noise. They did not prevent them from leaving. That should not be a concern for us. Speaking of our competitor, have you seen what their stock is doing? They have record sales and cannot even begin to meet the demand. Not even the American cars can compete for their share of the market. The longer we wait to get back into the game, the harder it will be to be competitive again. I would like to see a show of hands by all those who agree that we must make the move."

Of the ten seated at the table, eight raised their hands. The CEO looked gravely at the two who had not lifted a hand. He then asked each if he would like to tender a resignation. Both shook their heads in a negative fashion.

"If there is no further discussion, I assume that we are in agreement that a move must be made. I will be in negotiations in earnest as soon as possible. I shall let you know of any progress we are making. My advice would be to say nothing about the move until it is ready to happen. There will no doubt be some angry people when they learn of our decision. If we move repidly, we can avoid some of the frustration of those affected most. If there is no further business to be discussed, then I declare the meeting adjourned."

Negotiations began in earnest in less than a week. Representatives from the second company flew to Perdido to see what kind of offer they could get from Mr. Johnson and company. Charley had already met with his lawyers and laid out plans for a second company to make a move. He had acquired the land at what once would have been considered an extravagant price. Now he stood to make another fortune on the land alone. He knew that to appease his first client he would have to charge the second client more for the adjustment than he did for the first. It couldn't be a whole lot more, and he was prepared to extend them credit until they could be in production again. It would give Hans and Terry something to keep them busy again. It would also let them keep the host of deputies and moles they used to keep abreast of anything that might be happening in Perdido.

The work on Charley's house had progressed enough for him and Alice to make their move. In a way, he hated to leave the comfortable and familiar place that he had called home for quite some time. He knew also that he would miss watching his granddaughter on an every day basis. She was beautiful with her dark hair, which was in stark contrast to the blonde of his own daughter. They would become great playmates later, he was sure. Alice was anxious to have a house of her own for the first time in her life. She knew that moving that far away from the others was a greater risk, especially with all the neighboring trees. Hans hated the idea, but he was smart enough not to bring it up around Alice. He warned Charley to tell her to stay away from windows and not to take long walks around the house. Charley knew she would spend lots of time outside with her flower garden, and there was nothing he could do about that. He had Hans assign two men to to keep close watch on the area he feared most. No need for more than two, though Hans would have preferred twice that many. It was an argument he knew he could not win. Charley despised the need for such close scrutiny of his every move. He felt his privacy now might be a more important commodity than money. Life had been tougher before he became one of the richest men in the world, but he would have traded a lot of loot for just a little time alone with Alice.

The move took two days. There was load after load of things that Charley had not realized were accumulating. Alice was there to direct the movers, but Charley took refuge in his office until the move had been completed. He had no experience in this sort of thing, and he wasn't anxious to acquire any. He knew about where he thought most things would be located when the move was completed, important things like his easy chair and the big screen TV. His closet and the king sized bed couldn't be hidden, so if things like kitchen utensils were hard to locate for a while, he knew he could adjust.

Alice was a little perturbed that he was not there to help her make what she considered inportant decisions. She fretted needlessly for fear he would object to her placement of things. She kept the nanny she had hired first to look after her step grand-daughter. This had forced Billy to hire a new governess. Luisa had not recovered as fast as Alice and needed more help than Alice did in in taking care of a large spacious household. Luisa felt that a younger woman might be better at management of the house and the baby, but she hated to give up a woman who had years of experience with small children and housekeeping. She had decided to interview several candidates before making her final choice. Hans had insisted on a background check for any woman who applied for the position. Any one who had even a misdemeanor on her record was automatically eliminated from consideration. The job was one of the highest paying jobs for a woman in Perdido.

A long and well-qualified list of women had filled out the application necessary to obtain an interview. Billy had agreed to let Luisa make the final decision. He had long hours almost every day at the plant, and the arrival of a new company would not lessen his workload. He hardly realized that he was the son of the wealthiest man in Mexico, and soon to be one of the richest men in the world. He wondered what things would have been like if he had stayed in the United States and had gotten to play basketball. All that seemed so distant that he could not visualize any scernario except the one of which he was now a part. Some day maybe he would be able to relax and enjoy the fruits of his labor, but for now he never seemed to have enough time to enjoy his situation. His greatest joy each day was the time he could spend with his wife and daughter.

Diego was furious. He had never really had been sold on the idea that they would ever be given a piece of the pie in Perdido. He knew that his brothers still scoffed at his failed attempt with the French mercenaries. Now it was his turn to make fun of their acceptance of the word of his brother which he had said from the beginning would never be honored. He would have struck out blindly at Charley and his company if his brothers had not held him in check.

"Yeah, yeah, I know it wouldn't do us any good to blow the place apart. Nothing but a lot of satisfaction, if that chicken shit brother of mine was in the place when it blew up. How in the hell did he pull the wool over you guys' eyes? Now I could understand it, if he had only fooled a stupid son-of-a-bitch like me, but not you geniuses. Now that is remarkable."

"Okay, okay, you've had your laugh at our expense. Now tell me, do you have another brillaint plan? At least it didn't cost us half a million like your brainstorm."

"Whatever we decide, you gotta promise me that next time we take some action. I've had all I can take of the waitin' game."

"I hate to agree with anything he says, brother, but this time I gotta agree with him. The time has come for action."

"Okay, then you guys tell me what we should do. I told you they weren't worried about the challenge to the patent. He knew that even with political muscle on the other side that they had no chance of winning in court."

"Maybe so, but why would they be afraid of another attack after the French fiasco. It must have been our promise to keep the oil companies off their back that made them even consider our offer."

"You dope! They never considered our offer. They played us for chumps! They were just buyin' time until they could suck another car company into Perdido"

"Well Diego, I know you're not gonna like this, but I think our best chance is through the government. The present administration can see itself goin' into the toilet if things continue to go the way they been goin'. Losing so much of the new car sales to the Japs can only make things worse. The patent end of things is screwed. We can't win there, and we know it. But maybe we can find a hole in the NAFTA agreement that would limit the number of cars they can ship here."

"So when did you become an outhouse lawyer, brother."

"I've had lots of time to think about things like this recently. Also time to read up on them. Maybe you ought to try readin' something besides the funny papers, brother."

"Maybe, but what's the angle here?"

"I think because most of the parts are manufactured in Japan, the fact that they are assembled in Mexico does not give them unlimited distribution here in the States."

"Well, listen to you, brother. You sound more like the old man every day."

"You know, that's something I never could understand about you. Why have you always hated the old man so? Don't you know that he became rich and powerful by using his head and the law to get what he wanted. Now every time I try to do something like that, you let out a squawk like a sow litterin' broken bottles."

"Maybe so, but he wasn't above usin' force to get what he wanted. Remember it was his idea to blow up the boardroom and the supertanker."

"I haven't forgot. But don't you forget it was his use of his brains that blocked the extradidtion of Mr. Johnson when the State Department tried to get him back in this country. He knew the law, and he knew the right people to get his way. He was smart enough to see what the adjustment could mean when even the inventor himself couldn't see it."

"What political pull do you have that might be to our advantage?"

"None, right now, but I know the people in our organization have some of the best lawyers that money can buy. How do you think most of the big boys have stayed out of jail for so long?"

"Yeah, but that's mostly criminal law. What we're talkin' about here has nothing to do with anything criminal. Besides, I thought we agreed a long time ago to keep our connections with the mob out of this. They'll want the lion's share of anything we get for themselves."

"True, but even a small piece of what they got goin' would be better than a 100% of nothing."

"Do you think they'd be interested in tryin' to help us?"

"No, but I'm for damn sure they'd be in for helpin' themselves. If you guys agree, I'm gonna set up a meet with big man tomorrow."

"I'm okay with it. How about you, Diego?"

"I guess. We don't have a hell of a lot of options. If they say no, what then?"

"Then we let you decide. How do you like that? If you want an all out hit on them, I'll vote aye. If we can't get a piece of the action, why should we let our brother have it all?"

"Now that's what I've been sayin' all along, and right now, I don't give a shit what he says. At least we're gonna do something."

"Okay, I'll be able to tell you by this time tomorrow."

The next day Carlos went to see the big guy. He was frisked before he was allowed to go into the main office. He waited to be asked before taking a seat. He waited for the slightly balding man who faced him to speak before saying a word.

"And what can I do for you, Carlos?"

"Well, sir…………..

"Come on. Spit it out. I haven't got all day. You surely wanted something or you wouldn't be here."

"I do want something. I need some legal help."

"Really? What kind of trouble are you in? I hadn't heard anything."

"No, not that kind of legal help. It's just that……….

"Come on, say it. You know I was a big fan of your father. He was a man to be respected. Now, what can I do for you?"

"Could you arrange for me to have a talk with your best lawyer on civil matters?"

"I could if you'd tell me what you want to see him about. Does this have anything to do with your late father's enterprise in Mexico?"

"Yes sir, it does. We were promised a piece of the action down there, but they have reneged on the deal."

"So what you expect to gain by seein' my lawyer?"

"Well, I know you have many legitimate enterprises goin', and that you hire only the best lawyers to see that you don't get screwed by the so-called legitimate business men. This guy has a patent that seems rock solid on his so-called adjustment, and that is driving the oil people and the carmakers crazy. They can't compete, and it looks pretty bad for business here in the States. We've tried muscle against them, but it didn't work. We tried to break the patent, but that never got off the ground. If we could explain all this to one of your great legal minds, maybe he could find some way to help us out of this situation."

"Indeed he might, but what's in it for me and the organization if he can help you?"

"Well, we thought you might be interested in getting a piece of the action if we're successful."

"Just how a big a piece of the pie are you talkin' about, and what is the size of the pie?"

"Well, we thought 10% would be enough. The size of the pie as we speak is millions, but we're sure later on it will run into billions. The Japanese have already moved one of their plants to Mexico, and there is another one on the way."

"Yeah, I know. I'm not stupid. I read the papers. What good do you think a lawyer would do?"

"We're hopin' there might be a hole in the NAFTA treaty agreement that let's them send unlimited numbers of cars manufactured in Mexico to the States. If there is, we could threaten them with import taxes if they refuse to cooperate with us. I know that 10% doesn't sound like much, but 10% of billions is millions."

"Interesting concept. Well, I don't have any idea if there's anything he can do, but I'll set up a meeting with my best lawyer for tomorrow. I'll talk to him after he's talked to you and see it there's anything we can do to get the ball rolling. I still have a few political connections that might come in handy if he thinks we have a chance with what you're proposing."

"Thank you, that's all we're askin'. Just a chance to talk to someone who might know."

He left the room feeling good. He felt it had gone well. At least he had listened, and he was going to let them talk to his best lawyer. Carlos had hoped that would keep Diego on his leash a while longer. He had always been frightened that some day the older brother's temper would be the death of them all.

As a lawyer for his powerful client, the man had created a reputation of a man who could get the job done. He had listened with interest as his boss had explained what he could of the meeting he had just finished with Carlos de los Santos. He asked if there was any chance that they might succeed in blocking the unlimited number of Japanese cars that were destined to flow into the States. He could only shake his head and shrug his shoulders and admit that he had no idea what the treaty said about plants moving into the free trade zone from outside the zone. He would put his whole staff on the project if that was what the boss wanted. It was.

Carlos arrived a little early. He was even more nervous than he had been the previous day. He did not want to appear to be some ignorant goof who had no real idea what he was talking about. He shook hands with the lawyer and took a seat facing him across a desk. He was relieved to know that the man already had some idea of what he wanted. The lawyer tried to put him at ease, but Carlos simply could not relax. He stammered through a short speech he had rehearsed earlier in the morning. When he had finished, the lawyer nodded and waited to see if there was anything else Carlos had to say.

"Well, I must confess that I don't have the answer to your main question. I have no idea whether the treaty covers the movement of a manufactured product to a new location for the purpose of avoiding a tarrif, or any other purpose for that matter. It might be that even if there is no language relating specifically to such an action, some might insist the spirit of the treaty does not allow such a move. One thing I know for sure. You are certainly not alone in trying to slow down the rush of Japanese products into the States. The Detroit people and the oil companies are frantic to find some way to slow it down."

"How long do you think it will take to find out if there is a precedent that might delay the Japanese invasion?"

"That's hard to say. We'll start working on it right away. I'll put the majority of my staff on it. I know we can count on a lot of political support from several different areas. We have several senators who owe us a few favors. I don't really know about the House. I'll try to get an opinion from one of the senators before the week is out. It's really quite a concept. If all else fails, we might try a little saber rattling. We have threatened them before and been successful. It's hard to tell. Sometimes we pay too much attention to the opinions of third world countries. It's my opinion that we should disregard a whole lot of what these countries think or say. Enlightened self-interest should be our foreign policy in most case like this one."

"I agree. Well, I guess I've told you all I can about this matter. I won't take up any more of your time. Thanks for listening."

"That's what I get paid for, listening. I'll get back to you as soon as I hear anything, one way or the other."

****

He took the news back to his brothers and was surprised that Diego did not berate him for bringing back nothing that was positive. He could see that Jorge was encouraged, and he himself was pleased with the prospects. He knew how hard it was to wait. He wished there was some action he could take, but he was at a loss for what it should be. Another expensive failure or a suicidal mission like the one favored by Diego, was not to his liking. Better to try something along the lines of what his father would have tried. He wished he had the old man's connections and his ability to influence the actions of others. He also secretly wished he had returned to Mexico when his father had begged any one of the three to come home and help him take care of business. It had seemed like foolishness at the time, but now he could see that if he had heeded the call, he might have been in the enviable position of his youngest brother.

"So, brothers, it looks like all we do now is sit and wait. I think the big guy was impressed. He was lickin' his chops when I told him how much the company is worth and what it might be worth in the near future. I hate to get him and the organization involved in this, but I don't see any other way."

"Neither do I, brother, neither do I."

****

In Perdido, things were going so smoothly that Charley was extremely nervous. The production of new cars saw transport after transport leave the plant headed for dealerships. In the States, dealers could not get enough units to meet the demand. There was a waiting list, and buyers were willing to pay a premium to get the first available units.

There had been no attempt at sabotage or violence for quite some time. It was a strange feeling not to expect trouble on a daily basis. Hans was bored, and Terry had taken to drinking more than he ever had in his life. Billy had found more time to spend with his wife and daughter, and Charley and Alice had become accustomed to the uneasy peace. Meals were served on a regular schedule, and bedtime also had become routine. It was this regularity that Charley feared. Since he had first arrived in Perdido, he had never known anything like the tranquility that now prevailed.

****

The second of the Japanese companies was rushing to get its plant completed. They could not help but notice the prosperity their competitor was enjoyimg. They saw the loaded transports leaving every day and could hardly wait for the time when these same transports would be loaded with their cars and headed for their dealers.

In Japan the situation was worsening. Unemployment was growing at an alarming rate. The prosperity of the Mexican enterprise had done nothing to alleviate the problems of the Japanese economy. The government could no longer maintain the subsidies which had kept many Japanese businesses afloat while they tried to compete. Now there was a downturn in the world economy, and only a few of the more fortunate companies had not felt its impact.

The noise from the streets grew louder every day. Even now many other businesses were thinking that a move to somewhere else might be in their best interest. If not Mexico, then maybe somewhere else where labor might be cheaper and markets might be closer. There seemed little doubt that all the manufacturers of automobiles would follow the first two to Mexico.

Charley grew more restless with each passing day. His temper was short, and his patience with those around him was slim at best. He quarreled with Alice over petty things and snapped at Billy when things were not going his way. The babies annoyed him at times. Finally it was Hans who suggested that he might need to take it easy for a while.

"How the hell can I take it easy? You know all the crap I have to do every day. Who's gonna do all that if I decide to take it easy, huh?"

"I know you have more to do than any man ought to be pressured into, but since things have leveled off for a while, I think Billy and Juan could handle things for a while if you'd take a little rest."

"Yeah? And just where am I suppose to get this much needed rest?"

"I've got an idea or two. If we were in the States, I'd say a weekend in Las Vegas would be just the ticket, but since we're not there, how about Monte Carlo? Have you ever been there?"

"What the hell would I do in Monte Carlo?"

"You'd be surprised. For a person of your stature they'd roll out the red carpet. Swimming, dancing, golfing, gambling, and the very best cuisine in the world. It would give you a chance to unwind, Charley. I hate to be the one to tell you, but recently you've been no fun at all. You've pissed off everyone in the family, and that's not like you. Even one of the Japanese executives asked me the other day what the hell was the matter with you."

"Yeah, I remember. He forgot to pass on a memo that I left for his boss. I guess it really didn't amount to much, but it was just the idea that he didn't do his job. It might have been important."

"Yeah, it might have been, but it wasn't. That's the whole idea, Charley. You're lettin' piddley assed stuff get to you. I'm just afraid if you go on like this, it could affect your judgement on something important."

"Maybe you're right. I don't think I could get Alice to agree to leave the baby long enough to take any kind of vacation."

"I think you'd be surprised. She probably wants you to lighten up more than anyone else. She can get all the help she needs in takin' care of the baby. That's one of the good things about bein' rich. You can always hire the best help. Remember, that's how you got me."

He laughed as he remembered the circumstances that had led to the hiring of Hans. "You know, if we'd left it up to me, we'd have hung you right after you surrendered. It was the alcalde who decided you were worth saving."

"Yeah, I remember. He was a pretty good judge of character. Now, what do you say? Shall I make the arrangements for a trip to Monte Carlo?"

"First let me get in touch with Alice and see what she says. If she says yes, it's a go."

When he got home that night, he found that Alice was in a bad mood of her own. Both babies were crying and dinner had gotten cold while she waited for Charley. The frown on her face told him that dinner would not be a good place to broach the subject of a vacation. He decided that bedtime would be better, after they had showered and sat on the edge of the bed to shake loose the slippers they wore.

"Honey, I'm sorry about dinner. I didn't realize it was that late. I've had a lot of crap on my mind these last few days. I know I haven't been very pleasant to live with recently, and I know that you've been stressed out, too. What do you say we take a short vacation?"

"What kind of vaction? You know we can't just take off and leave the baby."

"I know we can't just run off, but I think we could hire a little extra help to look after the baby. Things are going pretty good right now. Billy and Juan could handle about anything that might come up."

"How long would we be gone?"

"Oh, I don't know, four or five days."

"And where would we be going, if I may ask?"

"Monte Carlo. Have you ever been there?"

"No, I haven't been. Have you?"

"No."

"Why go there?"

"Well, I hear it's really a fun place to be."

"I can't believe this is your idea. Who came up with Monte Carlo?"

"Hans gave me the idea. He said they have everything you could possibly want there, especially if they know you have money to spend."

"When would we leave?"

"As soon as we can make the arrangements, tomorrow or the day after. Would that be too soon?"

"No, not if we can get the extra help to take care of the baby. What arrangements need to be made?"

"Airline tickets and hotel accomodations. I think those can be made by computer."

"I think it might be best if we didn't let anyone know we were going. The computer might not be a good idea."

"You're probably right. On second thought, I don't think a commercial flight is a good idea. I'll just charter a small jet. That way if anything did happen, we could leave whenever we want to."

"My god, Charley! Charter a jet! That would cost a fortune!"

"So what? I have several fortunes. I haven't had time to enjoy any of them lately, and I think it's about time I did. What do you say? Shall I make the arrangements?"

"I say yes!"

****

The next morning Charley told Billy about his plans and asked him if he thought he could handle things for a few days. He was pleased to think his father thought he was capable of taking care of business, not to mention he had been hard to live with the past few days.

"No problem, dad. Leave me a number where I can reach you in an emergency. Would you like for me to arrange the airline tickets?"

"That won't be necessary. We're gonna charter a small jet so we can leave on a minute's notice if we need to. You could check the hotels and get and me a reservation at one of the best ones. No, make that the very best one."

"Will do. I hope you and Alice have a great time. Maybe you'll be in a better mood when you get back. Maybe Luisa and I can take off a few days when you get back."

"Sounds like a good ides. Let me know which hotel you got us booked into. It might be a good idea to talk to Hans about the hotels there. He's been there lots of times, so he surely knows the best place to stay."

Chartering a small jet had been no problem, and when Billy told the man at the resort who the reservation was for, the man was unbelievably polite. He wanted to know when they would arrive so they could have a limo at the airport to pick them up. He guaranteed them the best suite in the place and also the best of service. Billy decided to ask how much cash they should bring, but the man informed him they needed no cash whatsoever. He could sign his name for anything he wanted.

The flight was quick and uneventful. They landed and were picked up by a driver holding a large sign which read Mr. and Mrs. Charles Johnson. They got into the luxurious limo while the man stored their baggage in the trunk. He spoke perfect English, so Charley knew he was not an American. When Charley offered him a tip, he declined, saying that he would be at their disposal for the length of their trip and then if he wanted, he could give him a gratuity.

Once inside the hotel-casino, they were escorted to the desk to check in. The hotel manager took them personally to their suite and told them if they wanted anything to let him know. He gave them a brochure that told them of the many activities that were available. He mentioned tennis and golf, but Charley shook his head. Alice, however, wanted to know where she could get a swimsuit. The manager told her that one could be purchased there in the hotel giftshop.

"What do you say, love? You want to take a dip before we unpack and get some famous food?"

"I don't have a suit."

"Neither do I, but they can get both of us one. Come on, it'll be fun."

"Okay, that's what we came for—fun!"

The manager was right. Indeed they did have swimsuits right there in the gift shop. He had neglected to say that they were designer suits that cost a small fortune. Charley didn't even blink when he saw what the two suits would cost. He had made up his mind not to count the costs of anything they did while on vacation. It was about time he started to live like a millionaire.

"You know, Alice, I've never seen you in a bathing suit before. This is gonna be a thrill for me."

"I doubt it. It might have been before I got pregnant, but I'm still ten pounds heavier than before. You can't hide that in a suit like you just bought me."

"No, that suit doesn't hide much of anything. Just remember not to wiggle the old caboose like in the old days."

The water was warm, and they had decided to use the outdoor pool, rather than the smaller one inside the hotel. The ten pounds that Alice had not lost did nothing to detract from her still beautiful body. Charley could not help but notice the glances she got from most of the men who were sunbathing as she approached the pool. She leaped into the water and motioned him to join her. He was more cautious, touching the water with his toes before jumping in next to her.

"You'll ruin my hair-do if you keep splashing around like that."

"Not to worry. I'll bet you can get your hair done right here and get a complete make-over if you want one."

"So, you think I need a complete make-over, do you?"

"No, but I'll bet your're aching to see what some of these fancy hair dresssers might want to try on you. Just for kicks, why not give it a try?"

"Can I change the color?"

"Why? So you can go out and buy a whole new wardrobe to match your new hair color?"

"It's a thought. Is there any limit to how much I can spend on clothes and other stuff?"

"Yes, I'm glad you brought that up. Let's try to keep it down to six figures, Okay?"

"You're joking, right?"

"No, I'm not. Alice, I don't think you've looked at the books recently, but I am a man of considerable means. It would be mean spirited of me to limit my wife to a paltry sum for clothes and "other stuff "as you put it."

"The water feels great. I haven't felt this good in I don't know when. I'll race you to the other side of the pool."

She won the race and lifted herself up to the edge of the pool. He joined her there, and for a while they sat there with their feet dangling in the water. He put his arm around her, and for a few minutes their cares vanished.

Another short dip and they were ready for food. They dressed in the best they had brought with them. For Alice, that was no problem, but it was obvios that Charley was going to have to spend some money for clothes for himself.

"Sorry," he said. "You look like a million bucks and I look like I'm not even dressed for the prom."

"You'll do for now. We can take care of things after dinner. I'm sure they'll have something nearby that will be able to fix you up."

He let the waiter suggest something for them to eat, and neither was even sure what it was, but it was delicious. He didn't even look to see what the meal had cost, fearing it might lessen his enjoyment if he knew.

After dinner they went to an exclusive men's store where Charley purchased two suits, three shirts, and ties for a little over $3000. He signed his name and that was that.

They went back to the suite so he could change into his new clothes. Alice put on some fresh make up and waited for him to complete the change.

"Hey, love, you clean up pretty good. I've never seen you lookin' better. What are we gonna do now?"

"Well, what do you say we hit the casino? We haven't done any gambling in a long time."

"When did we ever, Charley?"

"The horse races in Oklahoma City. Have you forgotten?"

"How could I forget? The name of the horse you bet on was Miss Red Head, wasn't it?"

"Indeed it was. That seems like a million years ago. At least it was several million dollars ago."

"This seems so crazy. We go out and do anything we want and never mind what it costs. Do you suppose we'll ever get used to doing that?"

"I hope so. It's fun. What do you want to play when we get to the casino?"

"Well, about the only game I know is 21. I went to Vegas once and played a little bit, but I didn't have much money so I didn't play for long."

"I've never been in a casino in my life. I'll bet they have something somewhere that will explain the rules of all the games. I'll ask the hotel manager. He said if we needed anything to ask him."

He found that when he asked for the hotel manager, he was faced by a man he had never seen before. The man knew who he was and was just as eager to be of service as the first had been. He told them where they could get written material explaining the rules of all the games. He even volunteered to go with them and asked Charley how many chips he would like.

"I think $10,000 worth for a start."

"And for your lovely wife, how much for her?"

"Another $10,000."

After looking over the rules, Charley decided to try his luck at craps. Alice took off in the direction of the dollar slot machines. They had agreed to meet at the main cashiers in two hours if they became separated. The floor of the casino was almost full. Most of the table games had a full compliment of players. The crap table had no room at all, so Charley decided to work his way around to a bacarrat table which had an opening. He knew little about the game except that the magic number was nine. He sat down and watched a hand or two before making a wager. He saw the sign which said that the minimum bet was $500. He bought in for another full $10,000, and then looked around to see if others at the table had stacks of chips similar to his own. He saw that some had more and some had less, so he felt more at ease. He made his first bet and lost. After three straight losses, the gentleman on his right said, "The bank has been hot tonight. You might want to think about playing the bank's cards instead of the players."

"Thanks. I'll give it a try."

He then decided to double up and bet $1,000 on the next hand. The bank made a natural 9, and he felt somewhat better. After an hour and a half, he was up $6,000. He looked at his watch and decided to wait for Alice at the main cashier's cage. He waited for her to get there before cashing in his chips. She arrived at exactly the time they had agreed upon.

"So, how did you do love?"

"About six thousand ahead. How about you?"

"Well, if I had been smart enough to quit an hour ago, I would have been ahead about two thosand, but I just couldn't quit. I wanted to, I really did, but those coins just kept jumping into the machine. It's like they had a mind of their own. Did you play craps?"

"No, all the tables were crowded. I went to a bacarrat table and tried my luck at that. It was $500 minimum, but most of my bets were a $1,000 or more. It was okay, but the rules are so cut and dried that you really don't have many choices, just the player's cards or the bank's.

"You'll have to teach me. Don't let me get near those machines again. I know I can't stop. If I hadn't agreed to meet you here at this time, I know I would have played all night."

"Before we cash in, I'd like to talk to the casino manager. I really don't want all these chips in cash. Carrying around that much cash is just asking for trouble."

When the manager came to where they were standing, he asked what he could do for them. Charley told him he would like to leave a sum of money in the casino so he wouldn't have to worry about carrying it around. The man told him it would be no problem. He counted out the chips that Charley had and then had the cashier put the coins that were in Alice's bucket into a machine which counted them. He got the total and had Charley sign a piece of paper saying the casino was holding $28,000 for them. He asked if there was anything else he could do for them and then wished them a good night.

They went directly to bed and made love for the first time since the baby had been born.

For the next three days, they reveled in the pleasures of Monte Carlo. They took a sight seeing trip by bus and learned what they could about the history of the place. Each day they swam and and sunbathed. Three times a day they plunged into the food which never ceased to delight them. Nighttime was filled with gaming early and love making later. On the second night Alice had to place a call back to Perdido.She was relieved to find out that the babies were doing well, and that nothing of great import had happened in their absence. When the time came to check out, they left with reluctance and vowed to come again when they could stay longer.

****

The battle in the United States Senate had begun. The American economy was going into the toilet, and the losses suffered by the big 3 automakers were leading the way. Many consumers were happy. The gas mileage they were getting gave many of them new freedom or at least a return to the way things were before gas prices had balooned. Long vacations with travel by car were once again in vogue, and once again half the fun was getting there. Many of the once prosperous auto workers were now unemployed and making a lot of racket, but there were lots more automobile drivers than there were automobile workers. There was no great clamor among the majority of Americans to stop the flow of cars that delivered such great mileage.

Nonetheless, there was a vested interest that had raised a lot of noise about the unfairness of the Japanese. They had taken full advantage of the NAFTA Treaty. Now the catch phrase was "No more free trade. Let's have some fair trade." Those who had originally been if favor of the treaty and had urged its passage were now in the unenviable position of admitting they had made a grave mistake, a thing most rare among politicians. Those who had opposed the treaty were filled with glee as they watched their opponents try to backtrack.

At first there had been a proposal to levy a large tarrif on these imported autos, but the measure never came to a vote. Those in the know had correctly surmised that any tarrif levied against the manufacturer would be passed on to the consumer, making them unhappy without really doing anything to improve the American economy. The patent itself had withstood all the challenges that the oil companies and the big 3 had thrown its way. Now it seemed that the only way to stop the flood of Japanese cars into the United States was to either repeal the treaty or amend it such a fashion that those products which had originated in countries not linked to NAFTA could not be assembled in NAFTA territory and given unlimited access to American markets. It was a big gamble, for if the U.S. unilaterally decided to ammend the treaty, they faced a real challenge in the World Court. American popularity in Third World countries and even in the U.N. had shrunk to new lows. A change in the treaty could do little to enhance their prestige in countries affected by NAFTA.

The senior senator from Michigan was recognized by the vice-president. He walked slowly to the microphone and tried to put on the look of statesmanship. He opened by admitting that things were not going well for the American economy. He was quick to place the blame on the minority party. Now it was time for his party to take some vigorous action to try to turn things around.

"I know that every member of this body is aware that we have been overrun by foreign competition in the automobile industry. That competition is totally unfair. It was never the intent of the NAFTA Treaty to allow those countries not covered by its jurisdiction to ship their merchandise into our sphere of influence. There, these products are completed and shipped into our markets duty free while their markets remain closed to us. This has crippled our car manufacturers. Today I am going to introduce legislation that will bar the unlimited access of these foreign cars manufactured in Mexico or Canada or any other NAFTA country and then sent here to be sold. I hope those of you on both sides of the isle will support this legislation for the good of the country. It is time to put aside partisan politics and get this country moving again."

He sat down to a mixture of applause and catcalls. The next speaker could hardly wait to take his turn at the mike

"My how things have changed. When my party tried to tell you what might happen when you approved the treaty, you called it partisan politics. Now what *we* thought was un-American is a treaty which we signed. Now that treaty which the majority put into place is to be considered un-American. Why don't you tell this body what the real truth is, that the oil companies missed their chance to have this great Japanese carburetor because of their own greed, and that now the American car market is suffering the price of that greed. The man who invented this device is not Japanese. He is an American, but one who could not safely return to this country. He was forced into exile by these same people who are clamoring now for some remedy for their own stupidity and short sightedness. We are aware of the bind the Big Three are in, but I cannot in good conscience void a treaty we passed in good faith. Therefore, I have no alternative but to oppose any action on our part that would cause other countries to lose faith in our signed agreements."

As he left the podium, the cheers were louder and longer than those of the previous speaker. Even before the details of the new legislation had been presented, it was evident that it did not have enough votes for passage. The chief proponents of the measure now knew that the only hope they had was a rider to a bill that might have broader appeal. They would bring it to a vote just to see how many votes they would need to get something done on a rider. The number was a disappointing 16 votes.

Juan was the first to get the news, and he could hardly wait to relay the news to Charley. He had feared that something like a change in the nature of the treaty might throw a monkey wrench into the movement of the car industry to Mexico. Now he saw that it would take a lot of doing on the part of American politicians to accomplish a change of that magnitude.

He waited until Charley had time to unpack and relax before he told him the good news. Charley said, "I knew they'd get around to something like that eventually. Your father warned me that in time they'd have to try to void the treaty. He told me to be alert and try to bribe as many American politicians as necessary. He was certain that almost any of them could be bought if the price was right. I hope he was right. Is there anything else in the way of news that's happened while we were gone?"

"Not really. Everything is going so smoothly that it's almost scary. My greatest fear now is that my oldest brother may take it upon himself to make some idiotic play. The other two will try to hold him back, but sometimes there's just no stopping him. He is crazy!"

"Is there any way we can keep an eye on him to head him off if he decides to act on his own?"

"You'd have to ask Hans abut that. I have no idea how we can keep him under surveilance. Is everything okay at the plant?"

"Yes, I haven't heard anything negative. It's amazing how fast the second plant is going up."

"Yeah, when they saw what profits the first one made, they can't wait to compete again. How are the books going for us? Are we making money?"

"I don't think you have any idea how well things are going. At the rate things are progressing, you will soon be one of the ten richest men in the world. Right now you stand at number 13."

"I hope 13 doesn't turn out to be unlucky."

"It will have to hurry if it does because I'm projecting you in the top 10 in less than a year."

"That's hard for me to imagine. Your dad could see it, but he knew that I could never see what he called"the big picture." He was right. Even now, all I can see is the early start me and Enrique made working in the barn. That seems like years ago. Things have happened so fast. So many changes. It's even hard to remember what Perdido looked like when Alice and I got here."

"It certainly doesn't resemble the town I grew up in. I'd been away for quite a while, but now there's really nothing to remind me of my childhood."

"I guess in a way I'm adjusting to it. You know, when we went gambling, I thought no more of a $1000 bet than I would have a $2 bet a couple of years ago. Now the price of anything seems inconseqential. In a way, it kind of takes the fun out of buying anything."

"Well, I haven't gotten to that point yet, but I'm hoping some day I might."

"I think it will happen for you just like it happened for me if we can both live long enough to enjoy the ride."

****

The situation of the world became jittery. War between two or more of the oil exporting countries seemed imminent. This was not altogether bad for the people living in Perdido. As the nations of the world watched, the rival factions edged toward an armed conflict. The shortage of oil brought on by the reduction in production by the oil exporting countries had forced the price of a gallon of gas to new heights, and with each price hike, more and more people felt that they must own one or more cars with the adjustment.

Now military equipment had first priority. The plant had given first prority to its biggest customer, the United States of America. Every jeep, transport, personnel carrier, or anything else that ran on gas was headed to Perdido for the adjustment. Civilian vehicles were often forced to wait for days to get the adjustment, but most simply stayed in Perdido in the newly constucted hotels or motels until they could get what they came for. This, of course, was a huge boon to the economy of Perdido. Restaurants, fast food establishments, souvenir shops, and all sorts of touristy schemes thrived with the onslaught of those who came looking for a way to maintain their mobility with the gas mileage that only the adjustment could provide. Even people like Terry, who were affected most by the population explosion, treated the increase in the crime rate as job security. It was true that there were more petty thieves, panhandlers, grifters, and prostitutes than there ever had been before, but there was also more law enforcement on hand to control the situation.

Terry had become accustomed to delegating much of the authority he had to some of the deputies he had come to trust. It gave him more time to spend with his mistress, Teresa, and also time to enjoy some tequila. He stayed in contact with Hans to be sure he was on top of anything major, but he rarely became involved in the petty matters of day-to-day law enforcement. The central government had been generous in alloting enough judges for both a day court and a night court to handle things of a lesser nature. There had been a quick construction of a jail much larger than the one Hans had seen blown to pieces when the oil companies attempted to relieve him. Deputies were on duty 24 hours a day. Lawyers and bail bondsmen had followed the wave of petty criminals that always seems to follow the too rapid growth of a city. So while the rest of the world grew jittery, the vast majority of Perdido seemed only slightly alarmed.

Now came the first real crunch in quite some time. Three of the OPEC nations were standing in line to have their military vehicles adjusted. The line had formed when Uncle Sam had decided that the best way to insure an adequate supply of petrol was to have all his vehicles adjusted. The never stable situation in the Middle East had bubbled over with Muslem nations battling among themselves and never failing to look for a way to mix it with the Zionists.

Too much of a good thing--- America's civilians lining up to get their cars ready to go on vacation, and the American military fearing an oil shortage due to OPEC, insisting they had to be ready to support their Israeli allies if they were attacked. Already forced to run the plant 24 hours a day, now came the problem of the new cars from Japan. These new cars by contract had to be first in line to be adjusted . Someone would have to wait.

"Well, Juan what are we gonna do? We gotta tell someone they're gonna have to wait. They're gonna want to know how long, and I for one don't know what to tell them. What's your take on this?"

"It can't be the U.S. military. That would be financial suicide for us. If we put them off, they'll make life miserable for us. I think it's probably going to have to be our Muslim friends. I would suggest that the Saudis probably should get the first lick at the pot after we can satisfy the U.S. military. They are the least war-like of the three and least likely to attack one of their neighbors. If we can satisfy them, it won't seem as if we're anti-Muslim. Do you think there's any way we can speed up the work? Is there any way the mechanics can speed up the work, or is there any point in trying to hire more mechanics?"

"Negative to both questions. The quality of the work would suffer if we try to have them work any faster. It's a delicate operation, even for those who have performed the job hundreds of times. More mechanics would require more training for the new hires, and that would take away men who are now doing the job to train the new ones. I don't think that is an option. I agree that the U.S. military must come first. If we antagonize them, we run the risk the government might declare their national security is at risk and to hell with our patent. They just might find someone smart enough to put the thing together, and where would that leave us?"

"I agree. In the long term, is there any possibilty of enlarging the plant to make room for more mechanics?"

"Yeah, in the long term, but definitely not now. We have the money and the land, and we could train a lot more mechanics if we had the time. But as you know, we don't have the time. If a shooting war breaks out in the Middle East, we could be in a world of shit. We're bound to make some enemies no matter what we do. It's unavoidable. So we have to make sure that the ones who become our enemies are the ones who can do us the least harm."

"I think that would be Egypt and Jordan. Would you agree with that assumption?"

"Yes, I think so. Unless the situation changes, that's what I would recommend. What sort of relationship do we have with their embassies? Are we on good terms with them?"

"As far as I know. We haven't had any dealing with either up to this point, so I guess we haven't made any enemies in their direction. We don't have any direct dealing with the Israelis, and I think this a definite point in our favor."

"Why do you suppose we haven't heard anything from the Israelis?"

"Because they get almost all of their military equipment from the U.S. They have no need of our service as long as the U.S. sends them all their latest equipment."

"Yeah, I guess that would explain that. Well, how good are you at keeping the ones who'll be left waiting from wanting to attack us? We don't need any terrorist bombings or suicide missions against us. Your old man was a genius at keeping things like this together."

"Yes, so I've heard. I'll try to set up a meeting with the other two and try to put the best face on this that we can. I'll promise them more than I can deliver, at least enough to keep them at bay for a while. That's the best I can do.

"Okay, then just do that, Juan. Give it your best shot."

It was two days before Juan found himself face to face with the foreign ministers of Syria and Jordan. He had been involved in many important negociations before, but never one quite like this. He had spoken over the phone with both men and hinted at the bad news he would be forced to give them in person. Now he felt himself begin to sweat as he awaited the arrival of these two men. He had his secretary inform him when they were to be escorted to his office.

"Gentlemen, I'm so glad that you could come. I've been wanting to talk to you for some time now."

"Yes, of course, we have also been anxious to speak with you. You said over the phone that you might have some bad news for us. Can you tell us now what that news could be?"

"You get right to the point, and I appreciate that. Yes, we have received your order to have the adjustment performed on hundreds of vehicles, and I am afraid that at this time we are unable to accommodate you in this regard."

"Unable or unwilling? Are you afraid that the Muslim world might be able to protect itself from the Zionist attempt to control our whole territory?"

"Of course not. There are no Israeli vehicles targeted to be adjusted before those of your countries. The people who stand in front of you in this regard are the Egyptians who have already been sending a huge number of vehicles to be adjusted. I'm certain it is not your assertion that the Egyptians are part of a Zionist conspiracy, is it?"

"Of course not. We had not heard that they were the ones ahead of us in this regard. Can you tell us what type of vehicles and how many the Egyptians are sending?"

"No, I can't. That is not what my department deals with. I can only accept orders when Mr. Johnson tells me that he will be able to handle a certain number within a certain time frame. Now he informs me he will not be able to take any new orders for at least three months."

"But the Egyptians cannot possibly have that many vehicles, can they?"

"No, you are correct, but you must remember that they are not the only customer that we have."

"Yes, we are aware that many of the civilian population of the United States are lined up to receive the adjustment. We are also aware the American military awaits the adjustment of most of their vehicles."

"That is true. They were some of the first to recognize the value of the adjustment. Ours has always been the policy of first come, first serve. There has never been anything political in our decision as to who will receive the adjustment first."

"And what happens if war should break out in the next few days? What would that do to your "policy"?

"I'm sure that would not be my decision. As you know, Mexico has placed itself among the unaligned nations. My best guess is that in the order we have accepted the arrival of all vehicles is the order in which they will be adjusted."

"It is our greatest fear that many of these vehicles which you are adjusting for the American military will find their way into the hands of the Zionists. Nearly all of their military equipment comes from the United States."

"That may be true, but there is nothing we can do about that. We have no control over the final destination of any vehicle that we adjust."

"I see. May I be frank and candid with you?"

"I wish you would."

"My government is willing to pay twice as much for each adjustment if we can, how shall I say, be moved to the front of the line. Is there any possibilty that this could change the order of the adjustments?"

"I'm afraid not. We would then in all liklihood lose the business of those we bypass."

"I don't see that as a real possibilty. It is not as though they can take their business down the street, as you say. You have no competitors."

"That is true at the moment, but it may not always be so. Besides you have ignored our biggest customer."

"And who would that be?"

"The automobile industry of Japan. The potential business they bring to us far outweighs any military orders. For now, it appears that military vehicles are of prime importance, but I can assure you that when this crisis blows over, there will be millions of people who will want the blessing of the adjustment. Even countries such as yours do not have an infinite supply of oil. As that resource becomes more scarce, the price must go up, and as it does, our adjustment becomes more and more valuable."

"Then what shall we tell our governments when we return? That we cannot do business with you?"

"Of course not. Just tell them you are in line and will be adjusted as soon as we can get to you. I hope we will be able to serve you."

The two ministers looked at each other and shrugged their shoulders as if to say there was no way to take back good news to their respective governments. They stood up simultaneously and walked through the door.

As the trouble in the Middle East became more and more threatening, the more the automotive industry turned to the newest of the Japanese manufactured cars. With the flow of oil threatened, only the promise of the huge mileage that the Japanese cars could deliver stood between the chaos of an America that could not see itself immobilized. Prices were at an all time high, and relief seemed nowhere in sight. OPEC had long waited to claim some of the wealth of the United States, and now that chance had come. For one of the first times, there seemed to be a unity among those with oil to export. No one was using the latest price hike as an excuse to undersell their competitors. The price at $200 a barrel was firm and holding. Mexico itself had decided not to sell any of its oil to their neighbor to the north for less than the going rate. Threats of retaliation by the U.S. had not been effective. The threats had been ignored and totally disregarded by those who might have used this opportunity to ingratiate themselves to the industrial giant to the north. The feeling was that the short-term gain by accomodating the U.S. would be in the long run too costly. Let the Americans stew for a while when their population was forced to pay dearly for gasoline. This would insure a steady flow of Americans to Perdido to have their cars adjusted. Those who continued to drive their cars without the adjustment were like dinosaurs, headed for extinction.

Juan felt relieved that his meeting with the two ministers had gone as well as it had. He could not be entirely sure that his explanation of the wait the two countries would have to endure had been believed, but he thought he had at least bought them some time. His pretended ignorance of the fact that many adjusted military vehicles from the U.S were sent straight to Israel probably had fallen on deaf ears, but neither man had been outraged by his answer. He hurried to Charley's office to report the results of the meeting.

"Well, how did it go?"

"Okay, I think. It's hard to tell. They must know that a lot of military vehicles from the U.S. are sent to Israel, but I pleaded ignorance of that, and they let it slide. I don't know what they're really thinking. I can't read their thoughts. They hide what they're thinking pretty well."

"Your father used to say the same thing about the Japanese, but he had the gift of intuition. I hope you inherited some of that."

"I hope so, too. I'm not exactly an amateur at high level meetings between really big people. My job before this one gave me some experience in such things, and so far my intuiton had been okay."

"I didn't mean to insinuate that you couldn't handle these things. I know you have experience. That's why I offered you the job in the first place."

"Is that the only reason?"

"No, it's not. I thought your knowledge of how your brothers might act would be useful, but the biggest factor was that I saw a lot of your dad in you. I genuinely loved the old man."

"So did I. Sometimes I feel a twinge of guilt that I refused to return when he asked me to come home. At that time I was pretty taken with myself and thought that a return to Perdido would be a step down."

"Yeah, we all know hindsight is 20/20. What's your best guess about how long we can put off the Arabs before they get really angry. A lot will depend on the military situation over there. That's something over which we have no control. If there's no serious breakout of hostilites between Israel and her neighbors, we'll not feel the heat, but if things get hairy, who knows?"

"Yes, we have no control over things like that. What's the word with the Americans? Just how many of their vehicles are slated for delivery to Israel?"

"A lot. I don't have any exact figures, but my intuition tells me they think things are gonna pop real soon."

"Well, we're not going to change our policy until we have to, so just tell the guys at the plant to carry on business as usual."

That evening Charley sat down after supper to watch the huge new big screen HD television that had been delivered earlier that day. Alice sat down beside him on the couch and put his dinner on a TV tray. The news was playing, and Charley was paying close attention.

The first story of the newscast showed a riot in Japan. He shook his head and listened as the commentator described the efforts of the police to keep the situation under control.

"You know, Alice. I never dreamed that when I found the adjustment that some day it would be the cause of riots in Japan. It doesn't seem possible that I worked so long and hard to find something that has caused this much trouble."

"I don't think you can blame yourself for any of the things have happened along those lines. Your adjustment just came along at a time when the whole world was headed for a mess. The trouble in the Middle East has been going on for centuries. You can't take any credit or blame for what's going on there."

The scene shifted to Israel where tanks were rolling through the streets on the West Bank. The commentator told of battles between the rock throwing Palestinians and the well-armed Israelis. Again Charley shook his head, and this time he said nothing.

"You see, just what I was telling you. That kind of stuff has been going on forever. You don't have anything to do with any of that."

"I think indirectly I might."

"How so?"

"Well, if the Arabs could get their military vehicles adjusted to match the Israelis, I think things would settle down."

"Why can't you adjust their vehicles?"

"We can, but it's just that the Americans got here first. They ship a lot of their stuff to the Israelis. Hardly any of their military stuff is made there. I don't think it would be good business to tell the Americans that we have to delay fixing their stuff so we can fix things with the Arab countries. They might do any number of things that would be bad for our business."

"Such as?"

"Pressuring the Japanese to stop the flow of car manufacturing to here in Mexico. They could threaten to embargo all Japanese cars in spite of the NAFTA agreement. That would please a lot of American who've lost their jobs with the downsizing of the American car market."

"What else?"

"Well, I guess they could start harrassing the convoys of new cars headed for dealerships in the States. It wouldn't stop them, but it would really slow things down. It might cause other companies who are considering moving here to have second thoughts."

"It's all so complicated, Charley. How did it get that way?"

"I'll be damned if I know. I certainly never had any idea it would come to this. All I wanted was to give the American working-man a break. I saw that the oil companies and the car makers were screwing the American working man, and I wanted to do something about it."

"Did you have any idea that it would make you one of the richest men in the world?"

"Never crossed my mind. I knew I could make a lot of money, but I never thought it could be anything like this. Sure, I wanted more money than I could ever hope to make as a mechanic, but I never dreamed of this. I never could have imagined it if the alcalde hadn't been smart enough to see what he called "the big picture". I wish he was still around to handle some of the crap that's goin' on now."

"Don't you think Juan can handle it?"

"I hope so. I just don't know. He's so young. I know he's had some experience dealing with big things like we're running into now, but he's not the alcalde."

"Do you trust him?"

"I guess I do. I have to. He knows a lot more about the business end of what we have than I do. I don't really have any reason to distrust him except for the fact that his brothers are such miserable creatures."

"Well, he can't help that."

"I know, but I still think about it from time totime."

****

The scenes on the newscast shifted to the floor of the senate where a lively debate was in progress. A motion had been introduced to limit the sales of Japanese imports until there was evidence that they had opened up their markets to products produced in the States. The vote would not be taken until tomorrow, and the commentator was certain that the vote would be extremely close.

"You see. Just what I was talking about. They can cause a lot of grief if they go through with that embargo crap. I'll have to call some of my political friends tomorrow to see if there's anything we can do to head this thing off."

"How many political friends do you have in Washington, Charley?"

"More than a couple. Most of them I inherited from the alcalde, but there are others who we've bought. We spend a lot of money tryin' to influence what goes on up there."

"I had no idea you were involved in politics. You never talk about it."

"I'm never directly involved. I pay lots of influential people to lobby on our behalf. Juan handles most of it from down here, and he keeps me informed on what's goin' on up there."

The scene now shifted to Mexico. Charley was surprised to see that first his plant was pictured on the screen and then a close-up view of his house. The man went to great lengths to try to explain the tremendous growth of Perdido. He mentioned Charley by name but never mentioned how an American had been forced to move to Mexcio to produce a service so much in demand in the States. He finished the piece by saying that Mr. Johnson was the 4th richest man in the world.

"Well, he's a little behind on that one. My latest figures show that I'm number 2 and rapidly closing in on Mr. Bill Gates for number one."

"I find that hard to believe. A man who had to use the hard earned money of a lady of the evening like me just to get to Mexico is now about to become the richest man in the world."

"Yeah, I find it hard to believe, too. Did I ever pay you back the money you gave me for the trip?"

She laughed and nodded her head. Then she leaned over and kissed him on the cheek and got up and took their dishes to the sink.

In New York City, the brothers grew more restless day by day. On every occasion it was always Diego who screamed for more action against his brother in Mexico and his wealthy American friends. It was all the other two could do to hold him in check. Some if his plans were laughable, some bizarre, but all were far too dangerous to be implemented. It was more than just the money the brothers had hoped to obtain if they got what they felt was their rightful share of what their father had left in his will. Now it was a thing of honor. The name of de los

Santos had been relegated to a lesser name. An American name, Charley Johnson, had been elevated far above the proud name of the ancestors of the conquitadores. To Diego, and to a lesser extent, his brothers, this was a thing that could not be endured or tolerated.

"I'm tellin' you, brothers, somethin' is gonna haf to be done and quickly. Do you guys watch the news? Can't you see that those guys are gonna screw up and get involved in a lotta shit that's gonna shut down the whole operation? I got a plan."

"Great. What is it this time? Poison gas or a manufactured earthquake?"

"Okay, you two, make fun of any idea I come up with, but I don't see you two comin' up with any better ideas."

"So what's your latest bright idea?"

"A poular uprising. Let's start a propaganda campaign, and see if we can't recruit all the red-blooded Americans we can find who've lost their jobs in the auto industry due to the Japs. Lots of these guys got families and mortgages. If we put the blame on Mr. Johnson and the Mexicans, a lot them might be willin' to take matters into their own hands. What do you think?"

"You know, brother, for the first time you might be making a little sense. What do you think, Jorge? Is it possible our older brother has finally come up with an idea that has possibilities?"

"I don't know. It might work. What he says about the unhappines of the workers is true. They don't know what's happened to those great jobs they thought they had for life. A lot of them already own guns, but I think we gotta get better guns for them before we try anything big."

"How can we get started?'

"I'll ask the big boss if he'll contact the the family in Detroit, and see if they can start puttin' up posters around the union halls, advertisin' a trip to Mexico for those with enough guts to go down there and put an end to all this Japanese bullshit."

"What can we do in the meantime?"

"We can start comin' up with a cache of weapons they'll need if we can generate enough enthusiasm for the project."

"How many guys do you think it will take to have any chance of success?"

"I have no idea, but the more we can recruit, the better chance we have."

"How about transportation? They can't walk all the way down there."

"They probably all got cars. We could disguise the whole thing to look like they're all just goin' down there to get their cars adjusted."

"I suppose, but they'll need a leader. We can't just send them down there with no real plan and no leadership."

"That's no problem. I'll go myself. I'd like to get a shot at that worthless brother of mine."

"Brother, don't take this the wrong way. You have as much courage as anyone whoever carried the de los Santos name, but I'm not sure you should be the one to make up a battle plan."

"Are you sayin' I'm not smart enough to come up with a plan that would take care of these sons-a-bitches?"

"And what if I am?"

"Well, them I guess I'll have to start out by beatin' the livin'shit out of you, little brother."

"You see, that's exactly what I'm talking about. You think you can solve any problem with your fists or your gun. Wouldn't it be better to ask the big boss for help on this matter and see who he'd recommend as a planner for this project?"

"Then does that mean that I can't go along to see that things are done properly?"

"Not at all, brother. You can go, but I'd feel better if a man of the boss's choosin' was in charge of the plan."

"Will you contact the boss today to see if he likes the idea at all?"

"If I can get in to see him, I'll start today. If not, it'll be the first thing I'll try to get done tomorrow."

"Let's meet back here tomorrow at 5 o'clock. By then you should be able to tell us whether it's a go or not."

"Agreed. Tomorrow at 5."

At noon the following day, Carlos was admitted into the office of the boss. He had been thoroughly frisked before being granted an audience. He stood in front of the boss' desk intil he was invited to take a seat.

"And what can I do for you, Carlos?"

"It's about our problems in Mexico. I'm sure you're aware that things haven't been goin' too well for us down there in recent days."

"Yes, I see you haven't been able to gain any sort of concession from the owners of your father's great enterprise."

"And that is what I have come to discuss with you. My brothers and I think it might be possible to recruit enough disgruntled workers in the Detroit area who've lost their automotive jobs to make a hit on the people who're holdin' us up."

"Really, how can I be of service?"

"Could you get some of the Detroit men to put up posters around the union halls, advertising a trip to Mexico for all those who're interested in getting their jobs back?"

"I could. When would you want this enterprise to begin?"

"As soon as possible."

"Okay, on one condition. This must be done in such a way that none of it can ever be traced back to our organization. Who will be the leader of this expedition?"

"A man of your own choosing, I hope. My oldest brother would like to go along as second in command because he's familiar with the lay of the land."

"Your brother is a hothead. He cannot be trusted to make good decisions under stress."

"That is why we have come to you to ask who you would recommend for such a venture."

"A wise decision. I have two or three men who could lead this thing, but I'm not certain they would take the risk. The reward will have to be high to find the right man. I'll let you know tomorrow at this time if you'll come and see me again."

"I'll be here."

The next morning Carlos reentered the boss's office and once again waited before taking a seat. There were no formalities to discuss. Both men had been awaiting this conference and seemed to know that the decision about to be made could have a profound affect on the future of them both.

"I think I have found a man who will be willing to accept the leadership of this project which you have proposed. He is a native of the area, and he has experience in leading men. His name is

Jose Olivo. He was born 50 miles from Perdido and is familiar
with the whole area. He has been a member of our organization
for about 12 years. His loyalty to us has never been questioned.
This is important, because the people we intend to attack have
enough money to buy off anyone who can be bought."

"I agree. Loyalty is a thing that can't be overvalued. What experience does he have?"

"He has twice led groups of men into Central America to punish
those who have attempted to cheat us on large drug deals. He
has been succesful on both occasions, punishing those who have
cheated and returning with the money we were owed."

"How many men did he lead?"

"About thirty as I recall. It has been more than three years so I
cannot recall exactly."

"How many casualties were there?"

"Ours or theirs?"

"Both"

"I think we lost two men, and I think their losses were about
thirty."

"That's really a good ratio. How much money did you offer him
to get him to consider this venture?"

"That is really no concern of yours. Neither you nor your brother will be asked to put up the capital to finance this venture. We know if you are successful in gaining your share of your father's inheritance, that you will be most generous to those who have helped you."

"You're right. We could never forget that you're the one who made this possible. Have you had a chance to talk to the leader in Detroit to see if he can help us find volunteers for this venture?"

"Yes, he likes the idea. The posters advertising the project are being posted even as we speak. He is certain there will be so many that they will have to limit the number of the volunteers. He thinks there will be more than 200."

"Yes, that's probably an unmanageable number. I was thinking somewhere between 50 and 100. What do you think?"

"I leave those things to others. I never meddle in thing where I have no expertise."

"When do you think we'll be able to begin our journey to Mexico?"

"I was told that it would take about a week to prepare the men for the trip. He wants to rehearse an attack, and it will take a little time to arm the men properly. In the meantime, I must ask you to not let your brother screw things up by getting in the way. I'm reluctant to see him even be a part of an enterprise this big."

"Right. I'll do my best to keep him out of the way until we're ready to begin. Once again, I thank you, and I promise you'll not be disappointed if we're successful."

****

In Detroit, men had begun to gather at the Union Hall and were grouped around the signs that advertised the trip to Mexico. The trip was described as a way to punish those responsible for the unemployment in Detroit. The talk was loud and vulgar. Men boasted of what they would do if someone would just get them close enough to those responsible for their present condition. The loudest of those was a man named Harold, a man whose reputation for violence had earned him the nickname of Hardnosed Harold. He stood six feet six inches tall and weighed over 300 pounds. His fights with those whose opinions differed from his own were legendary.

"I'm tellin' you guys this. You may want to hang around here and do nothing, but I for one am not gonna put up with this shit. I am gonna go down there and see how many Japs and Mexicans I can kill. They're the ones responsible for my kids goin' hungry."

"How're we gonna get down there? I been out of work so long I couldn't afford to buy the gas to get down there."

"Yeah, and I had to hock my guns so I could eat last week. How am I gonna be able to kill Japs or Mexicans with no gun?"

"I don't have all the answers yet, but I'm gonna meet with this guy Olivo. They say on the poster that he has answers to most of our questions. He's gonna be here at the hall about noon. How many of you have enough guts to even come and see what the man has to say?"

Only a couple of men walked away while the others gathered around Harold to see what else he might have to say. They also clustered around several of the posters to see if there was any more information on them. The anger and frustration of unemployment now compelled them to try to do something about their situation. What had started as a mumble now became almost a roar as most of them were raising their voices in agreement with the comments of Harold.

Olivo strode to the center of where the men had gathered. He raised his hand to ask for silence. When the noise had subsided, he began, "Gentlemen, I have come to you with a proposition. I know what most of you have endured in recent days. I know of the turncoat American named Johnson who has taken his magic carburetor to Mexico to avoid paying taxes here in the States. I've learned how his connection with the Japanese has put all you loyal Americans out of work. I've had about all this I can take. Our government doesn't seem to give a damn about you and me. As long as they can get their own military vehicles adjusted, they're content to let you starve. I don't know how you feel about this, but I think I'll go down there and try to right this situation."

There was a roar of approval from the mob of men surrounding the speaker. Then there was confused mumbling as they waited for the speaker to continue his speech. He raised his hand again to ask for silence. When the men became quiet, he continued, "Today I will meet individually with any man who has balls enough to make the trip to Mexico with me. In the office I'll give you more details. It's a cinch that not all of you will be going with me. We can't have too many or we'll lose the element of surprise.

Make no mistake about it. These people are well organized and well armed. There is no doubt in my mind that some of us will not return. I may be one of those, because as your leader I will be out front. I am not afraid to die. What I am afraid of is slow starvation brought on by these people in Mexico who don't give a damn about you and me. I'm going into the office now, so if you'll line up, I'll start seeing you one at a time."

He disappeared into the main office, and the line began to form. No one tried to push his way past Harold, who had followed the man to the office door. He waited for only a minute before he knocked on the door and was told enter. The interview took no more than 15 minutes, and he left the office with a smile on his face.

Others followed Harold into the office. Some came out smiling while others came out scowling. Those who had been rejected were men Olivo had doubts about. Some were men with large families; others just didn't seem to have what it takes to be a part of an enterprise that would require some killing. In all, 40 men had been chosen to make the trip.

The next day Olivo met again with the big boss. He had been reluctant in the first meeting to agree to lead the assault on the plant in Mexico. He knew of the failures of others who had tried to attack these men in Perdido. He also knew of the reputation of Hans. He had been much younger when Hans had made his bones for the mob. He had seen him promoted to almost the top of the list of hit men before taking exclusive employment with the oil companies. It took a half million up front for him to agree to become the leader. This second meeting with the boss was his own idea.

"Good morning, Mr. Oretga. What can I do for you?"

"I would like a little more information about this venture I"ve agreed to lead."

"You'll have great latitude in this. You'll be given all the arms and ammunition that you require. You'll also be furnished with all the transportation necessary. What else would you like to know?"

"I'd like to know exactly what you hope to accomplish with this mission. I know we can't completely take these people out. They're too strong for that. I don't want to be part of a suicide mission."

"Yes, I guess now is a good time as any to go over this. I had intended to have this talk with you after you had a chance to work on the training of the men you'll lead. You're correct in assuming that we can't eliminate this problem with the force we'll be sending down there."

"So, exactly what do you hope to accomplish?"

"We hope to put doubts into the minds of both the Japanese who have already moved their base of operations to Mexico and others who are considering such a move. We don't want to totally discourage them. That might not be in our best interest. We hope to force the hand of those in control. There are those within our organization who by right of birth should have been given a large share of this operation on the death of their father. Clever lawyers have denied them this right, but we think we might be able to come to an agreement with Mr. Johnson and his associates if we can threaten them with the loss of the Japanese business. So, what we're hoping is that you and your men can create enough of a panic and confusion to make these people agree to take us on as partners."

"I see. Now let me get this straight. It really doesn't matter how many of them we kill?

"No, of course not. It also doesn't matter how many of the ones you lead are killed. Some must die. The more who are killed, the more sensational will be the headlines in the American papers. We want people here to be infuriated at the death of hard working Americans who lost their jobs and tried valiantly to do something about it."

"I see. Well, as I said, I don't plan on being a part of a suicide mission. So, whatever plan I come up with, I'll be far enough away from the heat to survive. I have half a million reasons to stay alive."

"Of course you do. Money does a dead man no good. How long will it be before you're ready to begin the journey?"

"I think about two weeks will do it."

He pulled a bottle from his desk drawer and said, "Let's drink to the success of your enterprise."

He poured a drink into two small paper cups and handed one to Olivo. *"Salud"* he said, and both men downed the drink. Olivo carried the cup out the door with him.

The next day Olivo began the training of those he had chosen to make the trip. He met them at Union Hall and told them to follow his car. He led them to an old deserted factory at the edge of town. In the basement was a setup for a shooting gallery. He had already stashed several automatic weapons to go with an impressive assembly of rifles and pistols. All of the men were familiar with the latter two, and a few with military experience had some knowledge of automatic weapons. When all the men had gathered around him in the basement, he made a short speech.

"Gentlemen, today we will begin to master some of the skills we'll need to be successful in Mexico. I know you're all familiar with most types of rifles and pistols. A few of you are also acquainted with automatic weapons. Those of you who have this expertise will serve as teachers to those who have no experience with this type of weapon. The type of automatic will be the AK47. We use these because they are easier to come by than the M16. Since those of you who have served in the army have never used the AK47, I will demonstrate it to you first, and then you will pass on what I've taught you to the others."

Seven of the men gathered around Olivo while the remainder huddled together and watched from a short distance. After a 10 minute briefing, several targets were set up at varying distances. Each man was given a weapon and a full clip. Five of the seven hit the target with their first burst. It took the other two the use of the full clip before they hit their targets.

Then the men were equally divided into groups with the seven as group leaders. More targets were set up, and every man had the opportunity to become more proficient before the morning was over.

After a short break for lunch, the men were given a short course in sniping with high-powered rifles equipped with scopes. All were given a chance from standing, kneeling, and prone positions. The attitude of the men was like that of a bunch of young men about to go on their first deer hunt. There was laughter aplenty, especially leveled at those who failed to hit their targets. Toward 5 o'clock, Olivo told the men to call it a day and to reconvene at 9 a.m.

The next day was filled with the use of grenades and a couple of small mortars. There wasn't enough room to actually use the grenades or mortars, so the lessons were strictly on the fundamentals and theoretical use of the weapons.

The third day was used to familiarize the men in the use of a bazooka. This was essential if the men were to run into armored units of the enemy. Once again the limited space for such a weapon kept the instruction on the fundamental level. There would be time later when space was provided for the men to actually use grenades, mortars, and bazookas.

After a week of this kind of training, the group set out for Texas. There they encamped on a huge ranch where they would have both time and space to practice the weapons they had not yet fired. Thirteen different vehicles made up the caravan which traveled south. Two men were hurt on the third day of practice when a grenade was dropped too close to the man who had dropped it. These two returned to Chicago.

****

Hans had been plagued by the recent inactivity. He was pleased when one of his contacts told him to be alert for a hit in the near future. The details were sketchy, but his informant knew that the brothers were behind the assualt. These days of idleness had not dulled his senses when it came to readiness against an attack.

He gathered his own forces and led them through several different scenarios. They were perpared for another helicopter assault, lightly armored vehicles, and suicidal attacks from a large force of ground troops. He thought it was best to tell Charley what he knew.

"What do you think we should do if we're attacked?"

"Protect yourself and your men as best you can. If at all possible, keep it as quiet as you can, Hans. We don't want the Japanese to get too edgy, and we sure as hell don't want the Americans to look on this as a bunch of martyrs. Do you have any idea when this attack is supposed to take place?"

"I only know it will be soon. My contact couldn't tell me exactly, but he thought it would be in a week. That gives me time enough to have a welcome ready for them when they get here."

"Do you know how they plan to get here?"

"My man said by car. That's all he knew."

"Why don't we just stop adjusting anything but military vehicles for the next week or two? That way, if a bunch of cars show up, we'll know it's them. Have the people at the plant put out the word that no more cars will be adjusted till further notice. Also tell all the deputies to keep you informed of any large number of American cars. Also, get bullet proof vests for any of our people at the plant who might be exposed to long range sniper fire."

"Good idea. I think you're starting to get the hang of this thing. Earlier you would never have thought of such a thing."

"Yeah, it's something I never thought I'd be good at. Don't forget. I've been shot at more than once, and I still carry a pretty good scar on my arm from the gunshot wound I got from a sniper. Can you get enough bullet proof vests before they get here?"

"I already have enough. The men hate to wear them, but I'll insist. I'll just tell them if they're caught not wearing one, they will be fired on the spot. That's all it will take to get their compliance."

"Okay, go ahead and do it. Let me know as soon as you get any more information. I'll tell everyone in the family to keep as close to home as they can. Let's double the guards around the home place."

"Done. I'll let you know as soon as I get the word. Anything else before I take off?"

"Just be careful. I need you."

The cars proceeded slowly on the way to Perdido. Two of the vehicles had minor breakdowns and had to undergo repairs. They were left behind as the others went on ahead. They planned to regroup some 100 miles before reaching Perdido. Some of the enthusiasm which had marked the beginning of the campaign was missing as the group approached their destination. Hot weather, strange food, funny tasting water, and insecurity have a way of making a long trip miserable. In spite of pep talks from Olivo and Harold, the men seemed less and less excited about their prospects with each passing day. The bravado of a lot of the men had disappeared when the two men were hurt by the explosion of the grenade. The lesson they had learned was that this was a deadly serious game. People could get hurt, and some might get killed. This was a sobering thought. The only one whose enthusiasm had grown on the trip was Diego. His only disappointment was that Olivo paid little attention to any suggestion that he tried to make in the way of a battle plan.

The only thing that Olivo had taken from his conversations with Diego was that they would be less noticeable if they were all equiped with local license plates. Long before they reached Perdido, he had each driver stop and remove the American plates and replace them with those he had acquired just after entering Mexico.

The caravan stopped about 50 miles from Perdido to spend the night in three different motels in a town called Valerde. It was there that Olivo first showed Diego a rough outline of his plan.

"This is the way I hope things will go. I know that you would like to get a shot at your brother, but that is highly unlikely. Our attack will be concentrated against the plant itself. I am told that your brother has an office there, but I'm afraid we will never be close enough for you to get a shot at him."

"What then are we gonna do?"

"We are going to arrange a line of snipers as close as we can get to the plant. We'll try to pick off as many of the workers and customers as we can. Then we'll just fade away into the night."

"How about the mortars and bazookas. Are we gonna get a chance to use them?"

"Yes, we'll open up with them to try to create as much confusion as we can. If they scatter from the initial explosions, we'll get a lot of good shots."

"What's the point of this? I don't see how this can affect them for very long."

"It won't. That doesn't matter. We didn't come down here to put an end to their operation. We just want to throw a scare into them. Hopefully, they'll be a little more reasonable in dealing with you and your brothers."

"How many men do you think we'll lose in the battle?"

"That's hard to say. It really doesn't matter. You and I will be far enough back to beat an easy retreat. We didn't come down here to get killed. The more of our people who get killed, the better. The outrage among the rest of the Americans will be far greater if we leave a string of dead Americans around the plant."

"Did the boss authorize this kind of attack? I thought we were comin' down here to hit these people?"

"That's why you aren't in charge of this operation. The boss knew your hatred of your brother might cloud your ability to make a rational decision. I came down here to make a lot of money and then go home to spend it."

"When do we attack?"

"Tomorrow when the shift is changing at the plant. That will add something to the confusion. Mechanics will be coming on duty as others are on their way home."

"Where are you and I gonna be?"

"Don't worry. Just stay close to me. You won't be in any real danger. As soon as the first volley is fired, you and I are gonna get the hell out of here."

Diego scowled, turned his back on Ortega and stomped off to his own room. This wasn't what he had come so far to do. In his heart he knew that whatever happened after the attack, there was very little he could do.

The battle at the plant lasted less than 20 minutes. For the first ten minutes, the attackers had fun sniping at the people as they scrambled around in chaos. It took Hans only ten minutes to have his people surround the leaderless Americans and less than ten minutes to silence every gun. Only three of the attackers were were left alive, and they were badly wounded. Only one seemed to have a chance to survive since his wounds were mostly to his legs. The other two had suffered wounds to both the body and the head. Those who had not survived had been riddled with fire from automatic weapons before they even had a chance to surrender.

Hans looked over all the dead bodies carefully, searching for the man he had been told would be their leader. He found no one who fit the description. He wondered who could have planned such a bungling effort. It was true there was some damage to the plant from the mortar and bazooka fire, and a few people had been hit by sniper fire, but overall this was still an amateurish operation. There seemed to be no plan to close in on the plant, and there certainly wasn't an easily accessible escape route for a group of their size. The men were obviously Americans, but one could not rule out the possibility that they had been hired by the Japanese. He hoped the one with leg injuries could last long enough for a quick interrogation. He was pretty sure these weren't mercenaries. Something more than money had compelled these men to take on such a hopeless operation. Maybe the survivor could clear things up.

Long before Hans had surrounded the attackers, Diego and Olivo had jumped into the best of the vehicles they arrived in and fled the scene. Olivo was driving and obviously had mapped out an escape route. In very little time he was headed down a back road that would get him away from Perdido. Diego said nothing until some thirty miles had been put between the assault and themselves. They came to a stop just before they were about to connect with a major highway. With no warning at all, Diego took from his belt the pistol he was never without, put it to the head of Olivo and pulled the trigger. Only a trace of blood spattered on Diego's shirt. He opened the door of the car and pushed the body out onto the deserted road. He then slid over into the driver's seat, fired two more rounds into the body, and closed the door. "*Vendejo*," he muttered as he drove off into the shadows.

He knew the area well. He had often been on this very road in his youth. He had no intention of returning to his brothers to tell them how little had been accomplished in this latest venture. His hopes of a showdown of sorts with his brother had been shattered, ever since Olivo had revealed his intention to make no serious attempt to hit hard at his father's heirs. He took a turn onto a road that ran almost parallel to Perdido. He slept the rest of the night outside the small town of Dolores and waited till morning to begin his assault on Perdido. As yet he had no definite plan, but he knew he must have a crack at little brother.

Hans was quick to organize a burial detail for the dead Americans. He knew that Charley didn't want pictures of a lot of dead Americans lying close to the plant. He knew that if word got out, the place would be overrun with reporters and photographers, neither of whom could possibly benefit Charley. He took what first aid he had and adminstered it to the wounded and rushed them off to the hospital. He followed close behind with two of his deputies.

The wounded were rushed into a wing of the hospital that was seldom used. Three different doctors were called on to attend the wounded men. Hans had a chance to ask each one what chance he thought the man he was treating would have to survive. As he suspected, the man with the leg wounds was the only one given any chance to recover. He was also the only one who was conscious. As soon as the bleeding had been stopped, Hans began the interrogation.

"Can you tell me what your name is?"

"Yes, I could."

"What is it then?"

"I said I could. I didn't say I would."

"I think you will. Do you know that the people who sent you down here have betrayed you? There's only three of you left alive, and two of them will probably be dead before morning. Your attack on the plant was stupid. Whose bright idea was it? Who was the leader? Do you know his name?

"His name was Olivo. He was the one who trained us before we got down here."

"Did you know that he wasn't among the bodies that we found? I know this man, and I can assure you he wasn't with you when we were attacked. He ran out on you and left you guys to be slaughtered. Who was Olivo workng for?"

"I really can't say for sure, but I got the idea maybe the mob had something to do with it. We had another guy whose name was Diego. He didn't train with us, and he spent a lot of time talking with Olivo. I think he was part of the group that sent us down here. How did he manage to escape?"

"My guess is he lit out as soon as the shooting started, probably before we had the place surrounded. This man was a Mexican, right?"

"Yeah, I guess. He looked it."

"You know, we didn't find his body either. There were no Mexicans found either dead or alive, so he and Olivo must have beat it together. They just dumped you guys and made a run for it. Why did you guys agree to come down here? Did they pay you a lot of money?"

"Naw, they didn't pay us anything. They just told us you people were the ones responsible for all of us losing our jobs makin'

American cars. They said it was you people who were puttin' the American car people out of business."

"So you guys thought you could just waltz in here, fire a few shots, and that would put an end to this whole operation? That was really stupid."

"I guess so. What are you gonna do with me?"

"That's a good question. Right now, I don't have an answer. We'll just keep you here until we decide what's best. My vote would be to shoot you, right here and now, but my boss is a whole lot more easy-going than I am. He may let you live if you continue to cooperate with us."

Hans left the hospital and went directly to the plant to survey the damage. There he found that 23 people had been hit by sniper fire and that six had been killed. The material damage to the plant itself was small. A day or two of cleaning up the mess would put the whole operation back on line in less than a week.

Charley had rushed to the plant as soon as he had heard the plant was under atack. The attack was over by the time he got there, and he went directly to his office, escorted by several guards. He waited quietly by the phone for Hans or Terry to tell him more about the situation. Terry was the first to call and told him that things were under control, but he had no details. Hans had decided to deliver his news in person rather than using the telephone. He arrived about an hour after the assault had begun.

"Charley, we got 'em all. They didn't put up much of a fight. There's only three left alive. I interrogated one and got some information.

It looks like the whole thing came from the American side. There doesn't seem to be anything that points to the Japanese. The man said a Mexican named Olivo was the leader of the group and there was another Mexican along who fits the description of Diego de los Santos."

"Did you kill or capture either one?"

"No, I don't think they stayed around very long after the shooting started. They turned tail and ran and left the others with no real plan of escape. It looked like a suicide mission, but from what I got from the prisoner, they didn't know it was gonna be like that. They were told they had a chance to shut down our whole operation and maybe get their jobs back makin' cars in the States."

"Well, can we get out a description of Olivo and Diego, just in case they're still somewhere in the neighborhood?"

"Yeah, we can do that. Unless they had a plane or a chopper close at hand, they couldn't have got very far."

"Post a $10,000 reward for anyone with information about their whereabouts. Let me know if you get any leads. Let's call it a night.

It wasn't until midmorning of the following day that Hans received the message about the discovery of the body some forty miles away from from Perdido. He took deputies with him and went personally to examine the corpse. The man carried no identification on his person, but Hans could identify the body with a single glance.

"Yes," he told the local magistrate, "I know this man. He is of Mexican origin, but he's long been a citizen of the United States. His name is Olivo. Can you give me any clues as to how he died and where the body was discovered?"

"We found the body about three hours ago. One of our locals was driving by and spotted the body lying on the road west of town. He stopped, thinking the man might need medical attention, but he quickly saw that the man was dead. He put the body in his truck and brought it here to us."

"And you are absolutely sure he's telling the truth, that he had nothing to do with the man's death?"

"Yes, we are certain. He can account for his whereabouts up to the time the man died. He is a local with no criminal record of any kind. As you can see, the man has wounds from bullets that came from close range."

"Yes, I can see that. Have you searched the area where the body was discovered to see if there were any empty shell casings around that would tell us what the murder weapon was?'

"No, we didn't think of that. We have very little experience in this sort of thing. We are a peaceful people. We have very few murders."

"Well, in Perdido we are not so peaceful. We have more than our share of shootings. Where can I find the man who discovered the body? I would like for him to take us to the place where he found the body. See if he can be excused for a while to take you there."

It was thirty minutes before the man arrived at the station to take them to the spot where he had found the body. He spoke no English, but one of the deputies acted as translator. He showed them the exact spot where the body had been lying. A close inspection showed a few small traces of blood, but there were no shell casings.

"Well, I guess we've learned about all we can from this examination. I think we might as well head back to Perdido. We thank you for your cooperation."

When he got back to Perdio, he reported directly to Charley. "I don't have many of the answers, but I did find out that the dead man was Olivo. He is or was a member of the mob. He was no doubt paid a pretty big sum of money to lead this bunch of amateurs down here to die. I would say he and whoever shot him had no intention of dying with the others. For some reason, there must have been an argument between these two and this ended the argument. I have a theory, but it's only a theory."

"And what would that be?"

"I think maybe one of Juan's brothers might have been the man who pulled the trigger."

"And for what reason?"

"That would be hard to say, but here's a couple of possibilities. He may have been disappointed that the raid, if you want to call it that, didn't go far enough. Maybe he had been led to believe that they were there to do far more than what they accomplished.

Maybe he thought he'd have a better chance of escaping on his own, that Olivo might slow him down. He might have known that if we questioned any survivors, they would disclose that there were really two men besides the others who were the leaders. That way we would be looking for two men instead of just one. If I'm right about this, I have a gut feeling that the man who shot Olivo may try somthing on his own."

"Any idea what that might that be?"

"Not really, but I think the next attempt will be personal. I don't think it will be directed against the plant. I rather think it will be you or your family, or if I'm right about it being one of the brothers, it wouldn't surprise me if the next target was Juan".

"So what do we do? Just lay low for a while?"

"No, I don't think that will be necessary. Just be very careful not to get into any situation which would give a man an oportunity to get close to you. Screen all your meetings closely for the next few days. Don't see anyone you don't know. Also advise Juan to do the same."

"Where would one of the brothers go right now if he knew we were after him?'"

"I have no idea, but I'll put out a description of all three to see if anybody around here has seen any of them. That's about all that I can think of right now. Have you heard anything from the Japanese?'

"Oh sure, they're scared shitless. I've done everything I can to calm them down, and I think they're not gonna panic. If nothing else happens in the next few days, they'll be all right. How many Japanese workers were hit in the plant last night? That's really important to them. They don't want to be in a position to have to send workers over here and give them hazard pay."

"Only one killed. Four others were hit, but they were wearing their bulletproof vests. How long will it take to repair the damage?"

"A couple of weeks, maybe. Hardly any of the damage is to parts of the plant where we actually do the adjustments. We can pretty much carry on business as usual. I got other things to think about right now, so I'll see you later."

"Okay, I'll talk to you again before the sun goes down."

Diego had hatched out a plan to strike at his brother again. It was risky, but he wasn't afraid. It was too humiliating to return to the States and tell his brothers what had happened in Perdido. He knew that his boss wouldn't be disappointed that Olivo wouldn't be coming back to collect the rest of his payment for leading the operation. After all, if what Olivo had told him was true, the boss would consider the operation a huge success. If all they had wanted was to throw a scare into the Japanese, they had succeeded.

He pulled into the hometown of the de la Rosas and went directly to their headquarters. He had visited there more than once when his father had tried to teach him about the marijuana business. His father's people grew the stuff, harvested it, and cured it in large barns, but he wholesaled the weed to the de la Rosas for a market that was largely in the United States. He also knew they were the ones who had killed his father when the old man wanted out of the business. He did not know if they were still harboring a grudge for the loss of their own people in the shootout that had killed his father. If they were still angry, his life wasn't worth a peso, but he had already made up his mind to give it a try.

He stopped in the anteroom and asked if he could see Alfredo, the man who he thought was in charge.

"Who wants to know?"

"My name is Diego de los Santos.

The man bristled when he heard the name and stood up and pulled a gun which he had concealed inside his coat. He pulled the weapon out and pointed it directly at Diego.

"What might your business be with Alfredo?"

"You're right. It's strictly business. You can search me if you want to. I have no weapons, and I come in peace."

The man edged his way over to Diego, put his pistol back inside his coat, and gave him a quick search. When he found nothing, he stepped back and once more pulled his pistol. He motioned for Diego to follow him up a short flight of stairs, and when they had reached the top, he knocked on the first door they approached. From inside he heard a voice which invited the knocker to come in.

It was obvious that Alfredo did not recognize Diego. He sat behind a large oak desk and did not get up or invite Diego to be seated. The man looked curiously at both men as if to ask with his eyes who this man might be and what his business was. Before he could ask, Diego said, "My name is Diego de los Santos. You haven't seen me for several years. I used to come here with my father when I was much younger. I know that your family had differences with my father, but I want you to know that what happened between you two and him was strictly business. I hold no grudge against you for what happened."

"So what brings you here? I'm sure you didn't come all this way just to tell me that."

"You're right. I came here on business. I have a proposal if you are interested."

"We are always interested in a good business proposal. Does it have anything to do with our marijuana business? What is the nature of your proposal?"

"No, it has nothing to do with that. I'm sure you're familiar with all of the big business going on in Perdido."

"Yeah, we know about it. What's that got to do with us?"

"Well, you know my father was co-owner of the big plant there that fixes carburetors. That's why he wanted out of the marijuana business."

"Yeah, we know all about that. He could have got out if he's been a little more reasonable. We wanted just for him to let his people grow for us. He wouldn't have had to do anything, just let them continue with business as usual, but your father was a very stubborn man."

"I'm well aware the old man could be very stubborn. That's not what I came here to discuss. This has nothing at all to do with his death or the marijuana business."

"What then?"

"Are you happy to see our youngest brother get rich from all the business that goes on in Perdido?'

"No, but why as the oldest son didn't you get a piece of the action? Why did the old man cut you and your brothers out?"

"I'm not really sure that he did. I think my brother and the American paid off some fancy lawyers to create a phoney will that gives my brother and the American everything. We've been in the States so long that we don't have the right kind of connections to win anything in a legal battle."

"Were you involved in the big blow-up we heard about yesterday?"

"In a way we were, though not directly. My employer sent the people down there to try to throw a scare into those peiople, but I'm pretty sure what happened down there won't make much of an impression on them."

"And who may I ask is your employer?"

"I'm sure you're familiar with "cosa nostra." My boss is a leader in that organization and like your family, they are always looking for a good business proposal."

"Tell me more. I'm interested."

"Well, if we can get them to change their minds about the will, they might give me and my brothers our share. Hitting the plant isn't really possible or practical. I can see that now. They are well protected by a man who was once a great hit man for the oil companies. If you should decide to help us, I know we could cut your family in for some of the profits. You have no idea what the company is worth. We don't even know how much, and I'm not sure if anybody really knows. They take in so much money every day that no one can really tell. We first thought millions, but now we think that's really too little."

"And what would be our share if we help you?"

"That's hard to say. I'm sure we could agree on something that would be agreeable to both sides. We could make it a flat sum, but I think if you took a small percentage, you'd be a lot better off."

"And what exactly do you expect us to do to become your partner?"

"First of all, I need a place to hang out for a short period of time. They're gonna be lookin' for me around Perdido. I need some time to let things cool down before I try anything."

"And after things cool down, then what?"

"I intend to kidnap my younger brother who's one of the big shots in the company. He's thrown in with the Americans and I'm pretty sure they'd be wantin' him back if we had him."

"I see. I kinda like this idea, but you realize I can't make any deal until I talk it over with the rest of the family. Are you willing to go to a family council and tell them the deal so they won't think I'm crazy?"

"Of course. How long will it take for you to set up a family council?"

"I think by tororrow. You can stay here in this building until I can get things arranged. Don't go outside for anything. We'll send somebody out for anything you need."

"Well, first I'd really like some new clothes. I got some blood on these from the bullet I put into the stupid *"vendejo"* who led this operation. I haven't ate in quite a while, so some food would be good."

"Okay, what size clothes and what do you want to eat?"

"Get me a couple of dark suits, 40 waist and 32 legs. Several white shirts, large, and a couple of ties. Nothin' flashy. I don't want to attract too much attention. Any kind of good Mexican food will do."

"And the money to pay for these things?"

"Here's $500 in American. That ought to take care of it."

"You realize if the family doesn't buy into your proposal, they'll probably want you dead."

"Yeah, I know that, but I think the rewards are worth the risks. I've always wanted to be filthy rich, haven't you?"

"Yeah, but I don't have the final say on something this big. There's a lot of danger to our family if we back the wrong side. You know there's no love lost between our families."

"Yeah, I know that, but I also know that your family, like mine, can put aside personal things when there's a lot of money to be made."

"That's true. You stay here until I get back. It'll take the rest of the day to round up all the members of the family. I'll let you know when to be ready to present your idea to them."

"I'll be here. I got nowhere else to go."

****

Juan and Charley spent more than the next three days in consultation with the worried Japanese owners. They had been hard to persuade that what had happened was an aberation, a thing which could not happen again. The final argument had been that they could not go back to Japan now, even if they wanted to. They had burned too many bridges. The friends they once had in the government no longer could be counted on to back them in these uncertain economic times. Charley had attended most of the meetings, but it was Juan who had been the most persuative in keeping the companies in Perdido. He had much of his father's knack of letting other people have his way.

As a week passed, things returned to nearly normal. All the workers continued to wear bullet-proof vests, and after the attack, it had been much easier to get the workers to wear them. The crews who worked to repair the damaged area worked around the clock to affect the repairs. Terry had been placed in charge of the security of the plant while the work was ongoing. He delegated most of the night time work to a couple of trusted deputies, but he was always present in person during the day. He was on call the rest of the time should anything happen. Hans was content to continue his search for Diego. He had heard that a man fitting Diego's description had been spotted in a nearby town shortly after the body of of Olivo had been discovered. He worked overtime with all his informants to see if the report could be confirmed, but no one could verify the initial report.

Diego had taken the advice of the de las Rosas family when they had told him to lay low for a while. He attended the meeting with the whole family to see if they would help him in his latest plan. They seemed lukewarm at first, but his first thought was that at least they had let him live. Finally, greed had taken over, and the idea of owning a piece of the gigantic action in Perdido had been too much of an inducement. They had agreed in principal to help Diego, although they had not been told exactly what their part in the caper would be. Diego held off on the details until he was certain that the family's desire for a return to power in this area had been properly fueled by the dream of untold wealth.

****

At the next full meeting of the family, Diego told told them exactly what he planned to do. This time there was more enthusiasm than there had been at the first meeting.

"I think the best time to try to grab my brother would be as he is leaving his office at the close of the working day. We need to set up a diversion that will keep Hans busy long enough for us to put the bag on my brother. He won't put up much of a fight. That's not my brother's style. He's a thinker, not a fighter. We'll stop his car by blocking the road from the plant after he's left the plant. He may have an escort. If so, we'll have to dispose of him. I think it might be best if we brought him back here to cool his heels until we've had time to contact them and see if they're willing to make any kind of deal for his release. If not, we'll just finish him off and dispose of the body. His loss would be quite a blow to them. He handles all the major transactions with the Japanese car companies, so I'm told. Without him, I think we might be able to strike a deal with them that will make all of us partners."

Back at the plant, Juan was engaged in talks with two car companies. He had pretty much convinced one that the latest trouble at the plant would not happen again. The other, however, was reluctant to accept his explanation. For more than an hour, Juan had shown him around the plant and explained to him the new precautions which had been put in place to prevent a recurrence of the latest attack on the plant.

At 5 o'clock he waited for the limo that was always at his disposal. He had a full time driver and a deputy who always rode in the back seat. He climbed into the front seat and told the driver to take him directly home. At times he stopped along the way to make small purchases like a newspaper, but his wrangling with the

Japanese had tired him, and he wanted nothing more than a good shower and peace and quiet before turning in for the evening.

From a small hill more than a half-mile from the plant, Diego and three of the de las Rosas watched. Diego held the binoculars first and passed them around when he saw his brother about to leave in the limo. He called their attention to the driver and the lone deputy as a bodyguard.

"Start the car. I know a spot where we can fall in behind them to see how he gets back to his place."

"Okay, just tell me how to get there."

"Take that old dirt trail off to the left. It'll intersect with his road in short order."

They pulled in behind the limo and followed it until Juan had arrived at his destination.

"This will be a piece of cake. Only the driver and one lousy deputy to protect one of their most valuable people. Not very smart on their part, wouldn't you say?"

"Maybe not, but maybe he takes a different route each day. We'll have to follow him for a couple more days to make sure of his route."

"Okay, this is Monday. What say we follow him two more days, and if he continues this pattern, we'll set up to grab him on Thursday?"

"Right, but only if he follows the same pattern."

For the next two days Juan followed the same pattern. No stops on the way home from work. His negotiations with the Japanese had been successful, and he was looking forward to a little R and R over the coming weekend.

On Thursday, he had finished all the paper work that had piled up on his desk while his conferences with the Japanese were ongoing. It was a little earlier than usual when he called for the limo to take him home. His early departure did not excite the curiosity of anyone closely connected to him, for his business did not operate strictly on a 9 to 5 basis. Often he had been forced to stay at the plant until long after 5, and occasionally he had been able to get away early if all his work was finished. He answered only to Charley, and Charley himself kept irregular hours.

The limo with the driver and the deputy were not long in moving to the spot where he always waited for them. He got into the front seat and exchanged pleasantries in Spanish with both of them. Most of his business was now conducted in English, but he did enjoy the occasional use of his native tongue.

About two miles from the plant, the driver headed down a narrow one-way street. There was a car blocking the way and a man lying in the street. The driver stopped just behind the car that stood in the way.

"What shall I do," the driver asked.

"Just wait a minute. I'll see if I can find out what happened to the guy in the street."

He walked over to the man stretched out full length in the narrow street. He bent over the body to see if the man was still conscious. The man was making moaning sounds as if he were in great pain.

"Are you okay?"

"It's my heart. My medicine is in my jacket pocket. Can you get it for me?"

As Juan fumbled for medicine in the man's jacket pocket, he rolled over on his side and displayed a pistol which had not been visible before. He said in a quiet voice, "If you make one false move, you're a dead man."

Suddenly a man rolled out of the back seat with a submachine gun. He opened fire on the limo and quickly dispatched both the driver and the deputy. Then the gunman walked quickly over to Juan and told him to get into the car that had blocked their way. He was stunned, but he did as he was told. He was surprised to see his oldest brother there with him in the back seat.

"Well, brother, we meet again. Have you missed me?"

"Yes, about as much as I would a good dose of the clap."

"Don't get smart with me, you miserable asshole. You don't know how much I was wishin' you'd do something stupid so my new friends could put you out of your misery."

"And just are these new friends of yours?"

"Not that it really matters, but these are a few of the de las Rosas family. Do you remember them?"

"But of course. How could I forget someone who murdered my father? I'm not surprised that you've aligned yourself with them. You're just the kind of scum that would go to them."

"Watch your tongue, brother. These people don't have my sense of humor or my compassion."

"Oh, yes, I'd almost forgot how humorous and compassionate you are. What do you hope to gain by kidnapping me? You'll never get away with it."

"Oh really? What's to stop me? By the time your American friends have discovered that you're missing, I'll already have you so far away they'll be of no help to you."

"I don't think so. There's no place in all of Mexico where you can hide me for long."

"Who said anything about Mexico? I'll be taking you to a place where Mr. Johnson would never dare to go."

"And where might that be?"

"In the good old U.S.A."

"And just how do you plan to get me to the U.S.A.?"

"That's for me to know and you to find out."

"And just what value do you think I might be to you? I don't really know anything about the carburetor business."

"We know that, but we also know that you're mostly in charge of the dealings with the Japanese. Without you, the whole deal with them might fall through. We think the Americans might be willing to cut us in for a piece of the pie to keep from messin' up the arrangement with the Japs. What do you think?"

"I don't really know. Charley is a really resourceful man. He might be able to close the deal by himself."

"You better hope not, brother. The only thing that's keepin' you alive is your value to the Americans. If you have no value to them, you have no value to us."

Because he had left the plant early, he was not missed for several hours. By the time the shot-up limo had been discovered with the two dead bodies, Diego and his new compadres had taken Juan back to the de las Rosas headquarters. They waited till it was almost midnight before they took Juan, blindfolded and hand-cuffed, to a small well hidden air strip which the family had often used in their own drug smuggling operations. Only a pilot was to accompany Diego and Juan back to the States.

Back at the alcalde's house Hans was furious. "I told him a dozen times not to take a oneway street, that it was too dangerous, but some people must think I don't know too much about security. Do we know who's responsible? Until we know that we won't really know how to organize a search for him."

Charley interrupted, "I don't think we'll have to look for him. I think whoever's got him will be contacting us soon. I doubt if it's the oil companies or their agents. I'd rather believe it's the work of the brothers."

"It does sound like something they might try. What do you suppose they think they can gain by grabbing him? He really doesn't know that much about the business."

"That's true, but he knows more than anyone else about getting the Japanese to come here. That's where we hope to change the millions we can make without them into the billions we can make with them."

"How long should we wait for them to contact us before we go looking for him?"

"Let's give it 48 hours before we go looking for him in earnest. If we haven't been contacted by then, we'll start our own search."

"Until then, I guess we just sit and wait."

"You can ask around to see if there were any witnesses to the shooting. I doubt it, but you can check it out. Just on the outside chance they haven't managed to get out of town, you can check with all your local contacts."

"Probably won't learn a thing, but it's better than just sitting around here and waiting for them to contact us."

"Let's try to give out that Juan has been called to Panama on personal business if anyone asks where he is. That should satisfy them for a while."

The small plane carrying Juan and Diego landed on an airfield not much larger than the one from which they had taken off. It was after midnight when they landed, and the only other sign of life was the car which had been waiting for their arrival. Inside the car were Carlos and Jorge. Jorge had been asleep while waiting for them to land, but Carlos had remained awake throughout the two hours they had been waiting.

"Wake up, brother. It looks like we underestimated our brother. He is supposed to have our youngest brother with him, but I'll believe that when I see it."

"Yeah, I've been a little skeptical myself. How he managed that I'll never know."

"I'm sure we won't be in the dark long. I'm sure he can't wait to tell us what brilliant stategy he used to get this far. I'm still not sure what having him is gonna do for us."

"He says that they may be willing to cut us in for a piece of the action if we let them have Juan back. Something about the work he's doin' with the Japanese car people. I have my doubts, but if it doesn't work out, at least he'll have the pleasure of killing him. It's something he's wanted to do for a long time."

"Yeah, I know. He never got over how the old man used to favor him when we were kids. I never let it bother me, but he thought as the oldest he should have been gettin' some of the things that went to Juan. Pull the car up closer to the plane."

Diego led Juan to the approaching car. When it stopped, he opened up the back door and pushed Juan into the back seat. His brothers offered no greeting, and he said nothing until the airstrip was behind them. Finally it was Jorge who said, "Where to now, brother?"

"Home base, I guess. Anything happen while I was gone that I oughta know about?"

"Naw, we heard the attack on the plant was a bust. How did you manage to put the bag on little brother?"

"It's a long story. Do you really want to hear it?"

"Yeah, if you can shorten it a little."

"Okay, do you remember the de la Rosa family?"

"Sure. They're the ones who killed the old man. What have they got to do with it?"

"If you'll shut up and listen, I'll tell you. After the attack on the plant fizzled, I manged to escape. I got in touch with the de la Rosas and made them a business proposition."

"Which was?"

"Help me nab little brother, and if they cut us in for a share, we'll give them a small percentage of what we get."

"How big a percentage?"

"What difference does that make? As soon as we start gettin' our share, I say we hire a few buttons and wipe out the whole family. I still haven't forgot what they did to the old man."

"I thought you didn't care about that."

"I don't, but it's the principal of the thing. Besides, I don't like the idea of sharing anything with those worthless bastards."

"You haven't said anything, little brother. What do you suppose the chances are they'll cut us in for a share to save your mangy hide?"

"I don't know. Mr. Johnson is a very resourceful person. I may not be nearly as valuable to them as you think. He may be able to get along fine without me."

"If that's the case, you haven't long for this world. If he doesn't need you, we certainly don't."

"There's one other possibilty. You may have forgotten about an employee of theirs named Hans."

"We haven't forgotten about the turncoat son-of-a-bitch. What's he got to do with any of this?"

"He told me once that if you guys ever tried anything else after you tried to hit the plant, he'd personally take all three of you out."

"Yeah, well, talk is cheap. You don't really think we'd be afraid of him, do you? He couldn't even take out a lousy mechanic when he was sent down there to do the job."

"That's true, but don't forget. He took out Toyota Man, and he was the best hit man the oil companies had. He always smiled when he talked about taking you guys out. I think it would be a job he'd really enjoy."

"Yeah, the same way I'm gonna enjoy slowly strangling you if they don't need your services any more. Is there anything to eat at the place? I'm starved. I haven't had anything to eat for almost 24 hours."

"No, we ain't got much grub on hand. We been eatin' out mostly, waitin' to hear from you."

"Well, let's stop and pick up some fast food on the way. How about you little brother? Are you hungry?"

"It would be a waste of my money to eat and then have you kill me. So I guess I'll just wait and see what they say about your proposal."

"Suit yourself. I'm buyin'"

"In that case, I'll have whatever you're having."

They pulled into a Burger King that advertised all night service in the drive-through.

"What'll it be, Mac?"

"Four whoppers, four large orders of fries, and four large cokes."

"It'll be a few minutes. I ain't got no help tonight."

"Make it snappy. We're in a hurry."

"Right, everybody's in a hurry these days."

It was several minutes before he handed the two sacks and the four cokes to Jorge. He handed the sacks to Diego. He grabbed a burger and took three large bites before he passed the sack back to the front seat. All three finished their burgers before giving anything to Juan.

"How the hell is he gonna eat anything with his hands cuffed behind him? You gonna feed him, brother?"

"You know better than that. He can wait till we get back home. Then I'll uncuff him long enough for him to eat. I don't think he has all the appetite that I had."

When they arrived at the hotel, Diego warned Juan not to make a sound on the way to the room. They saw no one along the way. As soon as the door was closed and locked, Diego removed the blindfold and cuffs. He pushed him into a reclining chair.

"Okay, little brother, you can eat. Let me remind you that if you make any loud noise or try to escape, this will be your last meal. Here's your food."

Juan ate only about half the burger and fries, but he did drink all the large coke. He had been thirsty before they had left Mexico.

He was tempted to ask for more to drink, but he decided not to press his luck.

"How long do you think we should wait before we contact them to see if they have any interest in our proposal?"

"I think tomorrow will be alright. We'll let him say a few words to let them know we have him and that he's alive. We'll give'em a couple of days to make up their minds."

"How much are gonna ask for his return?"

"That's negociable. We'll ask for 25%. They'll never go for that, but it gives us room to bargain."

"And just how much will we settle for?"

"Somewhere between 5 and 10 %."

"That doesn't sound like very much to me."

"Do you have any idea what 5% of billions would be? Well, my smarter than me brothers, let me tell you. It would be millions."

"What makes you think they can generate that kind that kind of money?"

"Because I've been doin' my homework. I know that if the Japs move their car makin' base to Perdido to be closer to the carburetor, they are gonna take in one of the biggest fortunes of all times. Every new car will come standard with that carburetor. Every car that doesn't have one will be a dinosaur. Every used car in America will be headed that way to get the adjustment. The military of several countries have already started to have all their rollin' stock adjusted. Isn't that right, little brother?"

"Whatever you say."

"I say I hope they need you bad enough to listen to what we have to say. I would enjoy killin' you, but I think I'd like to be rich even more than that. It's a win/win situation for me."

The brothers took turns standing watch over Juan. When morning came, none looked as though he had gotten much sleep. Strangely, it was only Juan who looked as though he had gotten any rest. Jorge went out for some fast-food breakfast after all four had awakened.

"Well, Juanito. I think it's about time we contacted Mr. Johnson to see what your value is to the corporation. Can you give me the number where Mr. Johnson can be reached?"

"I could."

"Will you give me the number or shall I have the pleasure of beating it out of you?"

"He might be at home, or he might be at his office. Which of the numbers do you want?"

"Both. We'll try his home first. Why don't you just dial the number yourself. That will save me the trouble of having to put you on the line later. If nobody answers at home, you can try the work number."

The phone rang only twice before it was answered by Charley. There was a slight hesitation before he said, "Hello."

"It's me, Charley."

"Where in the hell are you?"

"New York, I think."

Diego grabbed the phone out of his hand and said, "That's right, Mr. Johnson, New York. Now, I have just one question for you. Exactly how much do you think my youngest brother is worth?"

"My question to you would be how much do you think he's worth?"

"I think a small percentage of your corporation would be enough to satisfy my brothers and me."

"How small a percentage?"

"I think that's something we can negotiate, if you really want him back."

"Where and when would these negotiations begin?"

"Here in New York. You surely don't think I'd be stupid enough to go to your place, do you?"

"And you surely don't think I'm stupid enough to go back to a place where I'm a fugitive from both the oil companies and the government, do you?"

"So where does that leave us"

"I'd say we need a compromise. What would you say to Canada? Is that a possibilty?"

"Exactly where in Canada?"

"I don't know. Montreal, perhaps. I've never been to Canada, so it really wouldn't matter to me."

"When could you be there?"

"I think I could make it in about a week."

"Why so long? Why not two or three days?"

"Lots of paper work. Legal documents like this always require some lawyers if you don't want to take a chance on getting' screwed. Call me back tomorrow, and I'll be able to tell you exactly when and where we can meet and both be safe."

"Okay, I'll call again tomorrow at the same time. There better not be any stalling. I either want a piece of the action or a piece of my little brother."

"I understand that. I'll be waiting for your call."

Charley hung up the phone and looked directly at Hans. "Did I keep him on the phone long enough for you to get a trace on the call?"

"You sure did. I know exactly where he made this call from, but that doesn't mean that's where they're holding Juan."

"I know, but it's a starting place. What do you think? How long will it take you to locate them if I send you up there?"

"I don't really know. You gotta remember that I can't move as freely as I used to because I'm about as popular as leprosy with the oil people."

"No, I hadn't forgotten. It's just that I've gotten so used to you handlin' this sort of thing, I've almost convinced myself that you could handle anything."

"Thanks for the vote of confidence. Does this mean that unlike the alcalde, you're not worried that I'll try to get back with my previous employers?"

"I know he said that a man who works only for money could never be trusted, but I'm sure you believe you'll get a better shake with us than you would with the oil companies."

"That's right. Well, I have a few contacts up there that aren't tied into their mafia connections or the oil companies. If I can get there by tomorrow, I think I can locate them in no more than a couple of days. Just to give me a litle margin for error, when he calls back tomorrow, set up the meet for five days. That way he won't think we're stalling."

"Do you have any idea how you'll get him back alive after you find him?"

"Not really. This is the sort of thing you have to play by ear. You have to look at the situation and think about all the jobs you've done and see if this caper in any way resembles what's happened before. While I'm there, do you want me to eliminate the brothers so situations like this never come up again?"

"I'm not goin' to make that a part of the job, but I certainly won't shed any tears when you get back with Juan and tell me that the brothers had to be disposed of in order to accomplish your mission."

"That's all I needed to know."

"What special equuipment will you need?"

"I'll need the old man's private jet and a pilot to get me to New York. I already have about everything else I need."

"When will you be ready to leave?"

"An hour or two will be all I'll need to get a few clothes together and maybe a disguise or two."

"I'll call and have the plane ready in an hour. You don't have to do this if you don't want to."

"Oh, but I want to. I need a little chore like this once in a while to keep from getting rusty."

"Then start getting ready. I'll have the plane and the pilot ready in less than an hour.'

As soon as Hans had disappeared in the direction of his room, Charley turned to Alice and said, "I hope to God he can pull this off. I'm sure we can't do business with the Japanese without him. Our explanation of his absence won't satisfy them for very long. If they find out he's been kidnapped, it might queer the whole deal."

Alice went to him and put her arm around him. There was a strange smile on her face. He noticed and shrugged before asking, "What's the smile about? Is this a Mona Lisa sort of thing?"

"No, I was just thinking. Every time we think we're ready to get over the hump, something weird has to happen."

"Yeah, I know. Well, I hope he can pull this off, but if he can't ……so what? Even if the deal with the Japanese goes south, all that really means is that we'll have to settle for millions instead of billions. The American business alone will give us more money than we could spend in three lifetimes."

"I know, but I've kinda gotten used to the idea of being the wife of the richest man in the world. That would make me the First Lady, wouldn't it?"

"I guess so. I had no idea that you'd become ambitious. Why the change?"

"Because I'm afraid when this is over you may need the extra money just to protect yourself fom all the enemies we've made."

"You mean that I've made, don't you? You haven't made any enemies."

"Your enemies are my enemies. I'm sure I'm high on the list of people who our enemies would like to have gone."

"I'm sorry about that. If I'd known how many enemies I'd make, I'm not sure I would have ever taken it this far."

"I don't regret for a minute what you did. I'm proud of everything you've done. My life was nothing till I met you. At least I've been something for a while. It's scarey, Charley, but it certainly isn't boring. I've got a hunch that Hans will get Juan back, and we'll soon have Japanese neighbors."

Hans was ready to leave in half an hour. He had packed a couple of extra suits and shirts and very little else. He had taken an extra .357 in his suitcase in addition to the one he nearly always carried. He had already put on the first of two disguises which included a beard and mustache. As he was about to go out the door, he turned toward Charley and Alice and said, "Well, what do you think?"

"It's good. For a brief second, I wasn't really sure it was you."

"That's good, because most people are not gonna see me for more than a half second. At least that's the way it's gonna be if I'm gonna be successful."

Both wished him luck as he walked out the door to the waiting limo.

In another thirty minutes he was on the Lear jet and on his way to New York. He made very little conversation with the pilot. As they got ready to land, he told the pilot to return immediately to the airport nearby. The deserted airstrip on which he landed was less than thirty miles from the one that Diego had used when he had landed with Juan to meet his brothers.

He went directly to a pay phone and called a taxi. He told the driver to take him to a hotel which was very close to the one that he had pinpointed as the place where Diego had placed his call to Charley. He went straight to his room after checking in and picked up the phone. It rang several times before a man answered.

"Hello, Igor. It's me, Hans."

On the other end a man with a profoundly Russian accent said, "What? Hans? Where in the hell are you? I haven't even heard from you in years. I heard at one time that you were dead."

"Well, like the man once said, 'Recent reports of my death have been grossly exagerated.' Well, to answer your question, I'm here in New York, and I've been in Mexico. I'm hoping you can do me a favor."

"As long as it doesn't involve loaning you money, I might. In your line of work you're not a very good credit risk."

"No, this has nothing to do with money. All I'm really needing is a little information."

"What kind of information? Does it have anything to do with industrial espionage?"

"No, I just need the location of some people that I think are in New York."

"And who might they be."

"The de los Santos brothers."

"What do you want with those lowlifes? The last little job I did for them they stiffed me on the payoff. Who you working for now?"

"A group of people you don't know down in Mexico."

"Hey, I bet you're in on that carburetor thing, ain't you?"

"Yeah, sorta. The three oldest ones grabbed the youngest brother, and I believe they brought him here. I'm hopin' you can help me locate them."

"What's in it for me if I help you?"

"Ten grand if I find 'em where you say they are."

"You got that kind of money on you? I don't take checks."

"Yeah, I got the money on me. You don't have to worry about that, old friend."

"Well, I do worry about that. What you're asking is a risky business. These guys got mob connections, and if they ever even suspected that I was the one…"

"I'm not gonna tell'em. Are you?"

"Of course not. Listen, call me back in about an hour. I'll make a few calls and see what I can find out."

"Okay, thanks."

He hung up the phone, lay down on the bed and drifted off to sleep for about a half an hour. Then he got up and redialed the same number. When the man at the other end picked up, he said, "Well, have you got anything for me?"

"Yes, I think so. They have a room in a hotel very close to where you are now. The three of them keep a suite in the Boardwalk Hotel, but the doorman says he thinks there's four of them now in the suite."

"Thanks, old friend. I won't forget this."

"I hope you won't forget about the money."

"Not a chance, and thanks again."

He hung up the phone and went down the stairs, even though there were several flights of stairs down to the lobby. He avoided the elevator because he didn't want to run the risk of anyone seeing him close up. He walked briskly out the entrance and hailed a taxi. While riding toward the Hotel Boardwalk, he wondered how he could find out which suite the brothers were occupying without asking the desk clerk. He feared that the desk clerk might have instructions not to give out that information to anyone and report any inquiries along those lines. A thought occurred to him as he approached the hotel. He got out and handed the driver a nice tip. Just down the street, he spotted a telegraph office and headed in that direction. He waited briefly before leaving the message to be delivered to Diego de los Santos in the Hotel Boardwalk, room number unknown. The message said, "I have changed my mind. Canada is not a good idea. Call me tonight and I will give you three more places that I think we may agree to."

Charles Johnson

As the boy left to deliver the telegram, Charley stopped him at the door. He handed the boy a crisp new $100 bill and told him there would be another just like it when he returned if he remembered which suite he delivered it to. Then he walked outside and lit a cigarette. When he saw the boy returning, he reached into his wallet and took out another $100 bill. The boy was smiling as he approached.

"Well, did you get it delivered?'

"Sure thing. It went to suite 2578. The tight bastard didn't even leave me a tip."

"Well, this will take care of that," he said as he handed the boy the second bill.

He hailed another taxi back to his own hotel. He would scout out the Boardwalk tonight. He did not want to be seen there in bright daylight. When he got back to his room, he placed a call to Charley and told him he had located the brothers. He also told him about the telegram in case Diego called and wanted to know why he had changed his mind about Canada. Then he hung up the phone and decided to try to sleep until he had the cover of night.

At ten o'clock he got up and changed his disguise. He took another taxi to the Boardwalk and went to the main desk. He told the man he wanted a suite. In particular, he was interested in suite 2579 because he and his wife had spent their honeymoon there many years ago, and he wanted to see if it still looked the same. The clerk fumbled through some papers and was about to shake his head in a negative way when Charley waved two hundred dollar bills under his nose. He hesitated for a brief instant and then said, "Why, yes. That suite just became available."

"Good," he said as he handed the two bills to the clerk.

"Will you be needing any help with your luggage?"

"No, my luggage hasn't arrived yet. There was a big mix-up at the airport."

"Would you like someone to show you to your suite?"

"No, like I said, I honeymooned there, and unless they've moved it, I'm sure I can find it."

"Well, thank you and good night."

Once again he avoided the elevator in favor of the stairs. He unlocked the door, went in, and took a quick look around. There was no adjoining door between his suite and the one occupied by the brothers. That was a small disappointment. He had no definite plan as of yet to affect Juan's escape without a shootout with other three. He could quite possibly get all three, but if the lead began to fly, there was always a chance that he or Juan might stop one of the bullets. He also needed a way to make a rapid exit once the job was completed. Another taxi would have to do. He returned to his own hotel.

At 11 o'clock, he called Charley and told him to have the pilot ready with the jet as the same place they had landed at 4 a.m. He walked down the street and grabbed another taxi to take him to the Boardwalk. When he got there, he gave the driver three hundred dollars to wait until he returned. He entered again and used the stairs up to the suites. He extracted from his wallet a card which the hotels now used instead of room keys. This was a special key which he had had made for him several years ago. It was much in the nature of a skeleton key. It had failed him only once. Since this was an older hotel, he had every reason to believe that they were not on the cutting edge of room security. He slipped the card into the slot as quietly as he could. He swiped the key twice with no affect, but the third try gave him the click he was hoping for. He opened the door slowly with his left hand while he held the .357 in his right. When he could see completely into the room, he smiled. There was Juan asleep in a big recliner and no one else in the room. He eased his way over to Juan and tapped him gently on the forehead. As he awakened, Hans put his fingers to his lips vertically to indicate that he should make no noise. Juan stood up and stretched for a second before he slipped out the door just ahead of Hans. He pushed him toward the stairway and on reaching the lobby, they walked swiftly toward the taxi that was waiting.

"Why's the guy wearin' handcuffs?" the driver wanted to know.

"Because I'm a police officer, and he's under arrest. He's got some of his gang still in that hotel, so I suggest you stay away from there for a few days. If they knew you waited for us and drove us away from there, they might not be too happy with you."

"Yeah, but I didn't know…….

"That might not make any difference to them. Just stay away from there."

The pilot had the plane ready for takeoff as soon as they got on board. He asked no questions, and Hans offered no explanations. Hans and Juan had not spoken on their way to the airport. They had been in the air for sevaral minutes before Hans finally spoke. He said, "I might be able to get you out of those cuffs if you want me to try."

"It would be great if you could. My wrists are raw. I've been in these things for what seems like forever."

"Turn your back to me."

He did, and Hans fumbled through his pockets until he found a small hey. He had no idea if it would work, but he had unlocked similair cuffs with the same key. He fumbled in the semi-darkness until the key was inserted into the cuffs. Then he gave a gentle twist and heard the clicking sound that told him his attempt had been successful.

"Oh God, that feels great. I don't how to thank you. I was pretty sure I'd never get out of there alive."

"Think about that the next time you decide to go against my advice about staying away from one-way streets."

"Yes, I guess that was pretty stupid. How in God's name were you able to find me?"

"Partly luck and a little expertise on my part. The luck was Charley keeping Diego on the phone long enough to trace the call he made to your place. The expertise was having an old friend who got me the address of the place where they were staying. The rest was pretty simple since they didn't have anybody awake and guarding you."

"What would have happened if there had been someone awake inside the room?"

"That's really hard to say, but I'm guessing there would have been some bloodshed. I wasn't about to leave that room without you, dead or alive. Alive you're quite valuable to Charley's organization. Dead, at least we would know we could no longer depend on you to finish the negotiations, and we could have begun looking for someone else."

"Has anything major happened since I been gone?"

"Not really. Charley has convinced the people you were negotiating with that you had taken a well deserved vacation back in Panama. They were starting to get a little edgy, but Charley may have you lay low for a day or two to lend credence to the vacation story. How would you feel about a few days secluded before going public?"

"No problem. I think I could use a little time off to settle my nerves. Where will I go?"

"I don't know. That will be up to Charley. He may want you back on the job tomorrow, but I doubt it. If you're gonna lay low for a while, I suspect I'll be going with you. Charley's not gonna take any more chances on you being grabbed again."

"How long will it take us to get back home?"

"Not very long. Why don't you try to take a nap, and we'll probably be there by the time you wake up."

The pilot radioed ahead about thirty minutes before they were to arrive. Charley had Terry and a large bunch of deputies ready to escort them back to the house. Charley was the first one to greet them as they deplaned. He extended his right hand to each man and gave a big pat on the back to Hans. No one spoke until all three were safely back inside the limo that had carried Charley to the airport.

Once back inside the house, Hans asked Charley if Juan should stay out of sight for a few days to convince the Japanese that he really had been on vacation. Charley agreed that a couple of days might be in order. Then Charley asked Hans how he had been able to affect the rescue so quickly and with such apparent ease. He gave him a brief account of the major details and smiled when they looked astonished at what he had accomplished in such a short time.

"What do you think they'll do next?"

"I have no idea, but I think the oldest may be thinking about killing the other two if one of them was supposed to be watching Juan. I would have liked to seen their faces when they waked up the next morning and saw that he was gone. Do any of the deputies at the airstrip know any of the details about what was goin' on tonight?"

"I don't think so. We hadn't even told them Juan had been abducted. They've been warned not to say anything about tonight, but you never know. I think we can stick to the story about Juan's "vacation" since no one really got a look at him getting off the plane."

"Well, I'm ready to hit the sack. I haven't slept much the last few days. Juan can fill you in on what's been happenin' with the brothers, but I'm gonna wish you all good night."

"Okay, I'll let you know tomorrow where I want you to take Juan for the rest of his vacation."

After Hans had departed, Charley walked over closer to Juan and asked. "Do you know how close we came to hanging Hans when he surrendered to us? It was your father who put off the execution. He said one day we might need someone who had the skills Hans has. How right he was! Hans saved my life and

Terry's, too. The alcalde said a man like Hans can never be trusted, but after this thing, I think I do trust him. He had every opportunuty to make his getaway from us while he was on this latest gig, but he came back to us. I don't think money now can lure him away from us."

"He's a cool guy under pressure. He looked totally unafraid when he stuck his head inside that door. He didn't know what he'd find on the other side, but I think he was prepared for just about anything. I think he might have been a little disappointed that he didn't get to waste my three brothers. Come to think of it, I'm a little disappointed myself. But I can't tell you how glad I am to be out of there. He chewed my ass pretty good for not listening to him about taking the route I'd been taking to get home from the plant. I don't suppose the other two in my car might have somehow survived."

"No, they didn't make it. Don't worry about it. They knew it was a dangeous job when they signed on for it. That's the only way we can rationalize things like this when they happen. I used to blame myself any time someone got killed who was working for me or with me, but there wasn't a single one who didn't know it would be dangerous. My lawyer who got the patent for me was the first, but he had more warning from the oil people than just about anybody, but still he decided not to sell out to them. It cost him his life, and for a long time I felt responsible. They've tried to get me several times now, but there's no turning back. We're all in this for the duration. I'm sure you knew what your brothers were capable of when you agreed to become a part of our organization."

"What were you going to do if Hans hadn't been able to rescue me? I know from listening to them that they wanted a piece of the company. Were you going to do business with them?"

"You may not like the answer to that one, but the answer is no. I will never have anything to do with anyone who's mafia connected or with the oil companies. They killed some of my family, and I'm never going to forgive or forget about that. You'd best be more careful not to fall into their hands again."

"Yes, I will. I'm going to pay a lot closer attention to anything Hans has to say along those lines. I think I'm ready to try and get some sleep now. Where am I supposed to go for the next few days?"

"If you don't mind, I think you might be safer here than anywhere else. I can get you some of your things, maybe even a little paper work from the plant to keep you from being bored. Will you be up to doing a little work, or would you rather just take it easy for a couple of days?"

"No, some paper work would be fine. I think the time might pass faster if I had something useful to do."

"Okay, you tell me what you think I should be looking for tomorrow when I visit your office, and I'll pick it up. I'll bring it to you when I come home for lunch. Just make yourself at home."

The next morning Juan told Charley what he thought he might be able to find easily in his office. There were several files concerning his latest negotiations with the Japanese carmakers. He told Charley that the company in which he had the the least confidence might like to hear the sound of his voice to be reassured that he was on holiday. Charley was at first reluctant, fearing they might have the call traced and know he was not in Panama as they had been told. Juan could see no reason why they would have the call traced.

"I guess you're right. I'm getting' a little paranoid about things. I'm starting to think like Hans."

"That might not be a bad thing. He has great instinct for survival. If you can't find the files I want, call me here. I'm not really sure where I left them, but if they're not where I told you, I've got another idea or two about where they might be."

"Okay, if I find them, I'll bring 'em home by noon."

Terry was having mixed feelings about the way things had been going lately. He certainly didn't care to take on the risks to which Hans subjected himself in cases like the rescue of Juan, but he would have liked a little more notice of all the smaller details for which he was responsible. He had never dreamed of having all the money in the bank that he now had, He loved Teresa, but her recent past made him leery of proposing marriage to her. He had decided, however, to build a house close to the alcalde's old one, and move Teresa into it. He didn't think money would be a serious problem. He had plenty, and he knew he could get more if he asked for it. Acknowledging her as part of the project would also entail a security risk, but he had so many deputies under his command now that he could assign some of them to guard both her and his new house. When Charley returned at noon with some papers for Juan, he decided to ask him about a small piece of land for his new home.

"Say, Charley, have you got a few minutes?"

"Sure, what's on your mind?"

"Well, I been wonderin'…….."

"Come on, man. Spit it out. What do you want?"

"Well, I been thinkin' that I'd like to build a house of my own. I'd like for it to be real close to right here."

"Got any idea exactly where?"

"Yeah, you know that big grove of elm trees about a quarter of a mile north of here. How much would an acre or two around those trees cost me?"

"Well, technically, the land belongs to Billy, but I bet he'd let you have it for a song. You did save his life a time or two, and I'm sure he hasn't forgotten that. I'll ask him about it tonight at supper. Why the sudden urge to build?"

"Well, I'd like to have a place to move Teresa into. I think she'll agree to move in with me, but I'm not ready for marriage."

"I see. The alcalde urged me to marry when he found out that we weren't married. It's a Catholic thing. He said people here have a lot more respect for a wife than they do for a mistress. I think he was probably right. I've never regretted my decision."

"Yeah, but you know that she was a workin' girl before she met me."

"Doesn't matter, if she's no longer in the business. I think it would be better if you married her than just moved her into your house."

"I don't even know if she'd marry me. We never even talked about it."

"Only one way to find out, ask her. And don't put it off. Do it before you even start on the house. Let her have a little to do with how the house will set and what'll be inside it, and she'll probably be thrilled to marry you."

"You're prabably right. I'll ask her tonight. We're goin' to a show and then havin' dinner at the best place in town. She wants to show off the new dress I bought her last week."

"Do you have a ring? An eye-popping diamond might help her make the right decision. You thinkin' about a family later?"

"Hell no! I never even thought about marriage until just now. I'm a little old to be startin' a family."

"You're the same age as I am, and I sure as hell wasn't too old to start one. I think you'd make a hell of a dad. You're smart, you're well employed, reasonably good lookin', and even more important, you're rich. I think that makes you a great candidate for fatherhood."

"Maybe, but I think I better find a mother for my family before I start buyin' baby stuff."

"Right. Tell me tomorrow how everything goes tonight. I won't say anything about this until you tell me whether your proposal has been accepted."

"Okay, but go ahead and ask Billy how much he wants for the property whether she says yes or no. I really do want a house of my own. I've never had one.

Two days passed with Juan at the alcalde's house in seclusion. No one challenged his absence from the plant. He passed some time with the paper work Charley had retrieved from his office at the plant. From time to time he mused over the events which had led him to the position he was in today. He thought mostly of the hatred his brothers had for him, but that did not frighten him. He resolved to never let himself be at their mercy again. He would never underestiamate the warnings of Hans again.

On the third day he began negociations again with the Japanese carmakers. He told Charley he was almost certain they were at a point where he could assure him they were about to close an ironclad deal.

One week later it happened. Every major Japanese automotive company began making preparations to move their entire manufacturing enterprise to Perdido. The tax incentives were one of the major factors, but an unobstructed avenue into the lucrative market of the United States was the decisive thing. A compromise over how much of the work force would be local or Japanese had been the major obstacle. Finally it had been agreed that initially the workers at the plants would be 80% Japanese. Then as more Mexicans could be trained, in two years the Japanese would have 70%. Every two years the work force would be 10% more Mexican until a 50/50 ratio had been completed.

As word of the agreement became more than just another rumor, things in the United Staes became more unsettled. The American carmakers could already see the handwriting on the wall. They knew if every Japanese company was equipped with the adjustment, there would be no legal way of limiting the number of units that could be exported their way. They would simply be out of business in less than a year. Likewise, the oil companies could see that their hold on the American economy would only be a shadow of its former self.

In Washington, the howl was heard the loudest. It was no longer along partisan lines. Neither party wanted to be the scapegoat for the loss of the automobile industry, yet there seemed to be no grounds on which they could agree to blunt the movement of the Japanese carmakers to Mexico.

In the Senate, the majority leader took the floor as an impassioned debate was ocurring over the solution to the problem.

"Gentlemen, the time for partisan politics has come and gone. This great country cannot sit idly by while the Japanese are striking a blow that could be ten times worse than what they did at Pearl Harbor. At least this time we have some warning. We know that if we take no action to reverse what is happening in Mexico, that in two years there will be no American cars on the road. The current price of gasoline will all but bring a halt to the sale of American made cars. I see no prospect for the reduction in the price of gasoline. My friends tell me we are no closer to an agreement with OPEC to reduce the costs of oil. That is unfortunate but true, I fear. My friends and I on this side of the isle have a proposal which at this time I will make to the committee as a whole. We propose to put an end to American participation in the NAFTA agreement. This would allow us to close our doors to the importation of Japanese cars or to at least limit the number they can send our way."

A senator from the minority party stood and was recognized. He had a smile upon his face as he began. "I can't believe what I'm hearing. Back out of NAFTA now? Hasn't the President steadfastly argued that NAFTA is a great thing? How can his own party now stand up and say, 'Get us out of NAFTA.' Answer me that."

"I must admit that my colleague has a good point, but you must remember that not all of the president's party was as much in favor of NAFTA as he was. There was a considerable minority who opposed America's involvement in the agreement."

"If we agree to end American participation in NAFTA, what assurance do we have that the President won't veto any legislation that we pass?"

"We have no assurance. He may well decide for personal political reasons that he cannot reverse his position on NAFTA. Still, I feel we must give him the opportunity to change his mind."

"What reasons could he give for his change of heart in this matter?"

"I'm sure he would have no problem in finding a way to jusify his change of heart. You well know his adaptability to changing circumstances."

"Yes, we know he's flip-flopped on lots of lesser issues, but I think the senators on my side of the isle have a better solution to the problem.

"And what might that be?"

"Has anyone ever considered ignoring his patent and letting our own carmakers do the same thing he's doing?"

"Of course we've considered it, but I'm afraid we've waited too long to do that. We'll just get hung up in court, and before we can get it straightened out, the Japanese will be in complete control of the market."

Another Senator from the minority was recognized. "Have we no pressure we can put on the Mexican government to slow this thing down until we can straighten out this patent thing?"

"I'm not aware of anything. Do you have anything special to recommend? We've heard nothing from the State Department on Foreign Affairs."

"Has there been any slowing of the stream of American cars headed to Mexico?"

"No, the number seems to be increasing at a higher rate with every passing day."

"Could we close the border on some pretext for a while?"

"We could. But there's no point in that. When they re-open, they'll just flood the highways getting down there. We did that once before pretending it was a part of our War on Drugs, but they didn't seem to mind. They knew that as soon as we re-opened, the people would flock back down there."

"Well, here's a thought. What if we closed the border for health reasons? What if a mysterious disease suddenly has sprung up, and our health experts believed it had its origin in Mexico and is spreading throughout the United States, brought back by those who have been there having their cars adjusted?"

"What sort of disease did you have in mind?"

"Does it really matter? I'll let that go to people who are much more in the know about these things than I am."

"Not a bad idea. I'll have the State Department inform the Mexican government about the closing of the border."

Charley almost laughed when he heard about the closing of the border. He smiled when he remembered the first closing on the pretext of a War on Drugs and the hoard of Americans who had rushed to Perdido as soon as the border had been re-opened. It was also reassuring that even if no American cars came in for a while, there was enough military equipment waiting to be adjusted to keep the plant going full tilt for a year. He shook his head and almost giggled when he read the latest financial report he had gotten from Juan. The billions of dollars he now found that he controled caused him to reflect on what the alcalde had oftens said. He had told them many times that no one but himself could see what he called the big picture. No one but he had ever imagined the scope of what this enterprise had become.

****

Charley spent a few more hours each week at home with his wife and child. Since Hans' rescue of Juan, there had been very little to worry about. Things at the plant seemed to go fairly well even when he wasn't there. The people who worked for him knew they had to perform at a high level to maintain the high paying jobs they now held. The mechanics had vastly improved, and there were very few readjustments. More and more, Charley's main concern had become the construction of his new house. He made it a point to visit the site at least once a day. He tried when possible to have Alice accompany him on these visits. She loved those visits, especially when she got a chance to see the progress that was being made on the nursery. She could hardly believe the number of people who were working on the house itself and what seemed like a small army of workmen who were doing the landscaping. They were told by the head of the construction gang that the exterior of the house would be completed in less than two months. The interior might take another two months. No less than twenty deputies were on duty there around the clock guarding the workmen and making sure that no one was ever allowed on the premises at any time, day or night.

It was late in the evening when Charley and Alice arrived, accompanied by three bodyguards. Alice was reluctant to enter the house. She said, "Let me look around a little bit before we go in. What's that big hole in the ground in back of the house?"

"That, my dear, is going to be an Olympic size swimmimg pool. It will have two diving boards and a slippery slide for kids and grandkids. It will also have a hot tub nearby with enough room for eight or ten, just to the right of the big pool. I used to wonder if we could afford the expense of the water and all the rest of the things it takes to keep a pool clean and sanitary, but then I remember what the alcalde told me long before he died. He said, 'Carlos, you must give up the idea of wondering what things will cost. You must only decide what things you want and go get them.' I'm just now starting to get that feeling."

"I know, it's hard. How many people do you think have ever had so much money that they never had to consider the cost of anything?"

"Not very many. Maybe a few dictators, emperors, or kings. Maybe a few in the oil industry, the mafia, and a few industrial giants before the advent of the income tax. I have no idea how much money we really have, and Juan tells me there's really no way to know. He gives me a report each week, but he tells me they are never up to date because we make money faster than they can calculate it."

"Will this latest deal about closing the border for health reasons slow things down?"

"Not very much. We have enough military stuff waiting to be adjusted to keep us busy for quite a while."

"What will be in that place over there where they've cleared everything out?"

"That will be the main tennis and basketball courts. I know Billy will want the kids to have a place to come and swim and shoot hoops. He might have something like it on his own place, but I want the grandkids to always have fun at Grandpa and Grandma's. Are you about ready to go back?"

****

"Not quite. I want to take a little closer look at the setup of the bathrooms in relation to the bedrooms. I also want a better look at the closets. It wouldn't do any good to have all those new clothes and not have any place to keep them."

Back in New York, Diego had not gotten over the intense anger that had filled him when he had discovered the escape of Juan. He was tempted to take his anger out on his two brothers on whom he placed the blame, but they managed to calm him down before he killed them both as he had threatened to do.

"Stop pacing up and down, brother. It isn't the end of the world. I know you're disappointed, but we're not out of the game yet."

"How the hell could he have got out of here and disappeared without a trace? I know by this time he's back with them, and they'll never make a mistake like that again."

"I think the answer is obvious. It had to be Hans. You know, brother, he used to work for us. He must still have a lot of connections here in the city. We're not exactly invisible. Lots of people must know where we can be found. My guess is they must have put a trace on that call you made to them. I don't think they ever intended to make a deal with us. They were just stallin' for time. My guess is they would have sacrificed him before they would have agreed to become partners with us."

"Yeah, but even if that was so, I would've had the satisfaction of killin' that little high and mighty turd. Now were no better off than we were before, and they'll be even more careful not to let it happen again."

"I'm sure you're right about that. You'll just have to find a different way to deal with them."

"Have you heard anything from the de la Rosas?"

"Yeah, they let us know they're not very happy with us. They say the escape was a put-up deal to keep from payin' them what they think we owe them."

"Yeah, I kinda figured that's the way it would be. Do you think we should send 'em something anyway? I think if we send them an apology and at least a portion of what we promised, they might be talked into helpin' us again."

Eight months passed with little or no change in the international situation. The Japanese government was extremely unhappy with the auto makers, but powerless to prevent their moves to Perdido. The United States was in turmoil over the loss of their share of the auto industry, and the oil companies were frantic over the loss of revenue due to the impact of the adjustment on American cars. Only Mexico was happy. The impact on the Mexican economy was a classic example of the ripple effect. Perdido was the hub now of expansion and prosperity. Builders were present to accommodate both the Japanese and Mexican workers who had been displaced by the shift of the car manufacturing plants to Mexico. The housing industry was really booming, along with hotels, motels, and the food industry. Towns that had been close Perdido but had kept their identity, now became nothing more than suburbs The building of schools and hospitals was also taking place at a rate that only the alcalde could have envisioned. Terry could not believe the size of the jail whose constrution had been recently completed. He had recently bought himself a whole new wardrobe of uniforms. His authority now was over 700 police-men, and the new uniforms seemed necessary for a man of his stature. It had all happened so fast that he could hardly remem-ber the way things had been when he first took the job. At first he wanted to go back to being nothing more than a mechanic, but he knew now that he would never go back to that life again. Life seemed a lot more settled now that he had taken Charley's advice and married Teresa. He still put in a lot of long hours, but the sense of constant danger no longer enveloped him. He now had the finest Japanese luxury car for his own personal squad car. He no longer regretted his decision to come to Perdido.

Charley wondered how long it would last. He knew the situation they were in now could not last forever. Somehow, some way, the oil companies, with the aid of the American government, would find a way to regain control of what they had lost. He was surprised when a young man had knocked on his door one day. He entered the office and remained standing until Charley told him to take a seat.

"And what can I do for you, young man?"

"Just listen to what I have to say. That's all I ask."

"Okay, what do you have to say?"

"First let me tell you that I know who you are, and I know what you've accomplished."

"Go on. I know you didn't come here to flatter me."

"That's right, I didn't. I respect what you have accomplished. I'm glad somebody finally had enough nerve to stand up to the oil people. I know it's been at a great cost to you and your family."

"Go on. I'm still listening."

"Okay. Your adjustment to the carburetor was a thing of genius."

"I'm not so sure about that. I think something very similair had been discovered a long time before my patent. So what is your point?"

"The point is, I have something better than your adjustment."

"Oh really? Then tell me about it. I'm all ears."

"Well, to start with, it really has nothing to do with carburetors. It's a whole new concept. I know you must be familiar with the so-called hybrids, you know the ones that run on both gasoline and battery power."

"Yes, I know something about them. I know that up till now there hasn't been a battery that has enough power to take people on long trips without stopping to have their battery recharged. Go on with your story."

"Well, I think the key phrase is 'up til now'"

"Does that mean that you've indeed come up with a battery that can make long trips possible without recharging?"

"In a manner of speaking, yes. It's a whole new concept."

"Tell me about it."

"Well, up til now, even in the best of the hybrids, gasoline has still been the primary source of power. The battery could only supplement the mileage of the gasoline. My invention, if you call it that, is the reverse of the idea."

"Continue."

"Well, it works like this. The gasoline is only used to recharge the battery while the car goes merrily on its way."

"This is a theory then. Not necessarily a fact, right?"

"Not at all. It's a fact."

"Oh really? You've tried this then and it actually works?"

"Yes, it does. I'd be pleased to show it to you if you had the time to take a look."

"I have time to look at anything that's likely to put me out of business."

"I have no intention of trying to put you out of business."

"Then why come to me?"

"Because I know in the beginning you had lots of help getting your thing off the ground. You found a guy who had the money and the influrnce to get you started. I know you had and still have lots of enemies."

"Well, you're right about that. I had a lot of help and I still do. So what is it that you want from me?"

"Will you at least take a test run with me in an ordinary car that I've got hooked up in the manner I just described to you?"

"Sure, I'm not too busy right now. Where is this car you've got rigged up?"

"It's outside in the U-haul I drove down here. I didn't want anybody to know that I was on my way to see you."

"Will you need any help getting the car off the U-haul?"

"I can do it by myself, but some help would make it a lot easier. Where do you want me to unload it?"

"Just pull it right over there. I'll send a couple of guys over to give you a hand."

He got on the intercom and dispatched a couple of guards to help in the unloading. He wondered what must be going through this young man's mind as he tried to remember what it was like the time he had tried to explain to the alcalde what the adjustment could do. He waited for a couple of minutes before he headed in the direction of theU-haul. By the time he got there, they were already rolling the car down the ramp which had been placed at the rear of the U-haul. The car was 1998 Taurus.

As Charley approached, the young man was standing beside the vehicle. Charley said, "Mind if I take a look under the hood?"

"Sure, no problem. I want you to take a good look at what I've put together."

He opened the hood, and Charley could see that this was a thing he had never imagined. The battery was not as big as he thought it would be, and it was connected to a thing that somewhat resembled a carburetor.

"Want to explain how it works?"

"Simple, really."

"The same thing I said about my adjustment."

"Well, the battery itself is not that complicated. The thing that makes it unique is that the gadget connected to the battery is a thing which runs on gasoline and continues to recharge the battery while it's working to drive the car."

"And you've really field tested this thing?"

"Not once, but dozens of times."

"How much gasoline does it use?"

"Very little. A gallon would keep the battery charged for a thousand miles."

"You're kidding me, right?"

"Is that what people asked you when you told them what your adjusrment would do?"

"Yeah, I guess it was. How many people know about this thing?"

"Not very many. Most people just laugh when I tell them what it will do."

"Yeah, I know. That's pretty much the reaction I got at first. What can I do to help you? You know if this really works, it could put me out of business."

"I know that, but I think there's a way we can work together that would really benefit us both."

"And how's that?"

"Well, if I, or we, could get a patent on the way it works, you already have the car manufacturers here. With this device, we could make the gasoline engine obsolete. Even all the ones you've already adjusted would be coming back to have the adjustment removed in favor of what we could now offer."

"Why do you bring this to me? I already have more money than I could ever spend. Besides, there's the business of the patent and lots of other details."

"Yes, I know you don't need the money. I think that's a plus for me. If you decide to help me, you'll be doing it for other reasons. I guess the main reason is that you have experience at dealing with the people who'll be trying to stop me from ever getting started. Also, from what I've heard, you have a very personal score to settle with those people for what they've done to your family."

"You're right on both counts. I hate those people, and I've had more dealings with them than I even want to think about. You know, in a way, you're in about the same position I was in when I called on the alcalde for his help. He didn't need the money either, and he had a great dislike for the people who'll try to stop you. Explain what I could do to help."

"Well, I figure it would take about two years for it to happen, but here's what I'd like your help on. After I give you a demonstration of exactly what my device can do, I would like for you to call a meeting of all the car manufacturing companies and explain to them what can happen if they buy into my idea. Can you get me any help with my patent?"

"Not personally, but I do have some people who work for me who're experts at that sort of thing. The son of the alcalde would have to help you there. How would you propose to prove what your device can do?"

"It would have to be a secret thing. There's no way I would take it out on a public road. Besides there's always a chance that the whole thing might be a fake if the test isn't totally under your control and scrutiny. Could we build a little test course right here on your property and drive the thing day and night until you're satisfied that everything I've told you is the truth?'

"Yeah, I suppose we could do that. Tell me, is this the first vehicle you've tried this on?"

"No, not really. The first was just a kind of joke. My friend had a golf cart that was always running out of gas. He talked about switching to a battery powered one, and I jokingly told him I could build him one that ran on both gas and a battery. He bet me $200 that I couldn't do it."

"Then he knows about your invention?"

"Not really. After he paid me, I told him it was a joke and gave him his money back. Then I took the battery off when he wasn't around and returned the thing to its original condition."

"What's the furtherest you've ever driven without having to stop and have the battery recharged?"

"Just over 1000 miles."

"And how much gas did it take?

"A little over a gallon. The amount of gas that it takes to keep the battery charged is so small it's unbelievable. The secret to the whole thing is the chemicals in the battery. They're not expensive or hard to find. The fact that they're so easily rechargeable is the secret to the whole thing."

"What about speed and acceleration?"

"That can be controlled by the size of the battery. We'd have to do some experimentation to see how big the batteries would have to be for big trucks, off-road vehicles, and heavy equipment, but I'm sure if we work on it, we can figure it out."

"Then what you're saying is that essentially your thing will do everything my adjustment can do and almost completely do away with the necessity of gasoline."

"Yeah, I guess that's it. Will you consider what I've told you?""

"I guess I have to. I only really have two choices. Either help you put this project into motion or...have you shot. Just joking. I have business partners who'll have to approve this thing before we can even begin to get started. In the mean time, give me a little test run around the plant. Then get your gear and I'll take you to my place where you can stay for the time being. Does anybody know where you are and will they come looking for you?"

"No, I'm a loner. I have no wife or family. I know it's hard to believe, but a lot of folks think I'm weird. I'm taking a few classes at the University, but I don't think my absence will make anyone curious."

They walked to where the young man's vehicle had come to rest after being taken down from the U-haul. Charley said, "I'd really like to know your name. You can call me Charley."

"Mine's Avery, but everybody calls me Tink. I guess it's because I always like to tinker with things."

"Mind if I drive?"

"Not at all. It works exactly like any other gas-powered car. Here, take the key and we'll be off."

"Wait a minute. I'm not allowed to go anywhere without an armed guard. Get used to it. If we agree to become partners, the same will apply to you."

He got out of the car and motioned for a guard to come his way. The man looked surprised, but he headed in Charley's direction. When he got there, Charley told him to get into the back seat of the car. Then Charley turned the key and wasn't really sure that the engine had started. It was so quiet that he had to listen closely to be sure anything was happening under the hood. He drove toward an exit and told the guard he wouldn't be gone long. The guard opened the gate, and he slowly pulled away. He drove along a recently blacktopped road at about 35 miles an hour until he finally came to a stretch of straight road. He hit the accelerator and was surprised at how fast the Taurus leaped forward. He glanced into the back seat to see what the reaction of the guard was to having been thrust forward unexpectedly. The man said nothing, but there was a look of surprise. He then relaxed and assumed the same position he had been in when Charley had accelerated. He continued the drive for about three miles in a circular pattern, never leaving the property on which the plant was located. He returned to the same gate from which he had exited. He dropped off the guard at the same place where he had been standing when he saw Charley motion for him to come toward him.

"Okay, let's go to my office and talk. I won't be completely satisfied until I see what this thing can do on a really long trial. I'm going to set up a little road course right here on my own property."

They proceeded to his office and both took a seat. "It's not just the road course that worries me. I've got to find among my own people those I can trust to not only conduct the trial but also to maintain complete secrecy. I know of one or two, but they may have other duties at this time that won't allow them to begin right away."

"What will you do first?'

"First is the matter of a suitable road course. I want it to remain here on my property. I also think it might be a good thing if all the miles could be driven at night. We don't want anyone to think there's anything extraordinary going on. I want the test to cover 10,000 miles. I'll want the driver to keep accurate records of exactly when the battery had to be recharged by means other than the gas powered device, and also how much gas is actually consumed over the complete 10,000 miles."

"What are you going to do right now?"

"I'm going to call it a day here at the plant. I want you to come home with me. I'll introduce you to the rest of the family and other people you'll need to know if we go forward with this thing."

Alice was surprised to see Charley walking toward the house with a man she did not recognize. He seldom brought home anyone she did not know. She met him at the door. When he stepped inside the door, he paused long enough to say, "Hon, I got someone with me that I want you to meet."

"Well, tell him to come in, Love. Don't leave him standing outside the door."

He followed Charley inside and stood there looking sheepish while Charley fumbled for a suitable introduction.

Finally he blurted out, "This young guy's name is Avery, but he perfers to be called Tink. I think he'll be staying with us for at least a few days. He has a business proposition that I'll have to explain to Juan and some of the others. I'm gonna call a little business meeting tonight after supper. I'd like for you try to get hold of Terry, Hans, Juan , and Enrique, and both of my lawyers. It's okay if you don't want to cook for so many on short notice. I'll order out anything you think the others would like."

"How about pizza?"

"How about that, Tink? You got anything against pizza?"

"No, pizza sounds great. Can I get a shower before we eat? I've been on the road a long time."

"You have a seat. I'll have one of the deputies get your luggage."

They all took a seat and waited for the deputy to return with Tink's luggage. It wasn't much, just a solitary suitcase. The deputy set it down just inside the door and stood there waiting to see if there was anything else Charley wanted him to do. Charley just waved his hand, and the deputy slipped silently out the door. Charley told Alice to notify the others that their presence was requested for the evening meal, but she gave them no reason for this summit. All arrived a little earlier than she had suggested, but Charley made no move to explain the meetimg. When all had been seated at the table, a deputy brought in four large pizzas. Shortly thereafter, the young stranger came in and took the only vacant seat at the table.

Charley got to his feet and said, "Friends, I would like to introduce you to this young man. The only name he's given me is Avery, but he doesn't like to be called by that name. He prefers Tink, so that is what we"ll call him. He's an inventor, and he's come to us with an interesting proposition. He has come up with a device that he thinks will make our adjustment obsolete."

There was a stunned silence. They waited for Charley to continue with some explanation or crack a smile that would indicate that what he had just said was some sort of joke. For what seemed like forever, Charley just stood there, moving his gaze from face to face around the table to take in their reaction. Juan was the first to finally speak, "Could you be a little more specific, please?"

"Of course I can, and I will. What Tink has come up with, at least what he says he's come up with, is a battery powered means of propulsion that almost completely eliminates the need for gasoline."

"And you've actually tested this out?"

"Only for a short distance, but I was impressed enough to think he deserves a chance at a distance that proves his claim, one way or the other."

"Exactly what is his claim?"

"He says that components inside his battery can actually be recharged by a very small gasoline powered device while the battery is still taking the vehicle down the road. We took it for a short test run around the plant today, and I was impressed."

"Well, if it's true, what does it do to our situation?"

"Not to worry. He hasn't come here to threaten us. He wants to join forces with us to finally put an end to the stranglehold the oil industry has on the world. How about it, Tink? You want to tell them a little more about your idea?"

"Of course, I'll be glad to. First let me thank you for the welcome and the pizza. Gentlemen and Mrs. Johnson, first let me emphasize one point. Mr. Johnson was absolutely right when he told you I mean your enterprise no harm. It's no secret that I wouldn't mind becoming a wealthy man when all this shakes out, but I'd do it for nothing to put the oil people in their place. Here is the gist of what I propose. Since you already have all the Japanese carmakers here in Perdido, I would like to catch America's Big Three completely off guard. I propose that in two or maybe three years we suddenly put all the cars produced here on the market with a guarantee that any car purchased here will be able to get 1000 miles on a gallon of gas. Any car purchased anywhere else instantly becomes a dinosaur."

"Exactly how do you propose to prove to us that your idea will work?"

"Well, Charley thinks he can construct a small road course on his property very close to the plant."

"Won't people become curious seeing the same car going over the course day after day?"

"They might, but Charley thinks the whole test should be carried out at night. He said the driver, not me, will keep a very close account of what happens on the test drive. I have it hooked up to a 1998 Taurus, but I can hook it up to anything you want me to. A written record will be kept by the driver showing exactly how much gasoline is used on the test, acceleration, and the average MPH at which the car was driven."

"How about the battery itself. How large does it have to be to keep a charge that long?"

"It's only a little larger than twice the size of a normal car battery. It isn't the size of the battery that matters most. It's the chemicals inside and how they react to the power of the little gas burner that gives it the power to make long trips possible without having to stop overnight for a re-charge."

"How hard is it to get the chemicals that make the battery what it is?"

"Not hard at all. I'm sure we won't have any trouble finding all of what we need right here or very close by."

"Okay, I'm gonna take a vote right now of everyone seated here at the table. How many of you think we should pursue this thing any further? Let me see a show of hands."

Every hand went slowly into the air. Terry raised his a little more slowly than any of the others as his was the last to go up. Charley smiled as he turned to Tink and said, "This means we give this thing of yours a good, close look. There's still a few things to be ironed out before we get the Japanese involved."

"What are some of the details?"

"First, there's the matter of the patent. What do you think, Juan? It's gonna be up to you and that bevy of lawyers I keep employed. Can this idea get a patent?"

"That's hard to say. It surely can't be done in your name or in the States. You're about as popular up there as "aids." It will take a lot more money for this one than the one you got for your adjustment. But that's no problem. We have lots of money."

"What else might stand in the way?"

"Well, Tink, I know you're gonna think it's strange, but before we could seriously consider going into busines with you, there's something you would have to do."

"What might that be?"

"We'd have to have you make out a will, naming me as the only beneficiary. I know you think that's really weird, but I had to make the same agreement with the alcalde before we went into business big time. The reason is simple. If something should happen to you, we'd be left holding the bag. You know things can happen. I know you've heard about some of the close calls we've already had. Just ask Hans if you want to hear about all the close calls we've had. He's seen them all and even been the culprit in a few. You're shaking your head at that one. Well, before he became the head of our security, his assignment was to come down here and kill me and the alcalde. He came close a couple of times, but when he failed, the people who had sent him down here tried to kill him. He joined forces with us to keep them from killing him."

There was a look of astonishment on Tink's face. He looked at Hans who was smiling and slowly shook his head from side to side.

"Well, what do you think? Are you ready to make me your heir, or are you afraid this is just some elaborate scheme to do away with you and steal your idea?"

"I guess whether or not I'm completely sold on the idea, we can't go forward until I do as you say. I gotta have a lot of trust in you guys, but I do. That's why I came down here."

"I'm glad to hear that. I'll have one of my lawyers come here in a day or two to draw up the agreement. Juan, can you arange that?"

"Sure, no problem. We have several right now who don't seem to be too busy."

"Good, Terry, I'm gonna put you in charge of building the track we'll need to test drive his car. Keep it close to the plant and entirely on our property."

"When do you want me to start?"

"Well, yesterday wouldn't be soon enough, so get right on it. I'd like to have it ready to go by the end of the week. Use as many of your deputies as you need. Most of them haven't had to do a lot recently. If you run into any problems, let me know. I don't want this project to drag on. Tell the men it's for a new Japanese race car and not to talk about it."

When Charley got up from the table with a wine glass in his hand, he said, "I'd like to propose a toast before we all split up for the night. Here's to our new venture. May it be as profitable for everyone here as the original has been up till now."

****

Two days later the lawyer arrived and in less than two hours the will had been completed with Charley as the primary beneficiary and Alice and Billy as contingency beneficiaries.

Four days later Terry called to say that the track was completed. He hadn't had time for an asphalt job, so they had settled for oil and chat. He said he thought the test could be started that very night if he wanted to. When he got that report, he called Enrique. When Enrique answered, Charley asked, "How busy are you tonight, amigo?"

"Not very, why?"

"Well, I'd like for you to be the one who drives Tink's car. Terry says the track is ready to go, and I'd like to get it started tonight."

"Gee, I wish I'd known about this a little sooner. I could have got a little sleep. I don't think I can drive all night."

"No reason to. Let's just get it started. Drive until you think you need to stop. Don't try to set any land speed records. Just keep track of how many miles you've driven and at what speed. You can sleep all day tomorrow, and get in a full night tomorrow."

"How long is this 1000 mile trip gonna take?

"!000 miles isn't going to take all that long, but we're gonna be testing a lot more than that. We have to be sure this thing will work at any speed with the same results. Anybody who buys a car with this device is going to want to be able to drive it at any speed that he would with a gas driven car. So we'll be testing it out everywhere from 35 to 75 miles per hour. I figure it will take maybe three weeks. Be sure to take paper and pencil with you to record what happens."

"Okay, I'll start as soon as it's totally dark. I'll start the test at a slow speed because I won't be too familiar with the course. I'll try the faster speeds later."

"Sounds good. I'll have Tink fill the little gas burner. He won't be around during the test, but you can call him if anything goes wrong with the car."

"Okay, I'll call you or come see you when I've finished the 1000 mile test."

"Be careful."

Enrique arrived at the track just after 10 o'clock. He carried with him nothing but a thermos of coffee and a pencil and notebook. He found the car ready and waiting at the entrance to the track. He climbed in and started the engine. At first he wasn't sure the engine was running because it was so quiet. He eased out onto the track and set the cruise at 35 MPH. He glanced down and saw that it had an AM/FM radio. He also noted that there was a CD player. He told himself the time would probably pass a little faster if he'd brought some of his own tunes. At 4 a.m. he began to nod off, so he pulled back inside the compound and went to his own new pickup and headed for home. He took with him the notebook and wrote that he had completed 245 miles. He was certain he would be able to sleep till noon

Enrique woke up at 10 a.m. the following morning. His back was sore from the long ride of the night before. He heard his wife in the kitchen and called her name. She scurried to his bedside and asked what he wanted. He told her to fix him a light breakfast, and he then got up and got dressed. He knew he couldn't continue his test of the battery powered car until nightfall. He had little to do until then. He thought he might try to grab a little more sleep in the late afternoon, but for now there was nothing to do except for a few menial chores around the house. He also knew that his wife was skeptical about all this night work. Never before had any of his work been at the hours he had told her would be the usual in the coming weeks. He made a mental note to ask Charley to confirm his late hours with his wife. It would be difficult enough without one's wife suspecting that he was having an affair. He decided to go into town and check on his little brother Tomás. They had not talked for several days, and he wondered how following the police chief around as translator was affecting the boy. He loved Tomás dearly and was glad when he was around. He liked talking in English, and Tomás was the only other member of the family who spoke it since grandma had passed away.

He finished the breakfast his wife had thrown together and went quickly to his truck. It was still hard to believe this truck was really his. It was what once had been called a gas-guzzler, but with the adjustment, it no longer seemed to be constantly in need of gas. He remembered the wreck of a truck he had driven before when he had become Charley's first customer. He remembered that Charley had told him that his aptitude with tools would soon allow him to buy a new one if he dared join forces with them. He had been frightened then, especially when Toyota Man tried to kill Charley, but for now at least, he did not regret his decision to throw in with the American.

He didn't have any real idea where his brother might be at this time. He drove by the recently constructed police department and jail, but he saw no sign of Tomás or the Chief. He made a wide looping circle around the town until he spotted the easily recognizable squad car that Terry had been given as a reward for his past service. In the car were Terry, Tomás, and two of the deputies. He pulled in behind the squad car and parked his truck. Terry rolled down the window on the driver's side and asked Enrique if anything was wrong.

"No, Terry, I was just wondering if Tomás was real busy. If not, I'd like to have a chat with him."

"No problem. We aren't real busy now. You guys gonna go get something to eat?"

"Naw, I just had breakfast. How about you, Brother? I'll buy you lunch if you're hungry."

"Yes, I guess it's about time to eat. If the Chief doesn't care, I'll go with you."

"Go on, boy, and take your time."

They got into the truck and drove off toward that part of town that had recently given birth to to a host of fast food restaurants. Most of the new places featured Yankee style food, mainly burgers, but a few Mexican types had sprung up also.

"What would you like, brother?"

"I don't really care. What about you?"

"I'm not hungry. I had a late breakfast. How's everything going for you? Any problems?"

"Not really. I don't really have a lot to do. About the only time I have anything to do is when the Chief goes out himself to settle some domestic dispute. Other than that, I'm just along for the ride. How's everything with you?"

"It's been dull until yesterday. That's one of the things I wanted to talk to you about. Right now I'm in charge of a project that might change everything we've been working on."

"And what's that, brother?"

"Well, this is top secret. You can't mention this to anyone. The chief knows about it, but I don't want him to know that you know about it."

"Okay. I promise not to say a word to anyone. Tell me about it."

"Well, this young guy showed up at the plant a couple of days ago and showed Charley a new type of car. It runs almost exclusively on a battery and uses far less gas than anything we've ever seen. I'm in the process of testing it now. We're running all the tests at night because we don't want anyone to even suspect what we're doing."

"Why are you telling me all this, brother?"

"Because I want to ask you a favor."

"And what's that?"

"I want you to tell my wife that you're absolutely sure that I'm working late hours. She thinks I might be having an affair because I'm going to be gone at night for at least a couple of weeks."

"What shall I tell her you're doing?"

"Tell her it's top secret, and that you can't tell her what it is, but you are absolutely sure that I'm working and not runniing around."

"Okay, I'll tell her. I don't know if she'll believe me, but I'll tell her."

"Decided yet what you want to eat?"

"Yeah, let's try some of that new Mexican pizza that they're advertising in Pizza Hut. One of the deputies told me he thought it was pretty good."

"Okay, tell me where it's located."

"Turn here. It's about four blocks in that direction."

About thirty minutes before dark, Enrique headed toward the plant. He had remembered to take along several CD's, an extra thermos of coffee, and a couple of slices of cold pizza that Tomás could not finish for lunch. The Taurus was waiting at exactly the same place he had parked it last night. He thought correctly that it had not been moved from where he parked it. He opened the door and tossed everything he had brought with him into the passenger seat. The car started effortlessly, and he swung out onto the track.

By the third hour of his trek, he began to tire of the music. He shut it down and drank coffee in silence for a lap or two. He wondered if this wasn't going to be one of the worst assignments he had drawn since his work with Charley had begun. The thought didn't last long as he remembered the horrible days he had spent at the old school being the instructor for all the new mechanics who had come to learn to do the adjustment. He had hated that job since the first day. He always went home totally fatigued and dreading the next day. It had been an awesome responsibility. If he failed, the whole project might never have gotten off the ground. The task he was performing now could have been done by any number of other people. His teaching assignment could only have been done by Charley or himself, for they were the only two who knew how to perform the adjustment. This driving around in circles would surely be boring, but at least it did not put the fate of the whole project in his hands. At least, he didn't think so. He logged another 400 miles before he decided he'd had enough just before daylight.

The next night he finished the rest of the first 1000 miles at 35 MPH. He pulled the car in and headed for home. After breakfast, he called Charley to tell him that the first 1000 miles had been completed. He asked if the car would be ready to begin the 40 MPH tests by tonight. Charley told him yes, and he was glad that Charley could not see the frown on his face at this news, for he would have preferred to have the night off. He hung up the phone and headed for the bedroom to try to get some sleep before the heat of the day prevailed.

At the plant Charley and Tink were out to see what the effects of 1000 miles had been on the battery and the tiny supply of gasoline needed to keep the battery charged. A battery charger showed that the battey still had a little more than half of its original charge, and the gasoline used was less than a gallon.

"Well, Tink, so far, so good. Have you ever run as extensive tests as we're gonna do now?"

"Not at all different speeds. What else are you gonna check besides the charge left in the battery and the amount of gas burned on each leg of the tests?"

"We'll want to see how she accelerates, and we'll want to run some tests at varying speeds because people don't always drive at the same speed like we're having Enrique do."

"Have you mentioned to any of the carmakers our project?"

"No, I won't do that until we've had a chance to analyze all the tests results. I know they're gonna be hesitant to make a big switch. Right now they're really on top of things. It's hard to make big changes when things are going so good. "

"I suppose you're right. How would you rate the first test we just finished?"

"Great. If all the other tests are as good as that one, I have no doubt we'll be able to persuade them all to make the switch. Once one of them them switches, the others will have to follow suit or be out of business."

"I guess you're right about that. I wish I had something more to do right now than just sit around and wait for all the tests to be completed."

"Yeah, I know. I never was much good at just sitting around and waiting. Why don't you come out to the plant each day and see what's going on there. I'll introduce you to all the Japanese big-wigs in the carmaking industry. That way you'll have some idea how your battery will fit into the chassis of what they're making now. I know one size won't fit all."

"Okay, I'll go with you if you're heading in that direction."

"That's where I'm headed. Let's go see what Juan is doing."

They went to Juan's office and found him busily engaged on the telephone. He motioned for them to have a seat while he finished the conversation with a smile on his face. He hung up the phone and turned his attention to the two men seated opposite his desk.

"To what do I owe this unexpected pleasure?"

"Just killing time, really. How's everything going here?"

"Better than I expected. That call I just finished was from the man who's handling our patent request for Tink's device."

"Can I guage from your smile that everything is going well?"

"To say the least. He tells me that for the measly sum of $250,000 we can have the patent free and clear in six weeks."

"We certainly won't have any trouble with that amount. Who will get the money we paid?"

"He didn't say, but I have a feeling it will be split up among several. I can find out where the money goes if you're really interested."

"No, I really don't care. I suppose the pay-off will have to be in cash."

"No doubt. These people don't want anything that can be traced. How's the test results so far on the battery?"

"So far, so good. We've still got a long way to go, but it does look very promising. How do you think the Japanese will react when we tell them that we are changing directions?"

"Oh, they'll squawk. They've got the American car industry by where the hair grows short. They're not going to want to endanger their dominant position. We won't have to persuade the whole bunch to go along. If only one goes, the rest will have to follow suit."

"Who do you think will be the most likely to agree to make the change?"

"Couldn't say, but I would think the one that controls the smallest percentage of the market will be the first to go along."

"Sounds logical. Well, Tink, what do you say we mosey around the plant and see how everything's going with those who do the adjustments. It's been a while since I've seen one performed. Seems like forever since I've actually done one."

"How long did you actually work on the idea before you perfected it?"

"Years. I can't really remember how many. It was more of a hobby at first, but later it became an obsession. How long did it take you to work out your battery?"

"Not nearly as long as your adjustment. About a year and a half. I worked it out on smaller things like the golf cart before I even started to work on a full sized car."

"Have you told Juan what you'll need to start manufacturing the batteries. How many different sizes will you need to accommodate all the various sizes and types of vehicles we'll be working with?"

"That, I couldn't tell you. I'd have to see how much room we have under the hood for each model. Do you have the facilities to mass produce the batteries?"

"Oh yeah, we have the facilities to do just about anything. We'd naturally like to do it close to what we already have here. That makes security a lot easier. How much trouble will it be to teach the mechanics to install the little gasoline attachment to the battery to keep it charged?"

"Not very long, I think. You have tons of really good mechanics already working here at the plant. It shouldn't take long to teach them how to install my device. It isn't really as complicated as your adjustment. Will many workers be out of a job when we make the switch?"

"I don't think so. In fact we may need even more workers than we have now. I think we're gonna have to expand the plant again to accommodate all the work we're gonna have. We have plenty of room to expand. I own almost all of the land surrounding the plant."

"I guess I shouldn't worry about displaced workers. How big do you think Perdido will be when all this happens?"

"I think it will be second in size only to Mexico City itself."

"How big was it when you got here?"

"You wouldn't believe how small it was. Just a little jerkwater town, mostly owned by one old man. It's grown so fast that I can hardly believe it. I'll signal our ride, and let's head bck to the house."

****
.

Back in the States the panic had begun. No one was buying American cars. The whole of the American economy was in flux. Workers were being laid off, the inventory of new cars was staggering, and the sales people who were mostly on commission had to quit to find work that would feed their families. Politicians everywhere were hearing from their constituents. Finally, the leader of the House of Representatives had taken the bull by the horns. He had called for a joint session with the Senate.

The speaker of the House waited for some of the buzz from the assemblage to die down before he rose and walked to the podium. "Gentlemen, will the assemblage please come to order. The business we have today is so pressing that we cannot waste any time in idle conversation. We must get on with the business at hand. We have several speakers today, but before they begin, let me first outline why we have called this emergency joint session. I'm sure it is no secret to any of you that our economy is in dire straights. There are several factors to which some might point as a cause of this predicament, but most of those causes would only create arguments over politics. I think most of us can agree that the stagnant situation in the car industry is the chief cause of our economic downturn. I also think that the main reason for this downturn can be found in Mexico. Since the Japanese carmakers have all moved to Mexico, we have a problem that must be dealt with...quickly. You are all aware that under the NAFTA treaty there is no limit to the number of Japanese cars that can be unloaded here in the United States. You must also remember that I opposed the treaty when the Senate pased it, but I promised to stay away from politics. Some of you have asked why our own carmakers can no longer compete with the Japanese. Most of you know, however, that it is a device which only the Japanese have which gives them such a tremendous advantage in mileage. On that devise we've honored the patent til now, but we must decide here today if we can continue that policy. I have been assured by our own carmakers that they can put the same mileage in their cars if they're allowed to use this same device. It is up to us today to decide whether we should give the go-ahead to our own people to disregard the patent and begin producing cars that can compete with the Japanese."

There followed another buzz from the legislators as the Speaker paused to see what effect his speech had had on his audience. When order was restored, he continued, "It is now my priledge to surrender the podium to the Vice-President of the United States."

"Gentlemen, I have been instructed by the President to give you his position on the crisis we face today. It is true we have always honored the patents of those who have made a substantial contribution to society, but I'm afraid we may have to ignore this one which is having such a negative effect on our nation. When NAFTA was passed, we never imagined the Japanese would use this to try to take over the whole of our automotive industry. I fear this tactic of theirs is just as premeditated as their atack on Pearl Harbor, and in the long run, maybe more devastating. We all know that there will be legal problems if we ignore Mr. Johnson's patent. We know that world opinion will turn against us, and that we may face fines from the World Court, for they will surely rule against us. It is my own personal opinion, not necessarily that of the President, that if we face such fines, we should ignore them in the same manner we ignore Mr. Johnson's patent. I hear the dissention from some of you now, but let me ask you. Do you really fear the consequences if we ignore both the patent and the fines? I do not. Those nations that always vote against us in the U.N. will continue to do so in any event. We have few true friends in the world. This is the price we pay for being the leader of the world. The envy and jealousy of the have-nots of the world will always have them voting against us. I think this is no matter for real concern. If they don't like it, they'll just have to learn to like it."

He left the podium to a smatteing of applause. He returned to his seat as the Speaker rose to announce the next speaker. It was the Senator from Michigan. His criticism of the government's failue to act until now was both vicious and laced with sarcasm. The end of his speech was met with both cheers and cat-calls.

The rest of the session was filled with arguments on both sides. Those in favor of ignoring the patent seemed to be in a very small minority. Those opposing argued that if American began ignoring patents of one of its own citizens, it would not be long before chaos would ensue as all patents might be ignored in all countries. If that happened, the economy might in worse shape since most high-tech patents were held by Americans. The vote would be close and was not to be recorded, so no one's constituants would ever know how their representatives had voted.

The vote was close, but in the end, it was decided that American carmakers could use Mr. Johnson's idea, but they were expected to try to find some small detail that would allow them to claim they were not in violation of his patent.

It was too late for this year's models to be so equipped, but a huge advertising campaign would be started immediately. It would announce that American cars would be the equal of Japanese cars in the following model year. Not only would they equal the

Japanese cars in mileage, but American cars would be returning to the larger size cars that Americans preferred.

It was Juan who first got word of the decision to ignore the patent. Contacts of his reported this to him even before CNN had that news flash. He went directly to Charley's office with the news. He knocked on the door and went straight to Charley's desk.

"Have you heard the news?"

"What news would that be?"

"The Americans have decided to ignore your patent and to begin using your device on their own cars. You don't look surprised or angry at this news."

"I'm not. It was bound to happen some time. They couldn't let things go on the way they are forever. We've really upset the apple cart up there."

"What affect do you think this will have on us?"

"Probably very little. At least that's my hope."

"Why do you think it won't impact us?"

"Because I think Tink's device will make what we're doing and what they're about to begin doing obsolete. By the time they've spent millions, maybe billions, to retool their line and hire enough mechanics to perform the adjustment, they'll see what they've done is worthless. They've already lost most of two year's sales counting this one. I think they may be ready by the time next year's models come out to have some form of the adjustment on them. My hope is by that time we'll be turning out Tink's battery powered models. If so, they're gonna be stuck with a whole lot of cars in their showrooms. I think that might just be the end of the American car industry. They can't afford two more years like the last one. I don't think even the American government can bail them out of this. What do you think?"

"I hadn't realized your tests of Tink's idea were so convincing. Are they complete?"

"No, not completely, but enough for me to realize that our monopoly on the adjustment is about to come to an end. In a way this will make it easier to convince the Japanese to abandon the adjustment for the battery-powered car. They've come a long way and messed up the Japanese economy, so I'm sure they don't want to put all their eggs in one basket. As soon as the tests are completed, I want you to begin organizing a presentation. I will arrange for all the Japanese big-wigs to be there to hear your presentation. I see you shaking your head, but you know you're much better at these things than I am. Your father was great at it, and I know the fruit didn't fall very far from the tree. Like it or not, it will be your job to convince them to give up what they have now for what we can promise them in the future."

"How long will it take for Enrique to finish the tests?"

"A couple of weeks, no more. He's keeping good records to prove that what we'll say about Tink's car is true. I've already ordered the construction of the building where the batteries will be produced. I want you to look into that and see what progress is being made as soon as the tests are finished. We've got to be sure that we go on line with our new models just before the Americans introduce their version of my adjustment. I'd like a major advertising campaign in the States about a month before they come out with their new models. That won't leave them enough time to make any changes."

"Can I get a look at what Enrique's done so far?"

"Sure, but I'd wait a while till he's a little closer to bein' finished before you start working on your presentation to the Japanese. That will be the key to the whole thing."

"I don't think I've ever had an assignment that will put as much pressure on me as this one."

"Yeah, but I know you're up to the job."

****

For Charley the next two weeks had no sense of urgency. Enrique continued his nightly circles around the course that had been laid out for him. At no speed did the battery differ materially from the original experiment. Even the trials at varying speeds made no difference. The conclusion was that Tink's assessment of what his battery powered car could do was accurate. For Enrique the time had dragged on interminably.

For Juan, the time passed all too swiftly as he alternated between organizing his presentation for the Japanese carmakers and checking on the progress of the plant where the batteries and small gas motors were to be mass produced. The strain was enormous, and his usual easy-going, business-like demeanor had been replaced with a short tempered impulsive one. He snapped at all the people he had been ordered to oversee, and in no way resembled his smooth talking father. The construction of the plant for the manufacture of the batteries was moving at breakneck speed. He struggled nightly as he tried to put together a set of facts that would convince the carmakers that they must give up what they now enjoyed and embark on a thing that might risk everything. That concept was something that not one of them had ever even considered. Charley had given him only one more week to complete his presentation to the owners.

Charley could see the anxiety written in the faces of his family and the others who were privy to the great change that might be taking place. He tried to downplay the seriousness of it with a ready smile which belied his own misgivings. He wondered how the alcalde would have handled such a situation. He knew he held one advantage over the situation that the alcalde had faced. He needed no financial help. His adjustment had allowed him to accumulate enough capital to bring about the switch to battery power. If the rest of the world was ready to leave the internal combustion engine behind, he would be glad to show them the way.

The final week of testing had come and gone. Juan had finalized his presentation to the Japanese owners. He had rehearsed it for two nights, trying to anticipate any questions that might be asked of him. His only real comfort came from the thought that it would soon be over.

Charley had arranged the meeting between the owners. He had not told them the nature of the meeting or that all the other owners would be there. He had merely explained that this would be a meeting of great importance. None of the owners seemed surprised when it was Juan who showed up at the podium when the meeting was about to begin. They had had more direct dealings with Juan than they had with Charley.

"Gentlemen, I know you're wondering why you have been called to this meeting. He paused to give the translators time to relay what he had just said to those whose English was limited and then continued. "I feel confident that most of you are aware that the United States'government has decided that it is in their best interest to ignore Mr. Johnson's patent on the adjustment to carburetors."

He waited again until by nodding of heads he was certain that most of them were already aware of the situation in the States. Before he could continue, an elderly man wearing glasses stood up and asked, "How will this affect what we have now? Is there anything we can do to prevent them from copying what we have?"

"An excellent question and directly to the point. It could have a disastrous affect if we sit idly by and do nothing. As to the second question I think the answer is 'no.' We are powerless to keep them from stealing our idea."

Once again there was a buzz as the owners turned to each other to express their surprise and dismay to Juan's answers to the two questions. Juan waited for the shock to wear off as he saw the look of fear come over those who had risked so much in the move to Mexico. He smiled as he thought to himself that fear was good. If they were afraid of what the Americans were doing, they would be more ready to take the step that would alleviate that fear.

"Gentlemen, I did not call you here to frighten you or give you the idea that we are giving up. You are a part of the world that was not afraid of change. You risked almost everything in your lives to accept Mr. Johnson's adjustment and make the move to Perdido. The gentleman seated here at my right hand has come to us with something that even Mr. Johnson has acknowledged is superior to his adjustment."

Once again the buzz caused Juan to pause. He waited again until the room was quiet.

"I will try, if you will permit me, to explain the nature of what this man has invented. Gentlemen, what he has done is to signal that the end of the internal combution engine is at hand."

From that point on he had the undivided attention of every-one in the room. He explained first the concept, and then gave them the results of the tests that been performed. He went on to say that they had already begun the building of the plant that would produce both the batteries and the small gas motors He added that none of them would be held finacially responsible for any of the new buildings. His final argument seemed to be the one that won over anyone who might have refused to accept the new order. The argument was that if they worked together, they could very likely end the competition between themselves and the Americans in the manufacture and sale of passenger cars. The only remaining question was about the certainty of the patent.

"Another good question. We are certain that we can get a patent. It will cost a lot of money, but that is no concern of yours. The real question is 'Will the patent be honored?' The answer is prob-ably not. The question is then 'Why get a patent?' Because by the time they decide to ignore the patent, they will, in all likelihood, be on the verge of bankruptcy. They have sold very few cars in the past two years, so few in fact that one of the Big Three is already about to sell out to GM. It's a matter of timing. If we can put our new models out about a month before theirs, it will destroy any advantage they have gained by stealing our adjustment."

He could tell by the smiles on their faces that he had made a telling point. He continued by reminding them that not only would American cars be obsolete, but European cars, too, would become dinosaurs. He turned and took a seat as Charley approached the podium. Before he got to the microphone, everyone stood and applauded.

"Gentlemen, we thank you for your presence and kind attention tonight. We must have your approval before we can continue on this new project. Within a week we must have your answer. For any of those who do not wish to become a part of this new project, you can continue with what you have now. However, I must warn you that the future does not look bright for those who cling to the past and and cannot accept what the future may hold."

He walked over to Juan and gave him a hearty pat on the back. Juan smiled for the first time in days.

Charley said, "Your old man would have been proud of you. Your timing was great, and you were very convincing. I thought your point about putting the Americans out of the game permanently was a brilliant stroke. How many do you think will be willing to retool for the new models?"

"All of them, I think. No one dares to go it alone. It would be a bigger gamble to sit tight than to forge ahead with the rest. If a company fails, at least it will not be alone."

"What advice will you have for the owners when they come asking you what changes they should make in next year's models?"

"My only advice to them is to think big. I think bringing back cars the size of the old Lincolns and Cadilacs might cause a drop in the sales of SUV's and vans, but it's really hard to tell."

"How's the construction coming on the new plants for the batteries and small gas motors?"

"Better than I could have hoped. It will be rough finished in less than two weeks. The construction people work around the clock. They'll need more time to finish inside, but they should be churning out batteries and motors in less than a month."

"Great, I'll head on home and tell Alice and Billy what's happened. They've been on pins and needles ever since we decided to go this route. I'll alert Terry to double the security around the new plant. We can't have any slip-ups around there and hope to beat them in getting our new models out ahead of theirs. I'd like to see some of their faces when they start to advertise what their new line can do after they see what ours can do."

"Yeah, that would be a kick. How long do you think it will be before they see what they're up against?"

"No way to tell. I'm sure they have a few spies down here, and I'm pretty sure we may have excited their curiosity with Enrique's nightly rounds. About six weeks before we come out with the new ones, I'm going to declare a moritorium for adjustments on all passenger cars. We'll work on military stuff right up to the time we unveil our newest item. If we can maintain the schedule

I'm proposing, I think it will sound the death knell of the Big Three."

"I hope you're right, but I know they won't give up without a fight. I got a feeling we'll be seeing more of my brothers before long."

"I hope your're wrong about that. I'll ask Hans see if he can find out what they've been up to lately. He still has some pretty reliable contacts up north. Let's call it a night."

****

In the States, there was a sense that even though the carmakers had access to Charley's adjustment that all was not well. They knew of Enrique's nightly rounds, but they had no idea what the purpose behind them might be. Even though the carmakers believed there might be some light at the end of the tunnel, the oil industry did not. They knew that with the Americans now about to match the Japanese cars in mileage that their stranglehold on power was in danger. Even the people with underworld connections who had helped them in the past had no stomach for an attack on people as well entrenched as the people who were running the show in Mexico. Two of the three de los Santos brothers had already conceded that there was no way they would ever hold the trump card again. They had missed their chance when they had let their youngest brother escape. Only Diego still believed that there must be some way to get what he considered a part of their birthright. He burned with thoughts of revenge. If there was no way to ever claim his share of his father's empire, he would settle for the death of his brother. He had drawn up three separate plans for such a caper, but his brothers had only laughed when he had tried to get them to play the part assigned to each. They were willing to accept defeat. After all, they still lived the good life. They were comfortable, still maintained a certain amount of influence within their own assigned territory, and had more than enough money to maintain the life style to which they had become accustomed. They saw no good reason to give up what they had to go chasing rainbows with their brother on a return tip to Mexico. They hated Juan, but they had never felt the resentment that Diego had for the youngest. They knew he had been the favorite of both their mother and their father, but the knowledge did not rancle them the way it did Diego.

"So you guys are just gonna give up and let him have it all, huh? You laugh at me, but you don't have a better plan than me to kill the little bastard. Why?"

"Because we like breathing in and out. We found out how Hans got rid of that whole bus load of young punks that you had sent to Perdido."

"Yeah, brother, he got'em all and didn't even leave a clue. Not even a trace. I have no desire to disappear like that."

"Okay, then I'll just do it myself. I don't really need you two anyway. If you two hadn't gone to sleep on the job, we'd have either gotten a piece of the action or he'd be dead."

"Maybe so, but we're not ready to die just because we fell asleep."

"I'll be leaving tomorrow. Wish me luck, brothers."

"Luck, brother."

Diego did not realize that from the time that Hans had learned of his whereabouts in the City during his rescue of Juan that he had people watching all three of the brothers. Not a one of the three could make a move without being watched. Hans had been given quite a large budget to employ an army of spies to keep a close eye on the brothers around the clock. When Diego boarded a plane to Panama in the middle of the night, it did not go unnoticed. It was instantly relayed to Hans. Hans had warned them all that he thought Diego was fanatical and just crazy enough to attempt a suicide mission. He put men at every airport to intercept Diego if he tried to get to Perdido from that direction.

"It's interesting, Charley. We know that Diego is probably headed in our direction, but we think he's all alone. Both of his brothers can be accounted for back in the States. We aren't certain if he's gonna try something solo or if he's just comin' down here to set something up. We know he's a crazy bastard, one that might try something really weird."

"What do you think, Hans? How long will it be before he makes his move? Are we prepared for about anything he might try?"

"We think so, but you can never tell when you're not dealing with rational people."

"Well, keep me informed. I'll tell Terry to double the guards around everything we have. Has he used any disguises that our people at the airport might not recognize?"

"I don't think so. He's never been known as a great thinker. Most everything he's ever planned has gone South. I'm afraid he's gonna try something so weird that his brothers wouldn't go along with it."

"Any chance he might try to hookup with the de las Rosas gang again?"

"I don't think so. They sent us a representative the other day to tell us they no longer had any dealings with the de los Santos brothers. They remember well what happened to that bunch of thugs from the City who disappeared. I'm sure they don't want to disappear like they did."

"I'll go tell the family to stay inside for a few days. No need to take any chances."

For once Hans had been wrong. Diego had indeed made an attempt to disguise himself. He had gotten a pair of high rise shoes that made him appear five inches taller. He wore a long blond wig that matched his fake beard. He had shaved off his dark mustache and wore dark glasses. He walked with a distinct limp and used a walking cane to get to a taxi just outside the airport. When the driver spoke to him in English, he said he didn't speak the language. He said in somewhat broken Spanish that he wanted to be taken to some quiet motel on the outskirts of town. The driver complied and dropped him off at a small motel. The driver did notice that in addition to a very small tip, the man seemed to have no further use for the cane he had used while walking from the plane to the taxi stand. In fact, he left the cane in the taxi as he scurried to check into the almost deserted motel. He thought that behavior strange enough to report it to Hans. Hans had offered a substantial reward to anyone who could report the whereabouts of Diego. This man certainly didn't fit the description, but his behavior warranted a report to Hans.

Hans took the report of the driver himself. He was skeptical when the man described the passenger he had delivered to the motel. It was the same motel that Terry and Teresa had used on his first night with Teresa. The clerk did not recognize Hans and was reluctant to let him look over the list of residing guests. When he did finally realize who Hans was, he was more than willing to be cooperative. Hans looked at the ledger and saw that only one man had registered in the last two hours. He saw that the man had been assigned to unit no.8. Hans thanked the man and headed toward that unit. There was no light coming from the two-room cabin. He thought about calling for a back-up, but that wasn't his style. Besides, the man just might be who he appeared to be…some foreigner who was so tired from his long flight that he forgot his walking stick. He knew it would be risky to go barging into the place in the dark, so he decided to merely wait for daylight or for the man to make a move to leave the cabin. He returned to his car and positioned it in such a manner that he had a complete view of no.8. He would spend the rest of the night there if necessary.

When it was light enough to see, he peeked inside the small window but could see no one. He reasoned the man might be in the bathroom, shaving perhaps. If so, it would be a good oportunity to take him by surprise. He knew the door would be locked, but the door was a flimsy thing. He threw his shoulder into it and made an almost flying entry into the room. He screamed, "Come on out," but there was total silence. He listened closely but heard no sound. He stepped into the doorway of the tiny bathroom and saw that it was empty and probably had not been used for some time. He went back to the desk clerk and asked him if he was certain that the man had been assigned to unit no.8. The man assured him it was so.

For once Hans had underestimated the enemy. Diego had only been in unit no. 8 long enough to phone for another cab. He told the dispatcher to have the driver pick him up outside unit no.13. He left in the second cab and directed the driver to take him to a small town some thirty miles distant from Perdido. The driver was hesitant until he saw what a large tip he would get at the end of the long ride. He dropped Diego off at the office of another motel and headed back to Perdido.

Diego never entered the office to register. Instead, he walked almost a mile before he came to a somewhat larger motel. He removed his disguise completely except for his elevator shoes and put the whole thing in a trashcan before entering to register. He asked for a double room, explaining that his wife would be joining him later. He was assigned the best and largest room and was asked if he needed any help with his luggage. He replied that his wife would be arriving with luggage much later in the day. He went to the room and opened it but did not enter. The elevator shoes had started to wear blisters on his feet, so he decided it was time to be rid of them. He walked down the street until he found a small shoe store that was just opening its doors. He went inside and found a pair that fit him, paid in Mexican currency, and walked back to the motel. This time he entered the room and decided to get a little rest before putting his plan into motion.

Hans was puzzled. If indeed Diego was the man who had checked into this unit, how could he have left the premises unnoticed? The answer came to him suddenly and unexpectedly. He must have left in the same manner he had arrived …another cab! If that had been the case, then he would have to check with all the cab drivers who had been on duty last night. He got on his radio and put out an announcement that all cab drivers who had worked last night were to meet him at the jail. If any driver did not report to this meeting, he would be out of a job and quite possibly be facing criminal charges.

When all had assembled, they were asked if they had delivered or picked up anyone at the motel. The driver who had delivered Diego to the motel repeated his story. Then the second driver admitted that he had picked up a man who fit the description at unit 13 and taken him to the small town 30 miles away. He had forgotten the name of the motel, but it was the first one he had seen when he entered the town. No other driver had anything to report.

Hans took two deputies with him and got into his own car. He let one of the deputies drive while the other rode in the back seat. A half hour later they pulled into the motel that the second driver had described. Hans went in alone to question the desk clerk. He found the man cooperative. He showed him in the registry that showed no one but three women had checked in during the last eight hours.

Now Hans became angry. He was certain that he would find Diego here. Now it was time to rethink the whole episode. Something was certainly wrong. It was now almost a certainty that is was Diego who was playing games with him. There were only three other motels in the town so it did not take much time to check them out. In the first two, he was positive that Diego had never been there. No one even close to fitting the description had checked in or been seen by anyone in either establishment.

In the third, however, the desk clerk did say that a man had checked in recently. He did not fit the descrition that the driver had given Hans, but when he showed him a picture of Diego, he was almost certain that the man had checked in. He told Hans the man was in no.10 and gave him a key to the room. Hans placed one of his deputies at each exit and told them to shoot to kill if anyone tried to flee the premises when told to halt. Then he went to no.10, slipped the key into the slot, and slowly opened the door. Once again he felt frustrated. Moments before, Diego had vacated the room and thumbed a ride back to Perdido.

Diego had no idea how close Hans had come to finding him. He was rather pleased with himself. He had not had to face a single one of Perdido's vaunted security. If his presence in Perdido had been detected, he had certainly led them a merry chase. Now if he could just stay out of sight until nightfall, he would have a chance to enact the plan his brothers had laughed at.

He told the man who had given him a ride in an old pickup to let him off at a newly constructed roadside park at the edge of Perdido. He went onto the Men's Room to relieve himself. This new structure was a gift from the Johnson Corporation. Charley had not been stingy with the money he had earned in Perdido. Several new parks and playgrounds bore witness to that fact. Diego decided it was not only funny but also right to hide in a place built by the man he was trying to kill. He concluded that it would be safe to remain in the rest room till dark. He seated himself on one of the stools in case anyone came in to use the facility. He got up three times to stretch his legs briefly before reseating himself. When darkness finally came, he made his way to a little hideout very close to his father's house. He and his two younger brothers had dug a small cave out of a small hill that was a quarter of a mile from the main house. He hoped that all the changes in Perdido had not disturbed his childhood sanctuary. The opening was still covered with brush. He pulled enough of it aside to make his way into the small opening. Then he sat down in the cool dirt to relax. He examined the .357 he had concealed all day to be certain that it was fully loaded and functioning. Then he stretched out on the cool earth and waited for the dawn.

As day began to break, it was Tink who was the first to make it out of bed. He dressed himself and decided that a good brisk walk might improve his appetite. The excitement of having his work approved by Charley and the thought that he might be in line for more money than he had ever thought possible had made him a little giddy. He had been a little uneasy when Charley had insisted that he make out a will with Charley as beneficiary. His fear that he might be set up for an assassination had been put to rest as he had gotten to know all the people around Charley. Hans was the only one who made him nervous. He did not fear for his own safety when he was with him, but his reputation as a cold-blooded killer had an impact on his nerves.

He had strict orders not to venture very far from the sanctuary of the house. Nevertheless, he was determined to stretch his legs well before breakfast. He was stopped by one of the deputies before he had walked 100 yards. He told the man that he was just taking a stroll and would be back shortly. The deputy merely nodded. His command of English was minimal, and he thought at this time of day the walk must have been approved by those in charge.

He walked about 200 yards without stopping. He turned and looked back at the house. Because of a slight knoll, only the second story of the old house was visible. It felt good. It was the longest distance he had walked since his arrival in Perdido. He continued on at a slower pace.

Meanwhile, Diego had awakened and stretched. He was uncertain how he would get close enough to accomplish what he hoped to do. He heard someone whistling as Tink approached the dugout. He pulled the pistol and waited. Then it came to him. The only persons who knew about this place would have been one of his brothers. Since only one them was anywhere close, the approach could only be by Juan. What a break! The little weasle is going to walk right up to me. This is going to be a lot easier than I thought.

Tink walked past the opening and stopped. His back was all that was visible to Diego. He would have liked to have seen the look on his brother's face as pulled the trigger, but he could not wait. He pulled the trigger three times, watched the body fall to the ground, and began a swift retreat away from the body. He knew the sound of the shots would bring a host of security, and he knew he would be no match for them if they cut off his retreat.

The deputy to whom Tink had spoken, along with two others, made his way rapidly toward the sound of the gunshots. One of the others was the first to spot Tink's body on the ground. He signaled the others to come toward him. He turned the body over and saw that the man was lifeless.

When the other two arrived, it was decided that two of them should pursue the killer while the third would take the news back to the house. The dampness at the openng of the cave had left Diego's footprints clearly visible but only for a short distance. They split up and went in different directions, but neither ever caught sight of the fleeing Diego. He knew the land well, and he put as much distance as he could between himself and his pursuers. As soon as he was off his father's property, he thumbed a ride with an old man in a pickup. He rode 10 miles outside Perdido before the man told him he was going no further. He caught another ride in about twenty minutes, and this took him to a small town some 30 miles distant. From there he took a cab to a town large enough to have a small airport. At the airport he managed to talk a local crop duster into giving him a lift to a town large enough to have a commercial airport. From there he took the first flight, even though it was non-stop to Guatemala. Inconvenient, but at least it would make the rest of the trip home easy.

Charley was fuming. He screamed at the deputy who had not stopped Tink when he told him he was going for a walk. When the rest of the family got the news, it was Juan who spoke first. "Do we have any idea who fired the shots?"

Hans said. "Not really. I'm on my way now to check out the body. Do you want to come along?"

"Yes. I don't suppose I'd be any help, but I would like to see exactly where this took place. If the deputy described the place accurately, I might have some idea."

They left together with two more deputies. They had taken a jeep since there was no road leading to the cave. When they got to the crime scene, Juan said, "It's kinda what I expected."

"And why's that?"

"Because this is where my brothers used to come and play. They never let me in on any of their games, but I followed them many times."

"Why do you suppose he chose to shoot Tink? I would have thought that if one of them could get this close, he wouldn't have settled for shooting someone like Tink."

"Well, it was probably pretty dark when he fired the shots. You have to admit that Tink and I are about the same size. I'm sure this is the work of Diego. Neither of the other two would have been crazy enough to try something like this."

"He's gonna be hard to stop now. We should have got him right after he shot Tink. By now there's no telling how far he may have gotten or what direction he may have taken. Charley is more upset than I've seen him in a long time."

"Yes, I think he's afraid that Tink's death might queer the deal with the Japanese. It won't, you know."

"How can you be so sure?"

"Because Charley is his sole beneficiary. Charley now has complete control over everything."

"I guess you're right. I hadn't thought of that, and I don't think Charley has either."

Hans looked around and found three empty shell casings. ".357 caliber." was all he said.

"Yeah, that's the only kind that Diego ever carried. I'd bet anythng I'd ever own that he's your man."

When they got back to the house, Hans said. "Juan is pretty sure Diego is responsible for the shooting."

"How can you be so sure?"

"The location of the place is known only to family members. And the caliber of the weapon is the same as Diego always carried."

"Why did he shoot Tink? He didn't even know who he was."

"Juan thinks it was a case of mistaken identity. It was dark, and Juan and Tink were about the same size."

"That might explain it. You got any idea where he might be now?"

"No, but my guess is that he's a long way from here. We've searched the whole area around here and found not a trace. Just to be on the safe side, I've sent for some bloodhounds. He left a handkerchief inside the little dugout. We'll see if the dogs can pick up the trail. Even if they do, I'll bet he's long gone. You gotta nab someone like him immediately or you're not gonna get him at all."

Juan said, "Can you and I talk privately, Charley?"

"Sure, Juan. Let's go into the study."

Once behind closed doors, Charley asked, "What you got on your mind, Juan?"

"Well, I can see you're upset. We all are, but there is something about this that's not all bad."

"What might that be?"

"Well, I know you're worried about the deal with the Japanese falling through because of Tink's death, but consider. You're his only heir. His patent and all are now yours alone. The Japanese may feel more at ease dealing directly with you."

"That's kind of a cold blooded way of looking at it, but I guess you're right. How long will it take for me legally to become the sole owner of it all?"

"No more than a week. It might take longer, but I have ways of speeding things up."

"Is there anything else you want to talk about?"

"Not really. I just thought it might ease your mind a little to stop worring about the conversion of the adjustment to the new battery powered cars. I don't think we should even mention Tink's name to the authorities. If Diego thinks I'm dead, he won't try anything else in the near future. I don't think there are very many people who have any idea who Tink was or what he was doing down here with us."

"Okay, let's tell the authorities we are withholding the name until his relatives can be notified. That will hold them for a couple of days, and then we can come up with a story that will satisfy them. Let's go back and see what the others are doing."

****

Carlos and Jorge were caught completely off guard when their older brother walked through the door three days after the shooting. He smiled as he approached them. "Crazy, huh? You thought I couldn't get the little bastard, didn't you? Well, you were wrong. I got him."

"Are you sure, brother? We haven't heard anything about his death from the people we know and trust down there."

"Of course they aren't goin' to announce it. That would make their security look like shit, now wouldn't it?"

"Yeah, I suppose it would. How did you pull it off?"

"Well, you know that little cave we dug out when we were kids? I holed up there for the night when I got that close."

"How did you get that close, brother?"

"You know that disguise I came up with that you guys thought was so funny? We'll, it sure as hell fooled them. I'll give you all the details later, but let's just say I got to the old cave after dark. I spent the night there, and the next morning, who do you think came strolling right up to the entrance to the cave? Yeah, that's right, our little brother walked right past the entrance. He never even knew what hit him. I gave him three rounds in the back, and he was dead before he hit the ground."

"Congratulations, brother. I never thought you could pull it off."

"Now we'll just see how Mr. Johnson can get along without Juan. He handled a lot of big deals with the Japanese, I'm told. It would be quite a good thing for me if they all pulled out because little brother's not there any more. That would make my last trip down there worthwhile."

"While you were gone, we started hearing a few strange rumors."

"About what?"

"We'll, we heard that they have a whole new deal that would make his carburetor obsolete."

"Sounds like propoganda put out by the car companies to make peole think twice about runnin' down there to get what he already has."

"Could be, but I'm just tellin' you what I've been hearin'. How could that really help the car companies?"

"If Johnson's got something better, you can bet your ass, it won't be long before they steal it."

"If they really do have something, it won't be too long before we know. The new models come out soon."

****

Two months passed. It had been hectic with the change over. The construction of the building to produce the batteries had been completed in record time. Around the clock, three shifts had labored with overtime aplenty for all. No thought had been given to the safety of the workers, and accidents had taken the lives of several of the workmen. There was no concern for the lawsuits that surely would have followed if the construction had taken place in the States.

Before the onset of the new models to be released by the Big Three, Juan had engineered a huge advertising campaign in both the States and Mexico with a huge emphasis on the States. Huge billboards carried the message, and every major newspaper and auto magazine told of the end of the gasoline powered engine.

At first sales were slow and disappointing, but as soon as the early customers began to brag about what they were driving, the invasion began. Sales were so big that none of the Japanese manufacturers could begin to keep up with the demand. Seeing that Americans would pay almost any price, they greedily raised prices to unheard of levels. Profits were at an all-time high.

The exact opposite held true in the States. Sales had been brisk early, but as news traveled swiftly to the north, sales trickled down to almost nothing. Dealerships had stopped ordering as the new models piled up on the showroom floor and the adjoining lots. The American manufacturers screamed at the government for help, but no help came. So sure had the car-makers been that abusing Mr. Johnson's patent on the carbure-tors would bring them back to the top, they had overextended themselves financially, banking on the return of the customers they had lost to the Japanese. When few if any returned, huge loans that they had made to carry them through the lean times, came due. All three were faced with potential bankruptcy.

Economic times were not so good in other areas, and pleas for a bailout fell on deaf ears.

Chrysler was the first to go. It seemed ironic that to buy up what was left of the once proud company, GM had had to borrow money from the Japanese. The interest rate was enormous. The primary reason the Japanese had been willing to to loan them money was the hope it would lead to bankruptcy. That would allow them to take over the American factories and begin production of their newest models closer to buyers who did not want to travel to Mexico.

Ford was next to go. Once again it was GM with more borrowed money that cannibalized the second largest American company. GM was forced to sell what few cars they could at prices that were below the cost of making them. Those sales only provided the capital to pay the interest on the huge debts. Only a skeleton crew of all the workers in the American automotive industry was still employed. Only the depression of the 30's had seen higher unemployment, more bankruptcies, and poverty. The oil industry was trying desperately to convert to something other than gasoline to maintain some of the power they had wielded for so long. Plastics, fertilizers, and heating oil kept them afloat for a while, but only the huge reserves of capital they had amassed saved them from the fate of the auto industry.

Charley smiled when Juan handed him the latest compilation of the net worth of the company. Billions were already on hand and more were on the way. There was no way ever to accurately assess the value of the company. They simply made money faster than the computers could calculate. Juan had been right. It was not in the company's best interest to charge a flat rate to the Japanese for each unit they produced. Rather, he had correctly surmised that a percentage of the price of each vehicle sold would yield them the highest margin of profit. When the greed of the Japanese had raised the price of their cars with no real American competition, his company had profited even more than they had.

Juan sat comfotably in Charley's office. About the only duties he now had were to keep Charley informed of his net worth and keep his ears open to be sure that he knew what was going on in the States. Confusion seemed to be reigning in Washington. There was talk of impeachment of the President. None of the incumbents seemed to have a chance at re-election. Juan wondered why the look on Charley's face did not reflect his latest good news.

"What's the matter, Charley? Why's that look on your face? Things couldn't be much better, could they?"

"I suppose not, but I just have a feeling that where we are now is not the end of things. I know my countrymen pretty well. We got the best of them now, but I can't believe they won't bounce back."

"That's not the whole story is it?"

"No, I guess not."

"What is it then?"

"I really don't know. I thought when everything turned out so good for me and my family that I could be happy forever here in Mexico. Now, I'm not so sure. I know that that you and and

Hans and Terry and maybe even Billy and Luisa are pretty happy right where you are, but Alice and I have been talking and…"

"And?"

"And we'd like to go back o the States."

"Is that even a possibility?"

"I don't know. How much security can a man buy with all the billions you say I have?"

"I don't know. I'm sure Hans couldn't even answer that. What about the business?"

"I trust you. You're already a wealthy man. You have no reason to try to cheat me out of my share if I'm not right here. You know the business better than I do. There's not really much left for me to do. I fight the boredom almost every day."

"What would you do back in the States?

"I'm not really sure, but when Alice and I came down here, we came across a lake in the Ozarks of Misssouri. We pushed a stolen car off a cliff into the water to hide it. We've often talked about going back some day to see what the place looked like in the light of day."

"What would you do there?"

"I don't know. I just think I would be happier there than I am here. Alice has agreed to go with me if I decide to go. She's worried about the safety of our child, but we really aren't that safe here. If I decide to go, you'll be in charge of everything. I'll need for you to see about acquiring some real estate for me if I decide to go. It'll take a huge hunk of land because I don't want any close neighbors."

"How soon? "

"No real hurry, but don't put it off too long."

"You know you're going to have to make some readjustments in the way you've been living, don't you?"

"I've made lots of adjustments in my life. I'm hoping this one will be the final adjustment."

Charley and Juan's assessment of what might happen to the American car making industry and the giants of the oil industry had been accurate. Charly watched his net worth zoom until he passed Bill Gates to become the richest man in the world. The people of North America had regained the mobility they had recently lost. This part of the battle had been won. Only the return to his homeland remained.

(To be continued)